INVOKING INFINITY

INVOKING INFINITY (Archivist 1)

Published by Old Man in the CrossWalk
Productions 2021
Salt Spring Island, BC, Canada
www.oldmaninthecrosswalk.com

Library and Archives Canada

Doidge, Meghan Ciana, 1973 —
Invoking Infinity/Meghan Ciana Doidge —
PAPERBACK EDITION
Cover design by Damonza.com
Page break by Elizabeth Mackey Graphic Design
Illustration by Nicole Deal

ISBN 978-1-989571-30-9

ARCHIVIST SERIES • BOOK 1

MEGHAN CIANA DOIDGE

Published by Old Man in the CrossWalk Productions
Salt Spring Island, BC, Canada

www.madebymeghan.ca

Invoking Infinity is the first book in the Archivist series, which is set in the same universe as the Dowser, Oracle, Reconstructionist, Amplifier, and Misfits of the Adept Universe series. While it is not necessary to read all the series, **in order to avoid spoilers** the ideal reading order of the Adept Universe is as follows:

Cupcakes, Trinkets, and Other Deadly Magic (Dowser 1)
Trinkets, Treasures, and Other Bloody Magic (Dowser 2)
Treasures, Demons, and Other Black Magic (Dowser 3)
I See Me (Oracle 1)
Shadows, Maps, and Other Ancient Magic (Dowser 4)
Maps, Artifacts, and Other Arcane Magic (Dowser 5)
I See You (Oracle 2)
Artifacts, Dragons, and Other Lethal Magic (Dowser 6)
I See Us (Oracle 3)
Catching Echoes (Reconstructionist 1)
Tangled Echoes (Reconstructionist 2)
Unleashing Echoes (Reconstructionist 3)
Champagne, Misfits, and Other Shady Magic (Dowser 7)
Misfits, Gemstones, and Other Shattered Magic (Dowser 8)
Graveyards, Visions, and Other Things
that Byte (Dowser 8.5)
Gemstones, Elves, and Other Insidious Magic (Dowser 9)
The Amplifier Protocol (Amplifier 0)
Demons and DNA (Amplifier 1)
Bonds and Broken Dreams (Amplifier 2)
Mystics and Mental Blocks (Amplifier 3)
Idols and Enemies (Amplifier 4)
Misplaced Souls (Misfits 1)
Awakening Infinity (Archivist 0)
Invoking Infinity (Archivist 1)

More books in the Amplifier, Archivist, and Misfits series to follow.

More information can be found at www.
madebymeghan.ca/novels

For Michael
Who waded through the darkness
to bring me into the light.

I'D GIVEN MYSELF AND SISU TWELVE DAYS TO GET SETTLED into our new life before tackling my first official day as the head archivist of the magical archives at the National Museum of Ireland.

Our new kitchen was under construction, with the electrical and plumbing upgrades in the main rooms of the estate well on the way. I knew how and where to buy groceries, and had arranged a tutor for Sisu.

Totally under control.

Perfectly planned and executed, my to-do list had held strong through our transition into living among the Adepts of Dublin. With our secret identities firmly in place.

And then someone started releasing magical artifacts into the city, wreaking havoc on the witches and the werewolves. With me stuck in the middle, trying to sort it out with as few fatalities as possible. All while neutralizing the misused artifacts in question.

Thankfully, I was a quick learner.

And pretty damn indestructible.

Though the guardian dragons weren't going to be pleased by a few of my more creative choices when it came to the care and keeping of magical...well, magical anything. But that was my job.

Even, as some might say, my vocation.

I was the Archivist of the Modern World, after all.

CHAPTER ONE

BALANCING THE FOUR LATTES I'D BOUGHT FROM THE coffee shop around the corner on a Tupperware container filled with freshly baked blueberry cinnamon buns, I crossed through the darkened offices of the magical antiquities section of the National Museum of Ireland.

The nonmagical museum collections were actually distributed throughout Dublin, but the two main buildings—natural history and archaeology—were housed next to each other in the heart of the city, only blocks away from Saint Patrick's Cathedral, Trinity College, and the large park of St. Stephen's Green.

Caught up in moving and prepping for my new job, I hadn't had a chance to really explore the city yet. So I'd walked the twenty minutes to work, finding the early-November morning warm enough that I'd taken off my brown leather jacket and slung it over one arm, keeping my backpack secured over both shoulders, as always. I'd purloined the coat from my mother's closet, so technically it was vintage. A favorite dark-brown sweater, plaid skirt, tights, and laced brown boots completed my outfit.

The exterior door to the magical archive was tucked away at the side of the archaeology museum, which was built in the Victorian Palladian style—complete with an impressively grand colonnaded entrance that fronted a twenty-meter high domed rotunda. The unremarkable steel door that led to the archive was unmarked and locked, but it had yielded to my touch with only a slight push of magic. No automated lights had flickered on when I entered, so I left it that way.

I'd gotten up at 4:00 A.M. to bake the cinnamon buns, which were still warm and sticky. The lattes were for my new employees, though having never met them, I had no idea if they even drank coffee. Making the buns in the temporary kitchen currently set up in the basement of my newly inherited house had been challenging, but I wanted to meet my co-workers and start the first Monday of my first official job on the best of terms.

'House' still wasn't the right word. My new estate. Palace? Manor?

A name would really be helpful. Something that encompassed the scope of the estate. But I'd been a little too busy upending my life and overseeing the revitalization of the main house to come up with anything suitable. And my five-year-old brother's suggestions were a little over the top. Sisu, who had a habit of changing his own name on a whim, was the son of a demigod and had to be continually reminded that he was neither invincible nor the defender of all.

The so-called inheritance of the estate was part of my cover for being in Dublin in the first place. As was the job I was starting today. All subparts of a larger task given to me by the guardian dragons—to live and work among the Adept as a dragon archivist, posing as a Godfrey witch.

I was well qualified for the head curator position I was to undertake—though I had crammed about two years of studying into the last month in order to feel that way. But the spy mission was another thing altogether.

Hence, opening with the offering of coffee and cinnamon buns. My research had informed me that bringing occasional treats to the office was a customary bonding ritual among colleagues.

I crossed through the open office area, my eyes easily adjusting to the low light. Four desks occupied the corners of the large room, some neat and tidy, others piled with books, papers, and supplies. Shelving units and filing cabinets filled the walls behind the desks.

An enclosed office took up about two-thirds of the far wall. A name I couldn't read from this distance was stenciled into the obscured glass of the top half of the door. A clear path cut from the main entrance through the other four desks toward that door, with a corridor stretching farther into the building on the left, presumably leading to the bathroom and some sort of kitchen or eating area.

Energy radiated through the floor from heavy-duty wards, informing me that the main magical collection was archived below ground. As witches typically did when securing objects of power, sourcing their magic most often from the earth.

As I crossed through the main room, I wondered if there was also a more public collection. Something that the Adepts who called Dublin home could access without requesting specific items through one of the archivists or the librarian. If there wasn't, I'd need to look into the logistics of opening a small viewing space or even a library.

As I approached the office door, the name emblazoned across its glass came into focus—Celeste Cameron. It wasn't my own name, but the title printed underneath was mine—head curator.

So I'd found my office. Celeste Cameron had been murdered in an incident with a soul sucker entity over six years ago. An entity so powerful that it had also severely hurt my Great-Uncle Jamal when he'd been called in to deal with it, though he had managed to contain it.

I knew that the other employees—two archivists, a librarian, and a historian—had been maintaining the archive, but I'd been surprised to learn that neither the Byrne coven nor the witches Convocation had yet found anyone suitable to fill Celeste's position. Before the guardian dragons had arranged to appoint me. Not that anyone knew the guardian part of my assignment, excepting the head of the witches Convocation, Pearl Godfrey. The witch who oversaw all other witches was now Auntie Pearl to me and my brother Sisu. On paper at least.

With the lattes and cinnamon buns balanced in my left hand, I reached for the doorknob of the office, feeling the energy radiating around the door. Possibly a ward—but the office might also have been sealed after Celeste Cameron died. The fact that her name was still printed across the glass made the second option seem likely.

Power hummed under my hand, but the door didn't yield to my touch. I waited, feeling my way through the tenor of the energy, trying to assess its strength and purpose.

I could have waited until my employees arrived. But I'd come to work thirty minutes early to get a sense of the offices before meeting the people who were going to look at me as if I were simply a twenty-five-year-old witch who'd just come into her magical inheritance. A name and expectations came with that inheritance, but I'd have to prove I was qualified for the position I'd landed in.

Also, I had no doubt that the Byrne witches I'd already met, plus the members of the Conall pack helping renovate the estate, had already whispered bits of information about me to their friends and family.

So, since I couldn't actually control what other people said about me, or Sisu, I wouldn't worry about it.

Well, I wouldn't worry about it much.

I had still gotten up way too early to bake. To make a friendly first impression.

I twisted my hand gently, forcing the magic locking the door to yield to me. It resisted.

I applied slightly more pressure, but carefully. A broken door and shredded wards would result in questions—specifically, the question of why I hadn't waited to be given permission to enter.

But I didn't want to start out asking for permission to do my job, which was why I'd also given the boundary wards that had sealed the exterior entrance a slight nudge when I'd entered. Manipulating wards, or even breaking through them, wasn't beyond the abilities of any archivist talented enough to be a head curator, even a witch or sorcerer. And though I might have been still feeling my way through all the other aspects of the new life that had been thrust upon me, I was a good archivist.

I would eventually be a great one.

And all of that started today.

Magic stirred within my backpack. A press of warmth between my shoulder blades from Infinity, my personal archive. Not a warning. That always felt like more of a buzz. Encouragement, maybe?

Smiling, I pressed a touch of my own power to the door handle—and it yielded. The door popped open, swinging inward to reveal a large, dark office. The windows on the far side of the room were heavily shuttered. Which made sense, because now that the door was open, I could feel a humming energy emanating from the dozens upon dozens of magical items that occupied bookshelves running floor to ceiling along both adjacent walls.

I could feel the magic contained within Celeste Cameron's office even before I'd stepped through the secondary ward that stretched invisibly across the open doorway.

No.

It was my office now.

And either the wards were weak, or they hadn't been made to block the level of sensitivity I brought to the job. A higher sensitivity even than most other archivists—whether witches, werewolves, sorcerers, necromancers, or dragons—all of whom typically ranked as highly sensitive to magical items and creatures. It was practically the first line of the job description, right before a natural resistance to such magic. Otherwise that archivist's career would be cut dreadfully short.

I stepped through the doorway. Energy clung to me, trying to taste my magic, then slid off when it couldn't gain purchase. Because it was difficult to ward against a dragon. We were magic, descended from demigods. Not that it couldn't be done. But the witch who'd built the wards would have needed to know that dragons existed in the first place, outside of morality tales and mythology.

The boundary wards yielded completely. My front foot landed on a worn rug set just inside the door to protect the oak hardwood. And the buzzing of all the magic objects on the shelves increased.

A wide grin swamped my face.

This place already felt like home. Literally. The library at my mother's estate was filled with tiny touches of energy, just like—

Something slammed into the side of my head, getting instantly tangled in my already wild hair and obscuring my eyesight. Tiny claws tried to hook into my skin, failing at first, but then finding a hold on my bottom lip. The creature latched onto my right upper canine and started nibbling and suckling.

Yes. On my tooth.

I laughed.

Still somehow balancing the coffee and cinnamon buns in my left hand, I gently attempted to pull the creature off me. It clung with a tenacious strength that was usually only reserved for the starving. And since going for my teeth was a bit of a clue as to what I was dealing with, I understood that this creature did have a rather specialized diet.

I managed to transfer its front claws from my lip to my forefinger, tugging it away from me so I could peer at it. It assessed me with wide, dark-orbed eyes.

An imp. Known as a tooth fairy among various cultures. 'Imp' was a wide classification for magical creatures—some with wings, some without—that ranged in size from smaller than brownies to larger than pixies. This imp was the length of my forearm. Its eyes dominated its light-gray-skinned face, except for the overly large mismatched teeth of its lipless mouth.

"That wasn't nice," I said teasingly, holding it loosely so I didn't accidentally crush it. "You could have said hello."

The imp narrowed its eyes at me, then chittered discontentedly. It was unlikely it understood English, or spoke any language I could understand, but my tone should have—

The imp sprang free from my grasp, attempting to launch off the coffees and the Tupperware balanced in my other hand as it made its escape.

Four lattes in large paper cups with plastic lids didn't make for a terribly stable surface.

Scrambling for footing, the imp leaped for the nearest shelf.

The lattes slammed into my chest and shoulder, lids flying off to dump hot coffee all over me.

Shrieking—even a dragon wasn't completely impervious to heat—I lost hold of the cinnamon buns as well.

Hot liquid soaked into my hair and sweater, scalding the skin of my neck and collarbone, then dripping down my plaid skirt, all over my favorite brown boots and the rug.

The imp watched me warily from the shelf at eye level to my left. It chittered again, disconcerted.

"Yeah, that also wasn't nice," I said, sighing. Avoiding the liquid still soaking into the rug—though I was still dripping everywhere myself—I carefully stepped my way over to the book-strewn heavy oak desk. A box of tissues was set on a sideboard that ran the length of the shuttered windows.

I pulled out a handful of tissue and made a half-hearted attempt to blot the coffee from my face, neck, and hands. The imp crawled along the edge of the bookshelf, eyes pinned to me. It yipped quietly, then shied away as it came too close to what appeared to be a coronet of some sort—likely heavily spelled.

Squeezing handfuls of my hair in a fresh round of tissue, I crossed out from behind the desk, keeping an eye on the imp as I lightly ran my fingertips along the opposite bookshelf. I paused when I found an object that carried a hint of the imp's magic—a plain pewter jar.

The imp gnashed its teeth at me, shaking its head, then quivering. Though whether it was enraged or fearful, I didn't know.

The lid of the pewter jar had been tossed to the other side of the shelf it occupied, resting against a collection of spellbooks. I felt witch magic, both on the jar and the books. But with no easily discernible runes or other pattern for me to replicate, I wasn't going to be able to bottle the imp. Not without a concerted effort.

Which was okay, because I really didn't believe in bottling or caging magical creatures unless they were a threat. A serious threat, and not just to a few teeth from the recently deceased...or, if invited, to baby teeth left under pillows.

I touched the pewter jar, then the lid, trying to assess whether or not the containment spell on it had faded or if the imp had somehow managed to break free. But I couldn't sense any lingering residual that would indicate a spell had been broken or cracked.

More like it had simply been removed.

And from without, not within.

Someone had released the imp.

But when? Was it some sort of pet that had been caught in a stasis spell when Celeste Cameron had died, and...

No. I hadn't felt a stasis spell when I'd entered. Just the boundary magic, and the door lock. I glanced around. The shelves were dust free. The desk was strewn with piles of books and papers—half-finished work at first glance. A stasis spell should have been placed over the office and its contents until a new head curator could be assigned—though with six years having passed, any personal items must have been removed and shipped to Celeste Cameron's family long before. But whoever had done so must not have had the authority to completely clean out the head curator's office. Which made sense, since according to the reports I'd requested, the business operations of the archive—new acquisitions, including collections and digs—had also been on hold all that time.

I angled my head, trying to read a notebook lying open on the desk. Blue-inked handwriting filled half of one page. A journal, presumably work related. The date at the top of the page read: 'September 15, 2015.'

Three days before Celeste had died.

I knew that date, because my Uncle Jamal had tried to save her and nearly died himself.

So if there had been a stasis spell on the office, someone had removed it. Perhaps they'd anticipated my arrival? But if so, why not change the name on the door, or preemptively organize the artifacts and books piled on the desk and shelves?

I cast my gaze around again, checking for anything else lurking on those shelves. Anything else that might have been set free for reasons still unknown. I pointed at what appeared to be the skull of a rabbit one shelf over, raising one eyebrow at the imp. It was a really big rabbit. Its overly large single front tooth had been snapped off. Nibbled on. Then discarded.

The imp followed my finger, then paced back and forth on its shelf, chittering madly now. Apparently, dead rabbits weren't terribly tasty—even ones that were likely magical in nature. Otherwise, there was no reason a Cameron witch would have it displayed on a shelf.

I sighed, noting a roll of parchment tucked behind the empty pewter jar, likely the documentation for the imp. That would tell me—

Magic shifted in the outer office. Four energy signatures were approaching the main door.

And I was covered in coffee, with the cinnamon buns still upended in their Tupperware container. I should have cleaned up in the bathroom, not just half-heartedly with tissue.

I abandoned the parchment for later perusal, crossing to tidy up the mess of coffee and cups as best I could without supplies or knowing a cleaning spell.

Well, it wasn't that I didn't *know* a cleaning spell. It was more that my magic had a tendency to overwhelm such delicate and precise castings. Thankfully for my so-called undercover mission, magic and specific abilities weren't universal, even among witches.

The imp took the opportunity to launch itself from the shelf. Gorgeous, gray-veined, gossamer-thin, iridescent wings snapped out from its shoulders to mitigate gravity as it arced toward me.

I paused. I'd never seen an imp with wings. It glided more than flew, but it was rare and beautiful even in its monotone shades.

I turned slightly so the imp hit my shoulder instead of my head. It threaded its sharp claws into my sweater, chittering at me expectantly.

"Yes," I said, laughing quietly. "I'll get you some food, and then—"

A tall, red-haired witch strode into the office through the open door, easily passing through the wards. Glancing at me, then smirking at the now-snarling imp on my shoulder, the blue of her magic momentarily obscured the green of her eyes as she crossed all the way over to the windows.

Windows I'd deliberately left shuttered.

"No!" I cried, twisting my body in an attempt to shield the imp currently tangled in my sweater and my hair.

The witch threw open the shutters, systematically moving left to right.

Morning light flooded the room, radiating in from the east.

The imp cried out, pained, losing hold of my hair. I cradled it in my hands, pressing it against my chest to shelter it from the daylight now streaming into the room.

It was too late.

Or maybe the imp was just too malnourished to withstand any level of natural light.

The imp wheezed, shuddering. Its tiny clawed fingers weakly scrambled for a hold on my own. I wrapped my magic around it, trying to offer it comfort. Because I had no ability to heal it.

The imp convulsed, crying out again. Then growing quieter. Dark gray streaked its already pale skin. Its wings hung limply over my wrist, and the iridescent magic that had threaded through them faded, then disappeared.

"I'm so sorry," I whispered—hoping that even if the tiny creature didn't understand English, it would understand my intention.

It gazed up at me, dark-orbed eyes slowly graying.

It went terribly still. Its mismatched teeth caved inward, then dissolved. Then the imp completely crumbled into ash.

Behind me, the witch brushed her hands together. A superior smirk twisted through her Irish lilt as she spoke. "Well, that's a good start to the day."

Less than a minute had passed.

That was all the time it had taken to murder a creature so rare that I'd identified it more by careful guesswork than real knowledge.

The ashy remains of the imp filtered through my fingers, covering my coffee-soaked sweater and skirt, then sprinkling over the tops of my boots.

The unnamed witch stepped back around the desk. "I'm surprised it gave you any trouble," she said smugly. "With your...qualifications."

"You're fired."

"Excuse me?"

I finally raised my head, tilting it just enough to pin her with a withering look. She was taller than me by a couple of inches and older by two decades, dressed in a green silk blouse and dark wool pants. The imp's remains continued to filter down all around me, mixing with the dark liquid splattered across the floor and soaked into the rug. Speckling the white paper cups still strewn at my feet.

"You are fired," I repeated coolly.

The red-haired witch blinked at me, then she snorted. "You can't fire me. Just calm down. It was...nothing..." She flicked her fingers toward my feet. The coffee and ashes that had soaked into the rug and splattered the hardwood floor disappeared, as did the paper cups.

A cleaning spell.

She raised those same fingers toward me, still smirking. "Allow me to—"

"Enough!" I bellowed. My power punched through the room, coming up against the magic coating the walls and bookshelves, then flooding back to me.

The witch backed up, stumbling twice—and finally lost the superior smirk.

The three other Adepts I could feel standing just out of sight stepped up into the doorway, tucked behind the invisible ward that still sealed the room.

I ignored them.

For now.

"You work here, yes?" I asked the red-haired witch, drawing my rage within until it seethed white-hot just under my skin. It was a rhetorical question, since she'd crossed into the office without even knocking. I rubbed my fingers together. Not even a hint of the imp's magic remained in the ashes still coating my hands.

She had wiped its unique energy from this world. Utterly.

And she'd known exactly how to do it. Not all imps were allergic to natural light. In fact, most of them preferred nature, the outdoors, and sunlight. But the witch hadn't even paused to assess the situation or identify the imp upon entering the office.

Add that to the fact that the stasis spell on the office had been deactivated before I'd officially assumed the position of head curator. And the spell sealing the imp into the pewter jar had been removed, rather than degrading.

It was a game. A test of some sort. Or maybe the witch somehow thought that murdering a sentient creature would make her look good in my eyes. Her new boss.

It didn't.

She composed herself, stiffening her shoulders and finally answering my question. "Ayre Byrne. Archivist. I oversee the Celtic collect—"

"No. You oversee nothing, Ayre Byrne." Despite my resolve to be professional, to hold my anger in check, power laced through my words. "You work for me, and I am firing you."

"For what?" she sputtered. "For saving you —?"

"Saving me? From a tooth fairy?"

"That's...that's absurd."

"Gross negligence usually is."

Ayre's cheeks pinked, in anger not embarrassment. Her gaze flicked to the trio who still hovered in the doorway.

I kept my gaze on the witch, not remotely concerned about having an audience.

"You can't fire me," she repeated.

"Yet here we are." I swept my hand forward, lingering bits of ash caught within the gesture. "You're either completely ignorant, and therefore of no value to me as head curator of this institution. Or you just deliberately murdered a rare magical creature."

She sputtered.

I flicked my gaze finally to the three people standing in the doorway. Two men, a shifter and a sorcerer, and one younger woman, a witch. They shared a glance between them, showing concern but not surprise.

They weren't surprised.

"A prank?" I asked no one in particular. "A test?" I settled my gaze on Ayre. "Or did you just think it was important that I understood you were willing to murder an innocent creature?"

"This is ridiculous." Ayre drew herself upright, the blue of her magic flickering in her eyes. "You're completely overreacting."

"No," I said.

"I'm a Byrne witch!"

"I'm sure your coven will eventually forgive you. There must be some way you can make amends."

"Make amends! I've worked here for twenty years. I have seniority." She thrust a finger toward the desk. "I should have been the one to…" She stopped herself from completing the thought. Too late.

"If you were competent enough to fill Celeste Cameron's position, the vacancy wouldn't have sat open for the last six years."

"You dare?!"

I shook my head, dismissing her. Utterly tired of the conversation. I was sticky with coffee, and continuing to breathe in the imp's remains was making me sad. "Don't bother cleaning out your desk," I said. "I don't have the time to supervise you while you do."

Ayre clenched and unclenched her hands, power flicking around her fingers. As she considered attacking me, perhaps?

I waited.

The sorcerer hovering in the doorway cleared his throat. He was in his late thirties, his sandy hair just long enough to fall over his wide brow. "Might I suggest…there usually needs to be a component of proof…to fire someone for negligence." His accent was more British than Irish, at least to my untrained ear.

"Who would I need to prove it to?" I asked. "Other than myself? I am the head curator of the archive."

"The Convocation…" whispered the dark-blond witch. She wore her hair cropped and green-framed cat-eye glasses. She quickly snapped her mouth shut, her pink lips whitening as she presumably realized what she was suggesting. She was American by her accent—and the employee file I'd read.

"Fine," I said, completely amenable. "I'd be happy to review my decision with the Convocation. I assume the first step would be establishing the timeline and proving that Ms. Byrne set the imp free in order to prank me. Or perhaps to simply show me up?"

"Um…" The younger witch faltered, flicking her gaze to Ayre. "I, ah, guess so…"

"I'll have an independent reconstructionist brought in," I said, stepping over to collect the upended container of cinnamon buns. "And when Ms. Byrne's guilt is proven beyond a doubt, the expense of an investigation can be garnished from her final paycheck."

"Oh...it would cost much more than..." The younger witch swallowed, flicking her gaze to the fuming Ayre.

I set the Tupperware on the desk. "Well, let's see if I can offer a shortcut." I stepped by Ayre, crossing toward the doorway.

The trio, still not having even introduced themselves, stepped back. The shifter scowled when he realized he'd ceded ground to me without thinking.

Ignoring them, I placed my hand on the wall next to the doorjamb. Allowing my power to flow through me, I murmured the tracing spell I'd been practicing—modified from a grimoire that had been gifted to me by the treasure keeper of the guardian dragons. I had combined the spell with my own innate ability to assess magical objects by touch.

A thread of golden-tinted power spread across the wall, then feathered out into the office. The magic deepened into a medium blue as it picked up the residual I'd directed it toward. A blue wash traced a path from the door to the windows, looping back to tangle itself around Ayre's ankles—its endpoint.

She stiffened, but the energy was simply highlighting the path of her residual magic.

"Shall I continue?" I asked mockingly. I glanced at the trio in the doorway. "Or if I continue tracing Ayre's movements through this office, will I uncover multiple signatures?"

The younger witch blanched, then looked to Ayre.

"It means nothing," Ayre said. "I come and go from the office—"

"You lie," I said softly, pushing my tracing spell further. A secondary path of the same color and tenor—indicating it was Ayre's residual—stretched from the door toward the bookshelf. It touched a few spaces that might have previously held books, then settled to halo the pewter jar and the lid that had held the imp. "The office has been in stasis since Celeste Cameron died. But that spell had already been removed when I crossed through this morning. Shall I explain to you how to sense the difference between older and newer residual magic?"

Ayre Byrne's nostrils flared. "You aren't going to last more than a minute in this city if you piss off the coven."

"I'm not under the purview of the coven." Allowing the tracing spell to fade, I crossed back to my desk. "Don't make me escort you out."

"Escort me?!"

I looked over at the trio. I had memorized their bios, along with everything else that my lawyer, Tawny Sherwood, could find on the archives regarding my new position. Tawny had also helped Sisu and me get settled at our new estate. We'd needed passports, credit cards, and bank accounts, among many other things.

I settled my gaze on the dark-haired shapeshifter in his early thirties. "The archive's security is overseen by you. Owen Brady, is it?"

Clad in an indigo-blue collared shirt and black slacks, he nodded stiffly. "That is one of my areas of responsibility." His accent was Irish, but toned by all the education and travel that came with the intense study required to be an archivist specializing in dangerous collections.

"This is..." Ayre stuttered, though out of anger, not contrition. "You should...just...calm down. I don't need to be escorted from the building—"

"Fine," I said. "Call to arrange a time to clean out your desk. I'll put together an incident report if you'd like to involve the Convocation."

The red-haired witch flexed her hands a second time, opening and closing her mouth. I held her gaze steadily, adopting as calm an expression as I could. Though I could still feel an echo of the imp dying in my hands. Its magic crumbling into nothing. Over and over.

Ayre Byrne spun on her heel and strode out of the office, shouldering her way through the trio blocking her way to the main room.

Brady glanced at me. He kept his beard trimmed along his jawline—and likely had to sculpt it that way whenever he transformed to and from his wolf. That seemed fussy. But then, I didn't know many werewolves.

He huffed. Then, casually stuffing his hands in the pockets of his pants, he followed the irate witch out.

I glanced at the sorcerer and the witch still standing in the doorway, while tracking the other two with my other senses, feeling as Ayre lingered in the main room just out of my line of sight. "Were either of you planning on murdering another magical creature as a so-called prank for my first day?"

The sorcerer swallowed, smoothing his hand over his navy-blue suit jacket. It was a little snug over his shoulders and slightly loose at the waist, and I didn't doubt it was layered with protective spells. Unlike werewolves, I knew plenty of sorcerers. Suits and being prepared were both second nature to them.

The witch looked a little faint. She was only a couple of years older than me, and wearing a blue-and-white patterned dress over thick tights and wedge-heeled shoes.

Evidently, they had been involved in some aspect of the hazing Ayre Byrne had decided to give me.

"No," the sorcerer said. "I…I'm sorry it happened at all." He stepped into the room, momentarily offering me his hand. But as he passed through the wards, he faltered, curling his fingers in and dropping his arm.

Apparently, my magic was intimidating.

I wasn't covering my anger as well as I thought.

I deliberately dropped my gaze, shuffling through some of the books and papers on the desk. Preemptively tidying to cover getting my anger—and my magic—under control, though I knew I'd have to sort through everything a second time.

I hadn't even taken off my backpack.

"I'm Dusk Godfrey."

"Yes," the sorcerer said, smiling tightly. His accent was definitely British now, but not as clipped as the other London sorcerers I knew. "Jim…James Anderson. Historian."

Historian as opposed to archivist, meaning that James didn't work in the field. At all. No collections, no digs.

"Any connection to the Andersons of Books, Tomes, and Other Publications?" I'd noted his name in the bio Tawny Sherwood had provided, but it hadn't come with a detailed lineage. I'd only been to London a few times, but that bookstore was one of my favorites.

"Second cousin to Oliver. We don't get on."

"You manage the collection in general? Liaise with the public and other archives?" I asked, easing further into the conversation with questions that I already knew the answers to.

"I'm not a creature person," he said.

Joking, I thought, but I didn't get what was so amusing.

He cleared his throat. "Yes. I also focus on modern historical artifacts. Celeste was the ancient history buff."

The witch finally stepped forward, standing a few steps away from James. She kept nervously pushing up her glasses. I assumed they were mostly for show, though, since most witches had any vision problems corrected by someone suitably skilled in their coven.

"Crystal Pine," she said. "I'm on loan from the Boston Museum. Um, librarian. Assistant librarian, actually..."

"Assistant? Under whom?" I asked.

She twisted her fingers in the folds of her dress, then caught herself doing so. "Um, well. Celeste..." She glanced at James.

He ignored her, watching me, though he didn't appear to be looking at anything in particular.

Crystal hummed nervously. "She...Celeste died three months after I arrived."

"Ah. So you took over the head librarian duties but not the official position?" The bio I'd memorized had just listed Crystal as a librarian, without the 'assistant' attribute.

"Yes."

"Okay."

"I'd..." She hesitated. "Um, is that position something you...um, part of your job now?"

"You'd like to stay on in Dublin? Officially overseeing the main library?" I'd likely need to give Crystal a raise if that happened. Actually, all four of my new employees had probably had their wages frozen for the last six years. I hadn't dug into the budget or the funding aspects of the archive yet.

Three employees, I corrected myself.

"Yes," Crystal said firmly.

I glanced at them both.

Brady returned, stopping to hover just beyond the doorway. As far as I could feel, Ayre had left the building, though both the inner and outer wards dampened my range.

"As of now, you are all on six-month probation."

James stiffened, instantly indignant.

Brady smiled, chin dropping to his chest. Pack shapeshifters usually responded well to set rules and a clear command structure, so I wasn't surprised that he didn't protest.

Crystal just bobbed her head. Probation likely sounded just fine to her, because she wanted to be the official head librarian. It was only logical that she would need to prove she was up for the task, especially once I began authorizing new collections and acquisitions.

"I've been here seven years," James spat.

"But not working with me," I said coolly. "You might not like it."

He snapped his mouth shut, then spun to stride out of the office.

"Try to not murder anyone else," I said. "I'll check in with you after lunch."

"Check up on me, you mean," he snapped over his shoulder.

"Yes. That's more than enough time for you to get together a report on your current workload. Correct?"

"Correct," he snarled, then crossed past Brady.

The werewolf was chuckling quietly to himself.

"A written report?" Crystal asked brightly, practically bouncing on her toes.

"If you prefer," I said.

She grinned widely. Then she laid one hand on the container of cinnamon buns. "Are these for us? For coffee break? They look great, even a little…smushed."

"Yes."

"I'll take them to the kitchen."

"Thank you."

She snatched up the Tupperware and took off.

Brady watched her go with an amused gaze. Then he wandered into the office and flung himself down on the chair in front of the desk. "We knew about the prank with the imp," he said bluntly.

"Since I assume Ayre removed the stasis spell on the office to set it up, you wouldn't be much of a security specialist if you didn't."

He snorted. "Exactly. But...we didn't know the extent of it."

"The part where she murdered a sentient being, you mean?"

"Yes."

I stared at Owen Brady for a long moment. He didn't shift, didn't even blink under my gaze. Then I nodded once. Not appeased, but just...accepting that we were going to have to move on from the incident.

He snorted wryly, nodding to himself as if he'd weighed me and my truth in that moment as well. A wide, wolfish grin overtook his face. "Ayre Byrne is going to be a problem."

"You don't seem too worried about it."

"It had gotten boring around here."

"I like boring," I said.

He chuckled, levering himself out of the chair that he'd just sat down in. Owen Brady didn't like to stay still for too long. "But why do I have a feeling that boring doesn't like you, Dusk?"

I huffed a laugh.

"You'll find my main desk in the archive downstairs. If shit is going to go down, it usually starts there."

"Does shit often go down?" I asked, finding myself amused by the werewolf. "With what should be properly shelved artifacts?"

He shrugged. "Nah. Like I said, it's been boring. I get a lot of reading done, at least." He waved over his shoulder, then exited into the main room.

The smile slid from my face. The imp's ashes were drying on my coffee-soaked clothing. I contemplated finding the bathroom and cleaning up as best I could.

But I didn't.

I wasn't certain if I was punishing myself—or why. But instead of cleaning up, I pulled Infinity out of my backpack, sat down, and started trying to get the desk into some semblance of order.

I felt that press of warmth again. Like my personal archive was responding to my emotions, to my mood.

I was still working out all the new ways Infinity was...communicating with me.

Yes, the leather-bound, rune-marked book perpetually stuffed in my backpack when I didn't have it in hand had gained some level of sentience after I'd connected it to the Internet. Or perhaps as a result of Sisu and me having inadvertently visited the nexus—the seat of power for the guardian dragons—in the aftermath of that event, for a day that had turned out to actually be two weeks. Time moved oddly when crossing in and out of other dimensions, or dimensional pockets.

Or perhaps it was all part of the regular evolution for any personal archive. But I had no one to ask about that.

The ability to bind a personal archive was a talent specific to a rare subset of archivists. And each personal archive was unique to its wielder. Adaptive.

So I could dash off a note about Finny's new quirks to my Aunt Josephine, and wait months for her to write me back. If she wrote me back. Mom was still off on a collection. And Zeke was in Egypt overseeing the archives as Mom's apprentice. I could mention it in one of my letters to him, of course, but he was almost as new to having a personal archive as I was. Though he was technically over fifty years older than me.

That was a long story, though. And I had a job to do.

The first thing—literally right in front of me—was Celeste Cameron's work journals. A matching set occupied the shelves to my immediate right. I would have to scan the contents and then archive them all.

Time to get to work.

In the end, I cleaned up just a little in the bathroom so that I wouldn't draw too much attention to myself. Then, hiding the worst of the coffee stains under my leather jacket, I went out to grab some lunch—sandwiches and a pasta salad that I picked up at a nearby cafe. On my way back to the office, I cut through the main archaeology museum and wandered the first-floor exhibits, looking for residual magic in what should have been a completely nonmagical collection.

The museum was utterly gorgeous, for lack of any more poetic way to describe it. Splendid mosaic floors throughout depicted scenes from classical mythology, including a zodiac design in the rotunda, plus lavish majolica fireplaces and door surrounds, and carved wooden doors. The majority of the collection consisted of local archeological finds from the Bronze Age, the Viking era, and medieval times, though I knew the museum had some Egyptian, Cypriot, and Roman items as well. Everything I passed was beautifully preserved and displayed—and all of mundane origin. Which meant that, even without a head curator, my new employees had been doing their jobs.

I made a promise to myself that I would return when I had the time to truly enjoy it all—especially the Treasury and the exhibit called "Ór," aka Ireland's Gold.

I was, after all, a dragon.

As I returned to the front entrance of the main museum, my other senses drew me toward a paneled door all but hidden slightly behind and between two of the marble columns that supported the domed rotunda—marble that a nearby plaque informed me had been quarried in the counties of Cork, Kilkenny, Galway, Limerick, and Armagh. Traces of magic glimmered at the edges of the door, but I entered without resistance. The spell was obviously intended to mask an entrance from nonmagical sight, not to bar passage. I quickly slid the door shut behind me.

The neoclassical influence extended from the colonnaded entrance of the museum into the grand, empty room that stretched out before me. The smooth white marble floor was shot through with light-gray veins, punctuated by columns, studded with empty pedestals, and topped with a curved mosaic ceiling. The walls were bare, but capped with carved crown molding.

There was absolutely no way that the main museum would have chosen to leave a space this large, and just off their main entrance, empty—not even between rotating special exhibits.

I strode through the room, noting the benches set between the columns. The door at the far end was magically warded. And unless I was seriously turned around, I was fairly certain it led to the kitchen, bathrooms, and offices of the archive. I'd wondered why the bathrooms and kitchen were so large compared to the size of the staff.

I laughed, quietly delighted, spinning slowly to take in the space again. As I'd hoped, the archive was set up to host exhibits or showcases that could be opened to the Adept. Given the easy access to a kitchen, we could even host an invitation-only fundraising gala with food and drink.

I'd never curated a gala or an exhibit before. Never planned an event, or printed up invitations. But even though I hadn't seen the main archive yet—even though I had no idea if I could even put together a collection enticing enough to draw the attention of, and the donations from, the Adepts of Dublin—I was already grinning like mad and mulling over possible themes.

Celeste Cameron's desk had taken every moment of my morning just to sort through. It was filled with items that shouldn't have been left to lie around for six years or more. The head curator appeared to have been seriously backlogged at the time of her death. It would take me at least a week to organize it all. And I shouldn't have been adding to my work to-do list at all, but...

Maybe a masked ball?

An enchanted piano could be tucked into a corner. Art from multiple eras to decorate the walls. And the archive had to have some rarities tucked into its depths that I could haul out for one night. I felt certain that Crystal would be happy to help me plan an event for the upcoming holiday season.

Still smiling, I crossed to the opposite door, discovering that it did indeed lead back through to the offices as I'd suspected.

The kitchen and break room were empty as I passed. Embroiled in work, I'd skipped coffee break but noted that the Tupperware holding my cinnamon buns had been plundered. A tidy pile of mugs and small plates were drying beside a deep stainless steel sink. I'd thought about eating lunch out as well instead of getting takeout, but decided that making my presence felt, even from my office, was smarter while settling in.

A young girl was sitting behind my desk. Her dark-brown hair hung forward from her bowed head, covering most of her face. She appeared to be wrestling with a thick black leather book that I didn't recognize.

Brooke Byrne, though she preferred to be called Rook. Daughter to River Byrne, my interior designer. Unlike the rest of the pale-skinned, red-haired Byrne family—of the four I'd met so far, at least—her skin was golden in tone, just slightly lighter than my own.

No. I'd met five Byrne witches now. I had to include Ayre, though even a brief thought of her also recalled the feeling of the imp's death, crumbling into ash in my hands.

I shook off the thought before it completely dampened the little bit of lightness that finding the empty exhibition space had brought me.

Noting that the wards were still fully in place as I stepped into the office, I smiled at the young witch. We'd met only twice before, briefly. Once when her mother had stopped by with a budget for the estate renovations—and had been forced to embarrassingly talk me through electronically transferring funds to her design firm as a deposit. And once when River had dropped off countertop and cabinet samples.

The samples had all been numbered to indicate River's preferences, and honestly, I really couldn't see much of a difference. So I had just pointed to any sample that was numbered with a 1, resulting in River smiling and repeatedly clapping her hands as if delighted with my choices.

"Hello, Rook." I crossed toward the desk, setting my brown-paper takeout bag on the only corner I'd managed to clear.

The young witch started. Her magic likely wasn't mature enough yet to have picked up my approach while her attention was riveted to the book.

"Hey, Dusk!" She blinked her dark-brown eyes as if trying to focus on me. Her grip on the black leather book was intense, literally whitening the knuckles of both her hands.

That was concerning.

I reached out, silently asking for the book, already knowing that no matter what was going on, it was better for the young witch to relinquish it to me herself. Magic was like that when it tried to grab hold of a person—assuming magic was in play in some way in this scenario.

Grimacing, she passed it to me. "It doesn't open."

The moment I touched the hard leather cover, a soft vibration ran both ways up my spine. Not from my magic, but from Infinity in my backpack. My personal archive was warning me about something. Another aspect of the new bond we had established.

I inspected the cover of the book, then the unmarked spine. The black leather hadn't been broken in at all, though the edges were slightly damaged where two plain silver latches had been added. I saw no hinges, keyholes, or other obvious ways to unlock the book. The smooth-cut cream-colored pages, as well as the front and back cover, all appeared to be sealed or glued together.

The locked book hadn't been on my desk when I'd left for lunch—or I definitely would have felt it. But Rook could have pulled it off one of the shelves.

The secondarily warded shelves.

And even though she was a witch, Rook didn't feel to me like she had the magical ability to access such wards. Power matured with age for all Adepts, and females specifically often experienced a surge in their magical ability when they started to menstruate. As I had.

Rook had just turned ten. She'd informed me of her age herself the first time we met, when River had asked her if she wanted to play with Sisu and the Conall twins, ages five and six. According to Rook, ten-year-olds didn't play with so-called 'babies,' though they did occasionally share the same tutor for math. But only after attending a 'real school' during the day.

I set the locked book on the nearest shelf, next to the pewter jar that had once held the tooth fairy imp. I would need to investigate the odd tome further, but doing so now would only keep Rook's attention on it.

"We came to get lunch with you. To help celebrate your first day," Rook said, her gaze riveted to the now-shelved book. "But you weren't here."

I pulled the guest chair closer to the desk, leaving Rook in my seat behind it. "I bought extra. Sisu would complain if he knew I went for lunch but didn't bring him anything."

That tore Rook's attention from the book finally. She grinned at me. "I won't tell him if you don't."

"Deal." I pulled off my backpack and removed my jacket, folding it over the back of the chair. Then I put my backpack on. I liked to keep Finny close, especially when not at home.

She narrowed her eyes at me. "Do you have coffee spilled all over you?"

The browns of my sweater and plaid skirt were hiding most of the stains, though I knew I had to reek of coffee. And, to sensitive noses, the essence of the imp's death. "Yes. But it's dry now."

"Don't you know a cleaning spell?"

"No. Do you?"

She shifted slightly in the chair, her fingers flicking thoughtfully, but then admitted, "No. Not yet. I guess you...don't have a change of clothes at work."

"It would be a good idea, though."

I quickly rearranged the now-organized piles of books and papers on the desk, making a space in the middle for both Rook and me. Then I pulled out the sandwiches, setting one baguette in front of Rook and the salad in between us. I'd taken only one compostable fork from the deli, along with two small napkins, but she and I could share.

"Where's your mom?" I asked as Rook unwrapped her sandwich.

"Oh!" the young witch exclaimed. "This is the roast chicken and grilled veg from cousin Cove's cafe!"

"Your mom mentioned it to me."

Rook reached for the salad container, flipping the lid. "And the pasta salad!"

I laughed quietly. "Yes."

"Cove roasts the tomatoes, you know," Rook said, grabbing the fork and spearing the utensil into the salad. Stuffing her mouth impossibly full, she talked in between chews. "Aunt Del, short for Delta, provides the fresh veg from her greenhouses. Cove makes the garlic pesto from scratch too."

I took a bite of my sandwich. The baguette was crispy-crusted whole wheat that was slightly chewy in the middle, perfect to keep the sandwich from falling apart. The chicken and veg—grilled pepper, onion, and zucchini—were crazy tasty, with the aforementioned pesto spicing and all.

Rook happily dug into what was supposed to be Sisu's sandwich—but with her gaze still occasionally flicking to the sealed book on the shelf. I couldn't sense that any connection had been made between her and the book, but I decided it was best to keep her attention away from it for a little while longer.

"Where's your mom?" I asked again.

"We ran into Auntie Ayre," Rook mumbled through a mouthful of her sandwich. Her grimace informed me that 'Auntie' wasn't her favorite person to run into.

I could have said the same—especially since I'd told the witch I'd just fired to not return to the offices without calling ahead to arrange to clean out her desk.

"She insisted on talking to Mom. Alone. They went to that bakery one block over. I stayed here."

"And how did you get through the wards on the office door?" I asked casually.

"Mom knew the password. From, you know, before."

"Excuse me...a password?" Of all the idiotic...

"Yep. 'Gryphon.' It's a mythical creature with the head of a lion and the legs of an eagle."

"Other way around. Though nothing is set in stone when it comes to magical creatures."

Rook blinked at me over her half-eaten sandwich. "What do you mean? Like, mythical creatures exist?"

She had no idea. A so-called mythical creature was eating lunch with her right now. I just grinned at her, abandoning my sandwich to commandeer the fork and dig into the pasta salad. The oregano was very up front, but I quickly got used to the spicing and enjoyed it.

"Hey, Dusk?"

"Yeah?"

"Do, like…what does it mean, to be an archivist? Do books talk to you?"

I chewed, tilting my head as if I were considering her question. I could feel Infinity's energy pooling against my back, even through the pack and my sweater. "Sometimes. But not how I think you mean."

Her gaze flicked to the black leather book on the shelf once again.

"Did that book talk to you when you touched it?"

"Not exactly. It just…it felt like it wanted me to open it."

I nodded, giving her space to elaborate.

"I couldn't, though. Mom said I shouldn't touch anything in your library at the manor. She says you collect magical things? Same goes for in your office here, right?"

"Yes."

"It's just…" She frowned at the sandwich in her hand. "I was touching the book before I even saw it, really. Before I even sat down. I was going to work on my…stories, though I told Mom I'd do homework."

Magical compulsion. Though I wasn't certain why Rook would have felt it so intensely when her own magic hadn't manifested yet. "It's safe on the shelf for now, so we'll leave it there until I can get it properly catalogued."

Rook glanced around at the piles of books and papers occupying almost every centimeter of the desk. "That's your job then? Like a magical librarian."

"That's part of my job, but I also preserve magical items and…help with magical creatures, if needed." 'Help' in this case meaning relocate, contain—or only if absolutely necessary, dispose of. But Rook didn't need to know that part.

"Gran has lots of spellbooks, passed down through generations. I'm not supposed to touch those either."

"Totally annoying, isn't it?"

She burst out laughing.

Still smiling, we ate in silence. Rook didn't look at the book again. Whatever compulsion it held had apparently worn off. That was one of the oddly difficult things about being an all-powerful dragon. Magic that might affect others—those I really needed to protect—might barely register for me. Though, again, Rook did seem oddly susceptible.

"Thank you for joining me for lunch," I said, glad for the companionship after the tense morning.

"Thank you for sharing. I promise I won't tell Sisu." Her grin had a slightly wicked edge, though, so I had a feeling she might just store that info for later use.

That was fine. My brother needed to learn to share. And that was a lesson I wasn't particularly skilled at teaching, since it wasn't a strong trait of mine either.

Magic shifted through the outer office. Witch magic by its tenor. As far as I'd sensed, my other employees hadn't returned from lunch yet, so perhaps I hadn't needed to eat in the office myself. Though taking a seat at the witch-run cafe had felt oddly intimidating, as if doing so might expose me somehow. As not one of them. Even within a mixture of magical and nonmagical clientele.

I glanced over my shoulder as River Byrne appeared in the doorway, already smiling at her daughter.

"Hey, Mom." Rook grinned back, then crammed the last of the sandwich in her mouth.

River laughed quietly, stepping through the wards on the office without obvious effort. So the so-called password didn't need to be said out loud.

I was going to have to figure out how to replace the wards. Not only at the office, but in my own library as well. All my efforts over the last week had fizzled, as if I was missing some component. But whatever the key element was for me personally, I hadn't figured it out yet.

My Mom would have known, would have guided me, helped me. If she'd been available. But we still hadn't heard from her, or gotten any other news on her whereabouts. The collection she was on had kept her away for almost thirteen months now.

My heart pinched, then felt…hollow. But I pushed the pain away with the knowledge that the archive would have copious books on magical wards that might guide me in the right direction. I promised myself that I would ask Crystal for a list of recommended titles.

"River," I said, smiling.

The red-haired witch nodded, but kept her gaze oddly averted, taking in the desk and the remains of our lunch, but not me. She was dressed as casually as I'd ever seen her, in dark-washed designer jeans and a figure-flattering royal-blue cashmere sweater. A long gold chain hung from her neck, ending in what I thought might have been three entwined Rs. Metalwork crafted by her sister, Ravine, most likely. The youngest Byrne sibling liked to refer to herself as a metal mage.

The blond streaks hidden in River's hair made an appearance as she crossed around the desk to touch Rook on the shoulder, murmuring, "Would you give Dusk and me a moment?"

"What?" Rook cried, not bothering to moderate her tone.

"Please. Then we'll grab some ice cream."

Rook huffed, standing up with enough force that the chair flew back on its rollers. River caught it before it slammed into the sideboard running the length of the window.

"Like I can be bribed with treats," the ten-year-old said. But she grabbed her backpack from the floor, taking off for the door and calling, "Thanks for lunch, Dusk," over her shoulder.

"You're welcome."

Rook crossed through the wards, taking just enough steps to get out of her mother's sight, but likely still in earshot. Unless the office wards blocked sound for her. They didn't for me.

River tidied the lunch remains. I wasn't actually finished eating, but the witch's odd demeanor forced me to my feet to help her. Eventually, we swapped sides, and I sat behind the desk while she paced the other side of the office for a bit.

I pulled Infinity out of my backpack, setting it on the desk and tucking the pack into a lower drawer I'd cleared earlier. I didn't go out of my way to display my personal archive, but River had been in and out of my home enough that I had no doubt she'd already seen it. Sensed it.

"Does a talent for telepathy or empathy run in the Byrne coven?" I asked, breaking the silence.

River blinked at me, apparently thrown. "No. We all have earth affinities. Usually."

Her skin tone was at least three shades paler than her daughter's. I wondered what affinities Rook's biological father brought to her genetic mix.

"Why?" the witch asked tersely.

"Rook had a strong reaction to a book she found."

"You let her touch one of your books?!" River stopped pacing, gripping the back of the guest chair to glare at me.

I leaned back, setting Infinity in my lap and resting my hand on the gently humming archive. I just looked at River, confused—but also getting a little pissed at her odd behavior. I'd seen her just that morning. She'd been all smiles and gushing about Kellan Conall finally being free to start work on the custom cabinets for the new kitchen. The werewolf contractor was apparently more than worth waiting for, according to the Byrne witches. I'd already met his twin sister, Gitta, who was overseeing the entire renovation.

"Did you think that a ten-year-old could be left in this office without touching anything?" I finally asked.

River grimaced. "It wasn't my…"

I waited.

She didn't finish the thought, instead sitting down with a huff. "I have something awkward to ask you."

"For Auntie Ayre?" Yeah, I wasn't an idiot. I was also still covered in the coffee-crusted ashes of the imp that the elder witch had murdered just to get one over on me. Or whatever the hell her motivation had been.

Magic shifted in the main office as my new employees returned from lunch. I glanced at the clock set on a nearby shelf. That had been a long break.

River sighed. "As a favor to the Byrne witches."

"I don't trade favors with witches," I said caustically.

"Dusk…" River groaned. "I don't want to be having this conversation, to be caught in the middle."

"How could you possibly be caught in the middle of something that occurred between me and a former employee?"

River huffed. "She's my aunt. My mother's elder sister. I'm caught."

Elder. Meaning Ayre had been passed over for coven leader, then. That was interesting.

"It was just a prank, Dusk. And all of them were in on it. You can't punish one without—"

"It wasn't just a prank. Your aunt murdered what is commonly referred to as a tooth fairy. A creature so rare they're practically extinct."

"An accident—"

"Did your aunt fail to mention my trace spell?"

"No," River said. Then she continued cautiously. "But…no one recognized the spell you used. So the veracity is…in question."

"By whom?"

River closed her eyes for a moment, then spoke wearily. "Dusk, you don't want to be facing my mother instead of me, and her asking the same question, requesting the same favor."

"Favor? Or demand?"

"You're a witch, Dusk. I understand you're new to all this, but even as a Godfrey in Byrne territory, you are…a witch at the bottom of the pecking order."

I leaned forward, placing Infinity on the desk and pressing my hand to the archive. The bronzed leather warmed under my touch. River's gaze flicked nervously to my hands, then to meet my eyes. But she couldn't hold my gaze. She tried to smile as if to soften her as-yet-unvoiced demand, but couldn't hold onto the expression.

"Send your mother, then." My voice must have conveyed the depth of my ire, because River flinched. "I'd be happy to make a formal complaint. The Byrne coven doesn't want their witches going around murdering other Adepts. If, for no other reason, than the community isn't going to stand for it."

She scoffed. "Other Adepts? Please, that's just..." Then she trailed off, perhaps realizing what she'd been about to say.

"Sentience and intelligence is usually where that line is firmly drawn," I said coolly. "When it becomes murder."

A multitude of emotions flitted over River's face, mostly frustration and disbelief. I caught the moment she decided to keep up her side of the fight—despite knowing she wasn't going to win.

And that was seriously annoying.

Not only was I right, but I had a lot of paperwork to do before I could get home with dinner for Sisu.

And honestly, I'd been hoping that River and I were in the process of becoming...not friends, but at least friendly. The Byrne siblings had helped smooth the transition into Dublin for Sisu and me almost immeasurably. Of course, I was also paying what my lawyer described as a hefty fee for a good portion of that help.

"Imps are little more than...than...bugs." River stiffened her shoulders a little, though she still held her hands clasped before her. Perhaps that was protocol for witches, since most of them cast with their hands. Or at least they made a show of using their hands.

I, of course, knew better. River Byrne could access her magic and direct it with nary a flick of her fingers. Intent was all that was needed. She had an affinity for wood. Which meant that most of the furniture, shelving, and flooring in the office could be twisted to her will, most likely without her uttering a single word.

I stood, tucking Infinity against my hip as I crossed to the shelf holding the sealed book that had tried to compel Rook, along with the empty pewter jar that once held the tooth fairy. "I would have thought you'd be more interested in the fact that Rook was almost beguiled by a book that suddenly made an appearance on my desk. While I was out for lunch."

I could feel River stiffen behind me, her magic coiling in on itself. "That..." she sputtered. "That's just...another example of...your obvious..."

I grabbed the roll of parchment tucked behind the imp's empty jar, turning to eye the witch. "My obvious incompetence?"

River flushed. "I was going to say...youth."

"Oh? Wasn't my incompetence how your aunt justified murder? That she was somehow rescuing me? From a creature you'd personally classify as a bug?"

River flushed, clenching her hands together in her lap.

I handed the parchment to the frustrated witch. She accepted, but not without hesitating first.

"The term imp is a very broad classification," I said smoothly, crossing back around my desk.

River smiled slightly, as if she thought she might have somehow convinced me. She unrolled the parchment.

"You understand the shorthand?" I asked. "For the classification of a magical creature?"

Her smile became strained. "I do not."

"Top right-hand corner." I settled back into my chair. I'd already committed the report handwritten on the parchment to memory. That was how my magic worked. I remembered almost everything I read or saw. "The creature was collected by Celeste Cameron, who, as I'm sure you know, ran this archive for over twenty years."

"Of course I know," River snapped, frowning as she tried to read the official documentation I'd given her.

"Well, then, perhaps you'll trust her observations and conclusions."

"Dusk, please. I'm not suggesting—"

"I have a lot of work to do, River. We're only having this conversation because I thought we were...I thought we'd been building a friendship."

The red-haired witch swallowed, glancing at the parchment, then opening her mouth as if to say something.

She didn't, though, just returning her gaze to the parchment instead. She mouthed a few of the words—no doubt sounding out the Latin—until she got partway down the page. Her jaw tensed.

I knew she'd gotten to the 'reasoning' section of Celeste Cameron's notes. The section that said although the tooth fairy imp might be driven by instinct, it displayed a marked ability to reason and problem solve. It had been classified as mildly aggressive (unless hungry) but not hostile.

River didn't bother reading the rest. She allowed the parchment to roll up on itself again, holding it in one hand. She cleared her throat, not quite looking at me. "Be that as it may..." She corrected herself, starting again. "We all have different upbringings..."

I raised my eyebrows, actually interested in how River was planning to convince me that since her aunt was of an older generation, murder wasn't murder—for Ayre, at least.

But she faltered, looking down at the rolled parchment. "I liked you too, Dusk."

"I understand how witches work," I said.

River's head snapped up. "I'm not suggesting that...it's just for the sake of...this is not the right foot to start off on with the coven."

"I completely agree."

A smile formed at the edges of the witch's lips.

I squashed it. "Tomorrow, I'll let the entire staff go. As you indicated, they all knew what Ayre planned to do."

"What? Tomorrow?"

I deliberately mistook her confusion. "Well, firing them partway through their day seems petty. I'd thought the six-month probation was enough, but you've convinced me otherwise."

"You can't possibly run this entire archive without support—"

"I can. For however long it takes to find trustworthy employees who understand that letting a starving imp loose in my office as a prank, then murdering it, is wrong."

River shook her head. "This...Dusk, this isn't how this conversation should be going."

"This isn't how two witches communicate?"

She pressed her lips together so hard they whitened.

"Oh, I see," I said. "I'm supposed to just do what you say? Even though I'm the head curator of a major magical archive, I'm to bow to every demand the coven makes?"

"It's a request. A favor. To give my aunt a second chance. At least have a conversation—"

"We talked."

"Dusk! Ayre thought you were having trouble with the imp. Throwing open the shutters—"

"— had been her plan from the start. She waited for me to enter the building, then followed. With the other three lined up to witness her...what? Triumphing over me? Somehow? I, however, was focused on spilled coffee and the cinnamon buns I got up at 4:00 A.M. to bake. And the imp, which was under control."

River rubbed her face. "Ayre's job, her position, is important to my aunt. You don't want to make my mother…" She grimaced.

"Mad?" I asked evenly.

"You're a new witch in Byrne coven territory," River said sadly. "You don't want to be ostracized."

"Will Ridge feel the same way? Do I have to find another design firm?"

"Another design firm…" River blinked. Rapidly.

I couldn't help but push it. I was that angry. River had been gushing about helping me renovate the estate since the moment she set eyes on it. It was years' worth of work. "Since you don't like me anymore."

River stood up, set the parchment on the desk, and strode toward the door, speaking over her shoulder. "I'll send our final bill. The Conalls can work from the drawings as is until you can find another firm."

"River Byrne," I said darkly, slowly standing but keeping my hand on Infinity.

She spun to face me in the doorway.

"I am the head curator of the magical archives," I said dispassionately. "If another Byrne witch trespasses on my collection or puts anyone in harm's way by their actions, I will not be so lenient."

"Oh, yes?" she sneered. "A bug's life is more important to you than a witch's?"

"That's not up to me," I said. "But I'd be happy to refer the matter to the Convocation."

"My mother is on the Convocation!"

"One of thirteen votes," I said. "And how many seats do the Godfreys hold?" I already knew the answer—two—so I didn't wait to add, "And Celeste Cameron's cousin holds another, yes?"

"Yes."

I reached across the desk, touching the parchment roll that Celeste had written upon her collection of the tooth fairy imp. "The Cameron coven wouldn't want one of theirs besmirched."

"I really did like you, Dusk," River snarled.

"No. You liked my house."

The witch's jaw dropped.

I cut her off before she could offer a retort. "It was me who liked you. Enough to invite you in, to let you into my life when I was the vulnerable one, the new witch in town. If our roles were reversed, would we still be having this conversation?"

River snapped her mouth shut. Then she crossed into the main office. I felt her pause. She stepped back. "Please don't fire the others."

"I'll lay them off," I said, having already looked up the terminology and the notice required to do so. I'd asked Tawny Sherwood for the information before I'd even started the job.

River looked as though she was considering arguing with me. Then her shoulders slumped. "Ayre is their superior, and not just at work for one of them. If this was...premeditated, then they were just following orders."

I already knew that was true. "Then I'll stick with the six-month probationary period. Out of deference to the coven."

I might have sneered that last part.

River countered, "Three months. Most of them have been here for years. They're good at their jobs."

"According to Ayre."

The witch grimaced. "Dusk. You could at least—"

"I'm not even remotely in the wrong here," I said quietly, allowing a little hurt to filter into my firmly held professional demeanor. "You asking me for an open-ended favor only confirms that you know that. Or do I come across as so inept that you assumed I didn't understand—that I wouldn't understand—the magic backing the words of the next witch in line to lead the Byrne coven?"

River scrubbed her hand over her face. "Hell, I barely understand what a favor like that means. I was...being flippant." She locked her gaze to mine. "My mother won't make that mistake."

"I am not her witch to command," I said.

"You don't understand witches very well."

"Perhaps not. Is my life in danger?"

"No!"

"And what about Sisu? Will the Byrne coven go after a five-year-old to punish me for exercising my right, my duty, as Ayre's employer?"

"Of course not!"

"Then I'll expect your mother's visit. And your final bill."

River frowned, clenching and unclenching her hands. Then she walked away. Standing her ground.

Good for her. To take a position and stick with it, for family. That was noble. Completely irrational and illogical, but still noble. Loyal.

I actively ignored the way my stomach twisted as the witch I'd been starting to think of as a friend walked away. But it would be better to maintain some distance from the Byrne witches. Polite, but with no need to prove myself, as Pearl Godfrey had already suggested.

On a purely selfish level, though, overseeing the revitalization of the estate without River and Ridge was a daunting idea. Especially with the backlog currently surrounding me at work. I placed both hands on Infinity, breathing through a momentary bout of anxiety.

But…I could still feel the ashy remains of the imp stuck in the dried coffee coating me from chest to knees, as well as in my hair. And I still couldn't bring myself to brush it off any more than I'd already done.

If I'd been quicker, not so concerned with the damn coffee and making a good first impression, I could have easily secured the imp before Ayre had enacted the final phase of her hazing. And the imp would still be alive. Preserved and in stasis, yes. But alive.

Then again…if Ayre was a typical representative of the Byrne coven, then it was better for them to understand my perspective upfront. Now when they needed help with a magical artifact or creature, they'd know that my aid wasn't to be bribed or coerced. And that preserving life—including the lives of witches, no matter what the coven might now think—was of the utmost importance to me.

Yes, I knew how witches from old covens worked when it came to their so-called pecking order. I had just hoped it was one of those antiquated beliefs that the newest generation would at least ignore, if not actively reject.

CHAPTER TWO

UTTER RELIEF FLOODED THROUGH ME AS I PASSED through the ornate wrought-iron front gate and stepped onto the front path of the estate. From the street, the magical entrance appeared as an alcove opening up to a courtyard for a looming Georgian apartment building. But stepping through that alcove brought me onto a stone path slicing through an expansive lawn that had long been allowed to go wild, interconnecting with other paths all but hidden from view between craggy trees and misshapen hedges.

I wasn't certain I'd ever felt an emotional burden lift off me in such a visceral way before. I couldn't pause to enjoy it, though. I was forty-five minutes late for dinner with Sisu. He'd become so tyrannical about keeping to a schedule that I was regretting having put him in charge of Uncle Beckett's watch so we wouldn't miss any of our flights from Norway to Dublin. It was making it even more difficult to distract him from the life-altering move and leaving everything he'd ever known behind—including the brownies who ran our mom's estate.

The watch in Sisu's custody was a bit of magic that kept perfect time and tracked the date through any and all time zones—including tracking the year and century for any bearer who had a habit of slipping through time and dimensions. The watch would also help a time-lost bearer get back to the 'now' they'd left. Unfortunately for Uncle Beckett, though, he'd wandered off without the magical artifact one day and hadn't been seen since.

The watch liked to chatter on about the weather as well, though not with much accuracy. It was reportedly more accurate when predicting demon summonings—though the number of those it had had to track was thankfully low.

The sunset was barely tinting the horizon as I hustled up the front path, carrying enough Indian take-out to feed a dozen people. Or two dragons for a couple of evenings. I'd gotten poori to amuse Sisu, and I didn't want the puffy deep-fried 'balloon' bread to completely cool and deflate before I got dinner on the table.

The huge house—correction: manor—loomed before me, the lower left side lit up while the rest of the windows remained dark. It had been a terrible day. I'd struggled to ignore the lingering sadness that had set in after my fight with River Byrne. The confrontation with her Aunt Ayre had been far easier to ignore in the aftermath, but the residual magic of the imp's death had continued to echo all around my hands, no matter how much I'd tried to distract myself by getting Celeste Cameron's desk in order.

No.

My desk.

My office.

I stepped up to the ornately carved front doors—two slabs of dark-stained walnut set with images of wolves below and a raptor above. A light I hadn't noticed before was lit overhead, perhaps recently installed—or fixed—by the electrician. I, of course, had no problem wandering around with only a hint of moonlight or starlight to illuminate my path, but the warm glow gave depth to the doors' carving.

I awkwardly redistributed the bags I was carrying so I was holding them all in my left hand, then pressed my right hand to one door, to the neck of the great wolf carved there.

Energy swelled under my palm, pulled up from roots that threaded deep into the earth under my feet, and radiating through the thick-planed walnut wood. The entrance to the house had been carved from an ancient tree. River Byrne suspected that some of the branches actually stretched through the structure of the front of the house, and had made it very clear that no destructive renovation was to be done to those exterior walls. Ever.

Just thinking of River evoked a weird, anxiety-ridden reaction that I quickly shoved away. I didn't have much experience with face-to-face confrontations. It was hard to rebel against family members who came and went from my life with regularity, and I'd never had an actual job. I'd even ended my physical relationship with Zeke by letter.

Well, sort of. I'd changed the tenor and frequency of my letters to him, at least. Then I'd tried to simply leave him a note about my move to Dublin rather than talking to him…

I was dwelling on my inadequacies.

Not fun.

Or productive.

I focused on the energy lightly pulsing under my hand instead.

The tree that was now the front doors and their doorframe wasn't alive, of course. And yet it was. The dark, smooth wood warmed under my touch, as if greeting me. As if trying to soothe me further.

I stopped myself from speaking to it. It wasn't sentient. It was just that the house had been built for—or possibly built by—a guardian dragon, Jiaotu-who-was. She had tapped into the natural magic of the tree when having the front door constructed. It seemed likely that she'd used that same energy to ward the house and the property, but that magic wasn't something I could personally tap into and direct. Not yet anyway.

The door clicked open unprompted, swinging wide to reveal the marble-floored, cathedral-roofed great room that cut through the center of the manor, with more large rooms and a wide staircase branching off it.

The sound of pounding footsteps on wood flooring thundered toward me. Three sets. Then Sisu, flanked by the Conall twins, practically exploded into the main room from the dining room. The trio, each laughing madly as they jostled each other for position, made a beeline for me—though Sisu wasn't running anywhere near as fast as he could.

My five-year-old white-blond, pale-skinned brother took the lead, then made a dramatic show of suddenly stopping so he could slide the rest of the distance across the marble floor in his sock feet.

The other two, Neve and Lile, followed suit.

I had no doubt they'd been practicing the move, though technically they were supposed to be studying together under the tutelage of Bethany. The werewolf, who was an enforcer for the Conall pack, was the same tutor who worked with Rook twice a week in the late afternoons. I was surprised that Gitta Conall hadn't taken her girls home for the evening yet.

Sisu was in his typical outfit of navy shorts, a printed T-shirt, and a black hoodie, with baggy wool socks. The taller of the twins, Lile, was clad in forest-green-dyed jeans and a purple sweater, with a variegated scarf twined around her neck. Neve was in similar attire, but her jeans were bright blue with white-painted flowers.

"What did you get us for dinner?" Sisu asked in greeting—a young dragon always had his priorities in place, even when posing as a witch—then started relieving me of the take-out bags before I had a chance to answer. "Smells like Indian."

"Indian!" Neve and Lile crowed in unison, helping Sisu with the burden of carrying the food.

Neve and Lile were fraternal twins, six years old. And other than their general coloring and their eyes, they looked exceedingly different. Neve wore her brown hair in a long ponytail that was currently springing forth from the top of her head. Lile's slightly lighter brown hair was cropped short in a pixie cut so adorable that I'd imagined cutting my own unruly mane to match. Except my hair would then just spring up all around my head. Neve was shorter with delicate features, while Lile was taller and rail slim. Both of them blinked at me with identical and extremely unusual golden-green eyes.

A vibrant green was the typical color of shapeshifter magic, but the girls were too young to have manifested their wolves yet. Still, those eyes, and the fact that they almost kept up with Sisu, indicated that their power was definitely already making itself present in their speed and strength.

If I'd had to guess, that was most likely why Gitta Conall was homeschooling the twins, and why she'd had no problem offering to add Sisu to that arrangement when I'd asked her about schools over a week ago.

"Race you to the dining room," Sisu challenged, taking off with his bags of food.

"We set the table already," Neve announced before following my brother.

"I hope you had a good first day, Dusk," Lile said, sounding as if she was dutifully quoting someone. Likely her mother.

"Thank you," I said politely. "It was…eventful. Where's Bethany?" I could feel one other person in the manor, but by the tenor of their magic, it wasn't the kids' tutor.

Lile wrinkled her nose. "You don't want to know." Then she took off after her sister and Sisu.

Sighing, I followed, mournfully eyeing the stairs that swept up to the second floor on my right. I really wouldn't have minded a bath before dinner. But I was late, and I didn't want to be held responsible for Sisu's actions if he got too hungry.

I pushed through the thick layers of plastic that sealed off the section of the house currently under construction from the rest of it. Well, one of the sections. A bunch of the bedrooms had been stripped back and were in the process of being repainted or repapered, among other improvements—including the much-needed insulation the Conalls had already pumped into the walls and attics. Though I'd resisted the suggestion that actual walls of wood frame and plasterboard be added to the central tower so it could be insulated properly as well. The tower was constructed out of thick stone, including the narrow winding staircase, and I adored it as it was.

Apparently, guardian dragons didn't get as cold as a regular dragon did—that regular dragon being me. They might have just been far better at lighting fires, though, since there was at least one fireplace in each of the larger rooms in the house, and in all the bedrooms. Or the brownies who had once claimed the estate had been better at that sort of thing. Either way, when they weren't being used, the fireplaces were the largest culprits in the heat-leakage issue.

Instead of immediately joining the kids in the dining room, I had followed the slightly unusual power signature I'd felt the moment I set foot on the property, tracing it to the back of the house. I'd met most of the construction crew already—all Adepts of various kinds, mostly werewolves—but hadn't expected anyone to be working late except Bethany. She had agreed to stay through dinner for a couple of extra hours, because I had an appointment to meet Ravine Byrne's antiquities dealer later that evening.

Not that I expected the witch to keep our appointment now. Not after my run-in with her elder sister, River.

Though he was some sort of shapeshifter, the stranger looming over a temporary workbench in the middle of what was going to be the main kitchen was definitely not Bethany. He was working with some sort of tool—sanding, maybe?

He looked up as I entered, instantly and steadily meeting my gaze. The plastic sealing the doorway fell back into place behind me.

The air was slightly dusty. Bright pockets of light from work lamps set around the large space gave the room a bright white glow. The sounds of Sisu, Neve, and Lile chattering away in the dining room filtered through more thick layers of plastic encasing a doorway on the wall to my left.

I recognized the stranger, though I'd never met him. In his late twenties, he was the spitting image of his sister, Gitta—yet somehow looked nothing like her at all.

Kellan Conall.

Tall, broad-shouldered, and so well muscled that his T-shirt had to be cutting off his circulation at the upper biceps, he was one of the largest men I'd ever seen. And I knew plenty of warrior dragons, as well as the treasure keeper of the guardian dragons—Pulou. Though not as tall, Pulou had a body like a grizzly bear's from the neck down—and looked the part as well, thanks to the enormous mink fur coat he always wore.

Kellan's hair was dark brown, his skin a lighter brown. And his eyes were the same strange golden-green as the twins. Magic flared in those eyes as he took me in, staring at me as forthrightly as I was staring at him. His nostrils flared as he turned off and set down the tool he'd been wielding.

The sound in the room faded, including the chatter from the dining room. The moment seemed to physically stretch before us, as if some sort of spell had been triggered. Yet the warm but completely disconnected sensation I was feeling wasn't magic. At least nothing remotely conventional.

"Dusk Godfrey," I finally said. Was it possible to feel heavy, as if I were rooted to the plywood-covered floor, and yet lightheaded at the same time?

Apparently, yes.

He grinned, revealing white teeth. But the expression did nothing to soften all the hard planes of his face. He looked as though he could run through a brick wall, through multiple brick walls, without getting a scratch, let alone faltering.

That probably wasn't a particularly attractive quality to anyone except for myself…my hormones? My magic?

And yes, I was still staring at him. And he at me.

"My employer," he said. His accent was lilting yet still deep, as if his voice or the words themselves were pulled from the depths of his being.

There was something seriously wrong with me.

"Kellan Conall," he said, pulling off his gloves.

Energy shifted through the room, a slight breeze coming out of nowhere. It flitted around me in an unvocalized whisper, then stilled. My limbs loosened, as if I'd been freed from whatever spell had been freezing me in the moment.

Kellan's eyes widened, then dropped to my feet.

A branch bedecked with white flowers and deep-green leaves sat on my left boot. From a citrus plant.

I leaned down and plucked it up. A heady scent of honey and the taste of citrus tickled my senses.

Magic. Not just the scent of the flower.

My magic. Telling me I was in the right place or on the right path. Or in this particular case…

All right, I had no idea what it was telling me or urging me toward.

Kellan's nostrils flared. He could smell the magic too. And he had clearly seen the flower manifest.

That was surprising. Not that a shapeshifter could smell magic. That was fairly typical. But it was strange that he'd witnessed the manifestation. As far as I knew, the guardian dragons and Sisu were the only people who'd ever seen a bit of flora present itself to me before. Not even my mother or Zeke had ever witnessed that as-yet-unexplained aspect of my archivist power.

"Well," he drawled, "that's…unusual."

I didn't answer. My mind was whirling as I tried to interpret what had just happened, both with the citrus blossom and meeting Kellan.

If the blossom was a warning, then I was surprised Infinity hadn't stirred in the depths of my backpack.

I caught another hint of honey from the blossom as I tucked it away in the upper interior pocket of my jacket. I would press it into Infinity when I didn't have quite so many witnesses.

Brushing his hands over his torso to clear a layer of wood shavings away, Kellan stepped toward me. "We've been waiting for you. Sisu…or Algernon, as he insisted I call him for the first half of our day…assured me that you'd bring enough food home to feed us all."

Algernon. "Bearded," I murmured, focusing on Kellan's green eyes as he neared. They were shot through with lightning strikes of gold that might have been a manifestation of his magic. "Wearing a mustache."

Kellan's eyes narrowed in confusion. His apparently spellbinding eyes, given the way I was staring at him.

"That's what Algernon means," I said, somehow raising my hand and wrapping my fingers around the warm, slightly dusty hand he'd offered to me, breaking the tradition by which the Adept rarely touched. "English etymology."

"Ah," he said, tilting his head slightly and squeezing my hand firmly.

Was he noticing the golden tint of my own hazel eyes? Jiaotu might have masked my magical signature for my assignment among the Adepts of Dublin, but he hadn't changed my appearance.

"You smell like coffee…and death, Dusk Godfrey," Kellan said.

He had omitted something in the middle of that observation, and I found myself suddenly hoping that my breath wasn't awful.

Also, the fact that he could smell the imp's remains on me even over the dried coffee confirmed that his scent for magic was acute.

I removed my hand from his. My fingers and palm felt oddly chilled after the warmth of his touch.

He frowned, opening his mouth—

Sisu burst through the plastic-sheathed doorway that led to the dining room. "Dusk! The food is getting cold, and Neve says it's rude to start without you."

"She's correct," I said, stepping away from Kellan easily. As if I hadn't just been rooted to the spot.

"I told you." Sisu grinned widely at the dark-haired shifter. "Indian for dinner."

Kellan grunted noncommittally, loosening a tool belt I hadn't even noticed, then stepping back to place it on the plywood workbench.

I had to force myself to look away.

What was wrong with me?

Was there some sort of magic involved? Kellan Conall didn't read as a typical shifter, though his twin sister Gitta did.

Sisu snagged my hand, lifting up on his tiptoes.

I leaned over him slightly.

"It's okay, right?" he asked in a whisper. "Inviting everyone to dinner?"

"Of course."

Sisu patted my arm with his free hand. "Your magic feels sad." Then he took off, diving through the plastic sheathing the doorway with only a hint of disturbance.

"They've been practicing that," Kellan said, stepping around me. "Passing through the plastic. For at least an hour." He swept his arm out, effortlessly catching the sheathing in the gesture, then pausing so I could walk through the opening he'd created.

"And Bethany?" I asked.

He smirked. "Best for Sisu to tell you. Confession is good for the soul."

I sighed. "That's what I thought."

He huffed quietly.

I stepped past him and through into the dining room.

He leaned into me as I did so, murmuring, "Lingering sadness. That's what I missed. Coffee, death, and a lingering sadness. A strange combination, especially after your first day of work at your dream job, as you told my sister. Why do you smell of sadness and death Dusk Godfrey?"

Ignoring the overly personal question, I crossed to take a seat, pulling off my backpack and coat.

Sisu, Lile, and Neve had set one end of the table with mismatched plates and cutlery, all of which appeared to have been randomly pulled from the crates of china and tableware we'd found in one of the attics. Except for napkins that had been folded into floppy fan shapes, the long, dark-wood table was bare of coverings. The trio had filled variously sized crystal wine glasses with water.

Sisu climbed into the chair at the head of the table, reaching into the center to pull the lids off the to-go containers nearest him.

"That's Kellan's spot!" Neve protested. "He's the highest-ranked pack member in attendance."

Sisu laid a blistering look on the six-year-old werewolf on his left. "Dusk is the head of this household."

Neve sputtered indignantly, then looked to her uncle for support.

"It's an honor to be invited to share Dusk and Sisu's meal, Neve," Kellan said without heat.

We all found our seats—Sisu at the head, me to his right, Lile and Neve across from me, and Kellan to my right. We passed around the containers of curries, rice, and roasted vegetables, each serving ourselves.

Kellan dipped his spoon into the saffron curry sauce, testing it before sliding it across to Lile. "Be careful with this one. It's hot."

"I can handle it," Neve declared.

Lile smirked at her twin, but didn't say anything.

"I'm sorry," I murmured. Though I had been planning on feeding Bethany, I hadn't expected the twins and Kellan at dinner, so I hadn't thought about whether the food would be too spicy for a young shapeshifter. "The yogurt should cut the heat a little." I gestured toward a smaller container that hadn't been opened yet.

"Thank you," Kellan murmured, reaching for the grouping of extra sauces that had been abandoned in the center of the table. He tugged the foil-wrapped roti closer, folding a piece in quarters for both Neve and Lile, then himself. Then he slid the rest toward me.

We ate in silence for a short while, Sisu perched in his chair instead of sitting properly. The table, which came up too high on Neve as well, was slightly awkward without bigger chairs, so I didn't correct him. Lile was taller, so she had more clearance.

I scooped mouthfuls of rice and curry into a small piece of roti, as Uncle Jamal had taught us during his recovery at the family estate six years ago. Sisu tried to mimic my movements, but his fingers were still a little too short to pull it off. So he resorted to just stuffing a mess of food into his mouth.

Neve eyed him with amusement, but when she bumped her shoulder against her sister, Lile refused to engage. The pixie-cut twin sat with her back straight and her gaze most often on her uncle. Out of respect, I thought, rather than fear or worry.

I waited until I'd cleared half my plate before I looked pointedly at Sisu. "Bethany?"

I knew it would be better to get some food into my brother before tackling whatever had gone on that afternoon with his new tutor. Bethany, who'd been recommended by the Conalls and the Byrnes, had already been tutoring Neve and Lile. She'd been more than amenable to taking on Sisu and transferring to working out of the manor while the renovations were going on. I'd delayed starting work myself to smooth the introduction, and there hadn't been any issues last week. That I knew of, at least. Bethany wasn't overly chatty.

Sisu shrugged. "She went home."

"Voluntarily?"

He stuffed another mess of roti, rice, and vegetable curry in his mouth, talking around it. "Sure."

"That's so odd," I said. "Because she said that after Gitta picked up Neve and Lile, she'd be happy to stay for a few hours so I could run an errand with Ravine."

"I can go with you," Sisu said, not a hint of remorse in his bright-blue eyes. "I can help carry things."

"After you told her your plans this morning, Gitta took the opportunity to grab dinner with Len." Kellan spoke in a low rumble that did all sorts of odd things to my vulnerable insides.

That had to be some sort of magic.

Right?

Because my insides weren't vulnerable. They were covered in thick dragon hide.

"But Bethany wasn't able to stay?" I asked, keeping my gaze on Sisu.

"She somehow got herself locked in the wine cellar Len's crew uncovered last week while rewiring the basement," Kellan said casually. "Thankfully for Bethany, the wine hadn't turned to vinegar."

It wouldn't have. The entire estate had been held in a stasis spell before Sisu and I had unlocked it. Except for the interior of the greenhouse, where the gnome resided.

"Unfortunately," Kellan continued, "I was a little busy confirming the layout for the kitchen cabinets, and I didn't notice the distinct lack of tutoring going on until shrieks from the backyard drew my attention."

"I wasn't shrieking," Neve muttered. Her gaze fixed to her mostly eaten dinner, she wrapped her right hand protectively around her left forearm.

"Sliced through to the bone," Lile confessed, somewhat gleeful, somewhat disgusted. Her unusual green eyes—almost a perfect match to her uncle's—flicked between her sister, Sisu, and me.

I carefully curated another mouthful of my deliciously spicy but rapidly cooling dinner. "Locking up a werewolf is a difficult feat. Are there silver chains and cuffs in the cellar?" I was fairly certain there weren't.

"No," Neve mumbled across from me. "But..." She glanced over at Sisu. "We wanted to spar."

Sisu, still perched on his chair, glowered down at his now-empty plate. "Sparring is important!"

"But not what Bethany was hired to teach you," I said mildly.

"No," Lile said mournfully. "She didn't like the look of the sword."

Bethany wasn't an idiot. She'd been Rook's full-time tutor, then Neve and Lile's. She held degrees in English and history from Cambridge University, and before that, she'd spent four years at the European campus of the Academy, honing her magic with other Adepts.

"We could have used your daggers," Sisu said belligerently. "But you took them to work with you."

"You'd have me go unarmed?"

"You have Jiaotu's blade!"

"My blade," I said pointedly. I doubted the werewolves at the dining table would recognize the name of a guardian dragon, but Sisu seemed to need the reminder. "You locked Bethany in the cellar."

"Yes."

"How?" Because a mere lock shouldn't have been able to hold a werewolf. Bethany might have been initially cautious about breaking the door latch—or just breaking the door—but not after she'd been trapped for a while.

Still looking completely belligerent, Sisu pulled an object out of his pocket, setting it on the table. He removed his hand.

An old-fashioned key. Specifically, the master key that had opened the gate and the front doors when we'd first come to the estate.

Kellan grunted but kept eating. Apparently, he hadn't figured out the key part of the puzzle.

I sighed. I hadn't yet figured out how to ward the shelves in the library, or my room, or the house as a whole for that matter. But I also hadn't known that the key could be used to lock tutors up in the wine cellar. Therefore I hadn't hidden it. "How did you figure out the cellar could be magically sealed?"

Sisu shrugged.

"We tested it," Lile said brightly. "It works on every room with a lock."

"Lile!" Neve hissed.

Lile clamped her mouth shut.

Kellan huffed, then ate another large mouthful of curry. Laughing, but trying to cover.

I wasn't amused. The idea of Sisu's sword cutting Neve to the bone wasn't terribly funny to me. I pinned my gaze to my brother. "Did you do anything else to Bethany?"

"No," he said quietly.

"Have you hurt anyone else?"

He looked up at me then, eyes wide. "I never would. Never."

I raised an eyebrow. "How did Neve get cut, then?"

"Oh, I did that," Lile said.

"The sword isn't a toy," I said, still keeping my tone mild. "Bethany was right."

"We don't have any bokken to practice with," Sisu cried.

"And what are you supposed to do when you discover we don't have practice swords, or anything else we need?" I asked.

Sisu muttered the answer under his breath.

I waited for him to repeat it.

"Write it down on the list."

"Did you apologize to Bethany?"

Sisu's shoulders hunched up to his ears. "She left."

I glanced over at Kellan. "Is she okay?"

"She'll be back tomorrow morning. She just needed a long run, but didn't want to do so here without permission to enter your woods as a wolf. And I was here to watch the kids." He shrugged, collecting the last pools of curry sauce on his plate with a lazy swipe of roti. "The cellar is fairly large, as is every bloody room in this mausoleum, but most shapeshifters don't fare well in confined spaces. Especially not for more than three hours."

I threw a look at Sisu. "Three hours?"

"We forgot!" he cried.

"Then it took me some time to get through the stone wall." Kellan's tone hardened. "Someone failed to mention the key."

Sisu's face crumpled. He climbed out of his chair to wrap himself around the arm of mine, whispering, "I didn't know if it was supposed to be a secret."

"After you spent hours testing it with Neve and Lile?" I asked doubtfully. "You decided it might be too secret to tell Kellan?"

Sisu flicked his bright-blue eyes to the large man on my right, then dropped his gaze to his hands, clutching the arm of my chair. "The twins are trustworthy."

Neve smiled.

Sisu threw a look at Lile. "I thought."

The taller twin frowned sadly.

"We'll compose an apology," I said. "You can write Bethany a note and give it to her tomorrow. And she can decide what would be a proper punishment."

"What?" Sisu cried, then he checked himself, nodding dourly. "I understand."

I leaned forward to grab the key.

Sisu hissed excitedly. "What's that?!"

I froze. It was always smart to be cautious around anything that excited a previously dejected Sisu that much.

My brother carefully grabbed a coil of my hair that had fallen forward, pulling it in front of my eyes. "What's that?" he repeated reverently.

The tiniest pulse of magic sparked from something tangled in my hair.

"An egg…" I whispered.

Joy flushed through me, filling all the dark empty places that had been left by the death of the tooth fairy imp.

Sisu laughed excitedly.

The girls shrieked incoherently, then dove under the table to pop up and clamber around me.

"Gentle, gentle," I cautioned. "There might be more."

"Tell me, tell me," Sisu demanded.

"It's the egg of a tooth fairy," I said. "A very rare imp."

"What?!" Neve cried, bouncing on her toes.

"So cool," Lile gushed.

"We'll need a jar," I said. The excitement coming off the three was utterly infectious. "Glass, if possible."

"In my paintbox, Neve," Kellan said. "Dump the shims from the smallest jar. And the large flashlight, Lile."

The girls took off, plastic rustling in their wake.

"Let go of my hair for a second, Sisu," I said.

My brother looked utterly aghast.

"It's been stuck to me all day. It isn't going anywhere." I shifted forward in the chair, pushing it behind me.

Kellan set my chair to the side. "Along with the coffee and the scent of death."

"Something like that," I muttered, slowly kneeling on the hardwood floor, then settling back on my heels. Sisu followed along, rather than letting go of my hair.

The girls barreled back into the dining room. Kellan took the flashlight from Lile, switching it on. The beam was so bright it slashed through what had seemed like an already well-lit room.

Neve pressed the jar into my hands. A tiny empty mason jar. I flipped open the hinged lid and blew the dust out of it, though dust likely wouldn't matter.

"I'll do it," Sisu hissed excitedly. "Let me, please."

I knew I couldn't search my own hair, and tiny fingers would be better for the task anyway. "All three of you."

Neve, Lile, and Sisu snapped to attention before me, Neve grinning so hard it looked like the expression might actually hurt. Lile was alert and ready. And Sisu was as serious as I'd ever seen him.

"You must be very, very gentle," I cautioned. "The eggs will be fragile. Follow the glints of magic…Neve and Lile, can you see the glints?"

Sisu pointed at the hank of hair he still held around the height of my cheekbone. Both Neve and Lile leaned in, squinting. Kellan, standing so close I could feel warmth radiating from him, shifted the angle of the light, keeping it away from my eyes, but trying to help the twins see the tiny egg.

Neve cried out quietly, excited, "There, there, you see, Lile? It's round and gray, almost white." She flared her nostrils, leaning closer. "And it smells…it smells like…"

She blinked up at her uncle. "I don't know that smell."

"It's hard to pick up over the stale coffee," Kellan said gently. "It smells a little like dark, rich earth, yes?"

"Oh, yes," Lile said.

"Okay," I said. "You need to find each egg, if there's more than just the one, and very, very gently transfer them to the jar."

"Don't…shouldn't we put leaves and stuff in the jar first?" Neve asked.

"That's for bugs," Lile said. "Not eggs."

"And then we'll hatch them?" Sisu asked.

"That's not for us to do," I said, holding the jar by my chin. "We'll keep them safe while we figure out who to send them to." Mistress Brightshire, perhaps. The brownie who ran our family estate in Norway would know what to do to help preserve an imp's eggs.

Both Neve and Lile looked to Sisu.

He nodded to Lile, and she carefully took the hair he was holding.

"Gentle, gentle," Sisu muttered to himself as he leaned in and carefully plucked the egg from my hair. Holding it on his fingertip, he transferred it over, just able to get his fingers and thumb within the jar's mouth. It took an extra flick—the egg was sticky—but he managed to lightly drop it into the jar, then withdraw his hand.

We all leaned forward to gaze at the tiny gray egg. It glinted with magic again, and the girls gasped.

Sisu was grinning madly, as was I. The sorrow over losing the imp, feeling its unique magic fade from the world, loosened its steel hold on my chest a little.

"Imps?" Kellan asked from behind me with a doubtful grunt.

"Yes."

He waited.

I huffed, half-laughing, half-sighing. Then, not quite knowing why I was telling him anything at all, I added, "One was murdered at my office today."

"What?" Sisu cried.

"It must have deposited the eggs before that...when it was tangled in my hair."

"And spilling your coffee?" Kellan's tone was darkly amused.

"Tooth fairies are real?" Lile asked. Then she pulled back her upper lip and deliberately wiggled one of her front teeth.

"There aren't many of them left," I said. "So they're mostly considered myth now. But there was one in my office this morning, collected by the former head curator."

"And you let it go?" Neve asked, frowning. "And…it died."

"I didn't. Let it go. Or murder it. I don't…it was wrong. It is wrong to hurt magical creatures just because they're smaller than us, or scary, or different…" I trailed off, realizing I was on the edge of tears. And lecturing the kids.

Neve looked up at Kellan. If he responded to the look, I didn't see it.

"Let's look for the rest," Lile said. "If the imp left its eggs with you, then it must have known you'd protect them."

My heart squeezed in my chest. The transference had likely been unintentional, but I preferred Lile's interpretation of the events.

I sat still, holding the jar aloft as Sisu and the twins gently combed through my hair, dividing it into sections and murmuring quietly to themselves.

Despite being forced into an utterly passive role, which usually went against my very nature, there was something completely soothing about tiny fingers and the touch of fledgling magic running through my wild mane.

Kellan shifted position when the trio did. Pushing back the table a bit to make space, he ended up facing me, but still focused on keeping the flashlight angled away from my eyes.

I found myself staring at his large hands and muscled forearms, not able to look away without disturbing the egg hunt.

Not that I actually wanted to look away…

Neve found the second egg in the hairline at the back of my neck. She and Lile argued briefly about who got to transfer it to the jar, with Neve claiming ownership, then setting the tiny egg next to the one Sisu had already collected.

The right side of my head didn't yield any more eggs, which wasn't a surprise. The imp had mostly climbed around my left shoulder. But the trio decided they wanted to look a second time, changing tactics by lifting one layer of my hair at a time, from top to bottom. Kellan was commissioned to hold it tight in a messy twist at the top of my head.

Sisu found the third and final egg. He graciously let Lile deposit it into the jar, and I flipped the lid closed. Kellan let my hair go and it fell all around my neck and shoulders—warmed, I would have sworn, by his touch.

And since that was ridiculous, I ignored the feeling and focused on the jar in my palm, still feeling lighter than I had all day. Tiny pinpoint pulses of magic intermittently emanated from all three eggs. Ayre Byrne might have murdered one rare magical creature today, but we'd just rescued three others.

"Thank you," I said. And then, unable to contain my relief, I threw my head back and laughed.

Neve, Lile, and Sisu joined me, peals of laughter ringing around the room. Unleashed with our giddy joy, wild magic rippled outward, buffeting against the walls.

The energy that underpinned the manor responded to us, stretching. Almost like a cat did when someone offered to pet it.

That should have been disconcerting. I noted Kellan rolling his shoulders, though he might have been responding to the wild magic from all of us, not necessarily the house. But I was slowly getting used to it. Sisu had picked up that sleepy energy the moment he'd set foot inside, and he'd been trying to 'wake' the house ever since.

And that gave me an idea.

"Will you add a touch of your magic?" I asked, speaking to everyone. "To help keep the eggs safe?" I wasn't certain what body temperature the imp usually maintained, so I would just have to hope that the house was warm enough. But I knew that even the unhatched eggs of a magical creature likely needed magic to survive.

"How?" Neve asked, crowding closer.

"It's like…making a wish."

Sisu pressed against my right shoulder, cupping his hand on the side of the jar still resting in my palm. Lile did the same to the left, and Neve covered the front.

"A wish," Lile whispered.

"I wish…" My voice broke. I cleared my throat. "I wish…to keep the imp eggs protected. Safe." A tiny pool of my magic rose in my palm, coating the underside of the jar in a golden glow.

Kellan settled his fingertips on the top of the jar. I met his gaze—and for some reason, didn't drop it.

We stared at each other. But connected somehow, not confrontational.

Sisu, who practically had his nose pressed to the jar, whispered, "A wish for a safe place."

Neve, Lile, and Kellan murmured, "A safe place."

Soft touches of energy from each of them encircled the mason jar—a casting of pure intent. The golden glow took on a green tint, then faded.

"Do you want to put it on a shelf in the library?" I asked Sisu. "Not right next to the windows or the fireplaces."

He nodded solemnly, carefully taking the jar from me, then holding it before him. He took exaggeratedly careful steps from the dining room. Neve and Lile were practically plastered to his sides, hands hovering under the jar just in case my brother lost hold of it.

Kellan hunkered down before me, switching off the flashlight. Then he slowly reached for me, sliding his thumb across my cheek but not otherwise touching me. "You're crying," he murmured. Then he looked at his wet thumb as if it held something intriguing…as if it held magic.

And maybe it did. But before I'd met Kellan Conall, everything I'd read on the subject told me that most shapeshifters couldn't see magic. Scent it, yes, but not see.

The same way Kellan had seen the citrus blossom manifest.

"I've never had a magical creature die in my arms before. Felt its magic ebb from the world completely," I whispered. I still wasn't certain why I was sharing—except that having another adult around to talk to was comforting. "Not by my hand or any other's. I understand that sometimes such things are unavoidable, but that wasn't the case today. And I'm happy…for the eggs…that all is not lost."

"Who's responsible for the imp's murder?" Kellan asked. His tone was deceptively soft, but his energy shifted as if becoming aware. Ready.

"It's taken care of." I straightened, stepping over to the table, tugging it back into place, and beginning to collect the dishes. I didn't need the Conall wolves pitting themselves against the Byrne witches. That would make everything far, far worse.

It was already unusual for two disparate groups of Adept to occupy the same territory. But Dublin, and more specifically this whole part of Ireland, was apparently large enough that they coexisted without any overly obvious issues.

A large basket handwoven out of dark-green leaves and filled with mandarin oranges appeared in the center of the dark oak table. Another grin swamped my face. I left the rest of the dishes where they were, reaching for the last unopened container and setting it next to the oranges.

Kellan prowled around the dining room table, his narrowed eyes riveted to the oranges. He stopped just across from me, pinning me with that same look.

My grin widened. Shapeshifters liked to be in control of their environment. Which made complete sense, of course. It was one thing for me to come home with Indian food that was slightly too spicy and imp eggs in my hair. But it was a completely different thing for a basket of oranges to appear without Kellan sensing whatever magic had conveyed it.

I let him off the hook. "The estate has a gnome."

His glower deepened. "A gnome?"

I nodded—though I hadn't actually met the gnome that resided in the greenhouse face-to-face yet myself. I took the lid off the final to-go container, revealing gulab jamun. The syrup-soaked fried dumpling dessert was far too sweet for me, but was a favorite of Sisu's. "Dessert!" I yelled.

It took a moment, but then footsteps started pounding their way back toward the dining room.

I sat down, setting the cold remains of my dinner to the side and reaching for an orange.

Kellan took the seat across from me, perched on the chair that Lile had previously occupied as if ready to spring forward at any moment. The oranges had really disconcerted him.

"How is a gnome different than an imp?" he asked, the barest of growls underlying his deep tone.

Magic tugged at me, delaying my answer. A witch was knocking on the gate. And while the tenor of the magic was familiar, I was surprised to feel it. I had expected Ravine to cancel our planned trip to her antiquities dealer. I silently invited her onto the property, and preemptively into the house as well.

Sisu, with the twins on his heels, barreled into the dining room. Lile skirted the table to sit next to me, and Sisu and Neve took their previous places.

My brother folded his hands before him on the table, then looked at me. All innocence.

"Yes. You can have dessert—"

He made a grab for the gulab jamun. I snagged the container just out of his reach—and, given the way Kellan blinked at me, immediately regretted displaying how fast I could move in front of company.

"But..." I added, continuing as if nothing unusual had happened. Nothing unusual for the witch I was pretending to be. "You're still in trouble for upsetting Bethany. You still owe her a written apology."

Sisu adopted his mournful expression, nodding.

I pushed the container back toward him. "Share evenly, please."

Sisu half crawled onto the table, leaning over the container to count the small rounds of gooey, deep-fried dough. On my left, Lile carefully double-checked his math, a clean spoon already in hand for scooping.

"And the oranges?" Neve asked, reverently hushed. "Are they a gift from the gnome?"

"You met a gnome and didn't mention it?" Kellan asked, his tone slightly strained.

His niece bobbed her head, then shook it. "We tried to meet the gnome today, before I got hurt. But the greenhouse wouldn't open for us."

Kellan rubbed his forehead, frustrated.

I smiled at him, laughing inside. He'd thought watching the boisterous trio would be easy. Apparently not.

He caught my look, dropping his hand with a quiet grumble.

"Twelve!" Sisu exclaimed. "That's four each."

"No," Lile corrected. "There are five of us so..." Her brow furrowed thoughtfully. "So...that's..."

Five didn't divide evenly into twelve.

"Dusk won't have any," Sisu said, pushing Neve's empty, still-dirty dinner plate toward her sister, who had her spoon at the ready.

"I'm fine as well," Kellan said. "Though I won't say no to a gnome-grown orange." Gaze speared to me, he reached across the table and took one of the mandarins.

One of the front doors opened, so quietly that I was surprised when Kellan acknowledged it with a slight turn of his head. Perhaps it was Ravine's magic he'd picked up.

"Ugh," she cried out from deep within the great room. "It's raining again."

"It always rains here!" Sisu howled in reply. Then he went back to quietly arguing about the division of the sweet dessert with Neve and Lile. Apparently, though they had the math solved, there was some issue about which of the dough rounds were bigger than the others.

A tall, curvy woman strode into the dining room. Her shoulder-skimming hair was dyed dark brown and straightened. Wearing her typical oversized cable-knit sweater, slim-fitting black skirt, and high boots, Ravine Byrne took us in with a sweep of her blue-green eyes. She smirked at Kellan. "Kell."

"Vinnie." He curled his lip at her in greeting, peeling his orange.

Ravine huffed. She hated that nickname, which Kellan's sister also used. Narrowing her eyes at the bowed heads of the children, she pushed up the sleeves of her collarbone-baring sweater, revealing the gold Celtic-inspired bands that twined over her wrists and up her forearms. Then she inserted herself between Sisu and Neve, plucked one of the gulab jamun from the container, and popped it into her mouth.

Sisu and the twins howled in protest.

Laughing as she chewed, Ravine sauntered around the table, sitting next to me and licking her fingers.

Kellan looked between her and me, then asked me, "This is your date?"

"Yes." Ravine smirked.

"No," I said at the same time.

"What?!" Ravine cried dramatically. "I'm good enough to..." Her gaze fell on the younger trio, and she trailed off.

The kids, having come to some agreement about dividing their bounty, were watching her. Alertly. Mouths full and chewing.

Kellan chuckled.

I wasn't certain what Ravine had been about to proclaim, but apparently it was something she couldn't articulate in front of Sisu, Neve, and Lile.

"I didn't know if you were still coming," I said quietly, peeling my orange.

Ravine leaned across me, beckoning toward the kids. "You can give me at least one more." To me she said, "I would have texted if I had to cancel."

Pouting, Lile pushed the container toward the witch.

Ravine snagged a second treat, popping it in her mouth and gushing, "I love these."

Kellan ate a piece of his orange. Then he just stopped. Hand hovering in the air and everything. On pause.

I knew the feeling. The unnamed and unseen gnome grew life-altering oranges.

I ate my own piece, flavor exploding across my tongue. Then I met Kellan's gaze, smiling.

"A gnome," he murmured.

I nodded.

"Magical oranges?" Ravine shrugged. "I have an aunt who grows them."

Kellan grunted dismissively. "I've tasted your aunt's oranges."

Ravine's grin became sharp. "I know you have."

Kellan's expression darkened, flicking to me. Then he sat back in his chair, to finish his orange and watch over the kids. The change in position and focus was deliberately dismissive. Of Ravine.

She pretended not to notice, stealing the second half of my orange and eating a piece without further comment.

"I didn't think to check my phone," I said to Ravine, slowly making my way through the rest of the orange. "But I assumed that once you spoke to River—"

"River," Ravine snarled, "can go screw herself on this one."

Kellan's attention flicked back to us.

Sisu, Lile, and Neve were embroiled in a hushed argument that now included cutting the final sticky round of fried dough into three pieces. It was the size of those pieces that was being argued.

"She was very clear," I said stiffly, "that I would be on the outs with the coven, and that she'd be sending me her final bill—"

Ravine snorted. "Good luck getting that by Ridge."

"River quit the estate project?" Kellan asked, seriously surprised.

"She claims that Dusk fired her." Ravine eyed me pointedly up and down, then looked at Kellan. "It's pretty clear that wasn't the case."

"She took my refusal to rehire Ayre as…rejecting the entire coven." Crossing the coven was probably more like it, but I was growing uncomfortable with the conversation. With talking about River with her sister and Kellan.

"Does this have to do with the murdered imp?" Kellan asked.

I ate the final piece of my orange, as if that gave me a valid excuse for not answering.

Not at all fooled, Kellan pushed back from the table, pulling out his phone with a grumble that might have been, "Fecking witches." Then he strode out of the dining room, falling into pacing back and forth within the great room just beyond the open doorway, with his phone to his ear.

"What murdered imp?" Ravine asked quietly.

Now even more uncomfortable, I grabbed a second orange and peeled it instead of answering. Though I gave Ravine half.

She sighed, then nodded. "Do you still want to meet Doran?"

I did. I needed to cash in some of the artifacts that had been deeded to me by Jiaotu, Sisu's father and the guardian of Northern Europe, along with the house.

Ravine had offered to introduce me to a local antiquities dealer. Though when I'd questioned her further about Doran, she'd simply given me a mysterious smirk, then chirped something about how first impressions were always a better judge than foregone conclusions.

I had just grinned back at her. I was always up for an adventure or a mystery—as evidenced by the fact that I was in Dublin, taking on a clandestine role at the guardian dragons' behest, even though I still had no idea what exactly they wanted of me.

"I do want to meet him," I said. "I have more deposits to pay. And…apparently…a designer to pay out." The words sounded raw, even to my own ears.

"Bullshit," Ravine muttered. "River is too easily manipulated. And too…aware that she's expected to step up and take over the coven. In, like, twenty years. Mom isn't stepping down."

"I'm expecting a visit from your mother next."

Ravine huffed again. "Forget it. Ayre is the elder sister. She should be coven leader, except strength not birth determines such things. She should have also been doing your job. But she wasn't strong enough to even be offered the position, no matter how much she begged for it. Probably because she was the one who misidentified that damn mummy, or whatever the hell it was, in the first place."

"The one that killed Celeste Cameron?" And which had almost killed my Great-Uncle Jamal.

"Along with three other witches. Sucked them dry. Seriously injured Owen Brady. Took him six months to recover. Crystal and Jim were away for the weekend. Dating then, but not now."

"And Ayre?" I asked, rather amazed by the coven's ability to keep that big a secret. Granted, my uncle Jamal wouldn't have known the particulars when he'd stepped in to contain the creature. But even my lawyer Tawny hadn't mentioned anything in her notes on the museum archive.

Ravine's gaze flicked to the children. They were trading off swiping the syrup out of the container and licking it from their fingers. Sisu's bangs looked suspiciously spiky. Like he'd tried to get his face into the container.

"That's enough," I said, though without heat. I pushed the basket of oranges toward them. "Have an orange."

The trio complied—but not before lining the remaining oranges up and selecting the three biggest.

Sisu had found his competitive soul mates.

"It's weird, you know," Ravine said. "You grinning at them like that when they're being total brats."

"It makes me happy. All their energy in the house." I glanced over at her, holding her gaze. She hadn't answered my question about what had happened to Ayre during the soul-sucker's attack.

The dark-haired witch grimaced. The dusting of freckles she hid behind a complexion charm made an appearance, then faded back into her almost translucent skin. As magic often did under my gaze. Soon, I'd be able to see completely through the charm.

"Rumor has it that Ayre…distracted the creature and got clear." Ravine toyed with the orange peels.

I ate the last piece of my orange, contemplating what exactly a soul-sucking creature might have been 'distracted' by.

One of the witches who'd died?

"We all have asshole branches in our families," Ravine muttered.

Distraction techniques and lures were often an exceedingly smart first step to containing a rampaging entity or magical creature. I had once used Mistress Brightshire's green face cream to entice a pair of water imps so I could relocate them into my mother's pond at the old estate. But I didn't know a single archivist, didn't know any dragon, who wouldn't place themselves in the path of any danger in order to save…anyone.

Except I knew that being practically invulnerable to most magic probably contributed to that mindset. Plus, dragons were known to be a little obsessed about what we perceived as our duty—to protect the world and all the magic within it.

Ayre Byrne was an elder of her coven, though. Presumably higher ranked in their pecking order than the other witches who'd died. Possibly even higher than Celeste Cameron.

Her duty would have been clear to her as well.

Ravine cleared her throat uncomfortably. "River…"

"River?" I asked, trying to be polite but not quite making it all the way. Even my relief and joy from the discovery of the imp's eggs wasn't enough to ease the hurt I still harbored over River siding with someone who'd so casually murdered a rare magical being.

Someone who had possibly let witches die who should have been under her protection six years ago. Even if that someone was her aunt.

Yeah, I had no regrets firing Ayre Byrne. I actually hoped to never see her again.

Ravine sighed. "River…River ranks responsibility and duty to the coven over…everything else."

"I understand. Rationally, at least."

"Witches usually approach these sorts of incidents slightly differently."

"I get it, Ravine. River thinks I should have taken my issue with Ayre before the coven."

She nodded, not meeting my eye.

"As head curator, I'm not beholden to the coven. I read my contract very carefully and spoke with Pearl Godfrey."

Pearl was the head of the witches Convocation. The highest authority that the witches recognized. Of course, I actually took my orders from an even more highly placed governing body, the guardian dragons themselves. Pearl—now my great-aunt on paper—was just part of my so-called cover.

"I get it, Dusk," Ravine said softly. "I'm…I'm sorry that you and River are at odds over it, that's all. She'll miss your friendship."

"She'll miss my house," I said caustically.

Ravine snorted, then smiled sadly.

Kellan stepped back into the dining room, tucking his phone into a side pocket of his work pants, then leaning his shoulder against the jamb. "You're already late for Doran. You know how testy he can get."

Either Kellan Conall had prior knowledge of our plans for the evening, or his hearing was very, very good. Especially because he'd been carrying on a couple of phone conversations himself—one with his mother, who he'd referred to as 'alpha' three times, and one with Owen Brady.

Yes, I could also hear that well. Though out of politeness, I'd tuned the particulars out.

"Doran doesn't get testy," Ravine groused. "Especially not when he sees what Dusk has to offer."

Kellan narrowed his eyes at the witch.

She laughed. "I mean her artifacts."

"Brady will be shadowing you," Kellan said.

"What?" Ravine cried. "We don't need a bloody babysitter!"

Kellan's gaze flicked to me. "You should have let him know where you were going tonight in the first place. It's his job."

"This is private business," I said. "Owen Brady works for the archive."

"No," Kellan said.

I wasn't completely certain that anyone had ever said 'no' to me so definitively before. And with such utter arrogance. "No?"

"Owen Brady is your security specialist. Anything you do that involves Doran or the coven witches falls under his jurisdiction because of your position in Dublin." As he spoke of the witches, Kellan sneered at Ravine. "Your position in Ireland."

"What about Dusk's interactions with the pack?" Ravine spat. "Plan to have Brady oversee those as well? Or will you take up those duties yourself?"

Kellan huffed dismissively. Then, as if the conversation was done, he unfolded his arms and crossed toward the under-construction kitchen. "I'm happy to spend another hour or so laying out the cabinets, but then Neve and Lile will need to get to bed."

The twins, having followed the conversation with rapt attention, groaned in tandem.

"Want to play that memory game on the iPad?" Sisu asked, already clambering out of his seat.

Neve and Lile were instantly on his heels.

I sighed, casting a mournful gaze at the dirty dishes and containers strewn across the table. Apparently, I was providing dinner and cleaning up.

Ravine was eyeing the plastic-sheathed doorway through which Kellan had retreated. Hands on her hips, she shook her head. "Speaking of assholes."

She clearly knew that Kellan could hear her.

I started collecting utensils and dishes. "I always thought that was an exaggeration. Witches and werewolves not getting along."

Ravine shrugged. Then she noticed what I was doing, and with a flick of her fingers, vanished everything on the table except for the oranges.

I blinked at her.

She shrugged. "They're in the downstairs sink. But I can't actually wash them properly without access to soap and water."

"Thank you. I can wash them later." I collected my backpack and jacket, heading for the great room. "I just need to grab the items I'd set aside for your dealer."

Ravine trailed after me. "And change your sweater."

I abruptly altered course, toward the stairs and my bedroom instead of the library. "Two seconds."

"No worries."

I swapped out my combo of plaid skirt, sweater, and tights for an almost identical set of clothing. Yes, my wardrobe was rather streamlined, and I loathed shopping for anything other than books. Then before dressing, I stood bent over the tub and vigorously brushed my hair, hopefully removing most of the coffee-crusted imp remains.

I carefully double-checked the ashes and hair in the tub after I was done, finding nothing. I reminded myself of the three precious eggs that Sisu, Neve, and Lile had collected, but it still didn't quite quash the tiny void that had taken up residence in my chest.

Not wanting to hold up Ravine, or Kellan for that matter, I headed for the library. Not bothering with any lights, I crossed all the way through the empty vastness of the massive room to my desk in the far corner, by the darkened windows. With all the shutters thrown open and this far after sunset, it was chilly enough that I'd have to light a fire if I wanted to work after I finished my errand with Ravine.

The imp eggs glowed softly from an empty shelf that sat under the noticeboard I'd built a couple of days before. Sisu had chosen a spot as close to my desk as possible, but tucked into the corner so the jar was shielded from any sunlight that might filter into the room. Still, I closed the nearest shutters just in case.

A cream-colored envelope was pinned to the noticeboard. I hadn't been certain the board was working yet. My heart leaped in my chest as I stepped around the side of the desk to reach for it. Then I recognized Zeke's handwriting, including the way he always slashed a line under my name. I'd been hoping the letter was from Mom.

The two letters I'd pinned to the board the previous night were gone. One was for my Aunt Josephine, who rarely left the archive she'd built for herself in Crete, but who would probably appreciate an update. And one was for Branson, the sword master of the guardians, requesting that Sisu's and my training be resumed as soon as he could work out the travel logistics and timing. The fact that the trainer would need to pretend to be a witch or a sorcerer while the estate was under construction was going to be an issue. Warrior dragons were not big on subterfuge.

I left Zeke's note on the board. I would read it later. And I would send a note to Mistress Brightshire about the imp eggs. Though brownies didn't typically use noticeboards to communicate, I hoped that she would respond.

It had taken me a week to get the board set up properly. I'd excavated a painting—a horse-and-hound hunting party in a completely gorgeous antique gold frame—from among the smaller of the paintings stored in the central tower. Then I'd stretched a length of brown velvet across the painted canvas. Figuring out the anchoring spells took me far longer than getting the physical board set up. I had reviewed all the info I'd fed into Infinity on the subject multiple times—mostly pulled from family journals—but I'd still had to figure out how to anchor it with my own unique magical signature.

I had ended up diluting my favorite ink—dark brown speckled with 24-karat gold that was receptive to my magic—and staining the frame with it. Then I'd inked the two sets of runes Zeke had shown me on the frame's thickly papered back. One set that tied to my mother's estate, and one set that tied to the Giza archives in Egypt, where Zeke worked as my mother's apprentice.

I hadn't been certain it had worked, especially since I didn't have my Aunt Josephine's runed coordinates. But my letter to her had disappeared…though I knew it might just be pinned to the board at my mother's estate now. Or perhaps it had routed through my mother's noticeboard. I wouldn't know until Josephine responded.

Now I just needed to figure out how to ward the library. And then the house and property. I still wasn't certain that the spells that currently secured both wouldn't gradually wear off now that the estate had been pulled out of stasis.

I stepped back to the desk, placing my palm on the front face of the drawer on the lower right. It was larger on the inside than it appeared to be, and it had taken multiple tries to get the magical lock unlatched. The first three times I'd attempted to open it, I had actually needed to hold the deed to the estate in my hand, but the drawer clicked open for me easily now.

The chest of treasure that had been part of my so-called inheritance filled the bulk of the drawer, but I'd already set aside five items to take to Ravine's antiquities dealer. I assumed a small bag of gold coins would be the easiest thing for him to sell. I'd also selected a ceremonial dagger; a thin, jeweled coronet; two rings; and a bracelet I was fairly certain was of Egyptian origin, though it didn't carry enough magic for me to read it thoroughly.

I pulled the antique leather roll that Jiaotu had used to store the house deed, the master key, and the bone dagger out of the top right drawer, quickly filling its variously sized pockets with the coins and other artifacts.

As I expected, the leather portfolio shifted its dimensions to accommodate its contents. And it also apparently masked the magical signature of any item stored within it. Jiaotu had oh-so-casually given me a multitude of gifts. The simple-looking chest that held the small treasure trove was just as valuable, as it likewise appeared to dampen the magic of whatever it contained.

Ravine strode into the library. "Ready?"

I nodded, then paused to place the master key that Sisu had already pilfered from one of the upper desk drawers into the locked lower drawer. I doubted the magic sealing the drawer would stymie my brother for long, but it might give me enough time to figure out my own warding system.

I kept the most overwhelming of Jiaotu's bequeathals—the bone dagger crafted by a guardian dragon from the femur of an entity so powerful it had almost bested her—strapped to my thigh. And yes, the weapon was an even more weighty responsibility than the estate or my new job. I wasn't going to trust it behind any ward. When a guardian told me to keep the dagger with me at all times, even I listened.

Ravine touched the high back of the chair I'd placed before the desk so Sisu could sit with me while I worked. I had set two more chairs in front of the nearest fireplace.

"I thought you sent these off to be recovered?" she asked, her tone remote as if she wasn't focusing on what she was asking me. She ran a seemingly disinterested gaze across the old-fashioned phone on my desk that wasn't actually wired to anything, the rolled leather portfolio, and the twinkling imp eggs.

"Different chairs," I said. "If I'd sent them all at once, we'd have nothing to sit on."

The house hadn't come fully furnished. Many of the rooms were completely empty. But I had pieced together what I could find that was still functional, and had moved as much as possible into the areas we'd claimed—the dining room, two bedrooms, and the library. There was a smaller room to the right of the entrance that I was hoping to convert to a proper walk-in closet, but for now, I had just put up a few temporary hangers and tucked a table into one corner.

Throughout the manor, the walls were still bare. Except where Sisu had dug through the artwork we'd found crated in the attic—which I had deemed mostly hideous—and started placing pieces randomly around the house. Not hung up. He didn't have a ladder. Though I had no doubt he'd convince one of the carpenters, or even Kellan, to help him soon enough.

"You're new blood in a fairly closed ecosystem," Ravine said, apparently changing the subject at random.

"Sorry?" I double-checked that the drawer holding the key and the treasure chest was secure.

She shrugged, running her fingers along the top of the chair, tracing the smooth, ornately carved wood. "Everyone has tangled tongues with Kellan Conall at least once. Or Gitta, for that matter. The pack celebrations are always rather randy. Perfect for blowing off steam and not worrying about being…too much. But Kell is miserly when it comes to commitment."

I tucked the roll of artifacts into my backpack, nestling it against Infinity. I brushed my fingers along my personal archive's spine as I withdrew my hand, and it hummed contentedly. I zipped the pack. "I'm not following you."

"It's like Rook. River wanted a child, but being gay through and through, she didn't want to involve a coven witch. She deliberately got pregnant at a graduation ceremony at the Academy. My graduation, not hers. Thereby bringing new blood into the coven, but with none of the hassle of sharing custody with a casual lover."

That was a bunch of information in just a couple of sentences. And I wasn't certain it was my place to ask for clarification, so I just tried to follow Ravine's main point. "And…I'm new blood?" Except being a dragon, I really wasn't. Not in the way I thought Ravine was suggesting.

"The Conall pack does it more often than the coven," Ravine continued, somewhat ignoring my question. "Len Murphy, Neve and Lile's father, came over from the California pack and stayed. He and Gitta are constantly on and off."

Len was also the lead electrician currently working on the massive job of rewiring the estate.

"Aisling," Ravine continued. "The pack alpha, Gitta and Kellan's mother. She married and divorced their father, Odane. He's a Caribbean import. Married to their aunt now, father to their half-sister, Erin. And still beta of the pack."

My right palm was starting to itch with the urge to write all of this down. Ravine was unloading a lot of information, and I wasn't completely sure why. Except that I was posing as a Godfrey witch and was therefore this so-called new blood. "Your sister made my status within the coven very clear this afternoon."

Ravine grimaced. "I'm sure she did. And it's going to hurt like hell when Mom countermands her. One look at you, and the power you carry, and Mom is going to want you to stick around."

I ignored the way Ravine's comment about my power made me uncomfortable, like I was lying to her. As head archivist, I should be powerful. And whether or not I was posing as a witch, I was still the same person. Ultimately.

"For breeding purposes," I said, finally understanding.

She shrugged dismissively. "To strengthen the coven. You and Sisu."

"This is an odd conversation."

"Kellan's interest is hard to ignore."

"But by your own attestation, a witch and a werewolf aren't compatible."

Ravine grinned at me toothily. "They are. Owen Brady's mother is a coven witch. The shapeshifter magic is usually dominant. But most witches can't handle pack life."

"Which was your initial point, about the tangled tongues."

"You got me, babe."

"I'm not breeding stock."

Ravine shrugged. "Everyone is going to be after you, or want to be allied with you, for different reasons."

"Despite the issue with Ayre."

"Because of it, for some."

I gazed at her, trying to read between the lines.

She smiled, her expression a little tight.

"Consider me forewarned," I said.

She laughed quietly, as if relieved. Then she thankfully changed the subject once more. "Have you got the trinkets you want to sell to Doran?"

I ignored her use of 'trinkets,' though it felt slightly belittling. "Yes. I just need to say goodbye to Sisu." I headed out of the library, Ravine following.

A quiet buzz preceded her pulling her phone out of her pocket, then snorting. "I've got assholes coming at me from all directions today." Her thumbs flew over the screen, then she stuffed the phone back in her pocket with a smirk of satisfaction.

I crossed through the great room, heading toward the under-construction kitchen, where I could feel Sisu, the twins, and their uncle. "And Kellan is one of those assholes?" I asked Ravine quietly, slowing slightly.

"I thought you weren't breeding stock?"

I just gave her a look.

She half-sighed, half-grimaced. "We all grew up together. We're all assholes. We don't even bother trading off these days. I just thought you should know where you'd stand with him right away, since it was plainly obvious he'd already keyed in on you."

I disagreed, but I didn't argue the point. It was clear that Kellan didn't like the way I smelled. And that wasn't just about the stale coffee and the imp's ashy remains. Though I might have had some sort of visceral reaction to the werewolf contractor on first sight, then become hyperaware of him after, I was in Dublin to do a job, not dally with the locals.

"Are you internally monologuing again?"

"What?"

"You get a certain look on your face when you're talking to yourself."

I sputtered, working up a denial—and then realized she was right. "Yes."

"Something along the lines of…you've got a job to do and a brother to look after?"

"Yes."

Ravine suddenly flung her arms out to the sides and started spinning. She dropped her head back, laughing. "And this glorious, huge house. This palace."

"Yes."

She stopped spinning, grinning wickedly. "Houses like this are meant to be filled."

"Eventually," I said, hearing the tightness in my tone but unable to ease it. This conversation was far too close to the conversation I'd unwillingly participated in with Zeke seven months before. I was only twenty-five. Even for a witch, that was relatively young. And in dragon terms, I was still a fledgling. Biologically capable of bearing children? Sure. Mentally? No.

And I had Sisu.

Ravine nodded agreeably. "Eventually. I won't mention it again."

"Thank you."

She grinned amicably. "I get enough of it myself. But thankfully, River bred early and Ridge is older, so he takes the brunt of it. Plus…we have to clear up this garbage with the coven before we can get you truly settled."

"I thought you said it was fine."

Ravine shrugged offishly. "I'll make it so."

As we neared the plastic-swathed doorway, the sound of some sort of tool filtered through to us. The sander again, or a saw, maybe.

"I don't like to fight," I said. "But I will. For what I believe in."

"I already know that about you, Dusk. I knew it the first moment I realized that it was just you and Sisu alone in this huge, completely unsuitable house."

Sisu, quickly followed by Neve and Lile, burst through the plastic sheathing, barreling toward us. He flung himself toward me from a few steps away. I caught him, even though doing so likely revealed too much about my strength.

I would never, under any circumstances, drop my brother.

"We want to come with you," Neve cried, sliding to a stop before Ravine. Lile hung slightly back.

"Jesus, no," Ravine groused. "Your mother would have my head. Plus, I'm not a babysitter."

"Babies?!" Sisu cried indignantly, wiggling out of my arms.

I set him down. It was difficult to argue your maturity when being cuddled by your sister.

"We'll bring you back a treat," Ravine said.

"Ice cream," Neve demanded.

"And cookies," Lile added hopefully.

"A fire salamander for the pond," Sisu said.

The twins both looked at him, shaking their heads.

"You are so weird," Neve said.

"You're just jealous that I have a pond."

Lile started cackling. "She so is!"

"Am not."

"Are too."

"Enough!" Ravine cried. "The treat will be my choice. And you will be happy with whatever I select."

Much pouting met this pronouncement, but the verbal arguments ceased.

Ravine spun on her heel, heading for the front door. The four of us followed the dark-haired witch dutifully.

"Apologize to your uncle for us," Ravine said.

"For what?" Lile asked.

Both doors swept open without prompting, and Ravine threaded her arm through mine, tugging me outside. "We're going to be late."

"We are?" I asked.

"There's no way we can get to Doran's and back in an hour now. Kellan already knows it, but it's polite to apologize."

Ravine continued to tug me up the front path, as if she was afraid I would decide to stay.

In fact, I was feeling tired—and like I should just be curling up with a book in front of the fireplace. So apparently, the witch did know me already.

I glanced over my shoulder, catching sight of Sisu, Lile, and Neve hovering in the doorway. The dark of the night had encroached, but they were well lit from within.

"Stay in the house, please."

Sisu nodded. Neve and Lile dashed back inside, chattering away. The heavy dark-wood door shut.

Pinpoints of light sparked on either side of the path, leading toward the far gate. The estate responding to our crossing, not witch magic.

"Does the door do that often?" Ravine asked.

"Do what?"

"Open without a command...or did you open it, like nonverbally?"

I hadn't. I also wasn't quite certain how to respond. Wasn't quite certain what needed to be a secret. The house was doing its own thing, and I doubted I could curtail it even if I asked nicely. Thankfully, Ravine didn't wait for me to figure it out.

"A great-grandmother on my father's side had a house like that. Set out over the bluffs. After she died, it burned down partway through her memorial service. She wanted to be buried in the gardens. Silly bat wouldn't let us cremate her. But it was raining, of course..." Ravine gestured out into the evening, dark but partially clear. The earlier rain had paused for the moment. "So the coffin was put in the dining room for the main memorial service. Bloody house set itself on fire, taking her with it. Burned hot and fast. A few witches actually got hurt. It had been the sweetest house before that, though." She shrugged. "I was ten...no, nine. None of the Byrnes have been brave enough to rebuild on that property, though my Aunt Del farms the land."

I needed to record the story Ravine had just told me with such desperate intensity that my right hand felt like it was now on fire. I would remember the tale, of course. But I wouldn't get all the nuance and phrasing correct if I didn't commit it to Infinity right away.

Ravine smirked at me. "So yeah, the door to your palace opening for me on its own...twice...was a shock. But not unprecedented."

"I'm going to need to ask you a lot more questions...with names and dates. And how exactly a house chooses when and why to set itself on fire. That might be pertinent." I glanced behind me, just slightly worried about what exactly I'd inherited now. With the sun fully set, the massive house was aglow from within.

Ravine laughed. "Happy to oblige. Just don't mention it to River. Otherwise, you'll hear another round of 'witch business stays in the coven' again."

That thought diminished the bit of joy that Ravine's story had brought to the evening. So we just walked the rest of the way to the gate and the boundary wards that cloaked the estate from sight, crossing through in silence.

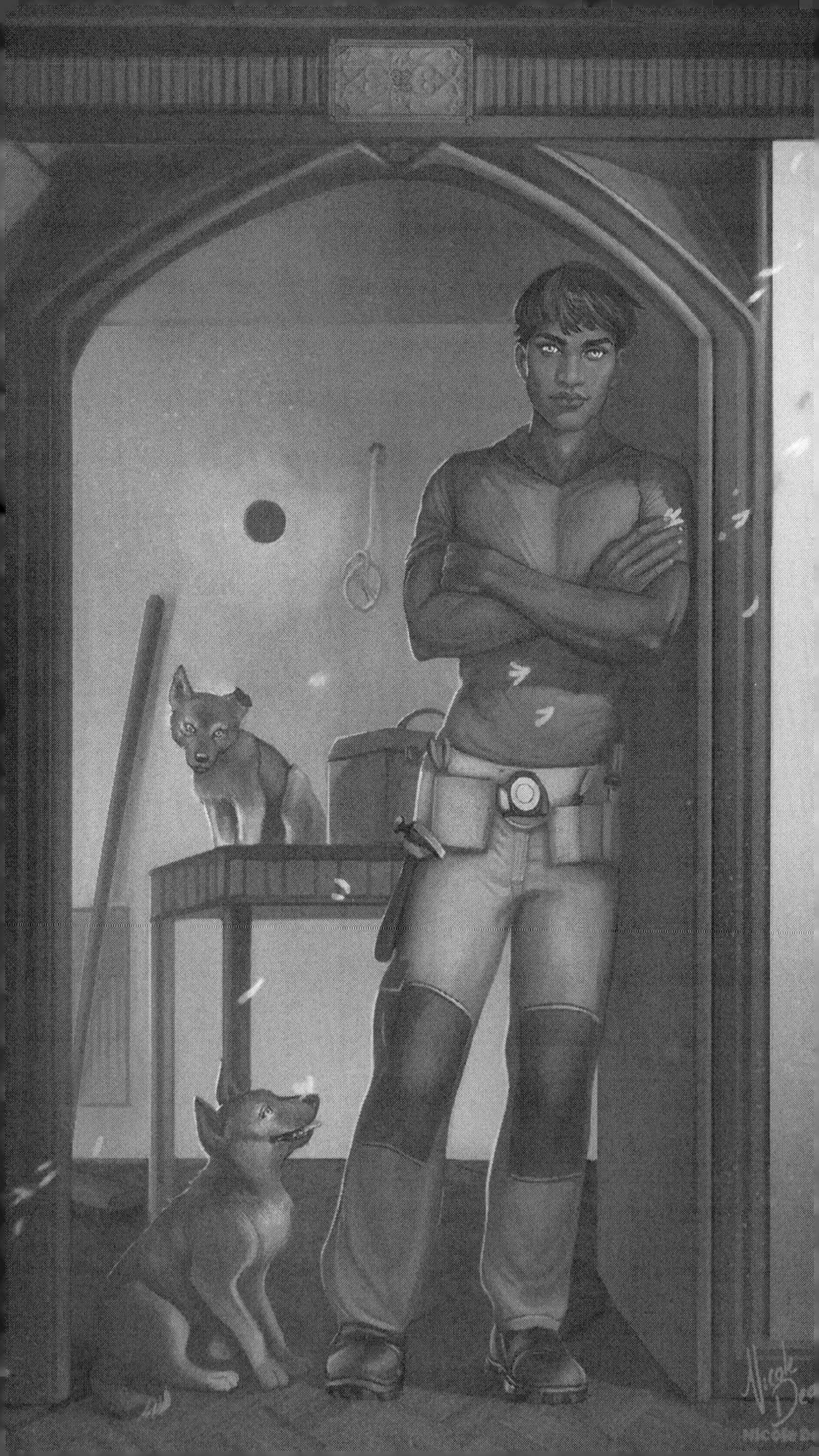

CHAPTER THREE

RAVINE DROVE THE TINIEST CAR I'D EVER RIDDEN IN. Granted, the only car I'd really been in was a regular taxi a few times. It was so tiny that she had backed into the parallel parking spot she'd found up the block and around the corner from the estate, leaving more than enough space for another equally tiny vehicle to park next to her.

"Electric," she said with a grin as she unlocked the car remotely. "I might be all sexy and edgy, but I am still an earth witch."

I was slightly nervous as I climbed in. Jiaotu's witch glamour was masking my magic but not actually suppressing it, and I was worried that a fully electric car wouldn't start with me in it. Thankfully, it did.

Ravine drove like a maniac, cutting through the city until I really had no idea where we were. I usually had a great sense of direction—when my feet were firmly planted on the earth. We left block after block of stone and brick buildings behind, entering what appeared to be a warehouse district. Then we abruptly pulled over by a large two-level building that appeared dark and abandoned.

Ravine climbed out of the car without another word. I followed.

A light breeze lifted my hair, bringing with it the scent of saltwater. I blinked, adjusting my eyes to the dark. Then I caught sight of the magic that edged the warehouse Ravine was already heading toward.

I fell into step with the witch, reassessing the area. "Are we near a port?"

"One of them."

"The one where most of the black market items pass through?"

Ravine flashed me a toothy grin. "You are quick."

"The magic disguising the warehouse gives it away."

Ravine blinked, pausing to scan the building. "It's…cloaked?"

"Sorcerer magic," I said. "Best guess. You can't …?" I didn't finish my question. It had been drilled into me from a young age that Adepts considered it rude to question each other about their magic. Plus, as a dragon currently posing as a witch, I couldn't share that sort of information in kind.

Ravine either didn't notice or didn't care. "I can see the runes on the door."

"You didn't think to mention you were taking me to an illegal antiquities dealer?"

"Where did you think we were going?"

I gave her a look. "To a legitimate antiquities dealer."

"Right…well, Doran pays better."

"I might have brought different objects."

She laughed quietly. "He'll take what you have to offer, then more, Dusk. You're the head curator of the magical archives of Ireland. Establishing a relationship with you—"

A beat-up black truck pulled up and parked behind Ravine's tiny electric car. I had no idea of the make or model, but the pickup looked old. At least while parked next to Ravine's ultramodern vehicle.

Owen Brady, dressed in a dark-wool jacket, worn jeans, and work boots, climbed out. He waved, then leaned back against the side of the truck, folding his arms. My so-called security specialist had arrived. Well, the archive's specialist.

"Obvious much?" Ravine muttered sarcastically.

"You'd prefer he skulk in the shadows?" I asked.

Ravine barked out a laugh. "Yes. Yes, I would. Then I wouldn't have to remember that he's a great lay who's now off the market."

I wasn't certain how to respond to that completely out-of-context bit of information.

Ravine snorted. "I told you. It's a small pond around here. As well as working for you at the archive, Brady is a Conall pack enforcer, currently engaged to Erin."

Erin. Gitta and Kellan's half-sister, I recalled. We hadn't met yet.

"Erin," Ravine sneered, "isn't big on sharing."

Brady chuckled quietly, his gaze trained down the road toward the water I could sense in that direction. He could hear every word Ravine and I were exchanging.

"You qualify a lot of your relationships based on who you can have sex with."

"You don't?"

I thought about it. "My pond is even smaller."

Ravine narrowed her eyes and tilted her head as if I'd said something interesting. "From before, right? Because your life has just opened way up. New job, new house..."

It was true. My life had just opened way up. But not in the way the metal mage, as she called herself, was implying. I might have been wrong about the usually strict divide between the species of magic users—though it was also possible that only Ravine slept with both witches and shapeshifters. But I wasn't a witch. It didn't have to be serious or anything, but dragons took other dragons as lovers. It was one thing to work among the Adept while trying to maintain Jiaotu's glamour, and completely another to be skin-to-skin with another magic user, worried about exposing my own power. And my strength for that matter.

Ravine's blue-green eyes flicked over my face. "Oh yeah? Left someone behind?"

I sighed, laughing quietly. "Not exactly. Just…it's nice to have someone to…touch. Someone who knows you."

Ravine laughed huskily. "I agree. It doesn't have to be all sweet kisses and rose petals, or undying love for that matter. But someone who knows how to touch you…that's hard to walk away from."

"Well, I wouldn't say he necessarily knew how to touch me," I drawled, caught up in what I'd read was commonly referred to as 'girl's talk,' even though I'd never really had someone to practice with. "But he took direction well."

Ravine threw back her head and laughed. The genuine joy in her voice filtered across the empty street, reflecting back against the warehouses toward us.

Still grinning at me, she pressed her hand to the door. Dark-blue glowing runes slowly appeared, pulsing in a ring around her hand.

Pulsing in time with her own heartbeat. Which Ravine undoubtedly couldn't hear.

That was oddly creepy. Even for an antiquities dealer illegally trading in magical artifacts.

The door clicked open. Ravine, still smiling, pushed through into the warehouse.

I glanced back at Brady. The werewolf enforcer was still leaning against his pickup truck, seemingly not at all annoyed by the misting rain that had started to fall on the drive over. Or perhaps we'd simply driven into a cloud of it. I raised my hand, waving to be polite.

He nodded, flashing me a smile that was more a display of teeth than a happy expression.

I stepped inside the darkened building.

The wards encasing the doorway tried to hold me back. They pulsed over me as if testing my magic—and not liking the results. Even through Jiaotu's glamour, my power wouldn't read as anything like benign. Not to anyone who had anything to hide.

And I didn't doubt that the illegal magical antiquities dealer I was about to meet had many, many things to hide. The location, the cloaking on the building that made it appear derelict, having to meet after dark—all of that made it obvious.

I probably shouldn't have felt as thrilled as I did, being a morally upright dragon archivist and all. But as I folded my power around me, drawing it in as deeply as I could, I also found myself grinning in anticipation.

The wards, presumably confusing my withdrawal of power for me actually stepping back, slid over me, lingering on my backpack.

I took a step, risking breaking the wards' attempt to hold me in order to get them to let go. I couldn't mask Infinity or the artifacts I was carrying. Not enough to completely disguise their magic with my own. That wasn't within my abilities. Not yet, at least.

The bone dagger strapped to my thigh crossed through the wards with nary a tug. I wasn't surprised. A guardian would have crossed through the protections on the warehouse as if human, and the dagger was guardian magic.

The wards released me, and the actual warehouse opened up before me. Pockets of residual magic came into focus first, then the black-painted walls, floors, pedestals, and shelving units.

Ravine was watching me, her eyes narrowed thoughtfully and ringed with the bright blue of her witch magic.

I was starting to get the distinct impression that the youngest Byrne sibling missed little when it came to people. It had taken only a moment, but Ravine had noticed my interaction with the wards.

I smirked at her, enjoying our outing more and more every minute.

She snorted playfully, then strode confidently into the cavernous room, ignoring every pedestal and shelf between her and a long glass counter that appeared to cut through the center of the warehouse. The black walls, ceiling, and floors did an excellent job of obscuring the dimensions of the room. Which was clearly intentional.

I struggled to not touch every single item I passed. Even the empty pedestals were lit with a single bulb on the end of a metal-encased wire, seemingly attached to nothing above it. An illusion that had nothing to do with magic, and everything to do with black-painted surfaces, high ceilings, and selective lighting.

The first shelf I passed was crammed with books on Irish and Celtic magic in general, with a number of duplicates that I assumed were various editions. More pedestals sat empty. The second bookshelf was devoted to spellbooks—specifically, witch magic.

A cherrywood jewelry box occupied the next pedestal. It was inlaid with rose-gold runes. I didn't have to touch it or even be able to discern those markings to know it contained something nefarious. Possibly something destructive.

So of course, I instantly wanted to collect it. To set it on my own bookshelves and run my fingers over the pink-tinged gold. Testing the magic the runes contained, then thwarting whatever curse lingered within. Not enough to break the box or destroy it, though. Just enough to disarm it. Then I might put it on my bureau and think about collecting some actual jewelry, to fill the box as it wanted to be filled…

Oh, yes. If I wanted it this much, the rune-marked box was powerful.

"Beautiful, isn't it?" a voice asked from out of the darkness.

Ravine, a few steps ahead, squeaked as she spun back.

I simply raised my eyes and pinned my gaze to the vampire lurking in the deep shadows a few steps beyond the pedestal.

Doran, I presumed. I'd had no idea he was a vampire. But I knew now why Ravine had been so circumspect—and why she'd wanted me to come to my own conclusions about him.

He was tall, slim. Of some sort of Asian heritage that was mixed enough that I couldn't distinguish it at first sight. His accent hinted at British. Or perhaps the tenor of his voice was just an artifact of having been transformed into a vampire? Of being remade by that dark-magic-tainted blood into the perfect predator.

I didn't know for certain. I'd never met a vampire before and had studied them only in passing. Even then, those studies had been mostly focused on how to identify and resolve any issues involving vampires. And training to destroy them, if necessary.

If Doran had been more keyed into his wards, if he'd even known dragons existed, he would never have allowed me entry.

Not that he could have stopped me. Even ancient vampires fell before dragons. Well, warrior dragons.

But as an archivist, my notions of good and evil didn't need to be quite so finely defined, or even so strictly enforced. Written accounts of vampire lore were exceedingly rare. And I certainly wasn't going to pass up an opportunity to add a chapter of my own on the subject to Infinity's pages.

The vampire's hands were shoved into the pockets of what I took for a bespoke suit jacket, given the perfect cut. His dark eyes widened slightly, perhaps surprised that I could see him.

"What the feck is wrong with you, Doran?" Ravine cried. "Scaring the shite out of a new client?"

The vampire stepped forward, allowing the darkness he'd been attempting to cloak himself within to fall away. It was a trick I'd seen other dragons utilize, but for which I had no ability.

"The jewelry box suits you," he murmured. "Dusk, isn't it?"

Ravine muttered under her breath with a peeved huff. "Apparently, we're skipping over formal introductions."

"Can you touch it?" I asked the vampire, genuinely interested. "Without it beguiling you?"

Doran grinned to reveal white teeth, impossibly straight. His hair was long enough to brush his suit collar, unkempt in a way that seemed deliberate. Because everything else about him was perfectly tailored. "Can you?"

I reached for the rune-marked box, not dropping my gaze from Doran. The magic that locked the lid slid over my hands, not impeding me in the least.

"Um, Dusk?" Ravine stepped closer, sharp-edged magic curled languidly around her wrists and forearms. "Maybe not such a good idea."

"But Doran requires a display of power," I said, smiling teasingly. Normally, such displays would be beneath a dragon. I, however, was masquerading as a witch with a very real job as head curator. Proving my abilities to someone like Doran only made sense. "Don't you Doran? With all your sneaking up in the dark?"

The vampire's expression blanked, but he matched my tone. "Perhaps I just enjoy the dark."

"Perhaps this is how creepy vampires flirt," Ravine muttered quietly—likely unaware that both I and the aforementioned vampire could hear her clearly.

I slid my fingers across the rose-gold runes etched into the warm cherrywood. The symbols hummed under my touch. I brushed my thumb across the empty keyhole. Then, smirking because the magic was practically singing instructions to me, I reached to the far bottom right corner. I pressed a series of runes as prompted to—for my ears only, I suspected. A small drawer opened.

Doran's expression tightened in surprise.

I took a tiny gold key from the drawer, placed it in the lock, then waited a beat for the locking spell to tell me which way to turn it.

Left?

No.

That released some sort of enchantment spell that felt rather malicious, even to me.

I turned the key right. The lock shifted. Pressing my fingertips to the top corners, I raised the lid. The jewelry box was empty, lined in deep-blue velvet with a divided cherrywood tray set in the top.

"It's beautiful," I murmured, lifting out the tray. The box was empty underneath. "Unfortunately, I don't own enough personal jewelry to justify keeping it for myself." I met Doran's gaze.

His dark eyes glittered, catching the light.

"Or perhaps you were thinking I should confiscate it?" I asked, smirking.

"And lock it in the basement of the museum?" A sneer that wasn't evident in his expression infused the antiquities dealer's tone. "Hidden away from the world? You'd make your predecessor proud."

"I don't need anyone's approval. And certainly not from beyond the grave." It was utterly crass to bandy about Celeste Cameron's unfortunate death. But I couldn't pass up the opportunity to take a jab at Doran's own state of undeath.

"No?" He glanced at Ravine, then back to me. A slow grin stretched across his face, completely humanizing him. Just for a moment.

A deliberate attempt to beguile me was layered within that smile, of course. Still, I found myself grinning back at him.

"What else are you hiding in the shadows, vampire?" I asked playfully.

He laughed huskily, once again unable to hide his surprise.

"Jesus, Dusk," Ravine muttered. "If I knew you liked to flirt with death, I would have introduced you earlier."

I snorted. "I'm only interested in the artifacts Doran's collected. And the ones he's about to buy. But he doesn't find me beguiling either, so fair is fair."

The dark-haired vampire barked a sharp laugh.

"Harsh," Ravine said, also laughing as she linked her arm through mine, tugging me toward the back counter. "Lay out your trinkets, archivist. We're on the clock. We don't need shapeshifters storming in to rescue you from nothing."

Doran suddenly appeared behind the counter.

I'd felt him move. But Ravine hissed, throwing an annoyed look at him as she snapped, "Stop showing off. We get it, you're the baddest boy in the dark."

Doran looked affronted. Then he bared his teeth in a sharp smile meant to intimidate. "Boy? I've marked over two hundred years, little mage."

Ravine's grip tightened on my arm, but her voice betrayed none of the fear that also stirred her magic. "With what? Your teeth?"

"Exactly."

"It isn't as scary, Doran, if you just go around announcing it."

"But the endorphins it causes you to release are just so…delicious."

Ravine jutted her chin at him. "Fine line, vampire. Fine line. And you're most definitely crossing it. And making me look bad by association."

Doran's gaze flicked to me. Then he straightened, smoothing his hands down his suit jacket, though it wasn't wrinkled. "My apologies, Ravine. Dusk's magic is intriguing."

"You aren't the first to think so," Ravine said sourly.

"Ah, the aforementioned shapeshifters? How has Dusk come to be under their purview?"

Ravine hesitated. "Just Owen Brady watching out for his new head curator."

Doran would be able to hear the partial lie—the hitch in her breath—as easily as I could.

I was starting to chafe in response to people talking about me while I was in the room. But something about Ravine's hesitation to reveal details about my life also pleased me.

I slipped my backpack off and pulled the leather roll from it—noting the way Doran's gaze lingered on the pack, rather than on the roll, as I secured it again over my shoulders. He could feel Infinity within its depths. Given their rarity, it seemed unlikely he'd ever laid eyes on a personal archive before.

Even given what little I knew of how vampires were made—their physical being literally overwritten by the power and blood of their maker—I would have assumed it was unusual for vampires to be sensitive to magic. But it made sense that Doran would be, given his chosen profession.

I unrolled the leather portfolio, removing each item without ceremony and placing it before Doran.

"I'll take it all," he said, without asking a single question or even touching any of the items.

"The coins alone are worth ten thousand," Ravine said before I could respond.

"More. Triple, even." The vampire tilted his head, watching me with glittering eyes again. "Roman gold. And the rings are intriguing. Sorcerer?"

"Those are," I said neutrally.

"And do you have many more?"

I just grinned at him.

He smiled, predatory. "The knife is purely decorative. And the coronet possibly worth more if broken down to raw elements."

I nodded. "Harvested for its magic, rather than the jewels."

"Exactly."

"That's your choice. Your business."

He nodded. "One hundred thousand for the lot. I can give you twenty thousand in cash now and transfer the rest."

Ravine looked at me expectantly.

I honestly had no idea if that was a fair price, but I needed the cash to fund the house renovation. And it seemed likely that Ravine would have piped up if she thought Doran was scamming me. "It's a deal."

He nodded, stepping along the counter and pulling out an iPad and a cash box. He started messing with the iPad, likely setting up the transfer. Thankfully, having gone clumsily through the steps with River the previous week, I now had the info he needed on my part memorized.

Ravine brushed her fingers against the bracelet I'd set on the counter. The one I thought was Egyptian, though not particularly old. "Do you have another of these?" she asked me quietly.

"Something similar," I said.

"I'd like to buy one off you."

"I pay better," Doran said without looking up from his tablet.

I looked at Ravine. "It's yours. Unless you'd prefer to take a commission from the sale?"

"The introduction to Doran is a gesture of friendship," she said quietly. "We can trade services for the bracelet."

I nodded. "I'll see what I have for you to choose from."

Doran slid the tablet across the counter toward me. It was ready for me to fill in my particulars for the transfer. "And the item you left in your bag?" he asked. His tone was cool, as if we'd offended him somehow.

"That's not for sale," I said, typing my account number into the empty box where prompted.

Doran didn't respond, simply taking the tablet from me and completing the transaction. Then, still silent, he pulled two short stacks of paper money from the cashbox and slid it across the counter.

I took it. Pulling my backpack off again, I tucked the money next to Infinity. The antiquities dealer watched my every move. I zipped the pack, securing it for the second time on my back.

Doran met my gaze. "I'm delighted to see what you bring me next time…archivist."

There was something pointed in the way he pronounced my title. It reminded me that Ravine hadn't actually gotten around to formally introducing us.

I just smiled at him politely.

I didn't mind playing games. But dragons didn't need to play games, not with vampires. Not even those pretending to be a witch.

Someone was stalking us. And it wasn't Owen Brady making certain Ravine and I made it back to the estate.

The werewolf had followed us for about ten minutes after we'd left Doran's warehouse, then turned off. Toward home, Ravine had said. But the stalker had keyed in on us only a couple of blocks from the estate. At first, they'd approached us from directly ahead, as if they'd been waiting at the gate, had seen Ravine drive past looking for a parking spot, then moved to intercept once we were on foot. But then they seemed to hesitate, backing off a block and letting us pass by.

It was only after they started darting in and out of the shadows behind us that I noted the predatory pattern to their movement.

Ravine had circled past the gate twice before being forced to admit there was no closer parking. And she had refused to simply drop me off in the No Parking zone with the large amount of cash I was carrying. What Ravine thought a regular purse-snatcher could do against me in the dozen steps from the curb through the estate gate, I had no idea. Even as a supposed witch, I was powerful enough to have taken over a head curator position. Which made me wonder what else was worrying her.

The coven? Doran?

At any rate, whoever was on our tail didn't know much about stalking prey. I had picked up the first hint of magic I couldn't immediately identify the moment I stepped from Ravine's car. It took the witch less than half a block to become aware of the sneaker-softened footsteps and the malicious figure darting from shadowed niche to darkened doorway. Except...well, calling them malicious seemed like an exaggeration. Because whoever had decided to follow us carried so little magic that I had no idea what kind of Adept was lurking in the shadows.

Sure, they could have been cloaked. But a cloaking ability powerful enough to make magic feel dim even to my senses would be a rare gift among the Adepts who walked the streets of Dublin.

I'd been in the city only two weeks, though. And I knew better than to make snap judgements.

Ravine, who'd been quiet on the drive back, stiffened, then glanced behind us for the third time. Her power shifted in that intriguing way around her wrists again. The bracelets she wore hidden under her long sleeves were more than just decorative, which made sense for a witch who named herself a metal mage. But whether Ravine pulled power she could then channel into a spell from their metal, or whether the bracelets themselves could be weaponized, I didn't know.

For a brief moment, that curiosity almost won over my usual common sense. I almost let Ravine turn and face our stalker. Just to see what she would do.

Then I reminded myself that I was building relationships and a reputation. Ravine wasn't a subject to study. She was a...friend. Or hopefully someone on her way to becoming a friend.

We rounded the corner, crossing in front of the Indian restaurant with Ravine still looking back over her shoulder. The small grocery store down the block was still brightly lit, but most of the other stores on the street were closed. Ten more steps put us near enough to the gate that opened to the estate that I could tap into the external wards—specifically the power that cloaked the estate from sight. At the same time as I reached for that power, I wrapped my arm around Ravine's waist and pulled her with me into the shadowed alcove. The wards encased us, gently snuggling us against the gate.

Ravine squeaked, her reaction slightly delayed. I had tried to move slowly, but apparently wasn't quite slow enough.

We waited there in silence, gazing out at the sidewalk and street. The sounds of traffic filtered in from the busier street a block over. The bulk of the upper-floor apartments in adjacent buildings were still lit, but the evening was generally quieting down.

Our stalker stumbled onto the sidewalk directly ahead of us, looking frantically around. She was slight, dark haired. And clutching something to her chest.

Ravine gasped. The sound drew the girl's attention to us, sharply.

Rook. River's daughter.

And she had the black leather-bound book from my office. The sealed tome that I was fairly certain had tried to beguile her.

Ravine's surprise turned to anger so swiftly I could actually feel her magic shift with her emotions. She pulled away from me, stepping forward from the wards masking us.

"What the hell, Rook?" she snarled. "You scared the shite out of me!"

Rook tilted her head. Like a bird might. Nothing particularly human about the gesture. A shimmer of darkly tinted magic shadowed her eyes for a moment.

Witch power read as blue—bright blue, not dark. Not verging on black.

Ravine pulled her phone out of her pocket, texting rather than keeping her gaze on the threat before her. "Does your mother know where the hell you are?"

Rook opened the book.

Or rather, the book fell open in her hands, silver latches hanging loosely. The black leather cover shifted as if composed of shadow, then solidified. The cream-edged pages flipped and then stilled. I could see handwriting flowing across the page, but wasn't close enough to read any words.

Rook opened her mouth.

She spoke.

But it wasn't words that poured forth from her.

It was magic.

I stepped forward, knocking Ravine aside a moment before the invocation hit her, taking it for myself. It skittered over me harmlessly. But I could feel its intent—to hold me, to take my mind and my body. And I didn't know Ravine well enough to know if she would have walked away from it.

Ravine shouted, again slightly delayed in her response. But Rook—or rather, whatever was controlling Rook—had no issue tracking my movements. She homed in on me with another odd crook of her head.

"How did you get the tome, Rook?" I asked, stepping forward so Ravine was slightly behind me, but not so far that I blocked the witch completely.

The ten-year-old lifted her chin defiantly. "It was mine to take." Her voice was a deeper, darker version of her usual lilt. The words had actual weight. More magic.

The pages of the stolen book began flipping again, faster and faster, as if the book was trying to find a spell. A spell that could counter me.

"What the feck is going on?" Ravine snarled, tucking in slightly behind my right shoulder.

Smart witch. She'd gleaned enough of the situation to know to not thrust herself between me and Rook.

Not Rook, I reminded myself. But whatever was influencing the young witch. Whatever had been hidden in the book so deeply that I hadn't picked up on it even when I touched it.

Or perhaps the book could sense danger, and had deliberately hidden itself from me.

That was a more terrifying possibility. Because I wasn't certain that I could get an artifact with that level of awareness away from Rook without harming her.

"I see," I said conversationally, taking another step toward Rook as I tried to visually assess how the spelled book might be tied to the young witch. If it wasn't, I should have been able to just take it from her. But if it had formed a bond, if it was somehow feeding off Rook, tearing it away from her could have deadly ramifications.

The sight of her being controlled was making me feel sick. But I couldn't risk killing her by being rash.

"How did you open it?" I asked.

The book settled in Rook's hands. Tilting her head in the other direction, she paused. To read the open pages perhaps? Or more likely, she was visually absorbing the power etched across the paper.

"Dusk?" Ravine asked, her tone demanding and tense.

"Rook came into contact with a book at my office this afternoon," I said. "It seemed to have attempted to beguile her, but she handed it over to me, and later left the office without even looking at it. I mentioned it to River, but she was..." I trailed off. River had been utterly dismissive of my concerns.

"Occupied with other matters," Ravine muttered.

Sure, that was a good excuse.

"Okay." Ravine's magic shifted around her hands. She was building a spell of some sort. "So we take the book. Then we figure out how the feck Rook got back into an office that's seriously locked down at night."

"It might be better to knock Rook out instead of making a grab for the book."

Ravine nodded. "I can do that."

The ten-year-old opened her mouth and vomited power at me. It was a spell as malicious as they came. Apparently, the book was no longer interested in subduing me, or using me. But instead of letting the tight torrent of power hit me for fear it would spill over onto Ravine—or, rather more selfishly, ruin my clothing—I redirected it around us with a sharp thrust of my own magic, coaxing the wards that cloaked the estate to absorb it.

The boundary magic gobbled the malicious spell up eagerly, as if it was starving.

That was something to assess at a later time. I mentally added it to my to-do list—and was thankful

I had no time to freak out about how long that list still was.

The malevolent power controlling Rook looked at me—that darkly tinted shimmer engulfed the young witch's eyes again.

Then she spun away and ran.

Ravine shouted, darting after her niece with me tight behind her. We chased the young witch along the sidewalk. With magic streaming out from the book in her wake, she was far quicker than she should have been. Though I was also checking my own speed.

Ravine stumbled as we veered left into a narrow alley, or perhaps some sort of maintenance access between two apartment buildings. Her high-heeled boots weren't made for running. I grabbed her elbow to prevent her from completely falling, but she wrenched free from me and released the spell she'd been building with a snarl.

Blue-tinted energy streaked toward Rook, slamming her in the back. The young witch went stock-still. The spell her aunt had hit her with twined around her, trying to strengthen its hold.

Ravine sagged against the brick wall, panting. She had put a lot into the spell, but quickly shook it off. Together, we steadily closed the distance between us and Rook.

"What was the spell?"

"Sleep," Ravine said—then added incredulously, "She's...fighting it."

She was. "Not she," I said. "It. The book."

Rook's head was thrown back, mouth slack, that darkly tinted power blazing from her eyes. I circled her, assessing the book without touching, looking for ties.

And now that it was partially highlighted by Ravine's quickly fading sleep spell, I could see the binding. It was black and seething, anchored deeply within Rook's chest.

It was also steadily gathering the sleep spell—and somehow siphoning it into the book itself.

In that, the once-sealed book shared certain qualities with an archivist's personal archive—if that archive had been utterly corrupted. But I quickly dismissed that notion. No matter how powerful they grew, personal archives couldn't be accessed or used by anyone other than the person to whom they were bound. And they didn't survive the death of their archivist. Nor did they control people.

Ravine reached for the book.

"Wait," I cautioned. "It's...burrowed into Rook."

"What?" Ravine's voice cracked. Raw fear flashed across her face—for Rook, not herself.

Rook's head snapped up. She looked me dead in the eye as she whispered, "I'll take the little witch, archivist. You might lock me away again, but you can't have her."

Then her eyes rolled back in her head and she collapsed. I caught her before she hit the ground, scooping her up and instantly bolting back toward the estate.

Ravine kept pace with me. "Dusk? Dusk?!"

"I'll get it off her, Ravine," I said, aching to run as fast as I could. "I'm just stronger on the estate."

I wasn't, really. But once safely in the house, I could act without worrying about the multitude of eyes that might be on us. Without worrying about Rook dying in the street.

Ravine accepted that explanation without question. Even if she mostly worked with metal, she was an earth witch, after all. She understood the power in that kind of connection.

I was surprised and pleased that the sleep spell had managed to stop Rook while she was in the grip of the spelled book—though I was fairly certain that Ravine wouldn't have hit her niece with anything potentially harmful—but I was still worried that in order to thwart the book's control I might need to put Rook, as its host, in jeopardy.

Then, in a heartbeat, I realized that I was discounting my own instincts, my own sudden need to get Rook back to the estate. I had already been able to use the estate's wards to thwart one spell manifested by the book.

Maybe I could do so again.

The gate came into view. Ravine darted ahead to open it, but it automatically swung wide in response to my presence. Perhaps even my growing terror.

Because I wasn't sure whether Rook, slung limply in my arms, was breathing anymore.

We dashed through the wards. That power instantly clung to Rook, collecting around the book specifically. I slowed, silently urging the estate's magic to suppress the power targeting the girl. To consume it as it had before.

Rook started convulsing, then foaming at the mouth.

"No!" I cried. "Stop!"

The boundary magic released us so quickly that I stumbled forward.

"Dusk!" Ravine cried, terrified. She was trying to take Rook from me, or perhaps to help me to hold her.

"Sorry. I hoped that would work. The library," I said, technically lying but trying to believe what I was saying. "I have more power in the library." That was true, of course, for most archivists. Unfortunately, I hadn't managed to tie the library to me yet, not even with basic wards.

I was going to have to use the bone blade.

We ran up the path to the house.

Both doors were flung open before we were halfway there. Kellan Conall filled the doorway, his eyes blazing green-gold. The color of his particular magic.

"What the fuck is...that?" he called out, all but roaring.

The house...shifted. Its energy, at least. As if responding to the power pouring off the shapeshifter, off all of us.

That energy reached for me, practically pulling me toward the door. I didn't fight it. There was power in the manor, in the walnut tree that anchored it, that I didn't fully understand yet.

I barreled toward Kellan. Ravine had flagged behind me. I could hear her sobbing breaths, but I didn't stop.

Kellan stepped out of my way at the last moment. The confused anger slipped from his face as he gazed at Rook in my arms.

The young witch was still. Utterly still. Still enough that I was even less certain she was alive.

Then Sisu was beside me, keeping pace as we darted through the house toward the library. Lile and Neve were shouting, but I wasn't paying attention to any of it.

I made it to the library, dashing to the center of the room and laying Rook down on the floor, across from the fireplace. It was blazing brightly. Kellan must have lit it. The ten-year-old's head lolled to one side, but she was still clutching the book to her chest.

Or the book was holding her. Burrowing in further and further while I hesitated. I just had to think...

I was surrounded by power.

I just had to understand how to use it.

Kellan, Ravine, and the twins raced into the library behind us.

"Sisu," I barked. "The grimoire from the treasure keeper." No matter how lightly the guardian dragon had bestowed the gift of the seemingly basic spellbook, I knew it would have been silly to not assume it was more than it seemed to be.

An exceedingly powerful book was trying to possess the little witch. But I had another powerful book on hand. And if the grimoire didn't work, I would use Infinity—though I loathed to put my archive in danger. The last thing I needed was for whatever was possessing the book to fuse itself to my archive.

I could lose the grimoire. It would hurt. But not fatally.

Lile and Neve fell to their knees on the other side of Rook's still form. I was vaguely aware of both Kellan and Ravine shouting into their mobile phones.

"It's that book," Lile cried. "That book is hurting Rook!"

Neve darted forward, catching me off guard as I reached to take the grimoire from Sisu. Kellan appeared, moving far too quickly even for a regular werewolf, snatching Neve away before her fingers could brush the book. Neve, then Lile, cried out. Neve sounded like she was in pain. I had no doubt her shoulder would be bruised by morning. I also had no doubt that her uncle had just saved her from far worse.

Ignoring the others, I set the grimoire just below the leather-bound black book, more on Rook's stomach than her chest. I carefully kept my hand on the grimoire. Sisu crouched beside me, ready for additional orders.

"Hush, hush," Ravine said, speaking to everyone else as she settled on her knees by Rook's head. "Is it okay to touch her?" she asked me in a whisper.

I nodded. "Yes. I'll let you know if that changes."

Ravine straightened Rook's head, gently holding her fingertips to the ten-year-old's temples. Then she began murmuring. A healing spell, perhaps. Magic glowed under her fingers, casting Rook's far-too-pale face in a light-blue glow.

"Rook's not breathing, Uncle," Lile whispered.

Kellan touched his niece on the shoulder, his expression grim. But he didn't speak.

"What else, Dusk?" Sisu asked anxiously. "Can't you just take the book? It's hurting Rook." He glanced at the twins, who were both huddled against their uncle.

Kellan stood ready, legs slightly apart, like he was ready to tear through anything that came at us. Anything.

I didn't doubt he would. I could feel the power coming off him. As could the house. The somnolent energy that only Sisu had felt when we'd first arrived at the estate shifted around us. Uneasily, I thought.

"We need to substitute another power source," I said, carefully lifting the bottom edge of the malicious book and sliding the grimoire partly underneath it. "We're going to try to get the book to latch on to the grimoire." I pressed my fingers against the bottom edge of the grimoire, giving it a kiss of my own power as I slowly slid it farther under the book Rook still clutched.

I met resistance halfway, right where I'd seen the seething magic attached to Rook's chest. I had to force myself to pause, to think over what I was trying to do mostly on instinct—convince the black book that the grimoire was a better power source than a young dying witch.

I desperately wanted to just tear it free. I knew I could conquer it easily. It was no match for my own power. But I didn't know if Rook would recover.

Wait…

I had detected the book's seething connection to Rook only because it had been highlighted by Ravine's witch magic. Meaning the black leather tome might have been witch wrought. Therefore it responded to witch magic…

"Ravine…" I said, still thinking.

"Anything, Dusk. Ask me anything."

"If it gets you—"

"Then it releases Rook. I have no problem pitting myself against it, if it saves Rook."

"In your hands, it might be harder to quell. Rook's magic hasn't even manifested yet."

"Tell me what you want me to do."

I sighed, feeling ignorant and a bit blind. I could still cut the bond between the book and Rook, but I knew it would be better for that malevolent magic to willingly withdraw. Healthier for the little witch.

The malicious book wasn't going to survive either way. Though I kept that thought shuttered in my mind as much as possible. If the book sensed that I was planning to destroy it—that I was so easily capable of destroying it—it would never let go of Rook.

"Reach around," I said. "Don't touch the book, or Rook. Press your fingers to the edge of the grimoire, and feed it your magic."

"Feed it?"

"It's just about intention."

"Like a wish?" Neve asked, hushed. "Like with the imp's eggs? A wish for Rook."

I smiled at the young shapeshifter, trying to be reassuring, though I didn't feel at all confident.

Ravine did as I asked. As the touch of her power wrapped around the grimoire, strengthening its own magical signature, I withdrew my own magic. Then I pushed the grimoire fully under the book.

Enticed by Ravine, the dark energy shifted, withdrawing from Rook and latching onto the grimoire.

Rook inhaled a deep, shuddering breath. One hand, then the other fell free to her sides. The black book had released her. The young witch didn't have enough magic to sustain it.

Ravine cried out, reaching for Rook with more healing power already pooling on her palms. I could feel the metal mage pulling energy not just from her bracelets but from the estate.

I snatched the book and the grimoire from Rook's chest, straightening and quickly crossing to my desk, Sisu at my side.

Only a sliver of moonlight filtered through the clouds to highlight the dark-wood desk, set in its corner between two sets of windows. I shoved the blotter to the side, knocking everything to the floor, clearing the desk except for the telephone set over runes in one corner.

I could feel the energy of the house shift toward me, pooling under my feet. In that moment, I realized—rather belatedly—that the desk was the same color as the front door. I had never tried to move it. Was it also anchored into the earth, into the sleeping tree?

Flipping their positions, I set the books down on the desk, the grimoire on top. I could feel the book that had held Rook in thrall trying to feed from the magic of the grimoire.

For a brief moment, I thought about simply tearing the books apart, possibly sacrificing the grimoire in the process. But I loathed being wasteful.

Kellan had ghosted my steps, standing close enough now to watch me, but where he could still keep an eye on Ravine and Rook.

Sisu pushed the chair out of place, standing on the other side of the desk. He placed his hands on the flat of the desk, watching me intently.

What if a book like this grabbed someone of Sisu's power? He was still young enough that his mind wouldn't be as naturally well shielded as mine, and—

I shook the dark thought away, hiking up my skirt and unsheathing the bone dagger.

"I'll help," Sisu said.

"No." Kellan stepped up to the edge of the desk, his gaze on the knife in my hand. His power was blazing from his eyes.

"I'll do it myself," I said stiffly.

"It's some kind of beguilement, yes?" Kellan asked, trying to sound calm though his power was boiling off him. "My ties to the pack make me immune."

"Not to everything," I muttered—but I knew he was right in theory. "All right. Lift the grimoire as I cut, please. Don't touch the other book."

"I'm not an idiot," he said, though without heat. He was already lifting the edge of the grimoire nearest him.

The book didn't want to let the grimoire go, but Kellan's strength wasn't just physical. As professed, he was also highly resistant to magic, as were most powerful shapeshifters. It was their inherent adaptability that granted them that immunity.

I slid the bone blade into the gap Kellan had created, effortlessly slicing through the energy attempting to bind itself to the grimoire. He lifted more of the grimoire as I cut, until he held the spellbook completely on its own.

Malicious energy writhed around the black-bound book, searching for another power source.

"Step back, Sisu," I said.

Both my brother and Kellan moved back from the desk.

The leather-bound black book flipped open, silver latches flapping uselessly. Still fueled by the magic it had leeched from Rook and the grimoire, its pages began to flip, searching for some way to bind or grab one of us now that it had been awoken.

But awoken by whom?

That was the question. And the major problem with everything that had just almost occurred.

It hadn't been Rook. That much, I was certain of. She didn't have enough magic or knowledge to break what I was now certain had been a binding placed on the book. That was why it hadn't opened in my office.

So who would put a book of such malignant power in the hands of a ten-year-old witch? Both times?

I might have been able to quell it. To figure out how to bind it again. But that wouldn't settle the bigger issue.

I might not believe in inherent evil. But I did believe in evil intent. And someone had unleashed this book on Rook. Used it and her to get to me. I had no concrete evidence, of course. But I couldn't see how it could have happened any other way. Because why have Rook wait for me in the deep of the evening outside my home? Why stalk me?

Another test?

If so, I was going to pass this one by following my own rules.

I brought the bone blade down on the center of the book, pressing my magic and my palm to the top of the knife's edge. The book's darkly tinted energy tried to grab me, but I sliced through its binding like butter, scoring the top of the desk.

The book split in two, convulsed, then stilled.

"We'll burn it now?" Sisu asked.

"Yes."

Kellan was watching me, not the book, his expression hooded. He glanced at the bone blade, nostrils flaring.

I hiked up my skirt and sheathed the guardian-wrought weapon.

The shapeshifter didn't say a word. He simply pressed the grimoire into Sisu's hands, leaned across the desk, and tore the book into tiny pieces. Sharp claws and magic slashed through paper and leather until it littered the top of the desk and the hardwood floor around us.

Sisu laughed, delighted.

Kellan huffed. "Just being thorough." He glanced over my shoulder at Ravine, who was cradling Rook in her lap. "Fire spell, witch."

Ravine looked up, readying some retort, but then Neve and Lile crowded around her.

"We'll hold Rook," Neve said.

"We'll make sure she's okay," Lile added.

Ravine gave up her hold on her niece, rising to cross to us. Her fingers flicked out when she was still a few steps away. Licks of fire engulfed the remnants of the book, roiling around it—but somehow not touching the floor or the desk.

Ravine cast with pure intent, as she had each time she'd wielded magic so far. No words, no circle. If her siblings—Ridge and River—were as powerful as her, together they'd be practically unstoppable.

Kellan grunted, satisfied.

Sisu was grinning widely. "So cool!"

The flames didn't ebb until the book was completely destroyed, burning through paper, leather, and the silver latches until there was nothing left. No ashes. And no burn marks on the desk or the floor.

Ravine looked at me. "Rook hasn't woken."

I nodded. "Let's get her into a bed upstairs. She might just need to sleep it off. But I'll see if there's any residual."

Ravine turned back to Rook. I ran my hand absently over the mark I'd scored into the desk with the bone blade. Energy shifted under my touch, and the desk...healed. And not by my magic.

I'd been right about the desk's connection to the house. Maybe even to the walnut tree.

Shivers of energy thundered up my spine as multiple people pounded on the property wards, not-so-politely requesting entry. At least a half-dozen witches and shapeshifters were waiting at the front gate.

Kellan carried Rook upstairs and settled her in Sisu's bed. The young witch was breathing steadily but hadn't woken yet. Ravine began pacing along the foot of the bed, occasionally throwing a look toward the door. I'd offered to greet the witches and shapeshifters approaching the house, but Ravine wanted me to stay with Rook in case she regressed.

Neve, Lile, and Sisu tried to crawl onto the foot of the bed. But Kellan, arms crossed and leaning next to the door, called to the twins, "Gather your things. Your mother is here."

Sisu instead perched cross-legged on the bottom corner of the bed nearest me, blinking sadly at Neve and Lile as they silently complied with their uncle's command. Kellan stayed behind, but the two burst into a run the moment they cleared the doorway.

So it was Neve and Lile—not Sisu or me—who opened the front door for the two werewolves and two witches who had marched the length of the front path to the house. I'd felt the determination of each of their steps, the property and the house somehow translating it for me.

I knew three of the four people crossing over the threshold now. And was somewhat surprised that the rest of the witches had remained outside the gate. I couldn't feel them as clearly beyond the boundary wards.

Was the Byrne coven concerned about how many of their witches were on the property at one time? Or concerned about me, specifically?

I should have expected that. After being condemned for caring about magical creatures. Would I face the same reaction now for rescuing a young witch from being bespelled by a malicious artifact?

Okay, 'condemned' was an overstatement.

"Dusk," Ravine whispered, her gaze on the door. I could feel the two witches and one of the werewolves ascending the stairs. The second werewolf had stayed with the twins in the great room. "Can you check again?"

I nodded, stepping toward Rook and hovering my hand over her chest. I didn't need my hand to do anything in particular, but when a witch felt for magic that sort of gesture was usually involved. I simply scanned the slumbering witch for any signs of the bond that the now-destroyed book had forced upon her.

As before, as far as I could see, no residual magic remained. Rook's quiet, almost inert magic was there—but simply as a hint of what she would eventually wield. It likely wouldn't have been enough for even me to have identified her as a witch if I hadn't met her mother first.

Speaking of whom, River Byrne burst into the room as if making a show of it. The door was already open more than wide enough, and no one was blocking her way.

"Get away from my daughter," she snarled, power lashing through her words.

Ravine's mouth dropped open.

I stepped back.

River brushed by me—rather than just stepping around—to practically throw herself over Rook, magic already welling under her hands. I had to stop myself from turning that brief bit of physical contact into a lesson that she should mind her manners in my home.

Apparently, I was still on edge. Still keyed up from seeing Rook in the grip of the book, feeling her dying in my arms. So, so much worse than the feeling of losing the imp.

An older woman stepped into the bedroom. Her hair was a vibrant red streaked with gray, and her green-eyed gaze was already on me. She held her power tightly coiled—so much so that if she hadn't been standing in the house, which was feeding impressions to me, I might not have picked her magic up without actively feeling for it.

Powerful Adepts often held their magic in check. It was easier to be underestimated that way.

"Dusk Godfrey," I said, forcing myself to follow protocol. "Archivist. Head curator of the magical archives of the National Museum of Ireland. Sister of Sisu."

"You should have greeted us at the door," the elder witch said coolly. She hadn't even glanced at Rook on the bed yet. "Invited us in."

"I asked Dusk to stay with Rook, Mom," Ravine said, clutching her arms across her chest as if holding herself in check. No. As if holding herself together. "Dusk got the book to release her, but Rook hasn't woken yet, and I was worried that there might be…lasting effects."

"Those effects are already rather obvious," the elder witch said.

Ravine swallowed some retort, then spoke evenly. "Mesa Byrne. Head of the Byrne coven. One of the thirteen of the witches Convocation. Mother of River, Ridge, and Ravine."

Struggling to remain polite, I gestured toward Sisu and said, "This is my—"

"No," my brother said, sliding off the bed to tuck himself against me. "People shouldn't come into our home and be nasty."

I had to actually twist my mouth to quash a smile.

Mesa looked utterly affronted.

Kellan barked out a laugh.

The elder witch rounded on the shapeshifter, who was still leaning back against the wall. "And why are you here, Kellan Conall? Have you made a conquest of the newest addition to the coven already? That's quick. Even for you."

The room went exceedingly silent. Almost as though the house was magically muffling everything, presumably reacting to me trying to keep myself calm. Contained.

Even as I struggled with my own reaction to the elder witch, anger etched itself across Kellan's face. His arms fell to his sides, deceptively loose. Not at all as if he was readying to attack.

"Mom…" Ravine whispered. "You are misreading—"

"You are a terrible person," Sisu shouted, pushing in front of me. "Get out of our house!"

The entire house responded to my little brother's demand. The entire manor. The entire property. Its power rose, pressing around us—trying to encase Mesa Byrne.

She gasped, eyes widening as her own power flared to hold her in place.

I shoved Sisu behind me. Just in case the head of the Byrne coven was about to lash back.

Then I stepped directly up against the elder witch. She was a couple of inches shorter than me. I locked my gaze to hers as I silently asked the house not to eject her. Not countermanding Sisu, because he had every right to dislike Mesa Byrne, but asking the magic that protected the property to wait for a moment.

"I have not hurt you or yours," I said evenly. "I have acted in good faith and to the best of my abilities. I am not your witch. I never will be. You can choose in this moment to be an ally, or you can take Rook with you and never set foot here again."

"More than good faith," Ravine said quietly. "You'd be planning Rook's funeral right now if it weren't for Dusk. And Kellan."

Mesa Byrne's nostrils flared indignantly.

The magic that coated the walls and floor flexed—as if in warning that it could grab her at any moment and eject her. I was fairly certain it wouldn't look good for the coven leader to find herself thrown off the property of a lower-status witch.

"I'm sorry," Sisu muttered, pressing his face against my hip. "I'm not trying to cause trouble."

"You aren't," I said, staring down Mesa.

"You are indulgent," she said to me with a sneer. "He'll never understand the proper way of things if you don't model the proper behavior for him."

"He knows who to trust," I said.

Mesa flinched.

Gitta Conall—Kellan's sister, mother to Neve and Lile—stepped into the doorway, dressed as if she'd rushed to the house from a fancy dinner. Glossy lips, high heels, and a flared skirt. She'd been lingering in the hall, perhaps out of deference. But more likely because she didn't want to get entangled in the situation.

"Sisu," she said after exchanging a quick glance with her brother, "would you like to say goodnight to Neve and Lile?"

Sisu looked up at me. "Yes?"

I nodded, and he peeled himself away reluctantly, glaring distrustfully at Mesa.

The elder witch's gaze dropped to him, and for a brief moment she looked regretful. She also took the opportunity to step away from me.

"I'll meet you at home," Kellan said without taking his gaze off Mesa.

"We could stay," Gitta said quietly, holding her hand out to Sisu. Her gaze flicked to me, the offer of allegiance clear.

My brother took her hand without hesitation.

Things were much simpler for shapeshifters. Their internal politics were just that—internal. They allied themselves with Adepts who brought welcomed or needed abilities to the pack, such as healers or clairvoyants, and didn't allow those relationships to become complicated. Because despite how much power they carried themselves, shifters generally weren't power collectors. Unlike witches and sorcerers.

"Sisu has an apology for Bethany," I said, instead of directly answering Gitta. I met his gaze. "Did you get it written?"

My brother nodded. "Neve and Lile helped. Do you want to read it first?"

I looked over at Mesa. "No. I trust you to do what is right."

The elder witch grimaced, but quickly blanked her expression. Then she crossed around me to finally address the fact that her granddaughter was unconscious on the bed.

I glanced at Ravine, who looked miserable. Then, stepping past Kellan, I followed Gitta and Sisu into the hall.

Bethany was there, standing with Neve and Lile. The statuesque werewolf was dressed in a long black wool coat layered over a T-shirt and blue jeans. The twins had donned their coats and backpacks.

"Everything all right then, Dusk?" Bethany asked, her voice low and rich. The tutor and pack enforcer's height and cascade of golden hair made her look like a Viking warrior who'd stepped from the pages of some bloody saga, but her accent was precise and clipped British. "With Rook?"

"We're not certain yet." I gestured toward my brother. "But Sisu has written you an apology, and I've confiscated the key."

"The key?"

"That was how he was able to lock you in the wine cellar."

She grimaced. "Magic."

I nodded.

Sisu stepped up beside me, holding a folded piece of paper out to Bethany in both hands. Then he bowed formally.

Fighting a grin, Bethany took the letter from him. "I will read it in the morning and offer any critique needed."

It was my turn to suppress a smirk. Nothing like taking every opportunity to educate. Oh, yes, I liked Bethany.

"It won't happen again," Sisu said, still staring at the floor.

Bethany looked at him for a moment, then glanced to Lile and Neve. Pointedly. The co-conspirators were apparently not as surreptitious as they thought.

I'd already guessed it was three against one. It was unlikely that Sisu would have come up with the idea on his own. Tutors were revered in the house of an archivist.

"I'll purchase some bokken for sword practice," I said.

"Already acquired," Bethany said breezily. "I'll bring them tomorrow." She tapped Neve on the shoulder.

The shorter twin took off for the main stairs without further prompting, Lile and Sisu on her heels.

Bethany met my gaze. "I owe you three bottles of what tasted like godawfully expensive wine."

I blinked.

"I have a bit of trouble with confined…confinement. Even in a wine cellar as large as yours."

"I'm so sorry," I murmured.

She shook her head. "I'll reimburse you. Or you can garnish my wages."

"Consider those, and any other bottles you'd like, an apology."

She grinned at me. "I'll take you up on that."

I laughed quietly. There were hundreds of bottles in the once-secret wine cellar. "It's not going to get consumed any other way."

Bethany chuckled, already moving to follow the kids.

I stepped back into the doorway, next to Gitta. Mesa was leaning over Rook, bright-blue magic pulsing from her palms as she made passes over her granddaughter's body in a clockwise motion.

After a few moments, Mesa straightened, placing a hand on River's shoulder. "There is nothing obviously affecting Brooke. She'll sleep until she is ready to wake. A mental trauma is...harder to heal. It just takes time."

River nodded.

Ravine, who'd been pacing again, sagged against the end of the bed. In relief, I thought.

Mesa turned, flicking her gaze over me, then to Gitta and Kellan. "I concur with Dusk's assessment. We will remain wary of possible long-term effects for Brooke. And I thank the pack for their assistance in this matter."

Gitta nodded stiffly. Kellan stayed silently watchful.

And that was it. The elder witch turned away, murmuring quiet instructions to River about setting Rook up at home and doing hourly checks for the next twenty-four hours.

"But the book," I said—speaking before I could check myself. Not letting the tension ease a bit further before dissecting it. "It would have needed to have been fully unlocked to grab hold of Rook the way it did. And the entire situation is odd, because Rook's power hasn't yet manifested, has it?"

Mesa straightened, throwing a look Gitta and Kellan's way. "Witch business."

Kellan's lip curled into a snarl. He cast a look my way.

"Thank you so much for all your help tonight," I murmured.

Gitta touched my arm lightly, already stepping back into the hall.

Kellan huffed, then uncrossed his arms and strode from the room without a word.

I looked at Mesa, trying to keep my expression placid and my tone calm. "You might consider this witch business—"

"You don't?" the head of the Byrne coven asked archly.

"The book was stolen from the office of the head curator of—"

"Who is a witch."

That was twice she'd interrupted me.

In my own home.

In my own territory.

Once again a coven witch was questioning my ability to not only do my job, but to understand its parameters and obligations.

I stepped farther into the room, not quite certain what I intended. Ravine stepped forward just slightly between myself and her mother, checking my forward momentum.

"It's been a long night," she murmured. "And Rook wouldn't be alive if not for Dusk."

"That isn't in dispute." Mesa's tone was stiff, unyielding.

I waited to see if she would articulate what exactly was in dispute. She didn't.

Silence stretched between us all. I could feel the shapeshifters moving through the house, then finally exiting. I had no doubt that Mesa could track their magic as easily as I could. Sisu lingered at the front door, likely watching them traverse the path to the gate.

"Explain," Mesa snapped.

Bristling at her tone, I actually had to stop myself from reacting as Sisu had and kicking her out of my house.

Mesa huffed, then amended her demand. "Please explain your supposition more thoroughly, archivist."

I sighed. Nothing was going to get solved if I didn't bend. Mesa Byrne wasn't the head of the coven because she was flexible and easygoing. And her grandkid was unconscious not a meter away. "The book was shelved in my office, behind secondary wards put in place by Celeste Cameron—"

"I am aware of the wards and the precautions Celeste had in place." Before I could chafe at the third interruption, Mesa shot River a glance, adding, "Neither your qualifications or your decision-making processes are in question by myself or the coven. The Convocation wouldn't have finally filled the head curator position if you weren't fully qualified."

Something I hadn't been aware of still clogging my chest loosened at Mesa's acknowledgement of my qualifications—even if it had been voiced only to chastise her eldest daughter for questioning my judgement in the first place. But I hated, just a little bit, that I'd needed the elder witch's approval at all.

River grimaced but kept her gaze on her daughter, her back partially turned to the conversation.

"I've spoken to Ayre," Mesa continued. "She might be able to manipulate my daughter, but I'm not so easily…led." River's shoulders stiffened, but she didn't otherwise protest. "My sister was directly involved in the circumstances that led to Celeste Cameron's death." Mesa paused as if expecting me to react.

I simply nodded.

"Which is why the Convocation never entertained Ayre's request to fill the head curator position. She's spent the last six years trying to improve her standing. The hazing gone wrong was…unfortunate. I don't wish the incident to color your relationship within the coven, Dusk. Though Ayre has her…supporters."

At that pronouncement, River whirled to look at her mother. "You don't think that I would even think about—"

Mesa waved her hand dismissively.

The incident. The murder of an exceedingly rare magical creature? That incident?

I opened my mouth to argue the point. To push. Then I reminded myself of the most important current issue.

"Rook was unable to open the book when she first got her hands on it. When I briefly examined it, there was no immediately obvious way to open it. Not without damaging it, of course. And since I had no clear understanding of its contents, there was no call to do so without further investigation. Either Rook gained the ability to thwart what I assume was an intricate locking spell in the last few hours, or she had help."

"Help?" Mesa asked coolly. "You're suggesting someone put the book in Rook's hands."

"I'm saying I hadn't seen it on my desk, of which I did a full inventory before lunch, even though Rook indicated that was where she found it. That she felt compelled to touch it. But she released it to me without protest, and seemed to forget it by the time River showed up."

"She also would have had to walk through multiple wards," Ravine said quietly. "The archive locks down when no employees are on site. A simple password would have done nothing."

"Unless Rook has underlying abilities," I added. "Also..." I trailed off. I really had no evidence that someone had armed Rook and pointed her my way.

"Yes, archivist?" Mesa snapped, testy—but not at me.

"Rook ran after attacking Ravine and me twice with minimal results."

"Minimal results?" Ravine snorted. "Not a terribly accurate recounting of how you countered the most malicious spells I've ever fecking felt without a single word or counterspell."

Mesa raised an eyebrow in my direction.

"The property wards that secure the estate are powerful," I said, only half lying. "As we've all felt tonight."

Mesa nodded. "Your point about Rook running?"

"The book was in control. Once it figured out it couldn't quell Ravine and me—"

"You. Couldn't quell you," Ravine said, snorting dismissively about her own involvement even though the sleep spell she'd used to stop Rook was far more elegant than anything I could have done.

"The book sought to preserve itself," I said.

"It was...sentient?"

"No...I don't think so. But I do think it could sense that I was able to contain it. I don't believe it or Rook would have chosen to track me on its own. But...that's just a feeling."

Mesa rubbed her hands together as if they hurt. "You think Ayre put the book on your desk."

"I have no evidence. But yes. I'd stepped out for lunch. It could have been one of my other employees...or River?" I glanced at the witch in question.

River shook her head, not looking at me. "I didn't even step into your office. Ayre waylaid me at the front door."

As I'd thought. "But…I'm sure it was just another test for me. It seems highly unlikely that Ayre intended Rook to find it—"

"Then who helped my granddaughter gain access to the archives tonight, and to unlock the book?"

I didn't say anything. Again, I had no evidence. "I'm sorry. I destroyed the book. It's not something I do lightly…"

Mesa waved her hand. "Perfectly understandable."

"Why not destroy it?" Ravine asked. "I burned it with utter fecking glee."

"We might have been able to figure out who'd touched it," I said. "Who'd opened it and put it in Rook's hands. That's not a talent of mine…" But a reconstructionist could have been called in. The Byrne coven might even have a witch capable of recalling scenes built from the tiniest deposits of residual magic.

Mesa crossed over to the bed and laid her hand on Rook's forehead. Then she looked to me, speaking formally. "Thank you for your actions tonight, Dusk Godfrey. For rescuing my grandchild to the best of your ability."

"I had help."

Mesa's gaze flicked to Ravine, and she offered her youngest a sad twist of a smile. "Yes."

Ravine ducked her head.

Mesa tugged a mobile phone from her pocket, then strode out of the room without another word. From the hall, I heard her start speaking to someone in Irish.

As if the head curator of the magical archives of Dublin, of all Ireland for that matter, wouldn't be able to translate that to English.

But no matter how insulting it was to be underestimated yet again, I didn't bother. I wasn't interested in interacting with the coven any more than I already had. Which was shortsighted of me, as an archivist who should have been collecting as many stories as possible.

But I was tired. Mentally weary.

Ravine was watching me, her gaze sad.

"Constant change is oddly difficult," I whispered to her.

Something shifted in her expression. Relief, perhaps. Then she covered it with a snorting laugh. "Yep. It will all settle."

"You don't sound particularly sure about that." I smiled, though I really didn't feel like doing so.

"Ravine," River snapped, trying to lift Rook off the bed. "Help me."

Ravine stepped around me. Rook's head lolled. The ten-year-old was too heavy for her mother to carry.

And I had carried her at a run, without effort, for a couple of blocks. Then all the way into the house.

Well, that might turn out to be an impulsive mistake. Though Ravine and Kellan hadn't questioned it.

"You're welcome to stay here for the night," I said. "It might be better not to move—"

"I know what's best for my own child," River said stiffly, still not looking at me. Then she cleared her throat, softening her tone. "She'll be more comforted surrounded by things she knows."

I couldn't argue with that. I was feeling terribly disjointed myself.

I stepped between the two witches, cradling Rook in my arms without another word. I'd already carried her once. Twice would make no difference now.

River grunted in surprise.

Ravine darted toward the door. "I'll bring the car around."

"Mine," River said, tossing her sister a set of keys. "It's a block north, halfway down on the left. We can all fit that way."

Ravine caught the keys, then took off down the hall.

I followed, holding Rook as gently as possible. River tucked up beside me, keeping her hand on her daughter's head. Her magic whispered across Rook's forehead in a way that felt like pure intent rather than a focused spell.

Sisu joined us in the hall, grasping the hem of my sweater. River and I didn't exchange any words. Or recriminations. Not even when the second side of the front door opened rather disconcertingly on its own so we could continue walking astride. River probably thought I'd opened the door with a silent spell. I hadn't. The house was just being helpful.

If Ayre Byrne was responsible for placing the book on my desk, even if she hadn't intended it to hurt Rook, she'd just lost River as an ally within the coven. If she'd been the one to let Rook into the office after dark, or to simply make certain that the book could grab the next person who touched it by leaving it unlocked and lying in wait, it wouldn't surprise me if the witches called a tribunal.

Except the fact that Ayre had apparently walked away from the negligent behavior that resulted in the murder and mayhem caused by the soul sucker six years ago might mean she was protected somehow. Perhaps by Mesa Byrne herself. But would that protection extend to include harm done to Rook?

Like the door, the gate opened for us without prompting, the property and the house responding to intention. My intention.

Three cars were parked at the edge of the sidewalk just beyond the gated alcove. It was technically a no parking zone, but I could feel shimmering walls of witch magic all around us. Distraction and masking spells, most likely. Too much magic for Ravine to expend when dropping me off or picking me up, but easy enough for a group of witches to cast. And a coven leader like Mesa could likely do far more with nary a word.

River dashed forward to a dark sedan with Ravine at the wheel, opening the back door and climbing in. Then she reached back for her daughter. Sisu detached from me momentarily, and I awkwardly laid Rook across her mother's lap.

The other two vehicles pulled away from the curb and drove off, carrying Mesa and the other witches I'd felt waiting at the gate.

River grabbed my hand as I stepped back. I almost broke the hold by instinct, but I forced myself to meet her gaze, readying myself to take another emotional hit.

I was practically impervious to magic, yet I was ending this day feeling completely battered.

"Thank you," River whispered. Her bright blue-green eyes were rimmed in magic, filling with tears. "I know I...I'm sorry. Thank you, for Rook."

I nodded stiffly. "It's my job."

River's expression twisted with some emotion I couldn't read, but I was already stepping back and closing the car door before she could speak again.

The sedan slid away almost silently.

Sisu wrapped his hand in mine. And, baby that I was, I clung to him, fighting back an uncharacteristic flush of tears. He pressed his face to my hip. I threaded my fingers through his hair as something broke in my chest.

I sobbed. Just once, stifling the next, then dashing the tears from my cheeks. The sky was misting, as always. I raised my face to the dark clouds that had completely occluded the touch of moonlight filtering through less than an hour before, welcoming the cool kiss of the rain.

Shadows shifted across the street as Kellan stepped into the edge of the dim light radiating from the nearest streetlamp. Our gazes met, my eyes shifting to accommodate the change in lighting.

His magic flooded his eyes. I wondered if he could see me in the dim night as well as I could see him.

And oddly, I just stood there staring at him. Finding comfort in his presence, even from across the street. I remembered magic bringing the citrus blossom to me when I'd first seen him in the kitchen. I recalled him tearing the book to pieces with vicious yet focused fierceness.

"Get some sleep, Dusk," he said, his voice pitched low but still carrying across the street. "It will all be easier tomorrow."

Sisu raised his arms to me, and I picked him up so he could wrap them around my neck. My little brother's weight anchored me further into the moment, into the earth. The whisper of the estate wards warmed my back.

"Goodnight, Kellan," I said, not bothering to raise my voice either.

He didn't respond, just watching us steadily as I turned back to the gate and crossed through onto the estate. Sisu waved just before we would have disappeared from his sight.

The property, and then the house, felt pleased to have us back. I ignored the concern that flitted through my mind at that thought—that there might come a time when the house tried to keep us. I would deal with that when necessary.

I was an archivist, after all. A dragon.

There wasn't much that could hurt me or hold me for long.

Instead of heading for the library to transcribe the day's events into Infinity, tuck the money I'd gotten from Doran into the safe, and write a note to Mistress Brightshire about the imp eggs, I carried Sisu upstairs. After forcing him to brush his teeth, I curled up in his bed until he fell asleep.

Drifting, taking comfort in Sisu's quiet snoring, I kept recalling and analyzing the way Kellan had been standing sentry across the street, heedless of the rain. He'd practically ordered me to bed. And I had obeyed. Eagerly.

He'd been right, of course. I needed sleep, respite. But was I so transparent? Or could he smell it on me?

Much later, climbing into my own bed in the wee morning hours, I realized that someone—likely Ayre, but possibly more people—didn't want me in the head curator position. Maybe they didn't want me in Dublin at all.

Given the shitty day I'd just had, it would be easy to walk away from it all.

But dragons weren't that easily intimidated.

CHAPTER FOUR

THE REST OF THE WEEK PASSED WITHOUT FURTHER incident, making me wonder if I'd misinterpreted the events of my first day at work. Much of that time was spent in Celeste Cameron's former office, working my way through her backlog. Most of which had just been casually sitting on her desk. Apparently, the former head curator had trusted the wards on the office explicitly.

I had come back from lunch on Tuesday to find my name etched across the glass door, replacing Celeste's. The block letters shimmered with residual witch magic—a gift from Crystal, judging by their tenor. I left the door open whenever I was in the office, but my employees were also buried in their own work, diligently implementing the new protocols I'd proposed after the incident with Rook.

Sisu had joined me twice before Owen Brady figured out we were returning for a couple of extra hours after dinner, and insisted on staying with us at the archive. The situation with Rook had everyone on perpetual edge. But keeping Brady from his life made me feel just as bad as asking Bethany to stay late, so I was forced to work the same hours as everyone else for the rest of the week. Well, mostly.

I had tried to trace the path of the maliciously spelled book from the moment I'd placed it on my shelf to it being removed from the office—and had discovered that a witch with light-blue magic so dim it was practically white had indeed retrieved it. That power signature could have been from Rook's immature magic. Or that of a witch who was ineffectually cloaking their residual. I'd never picked up Rook's magical signature well enough to be certain either way.

It had taken the ten-year-old two and a half days to wake up, and Ravine eventually reported that Rook's memories were a blank from after her gymnastics practice on the Monday. But aside from that information, I'd been mostly stonewalled by the Byrne coven. If the witches were conducting their own investigation, even Ravine was keeping quiet about the particulars.

And my own investigation was short lived. The moment the book thief had stepped into the main office, cutting a path between the desks, their thin trail had faded until it was hidden among all the regular comings and goings of other employees, as well as all the magical items those employees were working with.

Granted, I wasn't particularly skilled in casting witch magic, not even the tracing spell I'd adapted from the treasure keeper's grimoire. It was possible I never would be. But I was still working on tweaking that spell, as it was proving rather useful. Annoyingly so, given the circumstances.

Happily, the grimoire appeared to have withstood its contact with the sealed book relatively unscathed. Its true value—for me, at least—was the knowledge and spells it contained, not just the residual magic I'd used to bait the book.

It was late Friday afternoon when I finished reading the last of Celeste Cameron's multitude of daily journals, then set it on Infinity so my personal archive could copy its contents. I settled back in my chair to absorb the last words the former head curator had written before she'd been murdered by a soul sucker. Except for the occasional rare notation, Celeste had kept her always-detailed entries distinctly impersonal. As far as I could tell, reading between the lines as much as I could, she'd had no inkling of her impending death.

Perhaps it was always like that for archivists.

Infinity hummed, finished with the absorption. I could now recall any of Celeste's entries with a simple brush of my fingers and a focused intent. I set the journal in the final box of items I was planning to take down to the main archive.

The once-full bookshelves of my office were practically empty now. As I'd read about the acquisition of each book or artifact that had once filled those shelves in Celeste's journals, I determined what to keep and what to secure more thoroughly. Until I could figure out how to set my own unique wards on the office and the shelves, I didn't want anything remotely malicious or nefarious within reach of anyone who could get easy access to them. So other than a couple of shelves' worth of spellbooks and historical texts—witch, sorcerer, and necromancer—that were valuable to me for their unique content, I'd removed just about everything else.

I had kept the skull with the broken tooth, though. But only because I still believed it was too large to be the skull of a rabbit, and I wanted to identify it. And to understand why Celeste had kept it.

I was particularly interested in digging into a series of books that I'd found scattered throughout the office. Once I'd grouped them together, their presence suggested that Celeste had been researching ancient practices of so-called death magic. That was a broad classification, incorporating all aspects of necromancy, vampirism, zombies, ghosts, reincarnation, metamorphosis—as well as the actual harnessing of the so-called divine power of death. Dark subjects for a witch dedicated to the light. Though James had mentioned that ancient history had been Celeste's specialty.

I'd taken only a moment to flip through each text, but most of the content had seemed thinly researched and improbable. Even far-fetched. Still, I was intrigued by one book in particular: *The Mythology of Death and Its Many Goddesses*. Especially the sections dedicated to avatars and the creation of celestial creatures. The familiars of the gods, they were sometimes called. I'd only ever seen them referred to in passing before, and was excited to learn more.

I had no idea when I was going to find the time to focus on any personal research, though.

Tucking Infinity into my backpack, then slipping the backpack on, I scooped up the box of items to be archived and headed out into the main office. Despite the fact that no one else should have been able to even touch Infinity, I didn't leave my personal archive unattended, not for a second. Not even to simply hand a box of journals and a couple of final artifacts over to Crystal to be catalogued and shelved.

Paranoid?

Maybe.

Owen Brady was reading, his booted feet up on his otherwise bare desk, in the office space he'd claimed at the mouth of the hallway. From that vantage point, he could see the front door, as well as the corridor that led to the bathrooms, kitchen, and out into the nonmagical section of the museum. Also the stairs that led down to the main archive.

I glanced around. James had come in early—though not as early as me—in order to leave early for a weekend trip. His workspace in the far right corner was almost as empty as Brady's. Anything that couldn't be locked into filing cabinets or desk drawers had been relocated downstairs. On my orders. Though after what had happened to Rook, no one protested.

The news of the incident had traveled quickly—mostly via Brady, who was even more pissed than I was that Rook had somehow gotten the book despite his security measures. My new employees had practically all jumped me upon my arrival Tuesday morning. I'd given them extra duties instead of getting bogged down in details that were little more than gossip. In my opinion, at least. Still, everyone knew about it.

Brady's beard was as trim as always, and he was dressed casually in a plaid collared shirt and newer-looking jeans. Though he'd previously indicated he usually spent most of his time in the main archive below the offices, he'd been within two meters of me each day since Rook had been bespelled. He literally followed me to and from work, never once complaining that I walked.

I'd complained, of course. First to Kellan, from whom I'd received pointed silence and that golden-green stare in response. When I'd asked Gitta, she just grinned, bobbed her head apologetically, and said, "The pack protects its interests."

Which was an interesting turn of phrase. Was I the one being protected? Or was I under watch?

Used to Brady's presence after four days of being shadowed, I barely acknowledged the dark-haired werewolf as he silently stood, then slipped down the stairs to the main archive behind me. I could play the silent footsteps game as well if I wanted to. But having blown it on my first day of work, I was really, really trying to act like a witch. For the last couple of hours of the week, at least.

For the weekend, Sisu and I had plans that included all sorts of dragon activities, including a training session with Branson the sword master, plus one of his apprentices. Though I was slightly concerned that Kellan was going to want to work through the weekend. According to Gitta, he had a habit of getting obsessed about projects, and was already eyeing all the woodwork that needed updating throughout the rest of the house—including the walk-in front closet Ridge had designed.

I thought the woodwork was lovely as it was. But apparently, it was supposed to be oiled and sanded and goodness knows what else every few years.

The desk that sat just in front of the doors opening up to the archive was empty except for a phone. As expected, given that it was Brady's secondary workplace. But the wide wooden doors were closed and locked, which was rare during office hours.

Brady stepped around me. Tucking his book under one arm, he wrapped his hand around one of the ornate door handles. Then he waited as the magic sealing the archive entrance scanned his magic.

Crystal had been working on adding another layer of protection to the archives over the last few days, often to the point of heading home early, exhausted. Her delicate, precise work was evident in the freshly silvered runes etched along the bottom of one of the doors. She had added only three of that sequence of symbols to the second door. So far.

The magic accepted Brady's right to unlock the door, and he tugged it open with a quiet grunt.

Magical energy flooded out, my particular sensitivity picking it up even through the second layer of wards still sealing the massive room.

I lifted my chin, welcoming the deluge. "Thank you."

Brady nodded.

I crossed through the wards without impediment. Brady's step hitched enough that I belatedly thought it might have been a good idea to pause as if the wards had checked on me more.

A large light-oak desk sat before a narrow opening through a low run of wooden filing cabinets that bisected the entire width of the room. Each cabinet was about a meter and a half high, with one half filled with index cards and the other half filled with files. Each drawer opened up to a space larger than it appeared from the outside.

Behind the deliberate physical break of the filing cabinets, tall shelving units stretched out across what I assumed was the length of the entire museum, not just the offices upstairs. The outer walls were carved from bare rock, and heavily spelled. The Byrnes who'd originally overseen the construction were earth witches, after all. Open access to the hewn-in-place stone only strengthened the archive's warding.

Despite the disorganization I'd discovered in my office—and in general in the upstairs office space—the archive was pristinely maintained. Not a speck of dust, not a single burned-out light. No darkened corners for anything to get loose and hide within.

I set my box on Crystal's desk, stretching my senses into the archive to look for the witch.

"I'll help shelve," Brady said. "Crystal headed home early."

"The new warding is exhausting."

"She's pleased to be contributing, though...and it's not just about ownership."

Rook, he meant. All of us felt responsible for the malicious book falling into Rook's hands.

And actually, that feeling wasn't just limited to employees. James had indicated that the archive had seen an increase in donations from Adepts all across Dublin, turning in magical artifacts and ancient spellbooks. Most were fairly benign. But no one wanted to be the one whose family relic inadvertently caused another child harm.

Even Bethany had confessed to feeling like her protective instincts were on overdrive. River had contacted her to say that Rook was feeling well enough that she wanted to return for her regular tutoring sessions at the estate—that very afternoon, in fact.

Despite my workload, I was thinking of quitting early myself.

I wasn't quite certain how I'd grown so attached to Rook in such a short amount of time, and with relatively little interaction. But the same went for Kellan, Neve, and Lile. I didn't leave the house until they arrived every day, even if Bethany had already commandeered Sisu's attention.

I realized I hadn't actually answered Brady as he picked up my box and headed through into the shelves.

"Wait, we have to catalogue them first."

"No way. Crystal will have my balls if I file anything," he said cheerfully. "Best to shelve it, note the location for her, and leave it to her to fill out everything properly."

I was certainly capable of doing so myself, but I understood a librarian's territorial urges. So I followed Brady into the stacks without protest.

We didn't have far to go. The newer section, where Crystal was holding Celeste's journals until we got an answer from the Cameron family as to whether they'd like them, was in the front section of the fifth row. The sixth and seventh rows were mostly empty.

The overall collection was arranged by intake date, though artwork and anything else too large to shelve was crated and housed separately. But no matter where it was stored, every item in the collection was cross-referenced multiple times over—by creation date and era, magical signature, hazard rating, and on and on. The system was so complex that I still didn't have it all memorized, though I knew Crystal would be able to shortcut my hunt for specific relics until I had spent enough time in the collection. In fact, as soon as I got everything organized in my office, I was planning to ask her what items she'd recommend if we decided to host a holiday gala.

Brady set down the box before the set of shelves that held the first two-thirds of Celeste Cameron's journals, tugging a pen out from behind his ear and a pad of sticky notes from his back pocket. Apparently, he'd anticipated helping me shelve my last box, likely when he'd told Crystal to go home.

Owen Brady epitomized everything I'd ever read about shapeshifters. At least pack-oriented shifters. Wild wolves didn't form packs with the same strict hierarchy, but the magical combination of human and beast came with different instincts and urges—which benefited greatly from rigid order. Brady was bossy, through and through. He hid it under layers of what I was certain he considered playful charm, but it was always apparent to me that he was perpetually moments away from sprouting claws and ripping out the throats of his enemies.

Who those enemies were, I had no idea. But, that attitude, that readiness was apparent in the way he held himself, and in his smooth stalker's gait. That feeling, or perhaps my understanding of that feeling, had only sharpened after the incident with Rook. As the security specialist of the archive, Brady felt personally responsible for the ten-year-old gaining access to the offices and getting hurt—and equally responsible for not being with us when the book had used Rook to attack Ravine and me.

Given all that had happened, I was surprised that the coven still hadn't brought in a Reconstructionist. But as the week had wound on from the Monday evening of the incident into late Friday afternoon, I'd been forced to accept that the coven was either going to cover up or ignore what had happened. Either that, or they had already concluded their internal investigation without consulting anyone at the archive, including Brady.

Bethany, Gitta, and Kellan hadn't been quiet about the pack's reaction to being excluded from whatever the witches were doing. But other than a lot of grumbling, they understood it was coven business even if it had involved a theft from the archive. From my office.

As with Brady, I had started to recognize that Kellan Conall also epitomized the more controlling traits of a typical pack werewolf. Yet there was nothing deliberately charming or smooth about him. He just…was. And he didn't appear to care if he fit into a conversation, or a situation. His sister, Gitta, was far more diplomatic.

Okay.

I'd obviously been watching Kellan Conall far more closely than I really needed to, because my train of thought had just jumped way off the rails to include him in my increasingly obsessive recounting of the incident with Rook.

I pulled a gold-plated statue of a goldfish out of the box, stepping farther along the fifth row. I'd already given Crystal another two goldfish to shelve, not realizing they were a trio. The fish had been collected in 2002, so they were shelved near the end of row five.

Magic burbled up at my touch, giving me glimpses of the goldfish's creation and history. Like the first two, it was of Asian origin, designed to anchor protective wards. All three were designed to be set in a specific sequence within a home. They were especially effective if the front and back doors of a house aligned. Which meant that even with only a slight understanding of feng shui, I should have known the third fish was missing. And of course, now that I had the third fish, I was desperate to take the set home and work out their proper sequence.

They weren't mine to collect, though. And whatever research Celeste had been using them for, she hadn't mentioned it in her journals...

In fact, I actually wasn't certain why Celeste Cameron had shelved the relics in her office. Assuming she hadn't been interested in using them purposefully.

I slowed, thinking.

What if she had been interested?

Had the third fish been deliberately shifted out of place?

The first two goldfish I'd pulled from Celeste's shelves had been placed almost directly across from each other on a slight diagonal, the relationship between them plainly visible. The first had been set next to a number of the witch spellbooks that I'd kept. The second had been on a shelf next to the not-a-rabbit skull.

The third goldfish had been shoved to the back of a bottom shelf, placed behind a chest that had some sort of nullifying qualities. The chest held an intricate sorcerer-wrought mask that, according to its accompanying paperwork, delighted in making anyone who wore it dance until they died of exhaustion. Why something so dangerous hadn't been secured in the main archive years ago, I had no idea.

I tried to visualize a possible triangulation. If the third goldfish had been properly placed, what would the three have been warding?

I hadn't found anything all that deadly in Celeste's office. At least not deadly to me.

I paused before the shelf that held the other two goldfish. Then I slipped my hand through the magic sealing that shelf and set the third fish down next to the first two. I'd already sent a note to Crystal letting her know that I'd found another fish, but I made a mental note of the catalogue number she'd assigned to them so she could amend her records.

I was reading too much into it all.

Celeste Cameron had spent over twenty years overseeing the archive. I was fairly certain she hadn't cleared out her office with any regularity. Perhaps she hadn't felt the need to do so. It was completely possible I was overreacting, locking these minor artifacts in the main archive.

I turned away, intending to help Brady with the last couple of items in the box.

Then I noticed the empty section of shelving on the other side of the aisle. One unit over, at shoulder height.

That shelf hadn't appeared empty when I'd crossed through the stacks from the other direction.

I stepped closer, tilting my head back and forth and noting a flickering as I did so. One of the bonuses of being a dragon archivist was that I was partly immune to most magic, which meant I could see through a lot of spells. And until Rook had been so thoroughly beguiled by a book that hadn't felt particularly harmful to me, I hadn't realized that ability might be detrimental in my role as head curator.

An obfuscation spell had been placed on the shelf, or at least on one end of it. It was anchored to a small black stone that had been polished to a high sheen. Witch magic, but not Crystal's gentle power signature. And Crystal was a Pine witch, which meant her natural abilities were anchored in the written word. Anything she wrote in any language was laced with power, just like the runes she was systematically adding to the archives' doors.

An earth witch would cast in stone.

An earth witch would layer that stone with so much magic that its surface eventually smoothed into a sheen. So much magic that it might eventually fool even other archivists, all of whom were typically ranked highly sensitive.

I was jumping to conclusions.

I noted the catalogue number on the shelf, reaching to pluck up the black stone and smother its magic with…

I stopped myself a breath away from making a mistake.

This wasn't the first empty spot on a shelf I'd come across.

There had been obvious places on Celeste's overly full shelves where items had been removed, but I'd thought little of it. Archivists pulled items off shelves for further study or reference all the time. But…it was possible I'd jumped to the wrong conclusion about that as well.

"Brady?" I called quietly.

The security specialist was at my side before I turned my head to look for him. "Sniff out something interesting, boss?"

He was grinning, peering at me rather than the shelf I was pointedly looking at. I didn't know Brady all that well, but I already knew that grin.

I huffed a laugh. "I doubt it. There are lots of legitimate reasons artifacts are removed from the archive." The logical assumption was that James, Crystal, or even Brady himself were doing some sort of research. I currently had a set of spellbooks on my desk, all of which focused on warding magic. Crystal had curated the selection of texts for me from various eras, all pulled from the main archive. We'd been discussing my reading during coffee breaks.

That didn't explain the obfuscation spell, though.

Brady's eyes narrowed, taking in the shelf, then the others around us.

I stepped back, pointing. "What do you see there?"

"A box..." He trailed off, slowly pacing the length of the shelf and back again. "My senses are always a little overwhelmed in here...but..." His hand darted out, practically a blur even to my sight as he plucked the black stone from the shelf.

He looked at the stone in his hand, then looked at me. "No box."

I nodded. "Can you assess the magic on the stone?"

He shook his head even as he sniffed the stone thoroughly. "Witch...earth witch. That's a rather large pool in Dublin."

I nodded. Though the main archive would open only for select people, that didn't mean one of those people couldn't have purchased the spelled stone from a Byrne witch.

Brady flipped the stone in his hand, over and over. "Strong, though. Usually just moving it after it's triggered would break the spell. This one is trying to latch onto my hand. That might narrow down the pool of spellcasters."

I held my hand out, and he dropped the stone into my palm. Then he proceeded to run his hands over the empty section of shelving.

"After Celeste died, was an inventory done of her home?" I asked.

"Should have been," Brady said rather noncommittally.

I softened my tone. "That would have been your area, yes?"

He straightened, not quite looking at me. "Normally, yes. But, ah, it wasn't just the witches who the soul sucker took a chunk out of. Took me some time to…recover." He rolled his neck, then seemed to catch himself doing so. Showing weakness.

I focused on the stone in my hand instead of him, giving him a moment.

"The date, though…" He touched the catalogue number on the empty shelf. "It puts the collection of whatever was shelved here about four years before Celeste died."

I nodded.

"But …?" Brady shoved his hands in his pockets, grinning at me again. "What else is missing?"

"Possibly missing."

He hummed encouragingly.

"There were a few blank spots on the shelves in Celeste's…in my office. I first noticed them when I cast the tracing spell to prove that Ayre had released the imp."

"But you decided, logically, that there were lots of reasons books and whatnot would be moved around."

"Celeste's journals are detailed, but not that well..."

He smirked. "Organized?"

"They were written for her own reference," I said. "Not necessarily meant to be used by anyone else. But...I'd have to double check, of course..." I could, in fact, read any part of Celeste's journals through Infinity, but I wouldn't in front of Brady. My personal archive was exceedingly powerful, and not something a typical witch—not even an archivist—carried around in her backpack. "I don't remember Celeste mentioning a specific collection around this date." I gestured toward the catalogue number.

Brady shrugged. "The easiest thing to do would be to check the log to see if it's been signed out. Then check the catalogue to see what's missing."

My own thoughts exactly.

Brady held his hand out promptingly, eyeing the black stone I still held.

"This is my job," he said quietly. "If the power signature can be traced, it will be easier for me to do so when not in the archives."

He was right. And since it was his job, I didn't doubt he was actually a better tracker than me. He'd spent his life surrounded by the witches of Dublin, after all. And werewolves had a fantastic memory for scents.

So...trust.

I had no logical reason not to trust Brady.

I gave him back the stone.

He tucked it into his pocket and sauntered off, scooping up the empty box as he passed it and exiting the row.

I pulled Infinity out of my backpack and made note of the catalogue number, as well as the number on the neighboring artifact. That was a cracked but still lovely urn that looked vaguely Egyptian, though the blue runes painted on the thick white clay appeared to be a different style. I also noted the items shelved above and below.

Tucking Infinity back into my pack, I followed Brady to check the log sheet, mulling everything over.

Except for the oddness of the obfuscation spell, there were legitimate reasons that a section of any of the shelves in the main archive might have been empty. All archivists specialized in various topics throughout their careers. Celeste might well have been doing research at home. Maybe even writing a reference text. And with the devastation the soul sucker had brought down on the archive, any items she'd taken out might not have been properly returned.

Except for the obfuscation spell…

Moreover, Rook's run-in with the spelled book still bothered me. Because other than guesses and what-ifs that might have been born out of the grudge I held firmly against Ayre Byrne, I had no idea where it had come from or how it had ended up on my desk for Rook to find in the first place.

The spelled book could have been one of the missing items from Celeste's shelves. It could have been the item that Celeste had been using the goldfish to ward. Even worse, it could have been one of many items Celeste had been hiding behind the triangulated power of all three goldfish.

Maybe it all tied back. Maybe it was all covering up the same theft—of the spelled book. Except that still felt like an opportunistic attack that had been meant for me, not Rook. A relic plucked from Celeste's shelves and set on my desk for me to tangle with.

It would have been easy to blame me in the aftermath for whatever the spelled book had wrought, because I should have known it was in the office. Except it hadn't even tried to beguile me…

As it very well might have if I'd actually been a witch.

So with the book unable to target me, Rook had gotten tangled up in the second strike—or was it the third—against me. Against the new head curator.

What had Mesa called it? A hazing gone wrong?

And since Rook was seemingly okay, the coven had no inclination to investigate. No reason to find out what was really going on.

I was seriously jumping to conclusions. If any of this was true, if any of it reflected reality, I needed solid evidence that something had been stolen in the first place.

Thankfully, there were a few places I might get it.

The missing artifact hadn't been officially logged out. The card catalogue had a missing card between sequential numbers. And the corresponding file was also gone, though that wouldn't have been unusual if one of the other archivists was studying the artifact. Brady actually stuck his head in between the files, inhaling deeply three times.

He shook his head, frowning. "Just Crystal's scent. I'll check her desk upstairs, but…"

I understood. There was no way a librarian would have stepped beyond the main doors with an artifact that hadn't been checked out—let alone the catalogue card and the entire file. It was possible that such an act might actually physically hurt Crystal now, given how much of her magic she'd tied to the archive in the last week. That was one of the main reasons my Aunt Josephine rarely left the archive she'd built in Crete.

Wait.

In the last week…

"The artifact had to have been removed before Crystal started adding the extra protections."

"Yeah, I thought of that after you listed the precautions you wanted us to implement…after Rook."

"Ayre Byrne…" I said.

Brady interrupted me. "Listen…I…" He grimaced, then ran a hand through his hair.

I waited.

He huffed out a breath. "What were you going to say?"

"She came back the day I fired her."

"When?" he growled.

I shook my head. "I was out for lunch. I only know because River and Rook came to see me, and Ayre called River away. Actually, I can't even say for certain that Ayre even stepped back into the offices."

"James cleaned out her desk on Tuesday. I offered to do it, but I was a little busy trying to figure out how Rook got back into the offices, and your office specifically, after hours."

"And did Ayre pick up her personal items?"

Brady shook his head. "Crystal dropped them at the coven meeting yesterday, after Rook woke up and they knew she was going to be okay."

"Okay is…optimistic," I said cautiously. I hadn't laid eyes on Rook myself yet. But the long-term effects of being beguiled by a spell as malicious as the one that had been contained in that book were truly unknown.

Which is to say, completely dependent on Rook's immature magic...and any possible mental injury.

"You can say that again," Brady muttered, his gaze distant for a moment.

With four witches killed and my Great-Uncle Jamal incapacitated, I wasn't remotely surprised that even six years later, Brady was still recovering—even if just mentally—from the soul sucker's rampage through the archives. And I suddenly, very desperately wanted to ask all sorts of questions about the incident. I stifled the impulse, though, getting back on track. "So Ayre likely hasn't been in the office or the archive since I fired her."

"And the missing artifact might have been missing for much longer than that."

"Or it was among Celeste Cameron's personal effects...and has been unwittingly returned to her family."

Brady grunted in acknowledgement, lifting the sticky note on which he'd jotted down the catalogue number. "I'll check the desks and filing cabinets upstairs. Then I'll text Crystal to see if she knows who filled in for me when Celeste's belongings were being packed up."

I nodded, wandering back to the card catalogue.

"And what are you going to do, Dusk?" Brady asked, his tone slightly playful.

I shrugged. "Poke around down here for a bit. See if I can connect any...dots."

He chuckled, already crossing toward the main doors. "So secretive. Like I said when we met, things had gotten boring around here."

Brady had also said he had a feeling that boring didn't like me as much as I liked it. And given the events of the week—and I was only an hour away from finishing my first full week as head curator—I was slightly concerned that he might be right.

I pulled Infinity and my fountain pen out of my backpack, opening the personal archive to the first page. Using the date embedded into the catalogue number for the missing artifact as a starting point, I wrote a note.

Did Celeste Cameron mention any new collections or acquisitions in her journal in August or September 2011?

The inked words soaked into the otherwise blank page, disappearing as Infinity absorbed and processed the question.

While I was waiting for a response from my personal archive—which had been fed the journal from that year less than two hours earlier—I recalled the catalogue numbers I'd noted on the other shelves, looking up each in the card catalogue.

Each artifact had a corresponding card, as it should have. But only one had a notation tying it back to the missing artifact. According to the records, whatever had been removed from the shelf had been collected alongside the Egyptian-inspired urn.

Words started appearing on Infinity's pages. The journal entries. Speed reading for any highlighted mentions of a new collection, I flipped through pages and pages of copied text. Celeste was verbose and had a habit of jumping topics.

Unfortunately, nothing jumped out for me.

Sighing, I murmured to Infinity, "Keep those open for me. I'll read again, slower."

Infinity fluttered the edges of the indicated pages in response, making me smile.

I crossed to the corresponding filing cabinet to retrieve the file on the urn. It was thin, holding a single page indicating that while the urn held some residual witch magic, whatever was once contained within it had long been removed. A date of collection was noted—August

15, 2011—but nothing about where it had been found or why it was included in the main archive.

A final note was scribbled at the bottom of the page:

Unable to authenticate date/era or country of origin – C.C.

That was very odd. Everything I'd learned about Celeste Cameron indicated she was very thorough. So with no sense of where the urn had come from, why would she have felt the need to lock such a benign find behind the heavy-duty wards of the main archive. Why take up valuable space?

Granted, I was being overly cautious with all the items from the office I'd just added myself. But I had a good reason to do so, even in the short term. Rook.

I opened Infinity, intending to feed the archive what little info the file contained, when something caught my eye on the side of one of the journal pages that Infinity had recalled. At first glance, I had assumed it was just some sort of doodle.

I blinked. I blinked again, deliberately. The so-called doodle—some kind of magical code?—resolved itself into words.

Successful retrieval with D.

D? None of the current employees had the initial D in either their first or last names. So who else would Celeste have been on a collection with? And why call it a retrieval?

Had this been…an illegal collection?

Such things happened, of course. An archivist might hear word of an artifact they deemed dangerous, but which the current owner wouldn't surrender. Or some relic might have needed to be retrieved with the help of an Adept who wasn't an official employee of the Dublin archive. Perhaps Celeste hadn't trusted those employees? With Ayre being one of them, I could understand that sentiment.

It was also possible that Celeste was doing something untoward. Dealing in illegal antiquities. Though if the clandestine retrieval was connected to the missing artifact, which was also connected to the magically insignificant urn, why shelve those items in the archive, where they could be so easily found?

I flipped back a couple of journal pages, noting the date of the main entry—August 5, 2011, ten days before the collection date noted for the urn. It wasn't a sure thing that the so-called retrieval had happened in that specific range, since either date might have been noted as an afterthought. But it gave me an idea of the probable timeframe.

I tucked the file back in the cabinet and was in the process of closing the drawer when I caught sight of the edge of a dark piece of paper at the bottom. As if it had fallen out of one of the files at one point.

Pushing the files aside, I found a torn photograph stuck to the bottom of the drawer. It was easily small enough to have accidentally slipped out of a file as it was being pulled in or out of the cabinet. It looked as if about two-thirds of it had been torn off. The image was darkly lit, practically disappearing against the dark wood of the cabinet.

It was a picture of the Egyptian-inspired urn. It looked as though it was sitting on a shelf of some kind, a candle and a number of runes visible in the mostly unfocused background. So not just a shelf…

An altar?

I peered more closely at the urn. In the photo, it was cracked and its top had been set to one side. So it had been damaged and emptied before Celeste collected it.

Another object was barely discernible along the photo's torn edge. Not taking my eye off the image, I stepped closer to the nearest light.

"More golden runes?" I murmured. "On what?"

I squinted. And then my nearly perfect memory clicked what I was seeing into place.

I was looking at the corner of a rune-marked wooden box.

A jewelry box, to be specific. A box that I'd laid hands on four nights ago.

Successful retrieval with D.

D as in Doran?

Had Celeste Cameron gone on a clandestine artifact retrieval with the illegal antiquities dealer? Why?

I set the picture facedown on Infinity to take a copy I could retrieve whenever I needed. Then I placed the original back in the urn's file, adhering it to the folder with a touch of my magic. As it should have been secured to begin with.

And if I was grinning in anticipation of uncovering some mystery involving the former head curator, a vampire, and a missing artifact? Well, at least there was no one around to see me.

I glanced at the clock on the wall. Two hours until full dark. I needed to spend some time with the urn, to see if it would yield any info to my touch. Afterward, I would bring an early dinner home for Sisu, and ask Bethany if she could stay with him for a few more hours.

Then I had a vampire to interrogate. Civilly, of course.

Celeste Cameron had been correct about the urn. Its residual magic was dim. Whatever had once been held within it was presumably the reason it had been placed on the altar I'd seen in the torn photograph. As such, its connection to the missing artifact—however tenuous—might have been the only reason Celeste had collected it for the main archive.

Now all I needed to determine was whether or not the jewelry box was that missing artifact. And if so, why and how it had come to be in Doran's possession.

I was fairly certain that a vampire as obviously astute as Doran wouldn't have had anything quite so damning on display when he knew Ravine was bringing me—the new head curator—to meet him. Which meant it was unlikely it had been removed from the main archive, and more probable that the jewelry box had been part of Doran's haul from the so-called retrieval with Celeste.

Brady was sitting on his empty desk at the end of the corridor with his back to the rest of the main office, talking on the phone. "Find out for me, would you Ridge?" His gaze snapped to me as I crossed toward him. Then it fell to Infinity.

I was holding my personal archive in my left hand, the gesture so ingrained that I'd forgotten I was supposed to be more circumspect with it.

I was seriously the worst spy ever.

"I appreciate it. Text is fine." Brady ended the call. "Jim's and Crystal's desks and filing cabinets yielded nothing," he said to me. "I even checked yours, just in case you missed anything."

"Did I?"

He smirked. "No. I also can't scent anyone in there but you."

Not surprising. Even with Jiaotu's glamour to make my magic read as that of a witch, and even as closely as I tried to contain that magic, five intense days of being locked in the office was more than enough time to overwrite any older residual.

"You do have a pile of books about wards and boundary magic," Brady said casually. "Also more than a passing interest in death magic?"

The small collection of death-magic books had been Celeste's, but I wasn't interested in quibbling. "Yes."

He raised an eyebrow at me, waiting.

I didn't indulge him, instead getting him back on track. "Celeste's effects?"

He shook his head. "It's another fuckup. I'm sorry. Crystal had been here only a few months. And we were suddenly crazy short-staffed. Jim actually slept in the break room for three weeks."

"And Ayre?" I asked. "The soul sucker didn't hurt her, did it?"

Brady grimaced, then cleared his throat. "That isn't…clear. She was gone for about a month. It took me three months to even get out of bed…six to get back to work…"

"I see."

He huffed. "Listen, it was an insane time. I think we all did our best. The coven brought in a specialist, and then the witches were all on cleanup duty. The pack only cared if its members were in danger, which they weren't. Then whether or not I was going to fucking walk again." His tone thinned with stress.

Uncharacteristically, I closed the space between us, laying my hand on his arm. "It took the specialist seven months to even speak English again."

Brady's head shot up, meeting my gaze so frantically that I thought he might have been trying to read the truth of my statement in my eyes. "He saved my life…and I don't even remember it."

I nodded. "That was his job. That's…all of our jobs, with misplaced or misused artifacts."

"You've heard," he said quietly.

"Heard?"

"The rumor that it was Ayre who lost control of the creature."

I didn't say anything.

Brady's face twisted. "Ravine shouldn't be talking about shit she doesn't understand."

"Things happen, and you make the best decisions you can in the moment."

"Yeah, well…tell that to your new BFF."

I had no idea what BFF stood for. I allowed my hand to drop away from Brady's arm. He caught it and gave it a squeeze, then let me go.

"The most likely scenario," he said, his voice stronger now, "is that whatever is missing got boxed up in Celeste's belongings, and it's now sitting in the basement of one of her Cameron relatives. We'll find the person who did the boxing, and they can tell us where it was shipped. I've got Ridge asking around. He'll get more out of the witches quicker than I will."

"And the obfuscation spell?"

Before Brady could answer, he was interrupted by the ping of his phone. Which reminded me that I kept forgetting to carry my new phone with me. Despite the assurances Ravine had given when she purchased it for me, I was fairly certain the more contact I had with the new tech, the quicker my magic would fry it.

Brady glanced at his screen.

Then he just stared.

Lip curled in anger, he stood, grabbed his wool jacket off the back of his chair, and shoved his arms into the sleeves. He ran his hand through his hair, then spat two words in my direction.

"Ayre Byrne."

"She was the one who packed up Celeste's house?"

"Celeste's apartment, but yes. Don't go anywhere without me."

"And where are you going?"

"To Ayre's goddamn house. I'm not texting or calling. Again. She'll find it harder to dodge me face-to-face."

He was already pissed off enough that I couldn't imagine the witch managing to ignore him.

"You know it's most likely a coincidence," I said. I had proof—the picture copied into Infinity—that pointed in a completely different direction, though I wasn't ready to share that yet.

Brady narrowed his eyes at me, nostrils fluttering for a moment. "You're heading home for dinner with Sisu, right?"

"Right."

"I mean it, Dusk. Don't go anywhere without me."

I just smiled.

"When I said that thing about it finally not being boring around here," Brady said, "it's because your energy is intriguing. Intriguing is fun, Dusk."

My energy was intriguing, was it? Jiaotu's glamour might not be holding up against the shapeshifter's specific sensitivity to magic.

"You getting yourself killed because you go sniffing around something you shouldn't isn't fun," he added.

"Is there a lot of something that might kill me in Dublin?" I asked teasingly.

Brady shook his head. When he spoke again, it was just a whisper. "I've already lost one head curator."

That wiped the smile off my face. "It's archive business. If I find something that requires your attention, I will call."

"Text is quicker."

Right. He'd programmed his number into my phone on Tuesday morning, practically forcing me to hand the mobile over to him. "I'll text."

Brady pushed through the door, then paused. "Remember your obligations. To the archive and to Sisu."

That earned him a glare.

He shrugged. "Just making sure I have your attention. I got full reports from Ravine and Kellan about the incident with Rook. And let's just say you glossed over some parts."

"Some parts that now make me untrustworthy in your eyes?"

He shook his head in quick denial. "Not in the least. Parts that make you…the hero. And everything rash that comes with flinging yourself in the path of a dangerous object to save a child you barely know."

I opened my mouth to protest, but he cut me off.

"What power might that book have tapped into if it had gotten hold of you, Dusk? You might be young. Twenty-five, right? You might not cast simple spells like a regular witch, but I can smell power on you. So, fueled by you? That book could have razed Dublin to the ground before the witches even woke up to the danger."

"Then blame the person who put it on my desk," I said stiffly. "Not me."

"I'm just saying…learn the city, meet more of the players, before you rush headlong into whatever this is, okay?"

I didn't answer him.

I knew my job. I knew my talents and my limitations. I knew that Sisu was and would always be my first priority.

I wasn't quite certain what Brady saw in my expression, but he raised both hands, holding the door open with his foot instead. "Simple advice from your security specialist. My reputation and livelihood are tied directly to you. It's in my best interests to keep you safe."

Absolutely livid, I unhinged my jaw to tear his head off—and instead found myself saying, "I'll be paying Doran a visit after sunset."

Brady grinned at me. "Fantastic. I can't stand the vampire."

Of course he couldn't.

"I'll pick you up at…let's say 7:00 P.M. That's actually still early for the bloodsucker. Bethany can stay with Sisu."

"Fine."

He chuckled. "That was so hard for you."

"Shall I accompany you to interrogate Ayre Byrne?"

He barked a laugh. "Hell no." He let the door close behind him, then headed out of the building without another word.

See? I was capable of making rational decisions even when being goaded and having my judgement questioned. It was archive business, therefore it was Brady's job too.

No matter that I didn't need any backup, being a dragon with an epically powerful bone blade strapped to my thigh. But the witch I was posing as would, without question, bring a shapeshifter to meet a vampire.

CHAPTER FIVE

I ACCIDENTALLY ALMOST ACCOSTED A PIZZA DELIVERY guy waiting at the front gate to the estate as I darted into the alcove that magically concealed it. I'd forgotten an umbrella, and it was raining in earnest, hence the dashing home and darting around corners.

The delivery guy nearly lost hold of the five boxes of pizza he was carrying.

Five boxes.

Apparently, we were feeding shapeshifters as well as two dragons in disguise.

I couldn't help but smile. Then I really hoped I wasn't smiling about the idea of sitting across from Kellan Conall while eating dinner. Again. Dragons didn't crush on shapeshifters. Not even dragons in disguise.

"Hello," I said, pulling off my backpack to retrieve my credit card. "I didn't mean to startle you."

"It's paid for," he said a little gruffly, tugging his baseball cap down on his forehead. The nametag on his jacket said 'Dave.'

The gate swung open practically silently to reveal Sisu, with Bethany a few steps behind. I could see the long path leading to the house and the estate spreading out to either side, but only because I could see through the property wards that concealed the estate from magical and nonmagical sight alike. Delivery-guy Dave—like anyone else who might pass by—was seeing only a continuation of the courtyard.

"Pizza!" Sisu bellowed as if declaring war.

Dave flinched, spinning around so abruptly that he lost hold of the boxes for real this time.

I stepped in and rescued our dinner.

My brother was chortling so madly he was actually clutching his belly, partially slumped against the gate. Bethany shook her head, but I could tell she was attempting to hide a smile.

"Thank you," I murmured to Dave, stepping past him and practically hip checking Sisu through the gate with me.

Bethany reached past me, holding out a folded bill. "Thanks, Dave. I know it's on the edge of your delivery area."

"No problem, Beth."

I glanced back, taking in the goofy smile now stretched across Dave's face. He wasn't a werewolf, but apparently that didn't stop him from admiring the blond Viking warrior-goddess currently tipping him.

With a grin of her own, Bethany shut the gate and took the boxes from me. "The best in the city!"

"The pizza or the delivery guy?"

She barked out a laugh. "Both!" Then she looked pointedly at Sisu and said, "Last one to the house—"

My brother took off, not even waiting for the incentive that dangled on the end of Bethany's sentence.

"Hello to you too!" I shouted after him.

Bethany chuckled again, then kept pace with me up the path. It was still raining even within the magically sealed section of Dublin that held the estate, so that pace was fairly swift. I noted that a row of hedges to the far right had been trimmed into neat cylindrical shapes. Starting with the gardens and rose beds, the gnome had been methodically working through the property, which had been allowed to go wild for at least a few years before being put into stasis. I still wasn't certain if the gnome had been somehow confined to the greenhouse during that time.

"Bad day?" Bethany asked.

I blinked as we stepped up to the house. I'd probably been silent for longer than was polite. "No. You?"

"Same old, same old," Bethany said. "Everyone on their best behavior, still. We borrowed one of your Greek mythology texts today. It didn't smell like magic, so I thought it would be okay."

"Totally okay. I've locked anything worrisome in my desk for now until I get the shelves warded. But I don't keep anything in the house that might be dangerous." That was true. Because I kept Infinity and the bone blade with me at all times.

The front door opened of its own accord. Bethany flinched, a reaction so subtle it was practically just a shifting in her magic.

Sisu came tearing around the house from the left, greeting me as if he'd only just seen me, "Dusk! You were so slow, I did an extra lap."

Right. Sisu had apparently forgotten he wasn't supposed to be all that fast, though he'd been practicing with me every evening, learning to cloak his power. And I was managing to be just as forgetful about remembering to pretend to be a witch. Perhaps willfully so.

I glanced at Bethany, who strode through the open doorway with no indication that anything unusual was going on.

Even young shapeshifters could move quickly. So it was possible that Sisu's speed didn't seem unusual to a werewolf. But it was also possible that we weren't fooling anyone, and that our cover was already partially blown. Which would mean that the Conalls, and Ravine for that matter, weren't inclined to out us.

Warmth that had nothing to do with the actual temperature inside the house flushed over me as I crossed the threshold. A greeting, I thought. With my gaze caught on the soaring cathedral ceiling as always, it took two more steps into the massive great room for me to realize that I was dry, even though I'd just been dashing through the rain for a good twenty minutes.

That flush of warmth hadn't just been a greeting, then.

"Is that self-preservation?" I asked the air teasingly, still intrigued by what appeared to be the slow awakening of the house. Of the entire estate, perhaps. Or at least I'd be intrigued right up to the moment the house decided to set itself on fire, as Ravine's grandmother's house had done.

The house didn't answer me. Which, given the week I was still in the process of finishing, was probably a good thing.

I stepped into the temporary walk-in closet that Sisu had started referring to as the cloakroom—a hint that he wanted a cloak of his own, I assumed. I hung my jacket and backpack on the temporary hooks, then crouched to unlace my leather boots. Ridge had sketched a gorgeous design for the room, matching the dark woodwork that appeared throughout the house, but adding cupboards, shelves, and a full-length mirror.

I hadn't seen River since Monday, but no final bill had appeared. Ridge had dropped in each morning to check in with either Kellan or Gitta about the progress of the job, and whether any of the plans needed clarification. So Ravine had been right about Ridge not walking away from the estate project.

I turned my head to find Kellan filling the doorway. I'd felt his magic a moment before. Even clad in work boots, he moved practically silently through the house. Except when he was wearing his tool belt, which he wasn't.

His arms were crossed, biceps once again challenging the integrity of his short sleeves.

"You must go through a lot of T-shirts," I murmured, grinning at him teasingly before I could stop myself from articulating the thought.

He blinked, clearly confused, then said gruffly, "Most contractors do."

Of course they did. For perfectly practical reasons. I would just leave it at that and stop ogling him.

I straightened and set my boots on the rubber mat I'd bought as soon as I realized it pretty much rained constantly in Dublin during the autumn. Or misted, rather.

I wasn't oblivious to the fact that Kellan Conall stared right back at me while I was caught up staring at him. I was just fairly certain he did it for an entirely different reason—a suspicious watchfulness that had only grown after the incident with Rook.

And that was a good thing. Nothing positive would come from any sort of mutual lusting after one another. Despite the fact that we were genetically incompatible, he would know in an instant that I wasn't a witch if I—

"Right there," Kellan said softly, flaring his nostrils. "What are you thinking about?"

"Dinner," I said, tugging Infinity from my backpack. My stomach rumbled in agreement. I'd eaten nothing since breakfast except the day-old turkey sandwich I'd left in the break room fridge for lunch.

Kellan snorted, his gaze dropping to Infinity for a moment.

"Are you blocking my way to the pizza for a reason?" I asked, still teasing playfully even though I knew better. It was honestly like my brain didn't fully function around Kellan.

He flashed me a brief grin. "Bethany likes to reheat it, so we have a couple of minutes."

"I didn't know you were staying for dinner. And Neve and Lile?" I shifted my focus for a moment—it took actual effort to tune him mostly out—reaching through the house with my other senses. "Oh, Rook is still here?"

"Pending pickup," Kellan said, his tone grim. "Wouldn't want her to stay in proximity of a bad influence any longer than necessary."

"Me?" I asked quietly, my stomach instantly hollowing.

Kellan sighed, then shook his head. "Sorry. Old business. The witches are just riled up because the pack wants to be involved in the investigation."

"Owen Brady said he'd talked to you and Ravine. I thought that the pack was...satisfied."

"The pack is not satisfied."

I gripped Infinity tighter, then stopped myself from doing so when Kellan's gaze dropped to my hands. Again. "I would never hurt—"

"Not you," he snapped, then grimaced. "Ayre Byrne. The witches have closed ranks. If she's willing to hurt Rook, then a member of the pack would mean nothing to her."

"If Ayre is involved—"

"You just sent Brady over to talk to her."

"He sent himself," I said wryly.

"It's his job. On multiple fronts."

"So he informed me."

Kellan flashed his teeth at me. It was more of a challenge than a smile. "Why does your...journal smell like you?"

I blinked. He meant Infinity. That was a rapid change of subject. "Because I'm holding it."

"And when it's on your desk?"

I gave him a hard look. "I thought Adepts didn't question other Adepts about their magic."

"We're just having a conversation."

"Pizza!" Sisu's bellow reverberated through the house.

I stepped by Kellan, through into the great room.

He leaned into me, but kept his arms crossed.

"Isn't that considered rude?" I said, still walking. "Smelling me without permission?"

He didn't answer.

I glanced back at him.

"My apologies," he said stiffly, looking over my head instead of at me.

I opened my mouth to...what? Tell him it was okay? To flirt with him some more? Except, of course, it was possible I was interpreting the interaction incorrectly. "Did you have something you wanted to discuss? About the renovation?"

He shook his head. But before I could press, Sisu, Neve, and Lile appeared before me, grabbing my arms and dragging me into the dining room.

And then Rook, looking tired and a little sad, was pushing herself out of a chair to wrap her arms around me.

I hugged her back. While the younger trio claimed seats and Bethany and Kellan opened pizza boxes and passed around plates, I just held the young witch for as long as she wanted to hold me, unable to speak.

I hadn't been sure that Rook was going to make it. But maybe witches weren't as fragile as they appeared. My questions and concerns could wait a little longer. I smoothed my hand over her back gently, wishing that I had more power. Specifically, the power to heal.

Sisu, Neve, and Lile were debating the best kinds of pizza, with Sisu arguing robustly for chorizo sausage, Neve for prosciutto, and Lile for salami and roasted peppers.

Rook pulled slightly away from me and said, "You're all wrong. It's Margherita. Tomato, fresh basil, and mozzarella rock."

"No meat?!" Neve cried. "Disgusting!"

Sisu and Lile chimed in with a roar of disagreement as well. Bethany and Kellan laughed.

Rook grabbed a piece of whatever pizza was nearest to her, settled back in her chair, and started eating as I found my seat.

I ignored the way Kellan tracked my movements. Just like I tried to ignore the memory of Brady accusing me of being rash, for thrusting myself into a dangerous situation to save a child I barely knew.

Ravine arrived a few minutes later, pausing for a piece of pizza before taking Rook home. She would have stayed longer just to spite River—her words, not mine—but Rook was actually trying to not fall asleep while chewing.

When they had gone, Bethany somehow turned cleaning up after dinner into a teachable moment for Sisu, Neve, and Lile, then settled the unruly trio into the front-facing room across from the cloakroom—which had been converted into a living room while I'd been at work. With a sectional couch, multiple matching chairs, as well as a huge TV. All as ordered, all paid for by the money I'd gotten from selling the artifacts to Doran. The contemporary furniture should have looked odd against all the wood trim and crown moldings and fabric walls, but it didn't.

It was starting to look a little like…home.

Sisu's and my home.

A manor house that made it exceedingly clear that it delighted in being filled with laughter and magic. To my senses, at least.

Neve, Lile, and Sisu were squabbling over movies when I retreated into the library to get some work done. We didn't have cable or Internet hooked up yet, but apparently Bethany could 'stream' whatever movie the trio eventually picked.

For the so-called Archivist of the Modern World, I was still woefully behind on a lot of things.

Kellan was already back to work in the kitchen. The countertops had arrived and been installed, so he was adding the gables on either end of the kitchen island.

I spotted the notes waiting for me on the noticeboard from the doorway of the library, dashing all the way to the far end only to find that neither was from my mother. I stuffed the disappointment threatening to sour my dinner deeply down, then read the plain linen card that had been sent by Mistress Brightshire, the head brownie of my mother's estate.

Scrawled in a heavy but neat hand, it simply read, 'Ask the gnome first.'

The imp eggs were still glowing softly on their shelf under the noticeboard. I had written to ask Mistress Brightshire if she would take custody of them, but apparently she thought the estate's resident gnome might be interested in becoming their caretaker. That was intriguing. Mostly because it was becoming more and more obvious that Mistress Brightshire had been popping over to secretly visit the estate, especially if she'd already met the gnome.

With no brownies on the estate, I was still surprised that the house wasn't accumulating more dust after weeks of construction, even with how diligent the Conalls were in sealing the rooms they were working on. I cleaned the temporary kitchen with regular soap and water every time I used it, and had similarly scrubbed the two bathrooms currently in use the previous Sunday.

Admittedly, I hadn't exactly enjoyed either task. But although the cleaning spell I'd attempted to cast from the treasure keepers' grimoire two weeks before had stripped the moss and lichen off a teak table and chair set I'd discovered in the rose garden just off the library, it had then taken off their finish to reveal bare wood. And what I assumed had been rusty fasteners—screws and bolts and the like—had just...evaporated.

So the table and chairs were now in pieces.

So no more cleaning spells for me.

I would take the imp eggs out to the greenhouse for the gnome tomorrow—at midday, when it was hopefully a bit warmer. I hadn't actually met the gnome face-to-face yet. I didn't even know their name.

I wrote a quick 'thank you' on Mistress Brightshire's notecard, crossed out my name and added hers, then pinned it back onto the board.

The second note was from Zeke. Presumably a follow-up to my last letter. But instead of reading it, I tucked it into Infinity and sat down to quickly write him on a separate subject. The odd markings on the urn that had been collected at the same time as the missing artifact had been bothering me. If they were runes, they weren't any I knew. And even visually, they felt almost...false. But not...intentionally? As if someone had adapted Egyptian symbols for some other purpose, or combined multiple glyphs from different languages.

Settling down at the desk, I opened Infinity and recalled the copy of the torn photograph with a brush of my fingers and a touch of intention.

I dashed off a quick note to Zeke about the particulars of the urn and the missing artifact I thought it paired with, sealing the request with my favorite gold-flecked brown wax. The letter disappeared a moment after I'd pinned it to my noticeboard, which I hoped meant he'd respond quickly.

While I waited, I pulled out a pencil and set about trying to sketch the urn. I didn't write with pencil often, but hoped that becoming more familiar with the urn's symbols might jog my memory or help me understand their function. As I copied the runes into Infinity, thereby imbuing them with my own latent magic, it began to feel as if the creator had layered the symbols with some intent I still couldn't read. And that the creator's intention had been nullified when the urn had been broken. Cracked open deliberately, perhaps?

The idea that I was actually feeling the magic in symbols I only had a picture of seemed suspect, though, so I decided it was more likely simply an older subset of runes—perhaps even hieroglyphics—that I was unfamiliar with. Or maybe I'd caught a glimpse of something similar in some book once, but not enough to recall the connection.

But Zeke would have dozens of reference books in Giza that he could access. And being able to determine the magic or the function of the urn might help me track down the missing artifact. Or at least understand what I might be looking for.

I was partway through a second sketch—intending to send it along to Zeke for his reference—when I felt someone brush against the property boundary. Not requesting entry, but alerting me to their presence.

Brady.

I assumed he would come in, if only to see the crazy estate I'd inherited that he'd no doubt heard so much about from other people. But I found I was actually pleased that he was content to wait at the gate. Perhaps he didn't want to get caught up reporting to Kellan.

Slightly disappointed that I hadn't already heard back from Zeke, I folded the half-finished second sketch, addressed it to him as a follow-up, and pinned it to the noticeboard. Unlike the first note, it didn't immediately disappear.

Grabbing Infinity, I hustled out of the library.

I stuck my head into the new living room to tell Sisu that I'd be gone only a little while—and was completely ignored by him, as well as Neve and Lile, while they peppered Bethany with questions about something animated they were watching. The TV was paused on what appeared to be the interior of a spaceship, and multiple characters wielding swords made out of light.

"I'm fine to stay with them for however long it takes, Dusk," Bethany said, sounding amused as Sisu jumped up to mimic the movements of the sword fighters, triggering a debate with Neve over his technique. Lile seemed content to just watch. Everything.

I hoped my brother remembered his own sword shouldn't glow. We were already revealing too much to the shapeshifters just by being in such close proximity.

Kellan was waiting for me by the front door, leaning slightly back with his arms crossed and head bowed. A habitual posture for him, though I hadn't yet determined what it meant.

"Brady has a good nose," he said without looking up as I grabbed my coat, boots, and backpack from the cloakroom. "The best in the pack for magic." He grinned widely. "Other than me, of course."

I snorted, lacing my boots. "Is anyone better at anything than you in the pack?"

He shrugged, the grin lingering. "No one stronger or faster or—"

"More humble?"

He chuckled, the deep, throaty sound setting off some sort of strange physical reaction that started in my belly, then radiated…down.

Oh, that wasn't good.

"Brady and I will be fine," I said, acutely aware that I now sounded weird, stiff, as I covered my reaction.

Kellan straightened from the wall with a curt nod, all traces of teasing—flirting?—wiped away. "Doran resides in Dublin with the approval of the coven and pack. But he follows a strict set of rules."

"So he isn't out slaughtering innocents every night." I'd been trying for playful banter, but it came out sarcastic.

Kellan narrowed his eyes at me, as if I'd just insulted him. And I guess I had, by even suggesting that a vampire could run wild in his pack's territory.

"I have a few questions," I said, trying to hide my confusion over my reaction to him—and therefore my inability to converse like a normal person, or even keep our conversations purely professional. "In my capacity as head curator. It isn't a matter for the pack."

"You might be an independent contractor, but you aren't an island in Dublin, Dusk Godfrey," Kellan growled quietly. "If you need backup with the vampire, the pack will respond."

"I won't need backup."

"Either way, Brady will report back to me."

"Not his alpha?"

Kellan bristled. "My mother is far too busy to concern herself with the day-to-day workings of the archive."

"Too bad you aren't."

His upper lip curled in response.

And now we were fighting. I had no idea how the conversation had degraded so much, so suddenly. Except I was just trying to do my job, and Kellan was constantly telling me I wasn't capable of it. At least that was the impression I kept getting.

He blanked his expression rather than offer whatever retort he'd been about to snarl at me. He stepped slightly to the side, though he hadn't actually been blocking the door.

I exited the house without another word. It wasn't as if I hadn't expected to be checked up on by anyone. I just thought those questions would be coming from much higher up and with far less frequency. Maybe all this...interaction...was just what it was like to live among so many different Adepts. Many of whom had conflicting concerns. The pack, the coven, and the single vampire, all seeming to expect different things from the head curator. Me.

Kellan ghosted my steps up the well-lit front path, close enough that I could feel the energy rolling off him but not close enough that he was breathing down my neck.

Some part of me really wouldn't have minded feeling his hot breath on my…everywhere.

I was doing it again.

Damn it.

As we neared the gate, he cleared his throat, then spoke with what sounded like a forced politeness. "Would you allow Brady entry?"

"He didn't ask to enter," I said, my tone just as stiff.

"I understand. But being as he's your security specialist, I'd like him to be able to pass through the property wards, unless you choose to bar him at a later date."

"My security specialist," I echoed wryly.

Kellan simply inclined his head, not taking the bait.

I huffed, reaching for and opening the gate. "And did you have Brady constantly dogging Celeste Cameron's steps?"

"Celeste Cameron's tenure as head curator was…uneventful. You were attacked twice on your first day, and now you have a missing artifact."

So Brady had already reported to his packmate. Reported everything, not just where we were heading. I eyed the subject of our discussion as he stepped through the gate, casting his gaze across the breadth of the property.

"The artifact has likely been missing for some time," I said. "And Celeste's tenure wasn't as uneventful as you seem to think."

"Well, it ended badly," Brady said bluntly, pausing a step or two away with his hands clasped behind his back. His gaze was on me, not Kellan. A choice that seemed deliberate somehow.

Silence stretched between the three of us. I had questions for Brady but didn't want to have the discussion in front of Kellan, who really had no need to be involved in any archive business, as far as I could figure.

Brady flicked his gaze to Kellan briefly. The other shapeshifter was glowering, arms folded across his chest in his typical pose. Perhaps tucking his fists away was supposed to make him less intimidating. It didn't work.

But I was a dragon. And dragons weren't intimidated by shapeshifters.

I would just keep telling myself that.

"Shall we go?" I asked, stepping toward the gate.

Kellan huffed, then asked in a low voice, "Ayre Byrne?"

"Not at home," Brady said. "I left a message."

"In blood?" I asked mockingly.

Brady snorted, amused.

Kellan's glower deepened. "If that's what it takes."

"I might be jumping to conclusions," I said, though admitting that made me feel small. Insecure.

"In which case, no harm has been done." Kellan's nostrils flared as if scenting the night air. The rain had turned to the more typical constant misting. "Black or dark witches won't be tolerated by the pack. Not even if they are a Byrne."

"Dark doesn't always equal evil," I said quietly, aware that I was missing many nuances of the conversation, of the history between the pack and the witches. And perhaps between the pack and Ayre Byrne in particular.

Kellan glanced at Brady with a nod. The other werewolf stepped past me without another word.

"I'll see you tomorrow," Kellan said, turning back to the house before I could answer.

"You're working the weekend?" I asked. It had been made very clear to me by my staff that working the weekend was reserved for emergencies only.

"You want a kitchen sooner than later," he said, stalking swiftly away.

I shouldn't have been watching him walk, taking in his broad shoulders and the way his—

I shook my head, stepping through the gate to join Brady. The quiet rumble of the city increased, the traffic noise filtering in from the busier neighboring streets.

I closed the gate behind me.

"Your property is stunning," Brady said quietly.

"Come up to the house next time," I said.

He smiled softly, turning his shoulders in a way that indicated he wanted me to follow. "I will. And maybe you'll allow me to run in your woods once we know each other better. I could feel the power in the earth even in human form."

I fell into step with him. "Yes. The estate is ancient. Even wild in places." That wasn't the only reason it was imbued with so much magic, even near the gate. But Brady didn't need to know it had been built by a guardian. Brady likely didn't even know that dragons existed at all. Which was uncomfortably ironic, since I was walking right next to him.

I didn't like lying.

I hadn't known, hadn't anticipated, that maintaining a secret identity was going to be so difficult to...navigate.

Brady and I were colleagues, not friends, I reminded myself. Just as Kellan was a contractor in my employ, not...not...whatever else it was apparent my hormones wanted him to be.

"Did you contact Doran?" I asked, pleased that my tone sounded completely neutral. "Or are we going through the wards uninvited?"

"Can you? Without hurting yourself?"

I hesitated. "Do you know when I'm lying?"

"I haven't noticed you lying yet, but you do phrase things carefully."

I laughed. "Yes, I could get through Doran's wards. But not without ruining them, and that seems overly aggressive."

"Vampires only understand two things. Blood and power." Brady had led me to the older pickup truck he'd driven Monday night, moving around to and holding open the passenger door. "Tearing through his wards would get his attention."

"I already have his attention."

"I'm sure you do."

I laughed again. "I just need a couple of questions answered."

"You catch more flies with honey, hey?"

That sounded like some sort of aphorism, but I wasn't certain it was all that accurate. Especially not when applied to a vampire. I tugged off my backpack and climbed into the truck, remembering to pull on my seat belt.

Brady circled around and climbed into the driver's seat, starting the truck. The engine settled into a surprisingly quiet purr.

"Does Kellan hate Ayre Byrne because she almost got you killed?"

"No tribunal," Brady said, pulling into the street. "The incident just...swept under the table."

That was another expression I wasn't completely familiar with, but I understood it contextually. "And because four witches actually died and you survived..."

Brady grimaced, signaling, then turning right. "The pack didn't push."

"But anything having to do with Ayre will be a...trigger."

Brady glanced over at me, then said grimly, "You won't be able to remain neutral, Dusk."

"I've never been accused of neutrality in my life."

He barked a laugh, as if I'd torn it from him unwillingly. "Right."

Silence fell between us, questions whirling unarticulated in my head. Then, seemingly already more comfortable with Brady than I would have thought I was, I pulled out Infinity, flipped to a random blank page, and recalled the picture of the urn with a brush of my fingers.

I pulled out a pencil from my backpack, then set about sketching the symbols again.

Brady glanced over once or twice in silence as he drove, then said, "You don't need more light to see?"

Damn it. A witch would need more light. I opened my mouth to lie about Infinity being spelled, then just didn't answer.

Brady chuckled quietly to himself. "What about the urn bothers you? I went back and checked it in the archive."

"So did I."

"Its power signature is dim."

"It is. But the symbols are either so rare that I've never seen them before—"

"An impossible feat?" he interrupted teasingly.

"I am fairly well read," I said primly, drawing another chuckle from him. I smiled in return. I liked this easiness between us. It felt like...a possible friendship. As long as I remembered that everything said between us would be reported back to the pack.

But then, wasn't I technically spying on everyone myself?

"So the runes are rare...or ...?" he asked, prompting me.

"Or they're gibberish," I said. "A spell of pure intent."

"Intent to do what?"

"Exactly."

He hummed thoughtfully, but then didn't speak again as I traced and retraced the urn symbols all the way to Doran's warehouse.

Brady and I slipped through Doran's wards without resistance. The vampire was perched on the glass counter that bisected the huge, black-painted space, waiting for us with his legs dangling and the arms of his dress shirt rolled up. His suit jacket was slung over the counter next to the tablet he'd used to transfer funds to me.

The jewelry box that I'd spotted in the torn photo alongside the urn was still sitting on its pedestal as we passed. I didn't pause to compare the symbols to the photo, though. I could do that later. A direct conversation felt like the better way to deal with Doran. Because even knowing him as little as I did, it was clear that he liked to play power games.

I didn't mind playing games. Especially games I knew I could win. But ever since spotting the obfuscation spell on the shelf in the archive, I was feeling like things might spiral out of my control if I let them go on for too long.

Though what exactly those things might be, I had no idea. That was why I was about to attempt a cordial chat with an illegal antiquities dealer who I already suspected had a lot to hide—especially from the head curator of magical antiquities, and everything official that my job title implied.

As I drew near, I noted a light tracing of dust on the leg of Doran's dark-gray pants, as well as on the back of his hand and left forearm. The vampire had been going through new acquisitions. His dark-eyed gaze settled on Brady and didn't waver. Apparently, the security specialist was a bigger threat than just a witch.

Except given what I'd seen of the power even one of the Byrne witches could wield, I knew that Doran was seriously underestimating them as much as he was underestimating me. Ravine, specifically.

But I was still intensely jealous.

Yes, just at the idea that Doran had boxes of new magical antiquities to play with. Maybe even stacks of rare spellbooks and handwritten memoirs. Not that I'd ever admit my envy out loud. I had an entire archive to oversee, after all.

Doran cocked his head in my direction but kept his dark-eyed gaze on Brady. "I assume this isn't a friendly visit." Again, I couldn't place whatever underlying accent colored his mostly British cadence.

Brady leaned forward on his toes. "Just to get it out of the way…I know."

Doran frowned. The expression was little more than a subtle fold in his brow, but even in the low light, I caught it. "Know what, wolf?"

"I know that you were involved."

Doran laughed. The sound was somehow…chilly. "Any remotely untoward activities in Dublin, and the pack always assumes such. Why should whatever you're here to discuss be any different?"

Brady just glared at the vampire, not pushing his point. But I was fairly certain he wasn't talking about the missing artifact at all. I was also fairly certain that Doran knew that and was trying to deflect.

Brady finally looked at me, ceding the conversation.

"I've discovered that an artifact is missing from the archive…" I said.

"So naturally you assumed I was involved," Doran interrupted, smirking.

I gave him a cool look. Silence stretched between us until he waved his hand, asking me to continue.

"The artifact in question was collected alongside an urn with unusual markings…" I tilted my head. "And a jewelry box exceedingly similar to the one you have on display."

"It's not unusual for artifacts to be constructed in duplicate, refining the process."

"I have a picture. Shall I waste more of our time confirming it is the same box?"

Something glittery flickered across Doran's eyes—his magic, highlighted oddly by the sporadic pools of overhead light.

Brady tensed.

I smiled.

A slow answering smile bloomed across Doran's face. "I have pictures too," he said silkily.

Apparently, he wasn't going to deny anything. But he was going to play games. As I'd anticipated.

"You said jewelry box and urn," he continued, musingly. "But then you referred to the missing item as an artifact."

Brady growled something under his breath that sounded like old Gaelic. Doran and I both ignored him.

"Tell me about the collection?" I asked. "Where is the site located? What other items did you collect? Or was it a seizure? Other than Celeste, who were you working with?"

Doran looked at Brady pointedly, not answering a single question.

Brady snarled, then looked to me. "He's playing games."

"Most Adepts do."

"Werewolves don't."

Doran snorted derisively.

Brady's upper lip curled in response "Whatever you want to say to Dusk, you can say in front of me, vampire."

"We have very different opinions on many different subjects, werewolf."

I sighed. Either I was running around town worrying about a completely benign artifact that someone had misplaced—and the practically inert urn seemed to support that possibility. Or something absolutely terrible was in the process of happening.

Because for me, there was apparently no in-between.

The point was, the posturing was annoying and time consuming. "Please wait outside, Brady."

"What?! No."

"Doran isn't going to attempt to harm me," I said calmly. "I'm a valuable asset. And he isn't stupid." My blood was also poison to him, assuming he could even sink his teeth through my dragon hide. In his argument with Ravine, he'd claimed only two hundred years, though, so it was unlikely he was powerful enough to do so. Yet.

I, however, could skewer him through the heart with an exceedingly powerful bone blade before he even saw me lunge forward.

Not that I wanted to go around stabbing magical beings in the heart. I was a collector of rarities, after all.

Brady glanced between me and Doran, fury practically rolling off him. Then he turned and strode back through the warehouse. "I'm just a step outside."

Doran reached for his tablet, scrolling through what appeared to be hundreds of pictures of books, artifacts, and other antiquities.

I was struggling now to hold my jealousy in check. I did consider cozying up next to him so I had a better view, but dismissed that as overly familiar. I had my own boxes—and an entire major archive, damn it. I shouldn't have been so easily distracted by the mere idea of what the antiquities dealer had access to.

Okay, fine. I wanted all the books. All the artifacts. I wanted them all for me. I had a huge library to fill, after all.

Admitting it didn't make the need go away.

Doran found what he was looking for, pausing to select what appeared to be a half-dozen photos. "I'll email them to you," he said, not looking up. "Your address?"

I opened my mouth to rattle off my street address, then my brain caught up. I cleared my throat. "I don't have one." I almost added a 'yet,' but I had no need to give Doran an explanation.

He smirked. "A phone, at least? I can send it over Wi-Fi."

I pulled my phone out of my backpack—and caught Doran trying to take a look inside, presumably sensing Infinity.

I held the phone in my palm, then looked at him expectantly.

Nothing happened.

With a put-out sigh, Doran reached for the phone. I gave it to him. He angled it to read my face, then punched a series of icons—on both the phone and the tablet—before handing it back to me.

I swiped through the pictures that had appeared on my screen, studying each slowly, then returning to the first shot. I was fairly certain it was a duplicate of the torn picture of the urn from the file. But in the intact photo, a series of artifacts—including the urn and three spellbooks—were set on a shelf secured to what appeared to be a smooth rock wall. What I could see of the area behind the shelf was painted with the same glyphs, the same iconography, I'd copied from the urn.

"The mixture of symbols is disconcerting," I murmured, staring intently. As on the urn, the glyphs on the wall appeared to be based in Egyptian symbology—yet weren't.

"You should have been there," Doran muttered. "The entire space felt…oppressive."

I zoomed in on a specific symbol on the wall. It alone didn't match any of the markings on the urn. I turned my phone toward Doran. "This symbol is more Celtic, not Egyptian."

"I agree."

I flipped back through the pictures again, focusing on an amulet that was set in front of the spellbooks, on the other side of the urn. Constructed out of age-darkened gold and strung on a thick, wide-linked gold chain, the amulet had seventeen gemstones set into its face. Eight larger red stones were spaced evenly around its outer edge, with eight smaller red stones fixed around a single large golden-yellow stone at the very center. All topazes perhaps? The amulet was thick enough that it might have contained a small compartment within it.

I knew it could have been one or all of the spell-books that had been taken from the archive. But it was the amulet that drew all my attention.

Though it appeared to be well lit by multiple flashlights or witch lights, the photo that showed the amulet in detail—the third of the six images Doran had transferred to my phone—was blurred. And especially fuzzy around the gold setting where it wove between the larger of the red gemstones. True red topaz was rare, but given the orange undertone, I was fairly certain I'd identified it correctly.

I was also fairly certain there were symbols carved into the amulet's outer casing and on the links of the chain. But no matter how much I stared or narrowed my eyes, I couldn't bring them into focus.

"Magic doesn't photograph well," I murmured, more to myself than Doran. "Did you get a shot of the back of the amulet?"

"No."

"And the retrieval? August 2011?"

Doran smirked. "You are bright. It's not just your magic."

I ignored the implication that I glowed to his magically sensitive eyes. That wasn't a conversation I wanted to navigate at the moment. Or any time really. "The site?"

"Just outside the city—"

"On Byrne land?"

He frowned. "Why? Are you going to throw me on the witches' mercy, Ms. Godfrey?"

"So they don't know? I obviously can't see the entire room from your pictures, but it appears to be a tomb of some sort. Underground, yes? With what I'm starting to believe are personalized protection runes surrounding the items. A containment spell?"

His eyes glittering with magic again, Doran just stared at me, not answering.

I shook my head. "Why offer me the photos if you aren't willing to discuss them?"

He huffed. "Would that it were so easy. But we don't know each other, do we? And you are…newly arrived."

"And you've done something that you think is going to backfire on you."

"Perhaps."

"But you knew that Celeste Cameron could protect you."

"I knew she could keep these items safe."

Well, that was nasty. I was just in the process of getting the archive in order, after all.

"Because an underground tomb obviously not meant to be breached felt oppressive to you?" I asked. I could be a little nasty myself.

The vampire smirked, no humor in the expression. "Exactly."

"Secretly excavated from coven land? Without permission from the Byrne witches?"

He huffed—then decided to actually offer some clarification. "Conalls. Not Byrnes."

I swiped through the photos on my phone again. "This is clearly witch magic, not shifter."

"Yes. But the site is on Conall land."

"Explain."

Doran's dark gaze flicked away from me, then back again. I sighed, ignoring an odd impulse to pull out my bone blade. Just to give him a glimpse of it. Not to stab him, of course.

"Who else do you want to get involved?" I said. "If you don't trust me?" I flipped to the photo of the amulet, holding the phone toward Doran. "This is the artifact that's missing from the archive, isn't it? What does it mean for you if someone has stolen it with the purpose of using it?" I had no idea what power lay in the amulet, of course. But if the pack had locked it away, they were obviously wary of it.

He sighed, then casually placed his hands on the counter behind him and leaned back. As if I might be fooled by the casual gesture. "I was approached by a witch about eleven years ago—"

"Ayre Byrne?"

He blinked, then frowned. "Why waste my time if you know already?"

"I don't know the sequence of events."

"Ayre had done some research that led her to believe that some valuable artifacts were entombed."

"Under the protection of the Conall pack."

He nodded shallowly. "As you say."

"But Ayre didn't want the amulet, the urn, or the jewelry box for herself? Or was she looking for something specific?"

He shrugged. "Money. Her baby sister had taken over the coven. She'd been passed over."

"Money," I repeated, frowning. That didn't add up. Power was what most Adepts collected. "Why did you approach Celeste Cameron?"

"I couldn't even touch it," he said ruefully. "When I first went in. Any of it. I contacted Celeste, and she agreed to assess the situation. I might have failed to mention that it was Ayre who'd directed me to the site in the first place."

"You still paid her fee."

"I'm not an idiot. The spellbooks covered my expenses." He nodded over my shoulder, grinning at me suddenly. "Though oddly, no one seems to want the jewelry box."

I would have taken it in a second. I narrowed my eyes, knowing an attempt to distract me when I saw one. It was a technique my mother used on me often. And very successfully.

"I wasn't having it traced back to me if it got loose," Doran muttered. His gaze was still over my shoulder, as if recalling the feeling of the so-called tomb—or maybe the amulet he'd confessed to not being able to touch.

"If what got loose?"

"Hell if I know. It just felt wrong. Even to me. Which is some kind of irony." He grimaced ruefully, making fun of his own inherently dark nature. "But what do you think a pack of shifters would be protecting?"

I glanced through the photos again, still getting the impression that the garbled runes were supposed to be some kind of containment spell. But a spell of that magnitude, plus the underground tomb, would be an overreaction to just a few spelled items.

So what would scare the pack so much that they would put it underground, then have a witch—maybe even multiple witches—secure it?

"A magical creature? Or…an entity of some kind?"

Doran didn't answer me, which was fine because I was still guessing. I'd been following the same hunches all day, and they were definitely leading me somewhere.

"Take me to the site. Tell me the story Ayre Byrne uncovered that led her there, and then take me to the site."

"Make me an offer."

I looked him straight in the eye, then stepped forward, slowly closing the space between us.

The vampire held himself motionless, hands still placed behind him on the counter, legs still hanging loose.

"Look at me closely," I murmured.

"I'm looking."

"I'm an archivist. It's my duty to keep the city, the country, safe from whatever you might have helped Ayre Byrne release into the world."

Anger flitted across Doran's pale, chiseled face. "I was the one who brought Celeste Cameron in. I knew what I'd uncovered, and I entrusted her with the responsibility for it."

"But now I'm holding you responsible. It's not the retribution of the witches or the pack that you should be fearing in this moment—"

"Fearing," the vampire sneered. "I simply enjoy my life in Dublin. I would prefer to keep it unencumbered by whatever game…or test, perhaps…you're currently embroiled in."

"A test?" Well, that sounded like the antiquities dealer knew more than he was willing to let on. More about me and the first week of my new job, specifically.

"The amulet has gone missing on your watch."

"It could have been missing for years."

He blinked, then spoke thoughtfully. "Since Celeste Cameron died…"

He knew something more, or he was piecing something together. "You said Ayre Byrne wasn't interested in the artifacts she'd uncovered. That she just wanted money. A finder's fee."

"Correct."

"And you've continued to do business with Ayre…all these years?"

He didn't answer.

"Has that interaction increased or decreased since Celeste Cameron's death?"

The vampire's expression was stone cold. Unreadable.

I was on the right track. Ayre Byrne had been doing business with the antiquities dealer. For years. I had no proof that she'd stolen anything directly from the archive—not yet. But it was distinctly possible that she'd been redirecting items to the antiquities dealer that should have been added to those shelves.

I'd been about to threaten Doran's existence, but now I changed tack—to something I now knew would rattle him even more.

I stepped back, making a show of casting my gaze across the warehouse. "How many other items are missing from the shelves of the archive, Doran?"

"I don't question the sellers who seek me out," he said stiffly. "Just as I didn't question you."

I tapped my chin thoughtfully. "I've decided to authorize a raid of your holdings. That seems prudent, given what I know about the missing amulet that passed through your hands. I assume you have more than just this one warehouse? We'll demand access to any property you currently hold under your name or…any associates' names."

A glittering red sheen washed over the vampire's eyes, but was gone a moment after I caught it. His magic, much more fully manifested. Otherwise, he looked completely nonplussed.

"Of course," I continued, "if we don't uncover any stolen goods, then I'll feel a little…silly. But no one is going to hold that caution against me, given that I'm stepping into a position that's been vacant for over six years. Neither the witches nor the pack will think that a raid is a bad idea, will they?"

Doran could operate in Dublin only if he played within the rules the coven and the pack had set. He, and the function he performed, were actually a necessary part of the Adept world, in my opinion. But based on the little I'd gleaned from his interaction with Brady, he wasn't even remotely well liked.

He unclenched his jaw, coolly livid. "And if I tell you the tale of the artifacts as I know it, and take you to the site? This raid would be deemed...premature?"

"Well..." I tilted my head slightly. "I suppose it would be a good idea for you to do an inventory yourself. I'd be more than happy to look at any items you think might have...walked off the shelves of the archive. And I would trust you to return what you think might have made its way to you...accidentally." I hit the word 'trust' with extra emphasis. Then to sweeten the deal, I added, "I will also consider bringing you more of the treasures I inherited."

"Consider?"

"I could always go to a dealer in London."

"And be ripped off."

I smiled. "Do you think anyone rips me off, Doran?"

"Well..." He cleared his throat, looking at me for a long moment. "Not more than once."

I laughed.

He sniffed, not amused. I had a feeling that I might have just made an enemy out of a potential ally. But I wasn't certain how to fix it and get the information I needed from him at the same time.

"The relics were confiscated by the Conall pack when they helped depose a coven leader a couple of hundred years ago."

I blinked. Then I quickly pulled Infinity and my fountain pen out of my pack. Doran looked momentarily thrown as I set my personal archive on the counter next to him, opening it, and scrawling *Personal Notes: the Conall pack and the deposing of a coven leader, circa 1821* across the top edge of a blank page.

The words sank into the paper, ink and magic absorbed eagerly by Infinity.

"Well, now..." Doran breathed. "Isn't that magnificent."

I glanced up at him. "You were saying?"

He chuckled low and deep, slipping off the counter to lean next to me. With his gaze fixed to Infinity.

I had a feeling I had just taken a serious step toward the 'trust' part that every solid business relationship demanded.

The antiquities dealer took up his tale, sounding more and more delighted with every word of his that I transcribed as it was absorbed into Infinity.

"The deposing of the former coven leader left a space for the Byrne witches to fill. According to the info Ayre uncovered, in the process of fighting her ejection from the coven, the former leader used the artifacts in question to fuel her own power, combining whatever was previously contained in the urn with the power housed in your missing amulet."

"And what was in the urn?"

Doran shrugged belligerently. "You're the expert."

"The markings are either a crude attempt at copying Egyptian runes, or an exceedingly personal alphabet constructed by a subset of Adepts in order to anchor their magic."

Doran's gaze fixed to me for a moment. He wasn't exactly smiling, but the tips of his teeth were revealed. Not a hint of fang. "Black magic."

"Not necessarily. Though I suppose that depends on what was in the urn."

"If it was originally Egyptian in origin..."

I took the bait. "It's not big enough for a brain...or other viscera..."

Doran tilted his head encouragingly.

I let my gaze fall to Infinity, watching my inked words slowly fade from the page. I hadn't dealt with many dark artifacts personally. There just weren't that many lying around to be uncovered by archivists—mostly because they had a habit of turning on their creators or wielders, killing those Adepts, then burning themselves out.

"A preserved heart might have fit," I said quietly. I was thinking through the ramifications of someone—centuries ago—stealing a heart from a magical being...and keeping it.

I was suddenly exceedingly aware of the bone knife strapped to my thigh. The guardian who crafted it had done so from the femur of a powerful entity, using the bone's own magic to vanquish that entity. If it had been the heart of a powerful Adept contained in the urn, combined with whatever unknown power lay in the amulet ...?

"How many witches died?" I asked in a whisper. "And pack members? In order to depose the coven leader who'd armed herself with these artifacts?"

"I only have rumors and the bits of info that Ayre Byrne supplied." Doran paused, then added, "I mentioned what I knew to Celeste Cameron. I assumed she put together a report."

"The file is missing," I said. "It was just a random notation in one of her journals that clued me into you being involved. That, plus the jewelry box."

The vampire hummed thoughtfully, then said, "I might have asked around."

I laughed quietly. "And?"

"The witches are rather close-mouthed about it. Even those on the...outskirts."

"Witch business," I said, suddenly terribly intrigued about what would place a witch on the outskirts of her own coven. That would need to be a tale for another day, I expected.

Doran nodded. "Exactly. The Conalls are not at all forthcoming either."

"What picture do the bits of information you've pieced from various sources tell you?"

"That half the coven fell. Most dead. Their power used to fuel the black witch."

That was insane. And so, so much power that it should have been impossible for one witch to wield it. Though, even having no idea what magic was contained in the amulet, it was possible it was able to focus or contain the power the deposed coven leader had harvested from those deaths.

"How did they defeat her?"

"Three Byrne witches walked across a field of corpses, backed by two Conalls."

"Five in total? And only two werewolves?"

Doran grinned, leaning forward as if he had a great secret. A secret he'd be pleased to see recorded in Infinity. "Two of their twins."

Twins. Like Gitta and Kellan. Like Neve and Lile. There was some kind of power there. Oh, yes. The Conalls might turn into werewolves, but they most definitely weren't typical shapeshifters.

Doran smirked knowingly as he watched me put it all together, continuing to jot down notes in my personal archive.

"And the three Byrne witches? Were they siblings as well?"

Doran laughed. "You are quick, Dusk."

"The power of three," I murmured. "You barely have to be well read to see how often magically bound siblings appear in all…magical texts." I'd been about to say 'ancient magical texts,' except I wasn't certain that was the truth. The power of three, and the breeding of twins for that matter, was obviously alive and well in the Byrne coven and the Conall pack.

"They walked out unscathed," I said, filling in the blanks for myself.

"Alive, at least."

"With the Conalls in possession of the artifacts."

"Until Celeste Cameron heard of their existence. As an outsider, she'd already been studying the history of the pack and the coven, of course. When I came to her with the location of the site, I'd been surprised that she hadn't even questioned it. Now I understand."

"Knowledge is power."

Doran nodded. "As we both know."

"Why not leave the items under the care of the pack? Why move them into the archive? And so clandestinely that Celeste felt the need to hire you?"

"Instead of the employee who brought the idea to me in the first place? I think you probably know the answer to that already."

"Ayre Byrne."

"Indeed."

Celeste Cameron hadn't trusted Ayre Byrne. Ayre Byrne who was somehow also involved in the incident with the soul sucker…the Egyptian soul sucker…

Ah. Another piece of the puzzle clicked into place.

All this life-transition and new-job stuff was making me slow.

"Ayre Byrne oversaw the Celtic collection at the archive."

"Before you fired her rather resoundingly." Doran was grinning again, but still with no humor or joy in the expression. In fact, he looked like a large raptor of some kind…

The vampire reminded me of the raptor carved into the walnut front door of my estate.

Now that was an odd thought.

"Yes," I said, picking up the thread of the conversation again. "So Ayre's interest in artifacts once held by an Irish coven makes sense. Nothing potentially nefarious about how she came by that information in the first place."

"I'm not a witch," Doran said. "My understanding of what might have been considered nefarious by Celeste Cameron is based on observation and conversation."

I nodded, agreeing with him, but then continued on to my main point. Everything I was digging into was all somehow connected to one witch, going back at least eleven years. "But Ayre Byrne was definitely not an expert in Egyptian mythology."

That wiped the strangely predatory grin from the dark-haired vampire's face.

He didn't respond, so I continued. "And yet it was Ayre who was in possession of the sarcophagus containing the soul sucker, which ended up killing four coven witches, including Celeste Cameron."

I waited for Doran to confirm or deny my statement. But he just watched me with those glittering eyes.

"When you and Brady first spoke tonight, he said 'I know what you did.' He meant that you were involved in those deaths. In the attack that left him bedridden for months."

Doran tensed. It was subtle, just a few muscles in his jaw and shoulders tightening, then a slight shift of energy. But I felt certain he had almost made a move to attack me. Or at least was thinking about it.

"What do you want?" he asked, that accent I hadn't been able to place now thickly laced through his words. The vampire had dropped some of his imposed, civilized demeanor.

If I kept pushing, would I see the so-called monster lurking under his skin?

If I pushed him to attack me, would he then see me—and everything I wasn't keeping particularly well hidden despite Jiaotu's glamour?

Any trust we were building would be destroyed if either of those options played out.

"Hong Kong," I said, speaking before I'd even realized that I'd figured out his underlying accent, and that I was abruptly changing subjects.

The tense energy surrounding the dark-haired vampire eased slightly. He smoothed his hand across the glass counter, then plucked up the tablet to scroll through the photos he still had open. "You want something to do with Hong Kong?"

I smirked at him. "No. You come from Hong Kong, though you've almost subsumed the accent. I want to know how Ayre Byrne got her hands on a soul sucker disguised as an Egyptian pharaoh when she was an expert in Celtic artifacts."

"And I ask again, what are you going to do with any knowledge confirmed by me today?"

I sighed. "Keep cleaning up messes before they become deadly. I hope. Why? Does the head curator usually stand as judge and jury?"

Doran stared at me for a long while. Then he spoke. "Ayre Byrne acquired the Egyptian artifact from me. I can only assume she took it to the archive when she...couldn't do what she wanted with it."

"And what did she want with it in the first place?" I asked, already knowing the answer.

"For a smart girl, you ask a lot of redundant questions."

Ayre Byrne was interested in acquiring power. Eleven years before, she had convinced Doran that she simply wanted money. But something had obviously shifted.

Had she been trying to pull power from the soul sucker, not knowing what it was? And now, with her life and position set askew by my arrival, was she trying to do the same with the missing amulet? As a deposed coven leader had once done?

"Show me the site," I said. "I need to see everything not captured in the pictures. I need to touch any protections that remain."

Doran shook his head, just once. "I don't need to get involved any further than I am. The artifacts were in the possession and protection of the archive. I fulfilled the contract I inked with Celeste to retrieve them with her. Anything beyond that isn't my responsibility."

"Do you want to have a good relationship with me?"

"Do you want to have a good relationship with me?" he echoed mockingly.

"As previously mentioned, I can go elsewhere," I said, my tone deadly quiet. "But when you get in trouble? When you discover you've picked up something you'd rather not have so-called responsibility for, as with the amulet eleven years ago? Who's going to step in…without judgement…to save your ass?"

"My ass never needs saving."

"No? What if I take everything we've talked about to the Conalls or the Byrnes? Will you still be in business tomorrow? Even if I keep up my part of the bargain and decide that a raid isn't necessary?"

Doran bared his teeth in a hiss that quickly became a laugh. "Nasty, nasty, Dusk. Oh, I do like you."

"Then take me to the site."

"Get rid of your protection crew. I'll text you an address to meet me at in a couple of hours. I took the liberty of noting your number when I transferred the photos."

"Skulking through pack land under the cover of deep darkness."

"Would you have it any other way?"

Capping my pen and tucking Infinity against my chest, I turned away without responding. But damn it if I wasn't smiling. Again.

Since when had I become so attracted to untoward activities, as the vampire called them?

Since I'd gotten very, very bored training and looking after Sisu while effectively confined to my mother's estate?

I composed my face, blanking my expression before I left the warehouse. I didn't need Brady seeing me grinning like an idiot. He already saw too much of what I really was.

CHAPTER SIX

BRADY AND I SPENT THE FIRST HALF OF THE DRIVE home in silence, him navigating the brightly lit streets of Dublin while I rifled through everything I knew about Celeste Cameron in my head. Everything I'd gleaned from her notebooks, from the state of her office, and from what she'd collected.

That included the scattered array of books I'd grouped loosely together by subject matter, so that I could go through them thoroughly when I had a moment. Granted, those books might have just been randomly collected over many years. But if I added everything that Doran had told me about the history of the missing amulet into the mix…

Celeste Cameron had been researching death magic.

But why not do so openly? Why spread the books around when the rest of her office had been fairly orderly? Celeste's journal entries weren't personal, but they were detailed. Quietly verbose in places. I'd found references to every item in her office as I'd inventoried it. And I had assumed at the time that every item she'd personally collected had been shelved in the archive. But the journals contained no mention of the amulet or urn.

I would have to double check to be certain, of course.

"Could we stop by the archive?" I asked Brady, breaking the silence.

He nodded as he took a quick left. "You've got a lead?"

"An inkling," I murmured, suddenly itching to get my hands on the books I'd only finished shelving earlier that day.

It didn't take long to pick up the books I wanted from my office. I showed Brady the pictures I'd gotten from Doran, and he sent copies to his own phone. We discussed the amulet as being the piece that had likely gone missing from the archive, but I didn't mention the plan to meet the vampire later as the werewolf drove me back to the estate.

When we got there, a dragon was waiting at the gate.

The overhead light picked up lighter golden strands within his dark-blond hair, yet somehow also washed out his tanned skin. Arms crossed and glowering deeply, he laid dark-brown eyes on Brady and me, then offered us a stiff smile. He was wearing a three-quarter-length charcoal wool coat that I'd never seen before, over black jeans and laced boots similar to my own. But black, not brown. A large hard-shell suitcase was set off to the side of the gate.

Zeke.

He held his magic tucked away, as most dragons did when out among other Adepts and nonmagicals. Brady would easily take him for a witch. Another archivist, even.

"I was in London," Zeke said without preamble, answering a question I'd barely begun to formulate. "When I got your message. I was able to borrow some books that might help with your..." He glanced at Brady. "Your question about runes."

I blinked, partly out of surprise to hear that Zeke had been in London. And even more out of surprise that the Dunkirk witches would have allowed any sort of loan to take place. They oversaw the magical archives housed at the British Museum.

I also wasn't certain how Zeke could have gotten to Dublin so quickly, since I'd only sent his letter a few hours ago. A portal perhaps? At least for part of the journey?

"We have less than twenty-four hours to return the loaned items," he added stiffly, finally unfolding his arms and stepping forward to offer his hand to Brady.

The werewolf at my side glanced at me.

"This is Zeke. My..." I hesitated, realizing I hadn't worked out how I was going to present any of my relatives if they showed up unexpectedly. I had assumed I would have had more notice, since the estate library wasn't powerful enough for anyone to cross through yet. But archivists moved where they willed, or where magic willed them, so I really should have been more prepared.

"Fiance," my adoptive great-great-uncle supplied, smiling at me charmingly. "Zeke."

Brady huffed quietly, also surprised.

Yeah, I wasn't going to let that stand. "Generally, a proposal has to be accepted before such titles are bandied about."

Zeke's grin widened, his hand still held out to the werewolf. "Well, it's a work in progress."

Brady clasped his hand. "Owen Brady. I oversee security at the archive. Dusk and I were just conducting some…fact finding."

"Ah," Zeke said, releasing Brady's hand. "That explains it. Did you find what you were looking for?"

I shook my head. "More clues and a picture of an amulet that we think is missing."

"Well, I'll help in any way I can." Zeke glanced at Brady, clearly dismissing him.

Brady stiffened, then deliberately looked at me. "You're okay, then?"

"Why wouldn't she be?" Zeke's tone went suddenly cold. Hard.

Brady ignored him, still looking at me intently. I realized it wasn't the missing amulet that had him concerned. Apparently, a man showing up and claiming to be my fiance was worrisome.

"Zeke is a family friend," I said quietly. "He isn't here to hurt me."

"What?" Zeke snarled, utterly affronted.

I held my hand up to him. He huffed, then deliberately stepped back to the gate, ceding the conversation and the space to me in a show of cooperation.

And now he was going to be pissy for the rest of the evening. Hopefully, the pictures I'd gotten from Doran would distract him. And I, of course, was itching to get my hands on whatever books Zeke had brought, as well as to share those I'd just picked up from my office.

"I didn't mean to cause…stress," Brady said quietly. Having taken Zeke for a witch, the werewolf had no idea his words could be overheard.

"You didn't," I said just as quietly. "I actually asked Zeke for help. He must have decided it was easier to drop in than to write me back."

"Drop in," Brady echoed. "From London."

"I'll text you if I put together any…revelations." I knew that Brady would be a valuable asset in the field, but I also needed Doran to cooperate. I felt more than simply an itch drawing me into the investigation now. More a dim sense of…impending doom?

Perhaps it was just the conversation with Doran that had made me more anxious. Or that, combined with the idea that I was already failing spectacularly after only my first week as head curator. But either way, I could feel a looming shadow, a pending darkness, just at the edge of my mind.

I knew it was only my imagination. My possibly pathological need to have everything in order and in its proper place. In the end, everything that was bothering me so intensely might just turn out to be a blank spot on a shelf that was meant to be filled.

But what if it wasn't my imagination?

What if it was an as-yet untested aspect of my magic? Another layer of my magical sensitivity being triggered? I'd never taken on the responsibility for a magical archive. So maybe my slowly intensifying reaction to the missing artifact was part of that new responsibility.

Maybe, just maybe, something potentially nefarious was twigging my senses.

"Text me either way," Brady said, eyes narrowed on me as if he might have been waiting for me to elaborate.

"All right."

He nodded, glanced over at Zeke, then sauntered back up the block where he'd parked his truck.

I stepped up to the gate.

Zeke leaned in and brushed a kiss against my cheek. "I've missed you."

"We've gone far longer without seeing each other," I said stiffly, still pissed about him claiming to be my fiance. Though I understood why he would have opted for an easy explanation for his presence. Announcing that he was my adoptive great-great-uncle would have raised way too many questions—what with him looking only a few years older than me.

I unlatched the gate. "Why are you waiting out here?"

Zeke stiffened, and his tone cooled again. "I assumed there was no one home, and that you would prefer to keep your wards intact."

I sighed. Sisu would have felt Zeke knock. And, obviously, had known it was him and decided to not let him onto the property. "Five-year-olds are easily distracted," I said lamely.

Zeke didn't respond, simply grabbing his suitcase and following me through the gate.

We stepped through the boundary wards, and the full estate stretched out before us. Hectares of misty rolling grasses, a treed park, various paths, and one gigantic house ablaze with lights.

"Well..." Zeke drawled. "You did call it a palace."

Impulsively, I slung my arm through his, grinning. "Wait until you see the size of the library!"

He laughed quietly, tugging me closer, then striding up the front walk by my side.

Sisu was standing in the open, well-lit doorway of the house, hands fisted on his hips, legs braced, and glowering at Zeke. "You can't have my room," he declared. "And there aren't any other mattresses yet."

Zeke chuckled edgily, then opened his mouth with a ready retort.

I threw him a look.

He shut his mouth, settled his shoulders, and said, "Your boundaries have been noted."

Well, that was a surprise. Maybe he'd read a self-help book since the last time I'd seen him?

Zeke glanced at me, grimacing. "You said I wasn't...communicating to your liking."

Sisu lunged for Zeke's suitcase, and Zeke yielded it to him without protest. Sisu grunted as the weight transferred to him. "Books?"

"Yes." Zeke grinned widely. "Did you expect I'd bring Dusk anything less?"

Sisu just sniffed. Lugging the suitcase with him, he headed off toward the library.

Zeke cast his gaze around the massive great room and up to the cathedral ceiling, his expression neutral as he took off his coat.

Neve and Lile darted out from the living room as Sisu passed, talking over each other in not-so-hushed whispers.

"Did you ask?"

"Sisu, did you ask her?"

They each took a corner of the suitcase.

"Sisu?"

"Did you ask permission?"

"Not yet," my brother grunted.

Zeke was watching the twins and Sisu with narrowed eyes, as if trying to assess something. But then, catching me watching him, his expression softened. "I assume you have a mattress big enough for two?" he asked quietly.

"Whatever is going on between you and Sisu," I said, my tone unyielding, "fix it."

Zeke's expression hardened. "He's five, Dusk. He's just in a mood. He doesn't want to share you."

I stepped slightly closer so I could lower my voice. "He needs strong, loyal family members in his life. Guidance and training, yes. But mostly...love." I deliberately met his dark-brown eyes. "He is five. So if you can't act like his brother, then at least act like his uncle."

Zeke's nostrils flared indignantly. Then his gaze flicked over my shoulder.

I turned, spotting Kellan leaning in the doorway to the living room. Stepping past him, Bethany nodded at me, though her gaze was mostly on Zeke. It wasn't a nice look. Then she strode after the still-chattering trio.

I hadn't felt either werewolf before laying eyes on them. Actually, the same went for Neve and Lile. Was the house masking everyone's movements? If so, why? Because of Zeke's presence?

"Everything okay, Dusk?" Kellan asked casually.

"What right do you have to ask?" Zeke snapped before I could answer.

I looked at him. Hard. Unflinching.

Zeke smoothed his expression, then nodded. "Excuse me. It is your home."

"It is."

He glanced at Kellan once more, then turned and stepped through into the cloakroom to hang up his jacket.

I slowly took off my backpack and my own coat, giving Zeke some space before following. More so than the rest of our family, or even with archivists in general, Zeke was uncomfortable with change. A new house, new people, and...a new me? That was a lot to confront in a matter of minutes. Plus, assuming he'd flown and taken transit at least part of the way to get to Dublin, he'd still be dealing with the feeling of having been locked in a steel tube with countless nonmagicals.

"Everything okay?" Kellan asked again, far more gently this time.

"Yes," I said. "Apparently, no one answered Zeke's request to enter, so he's been waiting a bit."

Kellan smirked. "Well, it wasn't my place, after hours and all. And Sisu just...shrugged."

I snorted. I wasn't surprised that the property wards pinged for Kellan. That magic was adaptive, and he needed to know when his subcontractors wanted entry.

"I'm heading out now."

"Thank you for staying."

He shrugged, unfolding his arms. "I enjoy getting time with the kids. All three of them."

I smiled and nodded, oddly pleased that he'd included Sisu with his nieces.

Kellan crossed through the great room toward the under-construction kitchen, likely to make certain everything was shut off or out of reach. Not that anything was ever really out of reach for Sisu. Or the twins, I suspected.

"If you need any help, Dusk..." Kellan paused at the plastic-swathed doorway, waving his hand to encompass the room. "Other than with the house, I mean. The pack will back you."

"With the coven, you mean."

He shrugged. "Or if some pressure needs to be applied to a certain vampire."

I grinned. "Doran was very helpful."

"Doran is never helpful, not without reason."

I gestured at the house, then at myself, my grin widening.

Kellan laughed, having caught my inference—that I and my so-called inheritance were more than enough of an incentive for the antiquities dealer to at least feign being friendly.

The warm sound of the werewolf's laughter settled over me, and suddenly the space between us didn't seem so vast, even though he was almost at the other end of the great room. I glanced around at the house, thinking there might be magic at play that was so subtle I wasn't quite picking up on it.

"Thank you," I said, very aware of Zeke listening to every word we exchanged from the cloakroom.

Though why that would bother me, I had no idea.

"Goodnight." Kellan raised a hand in a brief wave, then ducked through the layers of plastic sheeting and into the new kitchen.

"Goodnight," I echoed. Then I stepped into the cloakroom to deal with Zeke.

My adoptive great-great-uncle was leaning against the front-facing wall, eyes closed. Like he was meditating?

I wasn't surprised. "Was the trip bad?" I asked quietly, hanging up my coat and retrieving Infinity, my phone, and the books I'd grabbed from my office from my backpack.

"No," Zeke said. "It was...fine. A commuter flight from London. I apologize for intruding without writing first. It just seemed like...you might need me."

"You're not an intrusion," I said stiffly. "You're family."

He huffed, then opened his eyes. "Actually, if I'm being truthful...London was just a stopover. I was already booked on a flight to Dublin. The Dunkirk witches have a door from the museum to Heathrow."

"A door...brilliant." Depending on the time of day and where the door opened within the airport, that would easily shave forty-five minutes off the trip.

He flashed me a grin. "Indeed. I got your letter, grabbed a few extra books, and made it to the gate with five minutes to spare."

"So…you'd already planned this visit."

He nodded, just once. "I had."

"Without warning me."

"Yes."

"Because you thought I'd say no."

"I thought you'd…defer."

I would have. Even without the current stress of tracking down the amulet, life was still unsettled. And when dealing with Zeke, I…well…I preferred to not be put in a situation that placed me in a defensive position. "I would have preferred to have the house ready for guests, yes."

He winced slightly. "I…didn't like the idea of you and Sisu all alone." Then his tone became pointed. "But apparently you have plenty of company."

I didn't answer. As was always the way with Zeke, I could save him from a fight, or I could just let him barrel right into one. I chose to let him barrel, as I usually did.

"May I ask who all the shapeshifters are?" he asked coolly.

"The local pack. Kellan is overseeing the construction crew and doing some finishing carpentry. As I mentioned in my first two letters."

"You mentioned getting some work done," he said wryly.

I ignored his tone. "Bethany is tutoring Sisu, along with Neve and Lile. I'm lucky she agreed to stay late so I could check out a lead, and finally figure out it was an amulet that was missing from the archive."

"Chatting with a vampire."

I just looked at him steadily, not liking the edge creeping into his tone. Again.

He sighed, frustrated. "I'm allowed to be protective of you. We are family." He hit the word 'family' with a bit of a snarl.

"Yes," I said. Because no matter Zeke's attitude, it was true. "I'm sorry if Sisu played games with the property wards. They will open for you now." I gave that little push of intention to the magic that edged the property, feeling the wards absorb and acknowledge it.

Zeke pushed off the wall, closing the space between us but stopping just short of touching me. "And will you instruct the house wards to mask my presence, as they apparently do for the others?" The question was low, and still edged in something I wasn't quite understanding. More possessiveness, perhaps.

"The house wards aren't yet under my control," I said, not quite certain what I was being accused of. Though, I assumed he also hadn't picked up the tenor of the shapeshifters' magic until he'd seen them.

Zeke frowned, tilting his head thoughtfully. Then he reached out and placed his fingertips against the nearest wall, doing so carefully. As if he was expecting…retaliation? "Interesting. Perhaps it plays favorites."

"The house?" I asked doubtfully.

Zeke simply smirked at me, not answering. His typical superiority was firmly back in place. "You said something about showing me the library?"

Sisu, Neve, and Lile had Zeke's suitcase open in the middle of the library, between the chairs and fireplace. The fire was down to embers. The trio was in the process of sorting through the books they'd removed from the case—while Bethany attempted to refold the few items of clothing they'd presumably tossed to one side early on.

She gave me a frustrated but apologetic grimace as I entered with Zeke on my heels.

"Magnificent," Zeke murmured under his breath, already trailing his fingers along the empty dark-wood shelves as he crossed farther into the vast room.

Neve popped up and hightailed it over to me. "Sisu has something to ask you, Dusk."

"Please say yes," Lile added, jumping to her feet.

I glanced at Sisu, but he was in the process of making neat piles of the books Zeke had brought, sorting them in some fashion that wasn't immediately apparent.

Bethany glanced over at Zeke, who was examining my desk, then said to Sisu quietly, "We can do it next weekend. With your uncle visiting now."

Well, that was going to get confusing. Sisu calling Zeke his uncle—as he should—versus Zeke claiming to be my fiance to Brady.

Damn it.

Honestly, some notice would have been lovely. But then, archivists rarely called ahead. Nor did dragons for that matter. I was probably going to have to get used to it.

"Adoptive uncle," I said awkwardly.

Neve took my hand and tugged me closer to Sisu and the suitcase. "Ask, Sisu."

Sisu glanced up from his piles of books. "I can be good," he said preemptively. "Act appropriately."

"Like making Zeke wait at the gate?"

Zeke was running his hand over the corner of the desk where a second ring of runes had been set. A magical drop point, used by Jiaotu when he'd sent me the treasure chest as part of my inheritance. He pulled his archive out of the back pocket of his jeans—a pocket the archive didn't actually fit in—along with a fountain pen, then jotted down the sequence of runes.

Sisu mumbled something under his breath.

I caught it, but waited for him to elaborate.

My brother stood, stepping around the piles of books he'd made, and peered up at me. "He was mean to you."

"When?"

Sisu shrugged. "I heard you arguing."

"The day we came to Dublin?"

"Before."

Ah. I knew the argument he was talking about—though truthfully, it hadn't been much of a fight. Mostly, I'd kicked Zeke out of my bed and then hadn't talked to him for six months. Which tied back to the false claim of being my fiance. Maybe one day, we would decide to formalize our—currently not happening—sexual relationship. But not now. Probably not anytime in the near future.

Bethany cleared her throat. "Perhaps we should leave."

"No!" Neve cried mournfully. "Please, Dusk!"

I grinned. I couldn't help it. Balancing my phone and my small stack of books on top of Infinity in one hand, I touched Sisu on his head lightly. "I can handle Zeke. Your relationship with him is independent from mine."

Sisu's glower only deepened. Apparently, that was the wrong thing to say.

I glanced over at Zeke, who had just unpinned a note from the noticeboard. Likely the sketch of the urn I'd sent him when he was already on his way to Dublin.

He was obviously completely disinterested in participating in the conversation.

I sank down to my knees, setting Infinity and the books to the side so I could meet Sisu's gaze as I offered him my hands.

He slipped his hands into mine.

"Family is very important."

"I know," he said begrudgingly, shifting his shoulders uncomfortably.

He would talk about it when he was ready. Which most likely meant when we were alone.

"Ask me what you want to ask me."

Lile jostled him with a shoulder.

"We…Lile and Neve invited me to a sleepover," he said, hesitating slightly with the last word.

"At Gitta's," Bethany supplied. "With both of us, and possibly Len there as well. If their regular date night went well." She winked at me.

Len Murphy was Lile and Neve's father. He was also the head electrician for Conall Construction and was currently rewiring the estate. As far as I'd figured out, he and Gitta had been separated but were now dating again. Though I wasn't certain if they'd ever been officially married.

"And we get to sleep in sleeping bags," Lile added in a rush. "In the rec room."

"And waffles for breakfast," Neve said, grinning madly. "With whipped cream and strawberries!"

Sisu squeezed my hands, desperately trying to contain his excitement. He'd never really had friends his own age.

And honestly, since I was about to sneak off with a vampire, it sounded like a great idea. Leaving Sisu with Zeke right now might just cause more problems between them. "You'll be polite—"

"Yes!" Neve crowed triumphantly.

Lile squealed, bouncing and clapping her hands together.

"No sword," I said, pinning my gaze to Sisu's. "No egg." My brother was still carrying the golden egg his demigod father had given him everywhere. I'd caught him sleeping with it under his pillow—and removed it—numerous times now. I still had no idea what it contained, or if it would hatch. But if it did hatch, it would be far better for that to happen at the manor.

Sisu nodded, plastering an attentive expression on his face to show he was listening. "I know. But I can bring a book, right? For a bedtime story?"

"Yes. One of your books."

Neve pressed against my shoulder, grinning madly. "We already packed!"

Bethany snorted, then mouthed *I'm sorry* to me.

I just grinned back. How could I not say yes? The glee of the trio was contagious. "And how about this. If all three of you would like to come back tomorrow, say around 10:00 A.M.? We can take the imp eggs to the gnome together."

A wide grin swamped Sisu's face. "To the gnome?"

"The gnome!" Neve crowed.

"Yes," I said as Lile danced around us. "We'll ask the gnome about caring for the eggs."

"Hatching them?" Sisu asked in a whisper full of anticipation.

"That will be the gnome's choice," I cautioned. Then I belatedly turned to Bethany. "Sorry, I should have asked if that worked for you?"

She shrugged. "You know they'll be up at dawn. Waffles will be consumed by seven. Technically, I'm off weekends, but..." She grinned teasingly at the trio who seemed to be hanging on her every word. "I've never met a gnome."

Another round of cheers exploded from three sets of young lungs.

"Perfect, then," I said, grinning widely myself. "Thank you."

Sisu flung his arms around my shoulders in the world's briefest hug. Then he raced out of the library with Neve and Lile on his heels.

I stood, staring after them but speaking to Bethany, slightly doubtful. "Have fun?"

She snorted. "I'm off duty the moment I get them home. Though my suite is just off the basement rec room. But Gitta and Len can handle getting them to bed."

"Expect many, many bedtime stories."

She smiled. "I think that might be Gitta's favorite part of the day."

"Mine too."

She raised a knowing eyebrow.

"Okay," I admitted. "Second only to tracking down potentially dangerous artifacts."

She snorted, then followed the squeals and shouts out into the great room. "Goodnight."

Zeke joined me as I heard the front door open, then shut, a slight smile softening his expression as he bent over to place a couple of logs on the fire. Then he grabbed a book from one of Sisu's piles. "Shall we get started?"

I handed him my phone, tapping the screen to show him the pictures Doran had given me.

"Well," he drawled, carefully swiping through the images. "That is a mixture of iconography." He paused on the blurry close-up of the amulet, squinting at it a little grimly. "And that is what I expected from your note."

"Egyptian origin, yes?" I said. "But somehow...converted by a Celtic witch?"

"Subverted, perhaps. Based on her...limited knowledge of what she was dealing with."

"Witch magic is all about intention," I said huffily, not certain why I was defending a witch I didn't even know.

Zeke just smirked at me. "Exactly."

"And sometimes magic moves as it wills," I added.

"I'm in agreement, Dusk. But neither truth makes unraveling your mystery any easier."

"Which hopefully means that whoever now holds the amulet is having the same trouble."

"Or it might simply be a prize to them. Something to be collected and gloated over."

I hadn't thought of that. That was actually the best-case scenario—other than it never being stolen in the first place, of course.

"You did say your staff did some sort of...prank on your first day?"

I had written Zeke about the incident with the imp, but hadn't mentioned the spelled book that had taken Rook. That hadn't felt like my secret to tell, not even to him.

Zeke pressed the book he'd picked up into my hand, settling down by the fire with my phone to study the photos and make notes in his archive.

I looked at the spine of the book he'd given me. *The Rituals of Death*.

"You think something was stored in the urn," I said. The same guess Doran had made. "Viscera?"

Zeke nodded, turning the screen of the phone toward me. He was studying the best photo of the urn. "Pottery, not limestone. And obviously the lid is plain, but inscriptions weren't typically used in the Old Kingdom period..."

He was comparing the urn to a canopic jar, used by the ancient Egyptians during the mummification process. Used to store specific organs removed from a to-be-mummified corpse. Of the two of us, Zeke was the expert in Egyptian history—and all that was now referred to as Egyptian mythology, but was actually simply tales of magical creatures and Adepts of power.

"If I can work out a basic alphabet..." Zeke was murmuring as he compared the half-finished sketch I'd tried to send to him with the photo. "I might be able to figure out what was stored in the urn."

"You're not the only one with an idea of what we might be dealing with." I passed Zeke the top book from the small stack I'd retrieved from my office at the archive.

He glanced at the spine. "*The Mythology of Death and Its Many Goddesses*? That's far-fetched."

"You're the one who thinks the urn was being used like a canopic jar." I snatched the book back from him, settling into my own chair with Infinity to read it.

Zeke sighed. "A broken urn paired with strange runes? It's a logical leap that it might have held remains of some sort."

"Well, your life would be rather meaningless if you weren't better than me at practically everything." I wasn't completely certain why I had to be so pissy about him coming to the same conclusion as I had, except it had taken me a ton of digging and multiple conversations to get to it.

Zeke looked up at me sharply. "I do have a few years on you, Dusk."

I just shook my head at him, opening Infinity on my lap so my personal archive could absorb the books—the ones I'd picked up from my office and the ones Zeke had brought—while I read them.

The screen of my phone flashed, drawing a disgruntled grunt from Zeke. The mobile was resting on the arm of Zeke's chair so he could reference the photos Doran had given me.

"What is this?" He leaned over to peer at the phone as if it might sully him somehow. "A…text message?" He grimaced.

"Doran," I said, still reading through the book Zeke had selected for me. *The Rituals of Death* was fascinating, detailing how the ancient Egyptians had a bad habit of entombing their so-called deities—aka Adepts of power—in such a way that they occasionally manifested. Yes, after dying and being entombed. A totally farfetched idea, but it was making me…anxious. And…I was almost completely convinced that the jumbled runes on the urn and the walls of the tomb were anchoring some sort of containment spell. But to contain what?

'Cairn' might have been a better term than 'tomb,' actually. Seeing as it was on Conall land. But I'd have to wait until Doran showed me the site.

"Did he give an address?" I said as I shut the book grimly. Zeke and I had barely had an hour to work together, and I already needed to change into something more appropriate for skulking.

"I'd offer to come with you," Zeke murmured, not answering my question. His attention was once more affixed to his own personal archive. He was refining a second set of runes, extrapolated from the ones that the witch had used in the cairn. "But..." He didn't finish the thought, frowning instead, then shaking his head. "I'm still not getting the logic here."

There were, in fact, a multitude of reasons Zeke shouldn't come with me—starting with how Doran might well refuse to take me anywhere if I brought anyone. But also because without Jiaotu's glamour, he wasn't going to be able to pass for a witch as well—or even as badly—as I was. Not long term, at least.

I closed Infinity as well, my mind still whirling with all the information I had just crammed into it. "I still don't understand how a witch could pull power from whatever was in the urn, combined with whatever was in the amulet."

"Not without getting your hands on the amulet," Zeke grunted, still focused elsewhere.

"A necromancer, maybe...fueled by slaughtering half the coven..."

"But there was no mention of a necromancer in the vampire's tale."

"True." I had filled Zeke in on my conversation with Doran. "But he admitted to having barely pieced it together. And factoring in the witch's intention two hundred years ago...and maybe again now..." I sighed, scrubbing a hand across my forehead. Witch magic—most magic, really—was all about focused intent.

"An intent we haven't yet confirmed."

"But we do know that the witches believed the artifacts were of Egyptian origin, based on the odd nature of the runes used to contain or protect the amulet and the urn when they were in the cairn."

"You'll know better once you inspect the site."

"I'm not an idiot," I snapped. I didn't need to be schooled about gathering all the evidence before leaping to conclusions. "But I'm also not running around town with an amulet that I believe contains enough power to destroy a coven."

Zeke shrugged. "I doubt whoever has possession of the amulet has any idea what to do with it. I still don't. It's probably just a prize on a shelf."

"We don't know how long they've had possession of it."

"Then just get it back," he said, slightly exasperated and suggesting it was just that simple.

And really, it was.

I just wasn't going to make any friends in the process. And I might lose a few could-possibly-be friends at the same time.

Zeke shut his archive with a snap. "It's possible this investigation…this hasty research is a waste of time. We retrieve the artifact and simply lock it away."

I smirked. "Really? Now that the mystery is literally shoved under your nose, now that you've come all the way to Dublin to solve it, you're just going to tuck it away on a shelf?"

Zeke smiled. Just a twist of his lips, but the expression was warm. "I didn't come to Dublin because you enticed me with garbled runes that may or may not be Egyptian replicas."

I didn't know quite what to say to that, so I simply stood and reached for my phone.

Zeke snagged my wrist in a light hold. I immediately broke his grip as I straightened, finding two messages from Doran:

>*The museum.*

>*Thirty minutes.*

Zeke's touch had been warm and gentle, and meant to be inviting. But I'd already made my boundaries clear.

"I'll await your return," he murmured, once again balancing his archive on his knee and opening it to the runes he was still deciphering.

"There's food in the downstairs kitchen," I said, turning away.

He nodded, his dark-blond hair falling across his brow, eyes downcast. "I'll wait until you return," he said again.

His words were heavy with innuendo. Unfortunately, it wasn't the suggestive, fun kind. It was asking for all sorts of things I wasn't prepared to give him.

The tough thing about sleeping with your adoptive great-great-uncle? Breaking up wasn't as clean as one might wish. Plus there was the whole 'perfect pairing' thing when it came to genetics and familial ties and so forth. More things I didn't want to be thinking about just yet. I wanted to experience at least another seventy-five years of the life I was just beginning to make for myself first.

I headed upstairs to change. If I jogged briskly, I could still meet Doran in time. Then I remembered I was supposed to text back. It was only polite.

I'm on my way.

The vampire stepped out of the shadows as I neared the gated drive that led to the archaeological branch of the National Museum of Ireland. I didn't flinch at his appearance, which seemed to disappoint him.

I had jogged from the estate, quickly and imagining myself slipping through the shadowed streets—though that particular talent eluded me. No one had followed me, but it was good practice.

Doran swept his gaze over me, smiling tightly. "Just had that gear lying around, did you?"

I was wearing dragon leathers, though I'd partly disguised them with an overly large thin black sweater that fell down to the middle of my thighs. The long sleeves hid the daggers sheathed in gauntlets on my forearms. The black lace-up boots were resistant to a multitude of conditions, including magic, heat, and water. And, of course, I had Infinity in my backpack.

The sweater was also long enough to conceal the bone blade currently occupying the built-in sheath on my upper right thigh. I would have to yank the sweater up to pull the blade, but it was better than simply displaying it. There was no way that an antiquities dealer like Doran wouldn't instantly know what he was looking at if he laid eyes on the weapon.

The way his initial assessing gaze had lingered below my waist let me know he'd already sussed out that I was wearing a weapon of some sort.

"I am an archivist," I said, raising my chin slightly and keeping my tone cool.

The dark-haired vampire was dressed in dark clothing as well. Some sort of tactical pants—based on the multitude of pockets—and a black hoodie to partly cover his face, though he currently didn't have the hood up. Plus black boots that were bulkier than mine.

Doran made a show of pacing around me, eyes gleaming with what I thought might be mischief. I was still figuring him out.

"No sword? That outfit practically screams for a sword. Though the hair won't do."

I'd left my hair to do what it willed. Missy, the youngest of the brownies who oversaw my mother's estate, had always braided it in a tight queue for me before training sessions. But I couldn't do anything with it even if I tried.

"You seem more...at ease, Doran," I said. "I thought you were nervous about our little outing."

He snorted derisively. Stepping back in front of me, he offered what appeared to be a rough-hewn silver coin etched with a single rune. It looked like something that might have been melted down repeatedly, then perhaps stamped with different runes? Set with different intentions?

"To slip unnoticed through pack lands," he murmured, his eyelashes hooding his gaze. "Suppressing both the sound and scent of our passage."

That likely wouldn't have been a problem for me. As a dragon. But I was supposed to be a witch, and acting like a witch.

I would just keep reminding myself of that.

"Thank you," I said, carefully taking the silver coin by the edges. "The trigger?"

"You'll have to hold it next to your skin for a few minutes, then keep it on your person. Between your thumb and forefinger should be fine."

I smirked, mostly to myself, flipping the silver coin over. Each side was stamped with a different rune. Pressing a finger to each would combine the magic held within, triggering the spell. "Clever construction."

Doran grinned at me. "You expected the trigger to be blood."

"I wouldn't have been surprised."

He chuckled, darkly pleased. "I just purchase such magic, I don't craft it myself. And coven witches don't deal in blood."

I hummed in response, not completely in agreement based on the coven witches I'd had occasion to meet in the last week—or one witch specifically.

His grin widened.

"I'll be happy to reimburse you," I said.

"Spending the evening with you is all the compensation I need. Though you could return the coin at the end of the evening, for reuse."

"Of course."

A dark vehicle pulled up. I thought it might have been a smaller limo, but I knew very little about cars.

Doran stepped forward, opening the back door, and I climbed in.

We drove for some forty-five minutes, leaving the city behind relatively quickly, but then continuing down a long, straight highway for another twenty minutes or so before making a series of turns. The traffic was sparse. Doran was in the back across from me, and I had no idea who was driving. But not picking up any magical signature from the driver, I assumed it was a hired car.

The vampire spent the bulk of his time on his phone. Texting, I thought. Possibly answering emails? I pulled out Infinity, recalling a chapter of *The Mythology of Death and Its Many Goddesses* with a brush of my fingers.

I had already read through the section on Egyptian death goddesses. So, inspired by the mixture of runes on the urn, I skipped ahead and homed in on the Celtic incarnations of the same theme. The deities or entities that fell into the Morrigan mythos, mostly. I'd read numerous Celtic mythology texts while in the nexus, preparing for the head curator position. But it was always a good idea to gather information from multiple sources for comparison.

The Morrigan was often described as a trio of sisters, the names and powers differing for each so-called incarnation. They were associated mostly with war and fate, a harbinger of doom and destruction. But some cultures had also seen the goddess as a guardian.

Even the etymology of the name Morrigan was in contention. 'Rigan' most likely meant queen. But 'Mor' might mean terror, or monster, or nightmare depending on the region and language it was sourced from.

The jumbled and disputed mythos of the Morrigan was a perfect example of what happened when nonmagical people tried to explain or understand magical occurrences.

Still, incidents using any sort of remains—such as whatever might have been stored in the urn—usually meant a necromancer was involved. And necromancers had no need to channel the power of any death goddess. Likewise, I could see no obvious connection between any sort of death goddess mythology and a single witch with a stolen object of power. Not even if that witch were the head of a coven.

So...it was possible I'd been making connections that weren't warranted. The books I'd found in my office might well have simply been randomly collected by Celeste, not a secret research project at all.

"Is that where the runes are pointing you?" Doran asked. If he'd looked up from his phone—if he could even see what I was reading across from him—I hadn't caught it. Though I did tend to get wrapped up in reading. "I'd assumed they were...set dressing."

"Set dressing?"

He glanced up at me, waving a hand offishly. "For show. To scare off any tomb raiders." He grinned at that pronouncement for some reason. Perhaps he enjoyed the irony of being an undead vampire who was also a grave robber.

"But...you said you felt an oppressive power..."

He shrugged a shoulder. "From the tomb, yes. From the amulet, most definitely. But the urn was inert."

It wasn't exactly inert, though. I could pick up residual from it. Which confirmed that my magical senses were more refined than Doran's. Not a surprise.

The limo slowed. Doran opened his door and stepped out before the vehicle had rolled to a stop. I followed, slipping Infinity into my backpack and slinging it on.

We were on a narrow paved road in the middle of the woods. From my vantage point, I had no idea how deep the forest ran on either side. The waxing crescent moon was out, but caught partly behind some clouds.

"Coin," Doran murmured, closing the door and tapping on the roof of the vehicle. The limo continued forward.

I pressed the silver coin between my thumb and middle finger, then just held it as I watched Doran take in the environment around us, without even moving his head or feet. Magic sparked and then died between my fingers as if I might have inadvertently broken or overpowered the working cast into the coin.

But Doran just nodded at me, seemingly satisfied, tucking his own coin in the pocket of his hoodie. Then his gaze went remote again, utter stillness overtaking him.

Having never met a vampire before, let alone worked closely with one, I had to admit I found him and his senses intriguing. It was possible he was better suited to hunting in the dark than even I was.

After executing an awkward three-point turn that highlighted huge swaths of the forest with bright headlight beams, the limo sped off the way we'd come.

"I'll call the car again when we're on our way back," Doran murmured. Then he stepped into the underbrush that edged the road and all but disappeared into the deep shadows of the trees.

I followed him, mostly by his magical signature. I had a feeling that he might have been playing with me. Perhaps I was supposed to be a little frightened and beg him to escort me properly. But I wasn't certain I could play at being that kind of a witch with any consistency, so I didn't.

As the trees grew taller and thicker, the forest darkened enough that even I had to slow, blinking my eyes to adjust to the low light numerous times.

After about ten minutes of skulking, I tucked the silver coin in my front pocket and paused. I could feel something on the edge of my range. So about three kilometers away. But to my right, not straight ahead.

Abandoning Doran, who was still a ways ahead of me, I veered in that direction.

I heard Doran swear almost silently. Then he was beside me in an instant, brushing his shoulder against mine.

"Did I ruin your game?" I asked, amused. I felt dense underbrush scraping against my legs, but couldn't hear anything. The spelled coin was definitely muffling our passage.

"Perhaps I just wanted to impress you," Doran murmured. "Spend a bit more time. Make a show of it."

I flashed him a grin that I knew he could see even in the dark. "Next time."

He snorted. "Apparently not, with you. But then, the head curator position did sit vacant for six years, so I shouldn't be surprised."

He paused, raising a single finger to his lips.

I'd heard the sound as well, just a moment after him.

Something was moving through the forest, parallel to us. It sounded like a small animal. But when magic was in play, that meant nothing. This was Conall land. The Conall wolves would be able to move across it in utter silence if they wanted to.

Doran started walking again before I would have, but I fell in behind him, keeping pace.

The power I'd felt bloomed just ahead of us.

Not exactly hidden.

Which was odd, wasn't it?

We stopped at the edge of a small clearing, still tucked within the trees. Blazing with light, at least in contrast to the darkness otherwise surrounding us, an opening appeared to have been carved into a moss-covered mound.

I stepped into Doran's personal space, casting my voice as low as possible. "The cairn?"

He stiffened but didn't step away. Then he nodded, once. His gaze was riveted to the opening in the earth. It looked as though large rocks had been shifted to either side to expose an abrupt drop.

"Was it open like this before?"

"No," he whispered back, then hesitated. "And the rocks take a great deal of strength and magic to shift. Celeste and I were exceedingly thorough about covering our tracks before we left."

"You most certainly didn't want the Conalls to know you'd raided their cairn," I teased.

He huffed quietly, but in agreement.

The tomb had been protected by both physical and magical barriers, then. And was now sitting wide open. Exposed.

Well, there was only one way to see what was going on.

I stepped into the clearing.

Doran didn't follow.

I was about five meters from the open cairn when shadows shifted from among the piles of rocks to either side, forming into two exceedingly large light-gray wolves. Each of them pinned glowing white-orbed eyes on me, stepping forward. Each of their upper lips was curled in a silent snarl, revealing unusually long teeth.

They were silver furred, not light gray. I corrected my assessment as the cloud cover shifted enough for more moonlight to filter into the clearing. And their size and the length of their teeth would have been unusual only if they'd been actual wolves. Or even regular werewolves, for that matter.

Doran was beside me before I could caution him, hands raised and speaking in soothing tones. "Steady now," the dark-haired vampire murmured. "We're on archive business. This is Dusk Godfrey, friend of the pack. I'm merely escorting her."

The wolf on the right snapped its teeth. The one on the left lowered its head, flattening its ears back.

"Doran," I whispered. "These aren't Conalls."

"Not Conalls?" he scoffed.

The cloud cover shifted again, soft moonlight once more highlighting the pair as they faced off with us. Their fur glowed silver. It was subtle, but they were definitely surrounded by a magical aura. Their eyes blazed with that same power, condensed and intensified.

"Celestial wolves," I said, still keeping my voice low—thrilled and concerned at the same time. If the wolves attacked, both at once, I wasn't certain I could quell them without hurting them. And I most definitely couldn't protect the vampire without revealing I was more than a witch.

"Celestial creatures are a myth," Doran muttered, more to himself than me.

I'd seen sketches of celestial beings in multiple books about mythical creatures. But the information that accompanied those depictions was always scant. *The Mythology of Death and Its Many Goddesses* had an entire section devoted to celestial creatures, but I hadn't read that far yet.

"They typically manifest as familiars," I whispered. "For a greater being to draw power from."

"You've got to be joking," Doran said under his breath.

The wolves lunged without warning.

Doran and I sprang apart. Claws and then teeth barely missed me as the wolf aiming for me twisted awkwardly in midair. But I was already dashing back through the woods.

Doran slammed a punch to the side of the second wolf's head, then darted after me. I wove to the right, intending to circle back, but he grabbed my arm, hissing, "Keep straight. The road is nearby."

Of course it was. He could have driven in farther, but that would have ruined his walk-in-the-dark-forest-with-a-vampire game.

"You go," I said, twisting out of his hold. "I'll quell the wolves."

He swore vehemently in Hong Kong Cantonese, confirming again that I'd been right about his accent. Though now really wasn't the time to be smug about it.

I was aware that I needed to keep my pace in check, though I had no doubt that I was already running too quickly and too nimbly for a witch. But that meant I was letting the wolves get too close. Grappling with the celestial creatures among the tightly spaced trees was sure to get us all hurt.

Another natural clearing abruptly opened up around me. Stumbling to a stop, I whirled to face the wolves only a few meters behind us.

Doran pulled a thick-bladed, single-edged silver knife out of what must have been an invisible sheath—because I flat-out refused to believe him capable of calling a blade to himself.

"No!" I cried. "You can't kill it!" Celestial creatures, the so-called familiars of the gods, didn't just manifest out of thin air. "The wolves aren't—"

The closest celestial burst out from between the deeply shadowed trees, lunging for Doran.

I knocked the vampire out of the way before he could bring the blade into play.

The silver wolf hit me hard instead, and we tumbled out of the clearing back into the thickly treed woods. I blocked my neck as the beast attempted to tear my throat out, got my feet up under its belly, and flung the wolf off me.

It flew, taking down a few smaller trees before hitting a huge tree trunk and falling stunned to the ground.

I gained my feet, racing back to the clearing where Doran was facing off with the second wolf.

"You can't kill it," I said again, a little breathless. I'd been letting my training slip.

Okay, fine. Cardio never had been my strong suit.

"I don't give a shit about preserving a beast that is currently trying to gut me, archivist," Doran snarled.

"It's not just that—"

The wolf lunged.

Doran stepped smoothly to the side, moving almost as fast as a dragon would have. He brought his blade down, aiming for the celestial's neck. I got there first, slamming a kick to the wolf's shoulder.

Bone crunched. The celestial flew back into the darkness-swathed trees. I winced.

Doran turned on me. Eyes blazing red with his magic, fangs bared. "Stop that!"

"Don't be an idiot!" I cried. "They're not just guardians protecting whatever the hell is going on in the cairn. Familiars have a multitude of purposes—"

Power shifted. Surrounding us, settling into a ring that vibrated with a deep hum of energy. The ring began slowly condensing, tightening around us.

Not the celestial wolves returning. Not yet.

Something else. Multiple somethings.

No...someones. Adepts acting in perfect harmony, hidden from sight and sound as if they belonged to the forest itself.

The clearing was suddenly edged with numerous wolves. At least a dozen. Their coats were various shades of gray, from light to brown to charcoal, lettingthem practically blend into the dark forest.The Conall pack had arrived.

CHAPTER SEVEN

I PICKED UP THE SPECIFIC TENOR OF THE WEREWOLVES' magic only after I'd laid eyes on them. I glanced beyond the ring that had closed in around Doran and me, slowly scanning for the celestials. I could feel their energy too, but it was muted as if they were waiting. Watching.

"What other purposes?" Doran asked, picking up the thread of our conversation like nothing else had happened. His tone was cool, casual, as he slowly crouched and deliberately set his large silver knife on the ground before us. Then he straightened with his hands up, glancing at me sideways.

"Celestials gather magic," I said, "feeding it back to their master...or mistress." The appearance of the celestial wolves had added another massive piece to the puzzle of what might have been contained in the urn, and the possible tie back to the stolen amulet. "And their deaths can be used to fuel massively powerful spells." I glanced at Doran. "Maybe even the invocation...of an avatar or incarnation."

He stared at me blank faced, but his dark eyes widened slightly as he realized what I was suggesting. Specifically, the idea of celestial creatures accompanying divine entities—or a manifestation of so-called divinity.

"They channel that power whether or not their death is brought about by willing sacrifice or an enemy," I added. "Hence my stopping you from beheading the wolves before we figure out what the hell is going on."

Doran swore. Under his breath this time, but still in Cantonese.

A woman stepped through the cordon of wolves, dressed head to toe in black knitwear, including calf-high laced boots. Power radiated from her even in her human form, as if gathered from the land and the wolves as well as what she carried herself. I knew before she spoke that I was looking at the alpha of the Conall pack. Kellan and Gitta's mother.

Aisling Conall.

As if brought forth by my observation, Kellan and Gitta, both in human form, stepped up behind the woman. Kellan was barefoot, wearing jeans and a black sweater. Gitta's black-knit turtleneck and leggings were skintight, but undoubtedly easy to move in or remove quickly if needed. Every other werewolf I could see—though I sensed still more of them deeper within the trees—was in wolf form.

A hunting party.

Aisling Conall was as tall as Gitta, just a hand's width short of two meters. But her skin was pale in the muted moonlight, and her hair appeared to be a deep red, almost in complete opposition to the dark hair and brown skin of her two children.

Doran bowed stiffly. A swift but deferential nod of his head and shoulders.

I met Kellan's gaze, smiling tightly. If he'd been pissed at me before, he was going to be in a rage now.

He twisted his lips. Not quite a smile.

"Alpha," I said, casting my voice louder than necessary. "Please excuse our intrusion onto your land. We were on a simple fact-finding mission for the archive that now has taken a turn."

"Quite," Aisling said, settling her hands on her hips. Her accent was a pure Irish lilt. "Since you've drawn our attention, plundering our land."

"Not us, alpha," I said. "And I wasn't referring to you, but rather the celestial wolves." Suddenly putting that piece of the puzzle together, I turned to Doran. "The celestials manifested as wolves! That makes sense, since we're on pack land."

"Not the time or place for revelations, Dusk," Doran muttered.

He was right. Aisling, who didn't appear to be more than a decade older than her children, was listening to our every word, but her impatience was palpable.

I turned back, intending to elaborate. "The cairn hidden here on your land—"

Aisling cut me off with a single word and a push of power. "Leave."

The command rolled around us, energy swelling to snatch up Doran and eject him from the property. Well, I assumed he'd been ejected. All I knew was that I lost sight of him almost immediately.

My hair took the brunt of the push, blown back from my face to churn wildly around me. But unable to even shift me off my feet, the power just slid around me and eventually faded. Completely ineffectual.

Aisling's mouth dropped open incredulously.

Every wolf went utterly silent, utterly still. All focused on me.

Honestly, I was a terrible spy.

How the hell was I supposed to have taken that expulsion as intended? It hadn't even forced me to fight for footing!

Kellan threw his head back and laughed. A full, braying-to-the-moon laugh. It was the tone of knowing laced through it that I didn't love.

His mother turned, looking at him with complete disbelief.

Then the celestial wolves attacked.

The first vaulted into the clearing from my right, sailing over the line of werewolves, its massive jaws unhinged to take Aisling in the throat. Smart of it to try to catch what it assumed was the most powerful Adept by surprise if possible.

The second tore through the line of werewolves behind me and slammed against my back. I twisted to keep it away from my backpack—and Infinity—but allowed the hit, letting it take me down. The beast and I tumbled once again into the cover of the woods.

I could hear yips of pain behind me, then a heavy silence as I wrestled with the celestial. I managed to twist so I was facing up, rather than getting my face ground into dirt and rock and underbrush. The silvered wolf clamped down on my right forearm—with which I'd been blocking my neck—then tried to toss me around.

Its magic was robust. I could feel it pulling power from the land...and from me!

That was extraordinary. It was like a solar panel for magic, but drawing it off from any source it could find.

And that confirmed my suspicions. Celestial creatures were always tied back—to a master, to a spell in progress...

I flipped over onto the silvered wolf's back, dimly aware that I had an audience. Or perhaps support troops? They were creeping through the underbrush, practically hidden among the dark trees. Only their glowing green eyes gave their movements away. Three werewolves, one in human form.

I freed my right forearm with a wrench that made the silvered beast snarl in surprised pain. A couple of its teeth had gotten caught in my armor, thoroughly shredding my sweater. Then I wrapped both arms around the celestial's neck and squeezed. Not tightly enough to tear its head off, but enough to cut off its air. It reared back, managing to take me right off my feet. Then it hit the ground hard with its two front paws, slamming me down onto its back.

That hurt all my soft parts, even through my leathers.

But it hurt the celestial more, possibly fracturing a few of its ribs, judging by how it started wheezing.

Dragons were heavy.

I got my feet under me, pinning the silvered beast beneath me as it thrashed and fought to breathe.

Gitta strode out of the woods, her intent gaze on me, not the celestial I was subduing. Her eyes were the bright green of her shapeshifter magic, but she otherwise blended almost perfectly into the night.

It occurred to me that wrestling a celestial wolf probably wasn't something a witch would do. Or could do. Some sort of spell would have been more appropriate.

As Gitta and the two wolves at her side steadily closed the space between us, I desperately tried to think of something to say that might sound like the end of a spell…even while continuing to subdue the celestial still fighting me tooth and claw.

Something…Latin, maybe? Witches didn't often use Latin, but it might be a good cover.

"Latin, Latin, Latin," I muttered, my mind completely blanking as I avoided the silvered wolf's claws and teeth—and tried to not hurt it too badly.

Infinity hummed against my back, through my backpack, feeding me the words I needed. Responding to my unvoiced request even though I wasn't directly touching the archive.

Et sic erit.

And so it shall be. "*Et sic erit!*" I repeated, trying to make the words sound magical.

The celestial sagged onto the forest floor.

Not bad timing with the Latin. But my sweater would have fared better with less wrestling.

"Move, Dusk," Gitta said. "I'll finish it.

I peered up at the werewolf. She radiated strength. The tenor of her magic was echoed by the two shifters in wolf form at her side. "It's fine," I said.

"This is pack territory," Gitta snarled. "Your word holds no sway here."

I slowly released the celestial, straightening but not stepping away. "Sometimes it's smarter to listen to your archivist than to assume killing is always the answer."

"And I told you to move."

Sounds started filtering in from the nearby clearing.

No. Not sounds exactly. A quiet but fierce undertone of energy. A silent battle was taking place.

Then I felt the low hum of power.

Pack magic, hiding the truth of what was going on from my senses. Until I'd focused.

Panicked, I scooped up the silvered wolf, laying it over my shoulders. It was so huge, I inadvertently knocked into Gitta as I sprinted past her. Her eyes widened in surprise. I'd moved too quickly for her to do anything else.

That fierce undertone of power grew, undulating around my ankles as I broke through into the clearing.

Kellan, in human form, was facing off with the second celestial. He was grinning manically. Half-healed gouges and bite marks marred his forearms. For some stupid reason, he'd actually pushed up the sleeves of his sweater.

The silvered wolf pacing across from Kellan was in bad shape, favoring its right back and left front legs. But it radiated power, even more than the celestial slung across my shoulders. Because as I'd suspected, fighting Kellan was strengthening it in a way that had nothing to do with its mortal life.

Or whatever power had replaced that mortal life.

Kellan lunged forward with no warning. The celestial reacted slightly too late, but still managed to twist its head away from the shapeshifter trying to snap its neck. It clamped its wide jaws down on Kellan's thigh.

Blood that I could feel more than see spurted freely. But Kellan only grunted, shifting his hold on the celestial's neck.

Gitta tried to grab my arm.

I yanked away from her, causing her to stumble. Then I bellowed, "No!"

My command boomed through the clearing, startling the other wolves so much that they dropped the magic they'd been emanating to dampen the sound of the fight.

Kellan cranked his head, looking at me with eyes that blazed with that golden-green power completely unlike his sister's or any of the other wolves'. He snarled viciously—at me. Then, digging his fingers into the silvered wolf's thick pelt, he managed to wrench the creature free from its hold on his thigh.

The celestial in Kellan's grip looked up at me then—or possibly at the wolf still slung across my shoulders. Its eyes blazed with silvered power, so bright it was practically white.

It stopped fighting.

"Kellan!" I shouted again. "It's fueling a spell! Don't…"

The werewolf snapped the celestial's neck.

"… kill…it."

The silvered wolf dropped.

Kellan fell to his knees and threw his head back in a triumphant howl. Then—impossibly fast—he slammed his hand into the celestial's chest and ripped out its heart.

I moved.

Not even thinking before doing so, I crossed the space between us to grab Kellan's wrist, holding him in place. My other arm fought to balance the unconscious celestial still across my shoulders.

The bleeding heart, pulsing with power, hovered only centimeters from Kellan's mouth.

Though his face was still mostly human, Kellan's teeth lengthened as I watched. As he fought my hold. So strong. Too strong for a shapeshifter. I was using all my dragon strength, not bothering with subterfuge in the moment, and I was still having trouble holding him in place.

"Don't…" I whispered pleadingly. Knowing I was going to have to hurt him to stop him if he wouldn't listen. "There's more going on here than you understand."

Kellan's upper lip curled into a snarl, and he darted his head forward. I was only holding his wrist, and was hampered by the weight of the other celestial.

An intense well of energy bloomed beside us.

Kellan turned his head sharply, still caught up in the fight, presumably thinking his dead prey was attacking him somehow.

The power that had fueled the celestial wolf stretched out into the clearing, brushing by me and Kellan. Then that energy began condensing. Compressing. Drawn back into the celestial's corpse.

No one else reacted to the boom as that energy exploded—meaning it was most likely audible only to me. The dead celestial's magic flooded the immediate area, then dispersed.

The body of the silvered wolf transformed into that of a young man. A teenager. Maybe sixteen or seventeen years old. His head was twisted toward us unnaturally. A huge gaping wound marred his chest. He was fully clothed—jeans, long-sleeved printed T-shirt, brand-new-looking hiking boots. A very distinct difference between celestials and shapeshifters.

Kellan dropped the heart. Shocked—momentarily terrified, even—he reared away, breaking my hold as he gained his feet. He scrubbed the back of his hand across his mouth viciously, streaking blood across his lower face. Then he bent over and retched.

I picked up the young man's heart, not a hint of magic within it now. Then I placed it back in the hole in his chest. The heart appeared whole. Kellan hadn't bitten down, not hard enough to tear flesh at least.

Another terrible shudder racked the werewolf, and I thought he might fall to his knees again. He didn't, but he was staring at the dead teen in horror.

Gitta stepped toward her brother. Slowly. Her hands were spread to the sides, as if she expected him to attack her.

In fact, every wolf in the clearing now had their eyes trained on Kellan, watching him as if they expected…something.

He took a shuddering breath, then another. His magic curled around him, tightening as if he was pulling it into him, as I often also held in my magic. He looked down at his still-bloody hand, then shook his head.

The tension that had been building in the clearing eased.

The celestial on my shoulders stirred. I allowed it to slide off, letting it slip down to lie in the grass and dirt that had been viciously churned up by Kellan and the other celestial's fight.

Then, sitting next to it, I laid the silvered wolf's huge head in my lap, stroking my fingers along its long nose and humming quietly. Hopefully soothingly.

The members of the pack, whether in human or wolf form, pressed forward. But as if in response to a silent command from Aisling as she crouched across from me, all of them except for Kellan and Gitta melted back into the trees.

The celestial whined, pained. But it didn't fully wake.

Aisling took in the form of the dead teenager, swearing quietly. Then she pinned her bright-green gaze on me, growling. "Explain."

"Celestial wolves," I said. "As far as I could figure out while running away and then fighting, they're gathering power for…something."

"Something?" Aisling asked archly.

"I'm in pack territory without permission, desperately trying to get you to listen to me," I said pertly. "I'm not going to start guessing without more evidence."

Aisling lunged forward, getting into my face. "You and that vampire raided the cairn tonight, and something you did released these wolves."

"No," I said, meeting and holding her gaze coolly. "We were investigating a theft from the archive. Doran and Celeste Cameron removed items from your land years ago—"

Aisling looked at Gitta sharply. Gitta shook her head, likely indicating she didn't know what I was talking about.

Kellan was still staring at the dead teenager, his expression a complex twist of emotions. Horrified, saddened, confused.

"We don't have a lot of time," I said. "By killing the celestial, Kellan might have triggered…"

"Something?" Aisling snarled.

"Yes," I snarled back.

She blinked.

Apparently, twenty-five-year-old witches didn't stand up to alpha werewolves.

I kept forgetting.

The celestial stirred, its silvered eyes opening in slits. It whined in pain again. I had probably bruised its throat badly, as well as crushing its ribs.

"I know," I murmured, still petting its silvered pelt gently. "It's going to be okay. If you transform, it might help you heal. Do you remember your other form?"

That was seriously improbable. But if the celestial could take its human form, we'd be able to question it—

Energy shifted through the ground, spreading under all of us…as if questing, looking for…

The silvered wolf in my lap stiffened. Its head reared back, panicked eyes catching my own.

"No," I whispered.

The celestial keeled over. And died.

Energy boomed through the clearing again, though quieter than when Kellan had killed the first wolf. The second hadn't gathered as much power.

Then the second celestial transformed into a fully clothed young woman, also in her mid to late teens. Her bright-blue eyes were still locked to mine, but lifeless.

"No..." I said again, completely ineffectually.

Gitta crouched beside the teen, leaning down to sniff her but not otherwise touching her. "This one smells familiar."

"Witch," Aisling said quietly. "Call the Byrnes."

The power that had reached out, demanding the ultimate sacrifice from the second celestial—its life—had retracted. Focused on not letting Kellan consume what I'd already guessed might have been human flesh, I hadn't noticed that sensation when the male teen had died.

But now I could feel that energy feeding into a deep well of power nearby.

The cairn.

I'd been played.

Possibly for the third time. If the imp had been a test. If Rook had been a test.

And while being tested, I'd revealed that I would hesitate to hurt or destroy what I thought I might be able to untangle instead.

Except this time hadn't been a test. Or at least that was what my instincts were screaming. But I would need way more evidence to convince the witches.

I had no idea whether or not I was the actual target of the events that had just unfolded. Doran and me being on-site at just the right time seemed like too much of a coincidence, unless the vampire was a stellar actor. So presumably, the celestial wolves had been called forth to fight the Conall wolves after the pack responded to the cairn having been broken open. Because that fight might have weakened the pack, even as it strengthened the celestials.

But for what? To call forth some sort of divine construct or avatar?

"What the fuck is going on?" Kellan snarled, as if finally waking up.

I stood, stepping around the girl and pulling my bone knife. A dark-gray wolf melted out of the shadowed tree nearest to me, tucking next to me. I picked up the familiar tenor of his magic—Brady in wolf form.

"Dusk?" Kellan's snarl was another even fiercer question.

"We're about to find out," I said without turning back.

An even stronger wave of energy exploded from the deep well of power nearby, flooding through the woods in a flash, hitting me around knee level.

I stumbled.

Beside me, Brady flew back, slamming into a tree with a nasty crunch. A quick glance told me that everyone else had also been knocked down. Except Kellan, who'd caught himself on one knee.

I lunged for Brady, scared that he'd been badly injured. But he took a shuddering breath even as I reached for him.

The wave of energy dissipated as if burning itself out.

The forest fell eerily silent—and, for just a moment, felt devoid of magic. I reached for that deep well of power with all my senses, but the cairn was empty of the magic that had been collected from the celestials.

I spun around, seeing and feeling nothing but the inky-dark forest all around me, but waiting...waiting for an attack that had to be coming.

I knew...I knew.

The oppressive weight on my shoulders and the tightness across my chest—a combination of anxiety and adrenaline—told me that the real fight coming this night hadn't even started.

Kellan stepped up beside me, close enough to practically envelop me in his heady energy, his warmth. His steady presence drew me away from all the thoughts of everything I'd already done wrong.

"I can taste it," I whispered, suddenly aware of the arid, earthy flavor coating my tongue.

"Yes," Kellan snarled, his bright gaze trained on the dark forest behind me.

I gagged, just once. Then I forced myself to ignore the residual magic staining my mouth, my senses.

Tightening my grip on my bone blade, I dashed into the forest, running with no magic to guide me in the direction of the cairn before I'd even made the decision to move.

Something very old had just woken up. Something very powerful. And very angry.

I was already too late.

The cairn was empty. As expected. The tight, oblong underground space was blackened, scorched. But not by fire, for lack of a better way to assess it on first sight. All the runes I'd glimpsed in Doran's photos had been scoured from the walls—so apparently they had held some power after all.

I was about two and a half meters below ground and crouching by a large, relatively flat rock. It looked as though it might have originally been part of the previously blocked entrance, but had been dragged into the middle of the space. I laid my hand on it, feeling for magic but not picking up anything. But based on what appeared to be an energy burn scorched into the ground in a pattern radiating out from the rock, it might have been used as a temporary altar.

Used for the transformation that had turned the teens into the celestial wolves? Then, drawing on the magic collected through the deaths of those celestials, used to power...an invocation? Of what?

An incarnation of divine power? A divine power rooted in death? In death magic?

A death goddess?

That was where all the mismatched pieces were currently pointing. The urn. The odd mixture of runes used to secure it. The amulet, the books that Celeste had collected, Doran's recounting of the deposed coven leader. The residual magic that still somehow coated my mouth. And the aching dread that had taken up occupancy in my chest.

Celestial creatures were the familiars of the divine. There was so little known about them, but that was key. Though if some sort of creature of ancient power had been unleashed on the world by the celestials' deaths, why hadn't it attacked us in the woods? Or at least tried to enchant us? To turn us into worshipers?

No. I was letting my fear of failure propel me into hasty conclusions. Plus, I kept circling back to the reality that death magic usually required a necromancer. And as far as I currently knew, there was no necromancer involved—not in the now, and not in what had happened two hundred years before.

Kellan was watching me, crouched at the opening to the cairn. I had jumped down easily—without thinking about it first, of course. But I made a mental note to remember to get him to help me up. To act like a witch. The wolves currently wearing fur refused to enter the cairn even that far, though Brady had tried to stick by my side. Once he'd caught up to me.

Gitta and Aisling were having rapid-fire conversations on their phones, pacing back and forth just beyond the entrance. The rest of the wolves had been sent out in hunting parties. With no prey. My senses told me that the incarnation of the goddess—and I was going to call it that, because I needed to call it something—was long gone from the Conalls' lands, along with whoever had invoked it.

Rubbing my fingers together, I murmured, "No residual magic."

"You need to start talking, Dusk," Kellan said. His tone was low, dangerous, and commanding. Containing nothing of the confused terror he'd previously exhibited.

"Oh?" I said offishly, though I was ready to move on myself. The cairn might have been rife with clues, but it wasn't going to help me catch the construct or avatar that had just been called forth. That might have just been called forth, I corrected myself. Because leaping to conclusions might also have me leaping past obvious clues. "Are you listening now?"

He snarled viciously. Then he scrubbed his hand across his face, as if he might scrub away the magic still riding him. And all the instincts that it had triggered.

I stepped toward him, hopping up on a rock, then reaching up to him. He blinked, momentarily surprised, but then grabbed my forearms and dragged me up. I scrambled for footholds, though he didn't seem to have much trouble with my weight. Dragons were heavy.

Utterly ironically for magical beings that used to have wings, we didn't much like being off our feet.

Kellan straightened, depositing me next to him at the mouth of the cairn, then releasing me.

For some reason, I laid my hand on his forearm—his arms were crossed again—and tilted my head back to meet his gaze. "There was no way for you to have known," I whispered, exceedingly aware of all the sharp ears nearby that might have been listening. "The celestials smelled like their magic, not the teenagers who'd been sacrificed."

"I could have listened to you a bit…earlier," he said with a wry twist of his lips. Then, as if unable to get what he'd almost done out of his head, he shuddered. "If I had…" He shook his head again, then simply said, "Thank you. For stopping me."

He dropped my touch along with his arms, stepping farther into the clearing where Gitta and Aisling were waiting, phones now tucked away.

Brady, still in wolf form, stepped up next to Kellan. He was limping. The last wave of the spell that had been ignited by the death of the celestials had injured a number of the wolves, but no one was hurt enough to need medical or magical intervention. Except for the female teenager currently lying a few feet away, but she was beyond any sort of healing. One of the wolves in human form must have carried her into the clearing while I'd been investigating the empty cairn.

Aisling pinned a gaze still full of her werewolf magic on me. "Explain now. We are listening." She tilted her head slightly, then added, "Archivist."

"You called the silver beasts celestials," Kellan said, prompting me as he watched a werewolf I didn't know carry the body of the male teenager into the clearing.

"But they transformed after...death as if they were shapeshifters. Except for the clothing."

Gitta stepped away, murmuring to the newcomer as the body was set down on the ground beside the other dead teen. Both the bodies had their arms flung out to the sides, so that their hands almost touched.

I looked away, but the image was already seared into my brain.

Kellan's focus was on the teenagers. Again. But Aisling was watching me intently.

Assessing my reactions? Maybe. Trying to decide if she could trust me? Most definitely.

"Divine magic," I said, clearing my emotion-clogged throat. "It requires a different type of sacrifice. The host must be willing. But that doesn't mean they can't be tricked."

Aisling grimaced.

Kellan grunted, proving he was listening.

Energy shifted from the direction of the road, or at least where I thought the road lay. Aisling turned her head a moment after I felt it, then Kellan did the same.

Gitta, standing by the dead teens, curled her lip in displeasure, sending the other werewolf back into the woods with a flick of her fingers. "Witches."

"We invited them," her mother said. She didn't sound much happier, though.

"The ritual scoured the cairn and the immediate area of all magic and also consumed all the power the celestial wolves had gathered." I kept my gaze steady on Aisling Conall and Mesa Byrne as I spoke, though I was aware of the others gathered in the clearing. "Robbed of their magic, the teens who had volunteered to be sacrificed—"

Mesa Byrne interrupted me with a snort of disbelief. The head of the coven was still formidable, even while dressed in jeans and a long cream-colored wool coat. Her gray-streaked red hair was swept back in a loose bun.

Ravine, to her mother's left, couldn't take her eyes off the two bodies lying just behind me. The metal mage had tried to introduce everyone when the witches first arrived, but her mother had cut her off with a list of demands.

Demands that Aisling Conall had skillfully directed my way.

So I told them what I knew. Doran's story, the missing artifacts. I told them quickly, and I was desperately trying to be polite—even as I was overwhelmingly aware that whoever was responsible for what had happened was getting farther and farther away. If it had been me, I would have already grabbed my prize and been fleeing the country.

"Not helpful, Mesa," Aisling snapped. "You weren't here. You didn't feel the power move through the earth."

Mesa stiffened at the rebuke, but didn't take her attention off me. "You're accusing a witch when the incident took place on pack land."

Aisling spun on the elder witch. An anger that I could literally feel clinging to all the werewolves sparked into an instant fury.

I raised my hand, getting everyone's attention before more violence could erupt—though honestly, I completely understood the impulse.

But I also knew we were going to need the witches to quell whatever force or entity or magic one of their own had awoken, or invoked, or released. The spell-burned husk of the cairn offered no clues to the exact nature of what we were now dealing with. All I had were suppositions. Well-formed speculation, based on as much evidence as I'd been able to gather. But still, acting rashly, based solely on suppositions, could get people hurt.

Well, probably not me. Or at least I was less at risk. And I needed to have been moving over fifteen minutes ago now.

"This is the third incident that has…started at the archive," I said, struggling to sound neutral.

"Which points to you," Mesa said stiffly, though without a hint of conviction.

"We're wasting time," Kellan snapped, continuing to pace a tight circle around us.

"I agree," Ridge said. The tall, broad-shouldered witch straightened from where he'd been systematically touching each of the large rocks that had once sealed the cairn. "The power might be stripped from this immediate area, but there was no mistaking the trail we crossed on the way in."

"From the road?" I asked.

He nodded, stepping over to crouch next to the bodies of the two teenagers.

"Did you see any cars heading out on the way in? Or Doran?"

Ridge shook his head, not looking at me as he gently touched the dead girl's shoulder.

"We'll split into teams," Aisling pronounced. "Kellan and Gitta with Dusk."

Mesa looked at the alpha sharply. "This is not an execution, Aisling. The coven will be responsible for any member—"

"You're a little late," Kellan snarled.

His mother raised the flat of her hand to him, and he instantly backed off. But when she spoke to Mesa, her tone was dangerously low. "I agree with my son. If you had taken care of your sister when she was the one who—"

"I didn't have enough evidence—"

"You didn't even conduct a trial."

"Our internal investigation—"

"She tried to kill one of my wolves!"

"She did nothing of the sort!"

Magic was roiling and boiling across the clearing now. On any other day, I would have been happy to simply watch, to stay in the role of the observer. A role in which I was, honestly, much more comfortable. Except what was unfolding around us might well be something that only I could fix—if I could only fully understand it first.

"I recognize her..." Ravine's sorrowful whisper somehow sliced through the argument between the alpha and the coven leader. I hadn't noticed that she'd moved to kneel by the dead teenagers. She was wiping tears from her cheeks. "I went to the Academy with her older sister..."

She sobbed once. Then, flushing a bright red, she slammed her hand over her mouth as if that would help her keep her emotions at bay. She struggled for a moment before she lowered her hand. "She wasn't...she didn't have enough magic to...her name was Jilly Dunkirk." She shook her head helplessly, then looked at her mother.

"A witch?" Mesa asked, her voice hollow. "From London? Or ...?" She cleared her throat, then asked Ridge, "And the boy?"

Ridge had been systematically going through the teenagers' pockets, peering at the various items he'd collected. "Stripped of their magic, as Dusk indicated. But not their possessions or cash." He didn't look up as he flipped open what appeared to be a passport. "That's…normally that would be shortsighted. Except I assume the teens were never meant to make it out of this alive." Ridge met his mother's gaze with a sigh, indicating the male teen with the passport he held. "William Medici. They appear to have been traveling together. They both have Leap Cards…transit passes…staying at the same hostel."

Mesa made a quiet sound of pain. Even if the teenagers hadn't wielded much power, there were now two outside covens involved—Dunkirk and Medici. Like the Dunkirks, the Medici coven, based in Italy, held a seat on the witches Convocation.

Everything was about to get much more complicated.

"I can't stand around discussing this any further," I said quietly. "My job, my responsibility is clear. The missing artifact, the amulet, is at the center of whatever's going on. I'm going to retrieve it before it can be used to harm anyone else."

Mesa opened her mouth, possibly to protest, possibly to agree.

I didn't give her a chance to do either. "It's likely that the entity we all felt awaken will require new companions." I eyed Aisling and then Mesa, deliberately not voicing my growing belief of what we were dealing with. The incarnation of a death goddess? Or, rather, a witch trying to invoke a death goddess? I didn't have enough proof, and I didn't want to waste time arguing. "If the witch had been successful in bringing the entity fully forth, or even if she'd lost control of it, she wouldn't have fled."

"Why not?" Ravine asked quietly.

"She couldn't have resisted using it against us," I said, keeping my gaze locked to Mesa. "Just like with the imp, and the book that ensnared Rook."

Mesa flushed.

"If Ayre Byrne was backed by the entity she thinks she awoke, or invoked, she would have stood her ground and tried to wipe out the pack. Gathering more power through their deaths. Am I wrong?"

Mesa clenched and unclenched her hands. "You're leaping to conclusions."

"I'm always happy to prove myself wrong," I said, utterly truthfully. "It makes the world a much, much more interesting place."

"Byrne witches don't go black!" Mesa sneered.

Silence met that pronouncement. Every pack member stared at the elder witch. Even Ridge and Ravine blinked at their mother.

Then Ravine said softly, "Oh, Mom...you know that's not true."

According to Doran's story, the deposing of the former coven leader had left a power vacuum that the Byrne witches had filled. But that didn't mean that deposed leader hadn't also been a Byrne witch herself.

"I will deal with Ayre," Mesa said brusquely. "If she is involved."

"Fine," I said. "Ayre is not my concern. She no longer works for the archive. But I will take the amulet from her. I will quell whatever she has released. And if she tries to stop me, I will not hesitate to neutralize her."

Mesa sneered. "Neutralize a witch decades your senior? Please. That's—"

"You had your chance to deal with the rot at the core of your coven, Mesa," Aisling snapped. "Once again, someone else is going to have to step in and—"

Mesa rounded on the alpha. "You just can't wait to get your teeth on my throat..."

River stepped silently into the clearing. I hadn't felt even a whisper of magic as she'd approached, but now that I saw her, I could feel the forest around her muffling her passage. She brought that muted energy into the clearing with her, her gaze locked to her mother.

In that moment, she was more than an interior designer, or a mother, or an earth witch. She was the scion of the Byrne coven. Next in line to lead. And something had most definitely shifted in the dynamic between her and her mother.

Mesa quieted, then stilled, twisting her shoulders to meet River's approach.

"Ayre dies for this," River said softly. "For Rook. For besmirching the coven over and over again. And for this..." She pointed at the bodies of the teenagers, keeping her gaze on her mother. "We won't stand with her, or protect her any longer from her own choices."

Mesa stared at her daughter for a long while, then nodded stiffly. "Ayre will be brought to trial."

"If she is involved, Ayre Byrne won't make it before a tribunal," Kellan murmured quietly to Gitta, though his gaze was on River—presumably unaware that I could also hear him. He sounded pleased, rather than bloodthirsty.

River flicked her gaze around the clearing, taking everyone else in. And then...the moment passed. She nodded to Aisling, brushing her fingers across Ravine's hand as she stepped over to join Ridge by the bodies of the teenagers.

Mesa took a shallow, shuddering breath, pressing her lips together so hard they went white.

"What do you mean by new companions?" Aisling asked, her tone a little too bright as she deliberately brought the focus back to where it belonged. "To complete the ritual?"

"Most greater beings can't exist in the world as it now is," I said dutifully, though I was so anxious to get moving that I had to stop myself from simply bolting from the clearing. "Assuming that's what we are dealing with. There isn't enough magic flowing naturally in the world anymore to sustain them, but they can gather the power they need. Usually through…followers, if you will. The celestial wolves weren't necessarily meant to die. Perhaps they weren't powerful enough, or hadn't gathered enough power."

Ravine looked at me, her eyes widening in horror. "She needs more powerful Adepts?"

I nodded. "Ideally young. Easily lured. I don't think those with more mature magic would be as useful. But that's entirely conjecture. I have no proof."

"Also harder to convince an adult to submit willingly," Ravine said. "And they have to be willing, right?"

"I believe so. But…" I shifted uncomfortably.

"Your guesses are as good as facts right now, Dusk," Kellan said.

"The appearance of the celestial wolves indicates that the entity either has divine roots, or that the magic used to contain it has…influenced it. Changed it."

"Meaning…if enough people believe it's divine, then it is?" Ravine asked doubtfully.

"River," Mesa snapped, cutting me off before I could answer. "Where is Brooke?"

I hadn't even thought about Rook. But Ayre had already targeted her once, had already successfully lured her. And as far as I knew—still with more conjecture than evidence—she had gotten away with it.

Meaning the pathways the book had forged in Rook's mind might be easy to reopen, to reform…

River, who'd been murmuring quietly with Ridge, glanced at her mother. "I dropped her off at Gitta's place on my way here."

"And nothing is getting into my house, or by Len and Bethany," Gitta said matter-of-factly. "But I suggest you make certain that others in your younger generation are well guarded tonight."

While it was highly unlikely that Sisu's magic could be harnessed—nor would he ever submit willingly to anyone—I was happy that he was at Gitta's as well for the sleepover.

River and Ridge instantly pulled phones out of their coat pockets. After conferring quickly, they started making muted calls.

"This has gone on long enough," Aisling said darkly. "I will have satisfaction."

Mesa flinched. It was barely perceptible, but my eyes caught it even with just the barest hint of moonlight overhead. "As I already said, if it turns out that Ayre is involved, I will not shield her from a proper tribunal."

"You should have turned the artifacts over to the witches Convocation two hundred years ago," I said, unable to keep my mouth shut about it any longer. That one aspect of the story had been bugging me since Doran told it to me. "When your coven leader slaughtered half the coven by tapping into the power contained within them."

"That's coven business," Mesa said stiffly. "And a mutual agreement we made with the pack."

"Not anymore. Not now that the archive and I are involved."

She lifted her chin. "We were tasked with protecting those artifacts centuries ago."

"Well, you've done a fantastic job. Your sister tried to get an illegal antiquities dealer to dig them up over ten years ago. If Celeste hadn't interceded, Ayre would have sold that amulet to the highest bidder, along with the tale about a black witch, and the pack and coven uniting to usurp her. That would have been a beguiling combination."

Mesa snarled. "You're the one who lost track of that amulet."

"In her first week on the job?" Aisling said coolly. "Down one employee within the first hour? An employee who shouldn't have had access to objects of any power level for the last six years?"

"That antiquities dealer cannot be trusted," Mesa said, on the defensive now. "He's a vampire."

"At least he knew better than to try to sell it," I countered. "Even out the cash Ayre practically stole from him. Because she would have known, wouldn't she? That it wasn't something that should be sitting on a collector's shelf?"

Mesa flushed. "Accusing a Byrne witch— "

"Shut up, Mesa," Gitta suddenly snarled, surprising even me. "Ayre might have hidden her trail on the way out, but the scent of black witch is all over the place from when she came looking for the cairn. What do you think led the pack all the way out here in the middle of the night?"

"Luring us," Kellan said. "For her beasts to slaughter."

"How do I know what you wolves get up to— "

I turned and walked swiftly away into the forest. The time for politics, the time for diplomacy, had long passed.

Kellan was at my side only a few steps into the trees, but then he veered abruptly right. "This way. No point in tracking her back through the woods. We'll grab a car, head into town. A second team will branch off and head farther out of town."

I followed him, checking my pace slightly as I remembered again who I was supposed to be. A witch wouldn't even think about tracking on foot for more than a few miles, not if she was on a deadline. Never mind running through woods she didn't know well.

A large wolf smoothly shifted out of the shadows on my heels. Gitta. That had been a quick change.

Kellan glanced over his shoulder, grunting in response to his sister's appearance. His eyes were glowing that golden green, presumably so he could see in the dark. Though maybe he was still just that riled up. His energy felt almost calm. Or perhaps like it was lying in wait. Ready.

"Gitta has the best nose in the pack," he said. "Now tell us exactly what we're hunting."

"Witch," I said, keeping it simple. Though I had felt the entity awakening, if it had left a trail of magic as Ridge had indicated, I personally hadn't picked up on it yet. But an earth witch might feel such things more acutely when surrounded by nature—or in Ridge's case, by stone—than I did.

"Ayre Byrne," Kellan spat.

"Most likely. But I honestly don't know for certain. And she could have accomplices." Like Doran. Though it seemed extremely unlikely that the antiquities dealer could have deceived me so thoroughly. "How far would your mother's command have sent Doran?"

"Just beyond the boundary, but he'd be barred from the entire property now." Kellan glanced back at me with gleaming eyes. "He couldn't have circled back, if that's what you're thinking."

"I don't think he's involved with what happened tonight. But he has been...connected with Ayre before."

"Financial connections. But there's no money in this...endeavor. Only death."

Well, that wasn't ominous or overly dramatic.

"And just in case I'm wrong..." Kellan smirked, clearly implying he was never wrong. "We're already tailing him back into the city. It's disheartening that you think so little of us."

Keeping our pace swift and steady, Kellan pushed effortlessly through the dark trees and underbrush, as if he knew where every root or vine already lay. I had to use my eyes. But as we crossed through the senses-dampening woods, a simple way to figure out exactly what we were hunting occurred to me. If there hadn't been so much posturing going on in the clearing, I might have already thought of it.

"Wait," I said. "The cairn was on pack land. You must have known—"

"No," Kellan spat, seriously pissed. "I had no fucking idea." He glanced back at his sister.

The medium-gray wolf at my side bared her teeth in a low snarl.

"Neither did Gitta. We'd been told it was an ancient burial site. For our very first alphas."

"It might have been at one point," I murmured. "It wouldn't have lent any actual power to what I'm assuming were containment spells. Any magic Adepts wield fades fairly quickly after death. But it would give it...significance."

"So that little wolves wouldn't go digging," he muttered.

"And your mother?"

"She knew," Kellan said. "But claims to not have understood the full power of the artifacts. Just that they needed to be locked away."

I wasn't at all surprised. In fact, the black witch from whom the coven and the pack had taken the artifacts might not have known what she was dealing with either. It was pure arrogance, though, that the Byrnes, and the Conalls for that matter, hadn't turned it all over to the witches Convocation.

Except in doing so, the Byrnes would have had to admit that one of their own had gone so dark as to slaughter half the witches under her protection.

"And before you ask the next logical question," Kellan said, "the witches insist they haven't been able to contact Ayre since the incident with Rook. They assumed she'd fled the city. Which sounds pretty fucking guilty to me. Brady is going to circle back with Erin to check Ayre's place. Though Mesa is sending her three as well."

Mesa's three—River, Ridge, and Ravine. A lot had clearly already been discussed between the werewolves and the witches, presumably when Brady had started pushing to contact Ayre.

"Are they up for confronting their aunt?" I asked doubtfully. As far as I knew, River hadn't even tried following the incident with the imp. Though now that Rook had been attacked, and with the dynamic somehow having shifted between her mother and her, maybe River was the perfect person to confront Ayre.

Though not if Ayre figured out how to wield the power of a death goddess incarnate, even if only partly manifested.

"They might all be heading into trouble," I murmured.

"They have us to back them," Kellan said with utter confidence.

I was fairly certain he meant Gitta and him. And I hadn't forgotten how he'd been the only one besides me to stay standing when everyone else had been felled by the backlash of the entity's awakening.

The forest ended abruptly, spilling us out onto a wide manicured green lawn that ran up to a large manor house. Every single light in the house was on, setting the entire structure aglow. Though I wasn't an expert in architecture, the design looked as though it might have been Georgian originally—but the centuries the Conalls had presumably occupied the place could be tracked through the numerous additions that sprouted from it.

At least a dozen vehicles lined the wide circular drive. Kellan led us to a large dark green SUV, opening the back door for Gitta and the side passenger door for me.

We climbed in, Kellan taking off an instant after he started the engine. He handed me his mobile phone without looking. I took it and placed it in the middle console so my magic wouldn't adversely affect it. Though I was already holding on to everything I had as tightly as possible, given my current company and situation.

In her wolf form, Gitta paced the back seat, alternating the windows she was looking out of as we pulled onto a narrow road, then turned right.

As far as I could see, the bulk of the property was forested. Which made sense for the pack. Witches would have razed most of the trees for gardens, filling the land with rare herbs and flowers.

Another trio dashed out of the woods to the far left, two in wolf form, and a large, naked dark-skinned man I didn't recognize. At full run, they jumped into a second vehicle.

"Odane," Kellan said. "Our Dad. The wolves are Brady and Erin." He glanced in the rearview mirror at Gitta, then smirked at me. "Don't worry. We keep extra sweatsuits in all the vehicles."

That wasn't surprising. Running around with a backpack while in wolf form wouldn't be terribly majestic or intimidating.

We drove in silence for long enough that I noted headlights behind us. As we approached what must have been the main road that Doran had taken into the back of the property, Kellan slowed and pulled over. "We'll let Gitta scent. It's unlikely she'll be able to pick up the black witch, but she'll be able to tell if cars have passed recently and what direction they took."

I stepped out as well, following Kellan and Gitta in wolf form up to the intersection, but then stepping away into the wild grass at the side of the road instead of following them onto the pavement. Gitta started systematically scenting the crossroads in a grid pattern. I turned my attention to the nearby fields, moving away until I felt I was far enough from the vehicle, and the others, to let my own magic loose…just enough to feel for any other magical signatures nearby.

It was interesting that the pack had started referring to Ayre Byrne as a black witch, as though some switch had been flipped, even though we hadn't actually seen her participate in the sacrifice of the teenagers. The willing sacrifice. Perhaps the werewolves had picked up something in Ayre's scent, but it honestly felt like something else to me.

Perhaps it was easier to hunt down a person if you thought they were evil? But I didn't equate darkness with evil in that way. For me, the rules of the hunt were already as clear as they needed to be.

An artifact of power was loose in Dublin.

It needed collecting.

And I was an archivist.

I moved farther into the field, hopping a low split-rail fence as two other vehicles pulled up. The first disgorged three more werewolves, while the second contained the Byrne siblings. The witches rolled down their windows, conversing softly with Kellan's father, Odane. But they quickly pulled away and headed into town. To check on Ayre's residence, presumably, as that had been the plan.

After a muted conversation with Kellan, the trio of werewolves followed the witches.

I sank further into my own senses, reaching, stretching. And there, on the very edge of my range, I could feel a smudge of…something. The tenor of its energy was deep and…aware. Not fully realized, though. But whether it was the same power that had woken in the clearing, I had no idea.

I opened my eyes to confirm that whatever I was picking up was in the direction of the city.

Kellan Conall was watching me.

He had kept a few steps back, but he was looking at me with an intensity that I didn't think anyone had ever directed my way before. There was something open and almost raw about the expression. And something within me responded to it. Not in a sexual way, but in an acknowledgement of…what? A familiarity? A reflection of…self?

He blinked and broke the spell. Then he shook his head, frowning. "Three cars. Two turned into the city and one away."

"Doran, the witch, and one other," I said.

He nodded. "And you?"

I stared at him for a moment, then gave in. It was extremely likely that I had already betrayed the fact that

I wasn't a regular witch. Hopefully the fact that I was considered powerful enough to be the head curator of a magical archive covered my…irregularities. "I can't pick up the witch at this distance, and especially not if she's in a vehicle. But I can feel…something…becoming aware or waking up. Either on the edge of the city or headed that way."

"Archivist," Kellan said with a grin. Well, more of a gleeful baring of his teeth. "What fine senses you have."

He moved for the SUV before I could respond, opening the door so Gitta could leap into the back seat again.

I followed.

CHAPTER EIGHT

KELLAN PULLED OVER AT THREE MORE SPOTS AS WE headed into the city, letting me step out each time to try to home in on the feeling I continued to pick up. Not a wrongness exactly, but something that didn't belong. It took two of those three spots for me to realize that what I was sensing was an intensification of the feeling—the instinct?—that had been driving me since I realized the amulet was missing. I had qualified that as a sense of doom and decided I was just being dramatic. But perhaps it had been the artifact I'd been picking up the whole time.

A series of text messages started erupting on Kellan's phone around the time I began recognizing buildings. We were probably ten minutes from the museum, but that wasn't the direction the feeling was leading me. I was itching to get my feet on the ground to hunt down the artifact properly. But with Kellan driving and Gitta in wolf form, that left me to read through the texts.

I read the messages from Odane out loud.

>The black witch's place is empty, has been for at least 48 hours. Though Erin and Brady are still fighting about the timeframe. I'm sending them to watch the archive but will stay here unless you need me.

Kellan grunted, then said, "Text back 'Okay.' But remind him to keep off the property without backup."

I texted as commanded, just as another message came through on the same thread.

>*River and Ridge are staying. Ravine insisted on going with Brady and Erin.*

"Three people on site is overkill," Kellan muttered. "Only an idiot would go home."

"Depends," I said. "How long has Ayre lived there? And does it have a basement? If she's accumulated a lot of power on the site, that might be hard to resist once she secures her...willing sacrifices."

He glanced at me, almost warily.

I shrugged. "Assuming I have any of this correct, what Ayre is trying to do takes a lot of power. And a witch is most powerful in her own territory. Her seat of power. Greater beings such as constructs or avatars of gods, or whatever else it is we might be dealing with, can form stronger connections to the real world through their celestial creatures. Ayre was obviously ahead of us on all of that, but maybe the first attempt didn't work out as she hoped."

"Right," Kellan said, though it wasn't completely clear what he was agreeing to.

A second series of text messages filtered in on his phone.

"More messages," I said. "From someone named Maura?"

"Aunt," Kellan clarified with a grunt. "Currently married to Odane. Erin's mother."

I read the new texts out loud, but they mostly just confirmed where the other hunting parties were focusing. One team was heading out of town and looking to pick up any scents. Another team had followed Doran to his warehouse and would continue to shadow him.

The third series of messages was from Ravine. The metal mage's texts were littered with typos, as if she might actually be texting without looking at the screen, or maybe doing so on the sly. The readability cleared up when she took off with Brady and Erin, both of whom were still in wolf form.

The witches, thinking ahead for what I believed might have been the first damn time since my initial run-in with Ayre, were covering all the points of power in the city. Like me, they had decided that if Ayre was going to create more celestial creatures, she'd need a place of power to pull magic from. Hence covering her house, the archive, the main coven house in the country, and a few other power-rich sites around town that I hadn't had remotely enough time to explore myself. Dublin Castle and Saint Patrick's Cathedral. Phoenix Park and the Dublin Zoo.

It was a smart plan.

But for me, hunting down the witch before she could even try to take another victim, willing or not, was a more direct approach. And to do that, I really needed to get my feet on the pavement and free my senses from the steel confines of the SUV.

As I opened my mouth to ask Kellan to pull over, the phone in my hand vibrated. The caller ID flashed a name I didn't recognize, but it was paired with a picture of Bethany. It took me a moment to recognize the golden-haired warrior, though, as she was sprawled across a bed, barely covered in a gray wool blanket.

I blinked.

Kellan glanced over at the phone. "Answer it, please," he said, voice slightly strained.

I pressed the green button, then fumbled around to put the call over the phone's speaker.

Before either Kellan or I could speak, Bethany's frustrated voice sounded out. "Is Dusk with you?"

"Yes," I said.

"Sorry, Dusk, I know you're busy with...something important, but Sisu is very upset, insisting on all of us leaving. It's his watch. You know, the one always chirping weird things about the weather?"

"His watch?" I echoed, slightly thrown by the abrupt change of subject.

"Yes, yes. I've got her," Bethany said, her tone remote like she'd stepped away from the phone. "Here."

"Dusk?" Sisu's voice came over the speaker, sounding so young. And a little freaked out.

"I'm here."

"Uncle Beckett's watch..."

My stomach soured. "What is it saying?"

Something clunked loudly, like it had bumped the side of Bethany's phone. Then a mechanical voice chirped.

"Glorious death approaches. All who see her shall worship in despair."

My heart started thumping madly in my chest. My mind was whirling.

'Glorious death approaches.'

Approaches.

Was that metaphorical or literal?

And *'All who see her?'*

Was the entity Ayre Byrne was playing around with capable of mass enchantment? On sight?

"What is going on?" Kellan snarled.

Sisu's voice rang through the phone. "Dusk?"

"I heard."

"You said it predicted demon risings."

"Stay in the house with Bethany and Len," I said.

"But..."

"Sisu!"

"Yes, Dusk." His tone was subdued.

Not waiting for me to explain, Kellan suddenly veered right, then right again, presumably now heading for Gitta's house. I didn't protest, though my racing thoughts were still trying to piece together why Ayre Byrne would go for...

Rook.

"Is Rook still with you?" I asked Sisu.

"No." My brother shushed someone in the background. "A couple of witches Bethany knows came for her about fifteen minutes ago. To take her to the main coven house? Is Rook in danger?"

How would Ayre have even known that River dropped her daughter at Gitta's...unless she was tracking her somehow? But River would have sensed a tracking spell on Rook. So I had to assume the young witch was safe, at least for now.

"Dusk?" Sisu asked again. "Is Rook okay?" More shushed whispers came through the speaker, then Sisu said, "Be quiet! My sister is thinking!"

Neve and Lile.

The twins were young enough that I didn't think their magic had manifested. But...what better raw material to remake the celestial wolves from than twin werewolves?

And where else would Ayre Byrne look for the young wolves other than their own home?

"The twins," I whispered.

"Yeah," Kellan said tightly. "I figured that out already."

"What?" Sisu asked over the phone.

"Listen, Sisu," I said, trying to keep the panic out of my voice. "If something happens, you head for the estate. Do you know the way?"

"Yes, but—"

"No, you stay with Zeke. I'll come for you."

"I can't leave everyone!" he protested.

"Of course not. But no one can get through the wards on the estate—"

"Gitta's place is warded," Kellan interjected.

I ignored him, still addressing Sisu. "And if the wards are somehow breached, you know no one can get by Zeke." Or the house, for that matter. "Bethany and Len will understand. If you have to run, run to the estate, bring everyone with you."

"Okay." The watch chirped in the background, repeating its prophecy.

"I thought you said it was a divine entity of some kind!" Kellan snarled, taking another sharp turn. The SUV listed heavily to my side. "Not a fucking demon."

"We're on our way," I said to Sisu before addressing Kellan. "It isn't a demon, and I have no idea of the accuracy of the watch, except for telling time." The werewolves didn't need to know about the watch's ability to slip unaffected through time, so I kept that part to myself. "But it's been documented on three or four occasions to predict demon summonings accurately. And the timing is…suspect."

"Len is going to do a perimeter check," Bethany said over the phone.

"No!" Kellan snarled. "Get the kids in the basement."

"We're already here." Neve spoke up. "We're having a sleepover."

Kellan closed his eyes briefly, as if hearing his niece's sweet voice had momentarily overwhelmed him.

"Neve," he murmured. "Stay with your sister. And with Sisu. Listen to Bethany, but if anything…happens, you head to Sisu's house, okay?"

"Okay!" the trio said in a chorus. Then they giggled madly, completely enjoying themselves as the adults all tried to not panic.

Infinity vibrated in my backpack, which was in my lap. A sharp, strong warning. I rolled down the window…and felt that warning in my bones. The wrongness all around us.

"How close are we?" I asked in a whisper.

"Fifteen minutes," Kellan said.

Gitta was pacing like mad in the back seat, growling quietly.

In the background, overriding the murmurs of the trio's conversation, the watch chirped another warning.

"Death approaches. Death approaches."

Kellan snarled. "Beth!"

"She's gone upstairs, Uncle," Lile called through the phone.

Kellan hit the gas, but he could only go so fast on the narrow streets. We would have made better time on a main road, though I assumed he was trying to take some sort of shortcut.

Either way, though, I would be faster on foot. "Is there an exit in the basement?" I asked in a whisper.

"Of course," Kellan snapped. "Two. One outside, plus a tunnel that leads into my place across the street."

Trust werewolves to have escape tunnels in the middle of the city.

"But they aren't going to need to leave the house," he said confidently. "A witch isn't going to be able to even breach the front door, let alone the wards, then get past Bethany and Len."

Gitta was practically vibrating with rage in the back seat. Infinity too, though without the intense emotion.

"Bethany?" I heard Sisu say.

And then something loud enough to hurt my ears even through the phone's tiny speaker boomed in the background.

The phone went silent.

The display flashed. 'Call ended.'

Kellan swore viciously, slamming on the brakes at a stop sign.

Without even thinking about it, I dropped Kellan's phone and was out the door before the vehicle had even rolled to a stop.

"Dusk!" Kellan snarled.

Gitta was into the front seat and out after me like a shot.

I ran straight down the street, not bothering with traffic lights or sidewalks. I ran straight toward the heavy miasma of power—witch power, it felt like—that lay just at the edge of my senses, growing steadily closer.

Gitta kept pace with me, even as I darted through the first alley and lost Kellan, who was still in the car.

Sisu. Sisu. Sisu.

And then the faces of the twins flashed through my mind. Oh, Neve and Lile.

No. No. No.

Gitta Conall lived in a terraced house with a small front yard. I knew it was her house before I'd even leaped the low iron front gate, because the front door was currently in that small yard—with the magical residual of a powerful break spell literally smoking at its edges.

I paused, crouching by the door to note that it was constructed out of reinforced steel, easily ten centimeters thick. It had an intricate locking mechanism.

I didn't have to touch the door to feel the witch magic that had ignored that lock, torn the door from its hinges, and yanked it into the front yard.

A huge medium-gray wolf leaped over me, racing up the front stairs into the house. Gitta.

I straightened. All my senses felt as blown wide open as the door, and it took me a moment to focus them. The magical protections were still in place over most of the house, but had been ripped away from around the doorframe—almost as if they'd been slashed with sword or claw.

The crumpled body of a werewolf in human form was sprawled next to a low rock fence to the far right, as if simply tossed aside. Len Murphy. The twins' father.

Other than Gitta, who I could feel moving systematically through her house, the structure before me was empty of magical signatures.

Sisu, Neve, Lile, and Bethany had either been taken or fled.

A vehicle squealed to a stop on the road behind me, calling my attention to how quiet the rest of the neighborhood was. The neighboring windows were all dark. A low hum of traffic filtered in from the adjoining streets. Whatever had happened when the door had been breached must have been magically muffled to not draw attention. As expected.

I stepped over to Len in the grass, crouching to touch his shoulder. Alive, but unconscious. I couldn't see any obvious wounds on him.

Then Kellan was beside me. After running his hands over Len to assess his condition, he scooped the werewolf up with absolutely no effort, even though Len was almost as large as he was.

"Dusk," Kellan snapped, crossing to the front stairs and taking them three at a time into the house.

I ignored the implied command to follow him inside, feeling Gitta on the second floor. She had checked the basement first.

The house was connected to the homes on either side, so I would have to cut through the house or circle the block to check the backyard, if there was one. And Kellan had mentioned a tunnel connecting to his house across the street...

Aware that I was feeling slightly adrift in my own body, possibly in shock of some kind, I stepped back to the path. Crossing onto the sidewalk, I focused my sense for magic across the street, then out around me in a tight radius. Casting wide wouldn't help me right now, since I didn't know this part of the city at all. I needed a direction.

I sensed the three werewolves in the house behind me. I sensed still-intact wards on a house across the street that I assumed was Kellan's. But the immediate area was devoid of other magic.

I knew there was a chance that Kellan's wards might block magical senses. But assuming they'd been placed by the same witches who'd applied Gitta's wards, I doubted they were strong enough to block me. Gitta's wards hadn't even been strong enough to block Ayre Byrne.

Because even though I hadn't seen her, even though I didn't recognize the residual witch magic that had torn the door off its hinges, I knew.

I knew who I was hunting.

I looked up, briefly considering going over the rooftops.

Then I instinctively turned right and jogged around the block instead. A narrow alley cut behind the row of terraced houses, but I didn't bother crossing to the back of Gitta's home specifically. Instead, I crouched, laying my hand on the pavement and calling forth the tracing spell. The spell I'd been modifying from the treasure keeper's grimoire.

I gave that spell a single intention with a magic-laden whisper.

"*Sisu*."

Power threaded out of me in a tight stream, instantly highlighting a strong wash of golden-tinted magic that stretched directly across the street from where I stood. As if Sisu had darted across the road and into the alley one block down. I urged the spell to sharpen. Its golden power resolved into a rope of residual magic that was accompanied by a thick line of bright green and two thinner lines of golden green.

Sisu. Bethany. Neve and Lile.

They'd run.

Now all I had to do was find out where they'd run to, before Ayre Byrne and the entity she was pulling power from did.

I pushed the spell, unraveling it before me so it threaded farther down the sidewalk. As before, it immediately crossed the street, veering right into what appeared to be another alley a block over.

"Dusk!" Kellan shouted behind me, sounding like he was deeper into the alley that ran behind Gitta's house. But I wasn't interested in talking, talking, talking everything to death.

I took off, my tracing spell leading the way. I didn't bother with pretending to be a witch this time. I'd been doing a terrible job of it all week anyway.

I just ran, focusing everything on the lines of power stretching out before me, barely seeing anything else.

If Sisu had climbed over a wall blocking an alley, I leaped it. If he'd skirted garbage cans or parked cars, I went over. I wasn't wasting another moment.

After about five minutes of full-out running, the trail of magic abruptly thickened, as if Sisu and the others had slowed, clustering tighter together.

Then my feet hit grass. I was in a hidden park of some sort. Perhaps a community green space tucked between rows of houses? I slowed, zigzagging through trees that were still losing their leaves, passing empty benches.

A large pool of bright-green power had accumulated at the base of what might have been an oak tree. I really wasn't looking closely. I had eyes only for the trail of golden power that beckoned me ever forward.

I walked through a sticky pocket of magic. Blinking, I focused on my immediate surroundings. A barrier of witch magic was hiding the area around the tree, which stood near the center of the park. But hiding what?

Then I saw Bethany.

She was…broken.

Her arms and legs were at impossible angles. Her torso was overly twisted. Or perhaps it was her pelvis that had taken so much damage that…that…

I shook my head, realizing that I'd been compromised somehow, and…

No…I had let my fear and anxiety drive me.

And now…and now Bethany was…dying? Dead?

Her gorgeous blond hair was splayed around her head. And her face...her face had been...crushed.

With not a drop of blood on her.

I fell to my knees beside her, moaning. I knew I had to keep going. I had to find Sisu. He might have been practically immortal, but he was only five years old. Instead, a terrible sob erupted out of my chest.

I'd never seen anyone so—

Bethany took in a ragged, painful breath.

She was still alive.

Oh, gods...she was still alive.

I moved without thinking. I wasn't a healer, but Bethany was a werewolf. She could heal in the same way as the dragons I'd occasionally triaged during training sessions. She just needed some help.

I checked her neck first. Impossibly, it didn't seem broken. That was good. I straightened her head anyway, running my fingers down either side of her vertebrae to make certain they were lined up as much as possible.

She moaned, pained.

"Sorry," I whispered. "Sorry, sorry, but it will help. If I get you sorted, you can transform easier."

I tried to figure out what was wrong with her hips next. Then, knowing it would hurt her even more than she already was, I shifted and straightened her hips and torso.

She made a garbled, retching noise. Then her head lolled to one side as she passed out.

Working quickly, I straightened her legs, then her arms.

Then I waited, my hands hovering ineffectually over her. I didn't want to touch her face, which seemed to have taken the brunt of the break spell that had been used against her—over and over.

A spell that had been uttered by someone wielding devastating power.

That was the best assessment I could make of the sticky pocket of magic I'd stepped into. Not blood magic. But so-called black magic had stripped this section of the park, burned through the natural magic that no doubt had once dwelled deeply in this pocket of nature, even as tamed and groomed as it was.

An earth witch amplified by an entity whose power was bent toward darkness could cast with that power. Would cast.

Bethany was still breathing shallowly, but nothing else happened.

The golden trail of Sisu's magic still stretched out before me. I desperately wanted to follow it.

I could have dragged Bethany out of the scoured pocket of the park, just in case it was that residual that was impeding her transformation. But moving her without her bones knitted together might actually kill her outright.

She made a low noise, as if trying to speak.

I leaned over her. "Transform, Bethany. I'm here. Transform into your wolf. It will help."

She made another noise, another word perhaps. I caught a glimmer of bright tears at the edges of her swollen eyes. As if her magic was leaking.

I laid my hand on her chest, but I couldn't feel her power shifting. She wasn't going to transform.

She grabbed my wrist so suddenly that I nearly wrenched free from her hold instinctively.

She tried to speak again.

And I realized her jaw was broken.

Her grip on my wrist was firm.

She was fighting. She just needed more help than I could give her.

I gently broke her hold on my wrist, reached up, and tried to shift her jaw back into place. Her entire body tensed, then vibrated with pain.

She managed to open one of her eyes to a slit of glowing bright-green power. "The…kids…" she rasped.

"I'll find them." I glanced at the golden trail leading me out of the park again. It was thinning. I pumped more magic into it, but it didn't thicken. So it was fading.

My heart was thumping wildly in my chest. I tamped down on the desperate need to run.

"Go," Bethany said. "Go, Dusk."

I thought about it. I really, really did. Leave Bethany, find the kids. It was what she wanted…but she needed to transform first. Then I'd know that she would survive.

She had put herself between the witch and the kids. She didn't deserve to be dumped in a park. To die alone.

I laid my hand on her chest again. "You need to transform, Bethany."

"Can't…" she gasped. "Something…blocking…go…go, kids."

"She's not going to kill them," I said, speaking with a conviction that I hadn't known was there until I heard myself voice it. "She needs to get them to a power source. And rituals take time to set up."

Bethany muttered something in disagreement, but I didn't catch the words. She was fading. I could actually feel it.

She was dying…like the imp had died in my hands. Also murdered by Ayre—

I shoved those thoughts away before they could fill me with even more doubt and fear. I had to think.

Bethany's ability to transform was being blocked…but what could be blocking her magic? I had straightened her skeletal structure as best I could.

I scanned her again, desperately ignoring the feeling of her life force slipping away.

No blood.

No open wounds.

The assault had been magical.

A break spell, or so I had thought…

Power stirred around me, whispering encouragingly. The fallen leaves shifted, gathering in Bethany's hair, on her shoulders and arm.

"All right, all right," I whispered. "I get it."

I didn't, really. But I understood that my magic was telling me to stay with Bethany.

I dropped the tracing spell, though it physically hurt to sever what felt like a connection to Sisu. I could pick it up easily enough after I got Bethany sorted.

I turned all my senses toward her, passing my hand over her as I felt for magic not her own. Just as I could with a magical artifact or a book.

There…

Right shoulder, left hip, and right leg. Pockets of witch magic. But their tenor felt a little…wild? Unstable?

Could I grab and tear those spots of malignant magic away from Bethany? Or would that make everything worse?

I needed some sort of nullifying or dispersal spell. But that wasn't how my power worked. I collected magical artifacts—

Energy shifted around me again, rustling my hair and bringing the scent of honey with a hint of citrus. A green-veined red leaf settled across the back of my right hand.

"Dusk?" Bethany murmured, every syllable streaked with pain. "The kids..."

"I'm here." I plucked the leaf off my hand. It might have been a maple, though I didn't know if it had come from any of the trees sheltering us. "They'll be okay."

I had no idea what the hell I was supposed to do with the leaves. Pausing in this dreadful moment to press them into Infinity seemed utterly stupid. But stymied as to other options, I shucked off my backpack and pulled out my personal archive. It hummed encouragingly. So, trying to follow my instincts, I just held it in my hands over Bethany for a moment, eyes closed, maple leaf captured in my fingers.

I collected magical objects...I occasionally archived those objects into Infinity...I also had my personal archive absorb knowledge from other sources, and I wrote...

My eyes snapped open.

I didn't know why my magic brought me flowers or leaves in the moments when I needed encouragement. But I always dutifully collected that flora, because it would be idiotic to ignore such gifts, even if I was subconsciously gifting myself.

I never knew what to do with those flowers and leaves, but I knew that Bethany had spells on her that had broken her bones and made it impossible for her to transform. Spells that needed to be removed. I couldn't tear the malignant magic from her without hurting her...

But I might be able to transfer those spells...and then feed that magic into Infinity. For my personal archive to absorb.

Holding Infinity in my left hand, I placed the green-veined leaf over Bethany's right shoulder. Pressing my free hand over the leaf, I reached through it for the malignant spell. I surrounded that dark-tinted magic with my own power, claiming it as I claimed every word

I inked within Infinity. Then I gently pulled on that combined energy, as I did when holding my own magic tightly around me.

But this time, I funneled it all into the leaf, not trying to absorb it myself.

Bethany cried out. More surprised than pained.

The break spell transferred to the leaf, somehow filling it even as it blackened its edges.

The injured werewolf sucked in a shuddering breath, then whispered, "They're coming…"

"The wolves?" I asked. But even as I did, I became conscious of at least five wolves headed our way from different directions.

Bethany didn't answer.

I pressed the spell-burnt maple leaf under my left hand, which was still anchored against Infinity. Then I plucked three golden oak leaves out of the werewolf's hair and pressed them to the second malignant break spell on her hip. I absorbed it into the leaves with far less effort this time.

Everything was always more difficult the first time, for me at least.

I could feel Bethany's magic shifting now, flooding into the places I'd unblocked.

I gathered the leaves resting against her arm…not immediately recognizing their shape…elm, maybe? Then I absorbed the spell from her leg.

Quickly, quickly, I flipped open Infinity and tucked the leaves into separate pages. I wasn't sure whether to ask my personal archive to absorb the magic altogether, or to just keep the three strong break spells I'd collected. They could be rather useful. When not applied against flesh and bone.

I hurried, feeling the wolves closing in and wanting to be gone before they found us. I didn't have the time to stand around explaining things. Again. And I could feel Kellan, followed by Gitta, close by.

As I moved to sling the backpack over my shoulder, Bethany grabbed my wrist.

"Thank you," she whispered. The bones in her face were already shifting. She was in the process of transforming. It looked painful. But not as painful as slowly dying under the break spells. "It...she only wanted Neve and Lile, but Sisu kept insisting that he go with her."

I huffed, half-sighing, half-laughing. And not at all surprised. Of course he'd insisted. "Ayre Byrne."

Bethany squeezed her one functional eye shut. "I've never seen a witch move that fast."

"She's getting some divine help."

Kellan burst into the park. He was still in human form, though his visage was terrible, bones misaligned, misshapen. It took me a moment to realize that he couldn't see us. Perhaps he'd been following my scent? Then he reached up with wickedly clawed fingers and tore through the edge of the sticky pocket I'd walked through without impediment. He laid eyes on Bethany through the shredded barrier and snarled, dark and vicious.

"Go," Bethany whispered, letting go of my wrist. Then her magic swamped her form, and she curled into herself with a sharp cry of pure agony.

Kellan fell to his knees beside her. His claws retreated into human fingers, the bones of his face smoothing.

I was up and running before he had come fully to rest on the grass.

"Dusk!" he shouted.

Four other wolves converged on the park. I snapped out the tracing spell, instantly picked up Sisu's faded golden trail, and ran.

I made it out of the park and one more block before Kellan was on my heels. Gitta was about a block behind him. I could feel pack magic whirling around us, as if to cloak our passage.

I glanced back at Kellan. His face still wasn't entirely human. He lifted his lip in a snarl, but didn't try to stop me.

"Don't slow me down," I snarled back. Then I picked up the pace.

CHAPTER NINE

RACING THROUGH YET ANOTHER PART OF THE CITY that I didn't recognize, I finally oriented myself as I darted across an overpass that cut across the River Liffey. Doran's warehouse was near Dublin Port at the mouth of that river, so we were running in the opposite direction. Kellan kept pace with me, but Gitta had fallen back a couple more blocks.

I had no trouble following the trail of residual power Sisu left behind. Even though given the distance we'd already crossed, how fast I knew I could run, and the fact that we hadn't caught up to them yet, it was obvious that Ayre Byrne had packed him, Neve, and Lile into a vehicle at some point, then kept to the main streets after that.

I slowed my pace as the structure and size of the buildings around us drastically changed. The boulevard widened, then became lined with large trees. The tightly spaced buildings filling most of the city gave way to detached homes on larger lots with wide lawns, trimmed hedges behind low stone or brick fences, and gated driveways. The architecture also became more varied, with modern homes mixing with Tudor and Georgian construction. Well, modern for a European city—meaning built in the last century or so.

It was an affluent area of the city, maybe an hour's walk from the museum. Assuming I wasn't completely turned around. I'd been keyed in on finding Sisu, not mapping Dublin.

Was Ayre Byrne so utterly arrogant that she would lead us right back to…

I slowed further, my breathing ragged. Sisu's trail led directly to a large house set at the top of a slight incline. It was mostly hidden behind greenery, not ultra-modern but definitely built in the last twenty or thirty years. Sisu's golden trail cut abruptly off at the gate set into a low brick wall, set just off the gated brick drive. My tracing spell apparently couldn't penetrate the heavy boundary wards that encased the property. Wards I could feel from more than a block away.

The house was ablaze with lights. Most of the other houses in the immediate area were darkened, tucked back on large lots and screened by greenery from the view of the road. I caught the flicker of TVs or computer screens through drawn curtains in a few upper windows.

Kellan swore viciously, his breathing as labored as mine. It was a mixture of English and Irish, some of which involved acts not anatomically possible without inflicting serious damage on a person.

But maybe that was his intent.

I wasn't going to be the one to hold him back. Not now.

I had chased my brother from one side of the city to another, only to end up staring at Ayre Byrne's house. Her seat of power.

"Where the fuck are the goddamn witches?" the werewolf snarled, looking around. "And Odane?"

Since he'd pieced an actual question together, I responded. "In the house." I slowed my pace again, but didn't bother trying to hide my presence or approach.

"You can feel that through the wards?"

The warding on the house was thick. Almost juicy. Blood wards, I assumed. Ayre Byrne would have needed to use more than just her own blood—but not Sisu's or Neve's or Lile's. As far as I could tell.

"No," I said. "I'm leaping to conclusions at this point. Either all the Byrne witches are in on what's about to take place in that house, or they've been...compromised." As horrible as the latter option was, I hoped it was the case. Because otherwise, we were about to go up against an entire coven—which would be seriously disastrous. Even I couldn't take on a full coven of united witches, plus the death goddess they were trying to unleash.

"Ridge and River aren't kidnappers," Kellan snarled. "And Ravine is still with Brady and Erin. The Byrnes aren't black witches."

"There you go," I said mildly, traversing the final few steps to the front gate. "You already have your answer, then."

Gitta flew around the far corner, barreling after us.

"Dad should have still been here," Kellan said.

He was texting. Having eyes only for the house and the golden trail of power that had led me there, I hadn't noticed him pull out his phone.

"Track him?" Kellan asked his sister as she skidded to a halt next to him.

Gitta immediately set her nose near the bottom of the gate, then sneezed viciously.

I'd already picked up what she'd scented—the earthy, musty scent of old death and decay. "There's an outer perimeter," I said to Gitta.

She huffed, then started sniffing along the edge of the road.

"The house is also shielded," I added, scanning those layers of magic as much as I could see them through the outer boundary.

"How do you know the kids are in the house?" Kellan asked.

"Can you see magic or just scent it?"

He gave me a sharp look, not liking being questioned about his personal magic. Then he shook his head, relenting. "I can see it."

That was an unusual trait for a shapeshifter. But I'd been fairly certain since the moment we'd met that Kellan could at least see my magic—including the citrus blossom that had presented itself to me in front of him.

I fed a bit more power into the tracing spell I was still holding, as I'd done when I used it in my office to highlight Ayre's path to and from the imp's urn. It threaded before me for about a meter, cutting off at the gate. It also stretched out behind us the way we'd come.

Kellan shrugged. "I can see that golden thread. I'd assumed that was your magic."

"Tracing spell, picking up Sisu, Neve, and Lile."

Kellan tipped his head to the side and narrowed his eyes, looking back and forth.

"Sisu is the bright gold. The green-gold is the twins." I almost added, 'Same color as your eyes.' But right now didn't seem like a great time to get into how his shifter magic didn't manifest in the same color as regular shifters.

"And the black witch?"

I shook my head. "Cloaked maybe? I'm a novice with these sorts of spells."

"Novice," Kellan scoffed under his breath.

Something warmed in my chest at his incredulity. Was I really so starved for praise? But I ignored it, stepping closer to the gate and trying to assess the magic sealing the house.

Not that it mattered.

I was entering that house and retrieving my brother, no matter what level of power I had to display in order to do so.

Gitta looped back to us, shaking her head slightly. Unable to pick up her father's trail or whereabouts.

"Ridge isn't answering his texts," Kellan said to her. "Ravine, Brady, and Erin are about twenty minutes away. Mom and the rest of the pack are at least thirty minutes out."

I touched the top of the gate, assessing the power that sealed it and finding nothing that would impede me.

"You can't just walk in there," Kellan growled, settling his hand on my shoulder. "Be reasonable. Wait for backup."

Ignoring him, I reached up, clumsily pulling my hair back at the temples to French braid it. The power sheathing the house was dense around the front door, but it thinned around what I assumed were the dining room or living room windows. Since those were about two meters off the ground, perhaps Ayre had decided they weren't a viable entry point.

Which was stupid of her.

Perhaps she didn't think we'd catch up so quickly. Maybe she thought whatever cloaking spell she'd masked herself with had also extended to her kidnap victims.

Kellan huffed—then shoved my hands away from my own hair to begin braiding it himself. He ran his fingers through to gather a hank of hair in each hand, then tightened each weave almost harshly. His touch was rough, fingernails scraping my skull, his power sparking off my skin.

But somehow it felt…right. Solid, proper. Almost like he was giving me his blessing, no matter how pissed he was about it.

Perhaps he was just trying to distract me. But it had the opposite effect. Sharpening my focus, slowing my heart rate.

I would slice through Ayre Byrne's wards and take back what was mine to protect. Sisu, Neve, and Lile. And the amulet. Then I would leave Ayre to the mercy of the pack and the coven.

Keeping my gaze on the house I was ready to storm like the dragon I was, I tried to ignore the delicious shivers triggered by the brush of Kellan's fingers and the warm kiss of his magic on the exposed skin on my neck as he finished the braid. Unsuccessfully.

I didn't have a hair tie. But having tamed my wild mane with impressive efficiency, Kellan twisted and tucked the tail at the nape of my neck so tightly that I thought I might have trouble getting it undone by myself.

His hands settled on my shoulders, then fell away almost reluctantly.

I stepped forward, laying my hand on the gate latch. The boundary magic nipped at my skin.

"Even five more minutes, Dusk," he murmured. "Brady and Erin are on their way to back us."

I glanced at him, smiling sharply. "I don't need backup, Kellan. But you can come if you like."

He shook his head, utterly frustrated. "So 'reasonable' isn't in your vocabulary?"

"Apparently we have different definitions of the word." I turned my focus back to the gate. "I'm sure it won't be the last time."

He snorted, amused despite being clearly pissed.

And I was being reasonable. I reasonably knew what I was capable of. But if Ayre managed to sacrifice Neve and Lile to whatever entity she had invoked, raising another set of even more powerful celestial wolves, then I was going to be in trouble.

Unleashing my magic, I flipped the latch as I slammed my hip against the gate, tearing through the boundary ward that secured it.

The gate flew across the front yard, embedding itself in the front face of the house. The house wards flickered.

Well, that was…a little more force than was necessary. If Ayre Byrne hadn't felt us at the edge of her boundary wards, she knew we were here now.

It was possible I wasn't playing it as cool as I thought.

Kellan grunted, impressed.

I muttered some random Latin under my breath, stringing together meaningless words. And knowing I wasn't fooling the shapeshifters at my side in the least.

Tucking my power away, I stepped onto the front path. The wards that encased the yard were gone, despite my trying to just open the gate, not take down the entire property boundary. But the house wards remained firmly in place, the feel of their magic confirming that they'd been anchored by blood—but holding none of Sisu's or the twins' magic, as I'd thought.

It made sense for Ayre to have returned to her power base. Especially if she knew the witches and the pack had already looked for her there and had thus cleared the site as a possible hiding place.

"At least tell me what we're hunting," Kellan demanded as I stepped off the path onto the trimmed lawn.

Crossing parallel to the house, I sized up the trajectory to the front window. "Not what," I said, understanding that he didn't mean Ayre. "Who."

"Who, then?" he snarled.

Gitta, still in wolf form, raced past us to the front stairs, nose to the ground. Then she looked at us with glowing green eyes, growling viciously.

Kellan nodded to her as if he understood her. Perhaps they were telepathically linked? That wasn't a typical trait for shapeshifters, but I already knew that the Conalls were different. Though Gitta's intent was clear to me as well, confirming that there were wards on the house. So perhaps I was reading too much into Kellan's gesture.

I focused on a response to his question, letting the last pieces, the last guesswork, fit together in my mind. "It could be the avatar or construct of one of many beings. Possibly a creature classified as a goddess of death by multiple cultures. In Dublin, in Ireland, it will most likely refer to itself as the Morrigan if it manages to fully manifest. Claiming those local beliefs for itself, even if the Irish no longer worship such deities, might help increase its power base. It takes on the myth to wield the power."

"But it's not the Morrigan. Not a real…goddess?"

"No. It's simply…an aspect of a once-powerful Adept trying to manifest in a world in which magic is dying. Or changing, if you prefer. Those who were once revered or worshiped as gods and goddesses don't walk easily on this earth anymore."

"Tell me how to kill it."

"You can't," I whispered.

Though I could. With the bone knife sheathed at my thigh.

I backed up a couple of steps, gathering my magic around me tighter and tighter. Kellan paced back with me, looking from me to the house, then back to me.

Then he grinned, laughing huskily. "What kind of witch are you, Dusk Godfrey?"

I shrugged. "I was raised a little differently."

Magic flowed and shifted around Kellan, growing, building in intensity. He tugged off his sweater, then the T-shirt underneath, flinging both into the yard. He kicked off his shoes, reaching for the buttons of his jeans.

I didn't pause to admire his...admittedly impressive physique. I didn't wait to see the beast that I knew was about to tear through his skin. I took three large, loping strides to build up speed. Then I flipped forward onto my hands and vaulted feet first through the front window.

The blood magic fueling the house wards came up against my dragon magic. It shattered as easily as the glass.

I landed on a sofa, tumbling forward awkwardly and slamming my knees down on the coffee table. The table collapsed under me, sending shards of dark wood in all directions.

Too bad. Even at a quick glance, I was fairly certain it had been an antique.

The room was otherwise empty. Of people. It was chock-full of furniture and knickknacks. Or what might have been called knickknacks if every decorative item hadn't held so much residual magic.

Ayre Byrne was a collector too. And she liked to put all her power on display.

Good to know.

Glass tinkling around me, I straightened as Gitta in wolf form flew through the broken window, vaulted prettily off the back of the sofa, and then landed next to me, completely avoiding the shattered glass and furniture.

A hulking monster that actually gave me pause came through the window next. In his beast form, Kellan was so large he had no need to jump in order to climb through the window, and he crushed the back of the antique sofa with a single massive clawed foot. He was easily two and a half meters tall. If his ears hadn't been flat back, they would have brushed the high ceiling.

The wide shoulders and glowing golden-green eyes were the only aspects of him that were immediately recognizable, other than the tenor of his magic.

He was perfectly proportioned. Nothing like the sketches I'd seen and the written accounts I'd studied. Most shapeshifters worked a lifetime to refine what they called their warrior forms, just to align their jaws. And some of them still couldn't properly talk even when they did. Covered in dark-gray fur, Kellan was so densely muscled that he looked as if he were wearing armor. His long nose fluttered and flared as he took in the room, smelling all the bits of residual magic. His canine teeth were easily longer than my fingers. He retracted and released his wickedly sharp claws as if flexing. Or perhaps warming up.

He tore the collapsed sofa in two with his feet, then casually stepped free of the mess and started for the wide doorway that appeared to lead to the front hall.

A spell triggered to his immediate right, set off by the magic that radiated from him like the sun at the height of the day. A crane-necked lamp tucked into the corner twisted, then latched onto his forearm, trying to hold him in place.

He tore it free, then proceeded to crush it into a misshapen ball of twisted metal and wires, completely snuffing out the malignant spell that had automated it.

Kellan Conall was no more a regular shapeshifter than I was a witch. Even beyond his unusual sight and sense for magic, he was bigger, stronger, and faster than any other werewolf I'd ever read about—matching my speed even as Gitta, in wolf form, had fallen behind.

I should have let him go through the window first and kept up my own pretense a bit better.

He stepped into the front hall, then looked back at Gitta and me. "Basement. I'll take point." His Irish accent was more pronounced in his beast form, but the words were perfectly articulate.

"After you," I said, having no problem with him clearing the way. "But the death goddess is mine."

A terrible, nightmare-inducing grin split Kellan's beast face practically in two. His dark-throated chuckle filled the room, shivering up my spine.

For the first time in my life, the instinct to run tried to seize hold of me. I brushed it away, though that did nothing to diminish the press of his power.

"Fine," he said, still grinning viciously. "But the witch is mine."

Grinning back at him, I simply rucked up my all-but-shredded sweater and unsheathed the bone blade, stalking forward.

Gitta took up the rear behind us.

Kellan crushed five more spells along the short route along the hall, then down the stairs. The basement was completely below ground. If the spells had been set for us intentionally, they weren't terribly effective. But my impression was that they were simply items Ayre Byrne had spent decades collecting. Items that really should have been tucked safely away in the archive. Items I was fairly certain she'd purchased or traded from Doran.

At the very base of the carpeted stairs, a sixth spell hit the monster that normally resided under Kellan's skin, trying to smother him. Very effectively. But once he stopped struggling and collapsed to his knees—thus bringing the spell restricting his breathing within reach—I was able to cut it away with three quick flicks of the bone blade.

Gasping for breath and still clutching his corded neck with one massively clawed hand, Kellan glowered at me.

That chastising glower of his was even more effective in his beast form—given the shiver of suppressed fear that ran up my spine when I tried and failed to hold his soul-blistering gaze.

That gaze fell to the blade in my hand, and Kellan curled his lip in a silent snarl.

I was completely aware that the bone blade was a dangerous weapon, even when wielded by me. In fact, when I'd sliced through the spell holding Kellan, it had felt for just a moment as though something beyond instinct might have been guiding my hand…

I would need to tie the blade to me, tightly. And to practice wielding it. I'd already added both items to my to-do list, but it would be better to bump them up to the top.

Just as soon as I cleaned up this current mess.

The door at the end of the short hall clicked open invitingly, drawing our attention.

Apparently, Ayre had decided to lure us into her basement lair. Either that or she was out of preset defensive spells.

Kellan regained his footing.

Gitta surged forward, practically launching herself at the door. Kellan caught her by the scruff of her neck, holding her back. She fought, snarling and growling, clawing at him.

Given that it was her children we were seeking, I was actually surprised that Gitta had managed to hold herself in check for so long. I felt as though there was a beast within me as well, ready to rip and rend.

"Peace," Kellan murmured, presumably trying to be gentle. But in his warrior form, everything that came out of his mouth somehow felt like a promise of death and destruction. Still, the dark promise apparently worked for Gitta because she quieted. Kellan released her.

She had scored the skin of his torso. And as it healed over, I caught sight of swirls of darker gray hair across his chest, looking like...

Looking like...some sort of runes.

I blinked, trying to bring the symbols into better focus. The hall was well lit, but I couldn't quite—

Kellan turned away.

Maybe his very different, exceedingly potent shapeshifter power was somehow magically shaped or boosted, not genetic. That made much more sense than him being some sort of shifter breed I'd never read about.

Kellan strode up the short hall and through the open doorway. His hulking form was instantly swallowed by a veil of darkness that lay beyond it. Gitta stayed tight at his heels.

Both of them had either forgotten that I was with them, or didn't particularly care. We had made our deal though, and I expected Kellan to honor it.

Sisu and whatever entity Ayre Byrne had awoken were mine to collect.

Closing my eyes to avoid any unknown effects of the unnatural darkness, I stepped after Kellan and Gitta, crossing easily through what felt like a wall of power. It shut tightly behind me.

So Ayre Byrne had been waiting for us.

A quiet chant rising from multiple locations filtered through to me. I opened my eyes to take in the candlelit room around us. The space appeared larger than the footprint of the house, judging it against the view of the exterior perimeter from outside. And it was stuffed absolutely full of earth-scented witch magic.

Kellan was directly in front of me. His massive feet, claws on display, were set at the edge of what appeared to be a wide circle of flat pale stones set into a tight-packed dirt floor.

Stone tiles, maybe? Made out of some sort of white or light-gray granite? It was difficult to distinguish colors under the golden wash of the candlelight.

The tiles, the circle, thrummed with energy.

I tucked up behind Kellan as I listened to that power rise and fall, noting that it followed the rhythm of the quiet chant—a song constructed from pure notes sung from multiple throats, but with no words.

Still, I knew magic when I heard it.

I placed my feet as Kellan had placed his, though his stance was too wide to be comfortable for long. Hiding behind him, just for a moment. Just in case the witch's senses weren't fine-tuned enough to pick me up when faced with an Adept who radiated as much energy as Kellan did in his warrior form. I couldn't see past him, but that seemed a fair trade-off for the moment.

Gitta paced back and forth at the edge of the circle, but didn't venture more than a meter to either side.

Presumably, the witch thought the sealed door behind us was enough to keep us within her reach, because she'd made no attempt to bind us as we entered.

"We've come for our children, witch," Kellan snarled. "If you force me to tear through your circle, I'll take your head in compensation."

He had torn through all the other magic he'd encountered without stopping to chat about it. So something about the circle was giving him pause.

I peeked around his broad shoulders, taking in the rest of the room at a glance.

Seven Adepts were laid out like spokes on a wheel just inside the large stone-tiled circle—including River and Ridge Byrne, four witches I didn't know, and one werewolf, Odane. They were all singing in low, sweet tones.

A benediction, perhaps?

A power base of seven with which to anchor the invocation Ayre was getting ready to attempt.

A large wooden table occupied the center of the room, set within a secondary stone-tiled circle. Something dark was splattered across those white stones—blood judging by its look, but I couldn't sense or smell it through the outer circle.

Neve and Lile Conall were huddled together on the table, holding hands. Their gazes were locked on the red-haired witch standing before them, not on their uncle or mother.

Cloaked in black over a lightweight black dress that fell to her lower calves and left her feet bare, that witch stood with her head flung back, silently singing the same sweet wordless tune as those she'd trapped in the outer circle. Or at least I couldn't distinguish her voice among the others.

Ayre Byrne.

Her hands dripped with the blood that had presumably been splattered across the circle surrounding the table. With no other source for that blood immediately apparent, it was an easy guess that it was her own.

I saw no sign of Sisu. I ignored a spike of fear at his absence, knowing that if it was his blood dripping from Ayre Byrne's fingers, I would have felt at least a hint of his power through any magical ward. The raw power of a dragon wasn't easily contained, and especially not the blood of a child of a demigod.

Ayre was wearing a familiar golden amulet, set with a golden-yellow topaz, speckled with red topaz, and slung on a thick gold chain. It pulsed with power in time with the chant, in time with the energy that anchored the outer tiled circle.

Ayre hadn't heard Kellan speak. She hadn't even noticed our entry.

So…was someone else in control? Had someone else lured us through the door, then sealed it behind us?

Someone acting through the witch?

Or someone controlling the witch?

A shadowed figure manifested slightly behind Ayre and to her right. It laid a pale hand on the red-haired witch's shoulder, leaning in as if to whisper to her.

The fingers of that hand were long, slim, and tipped in darkness. The face was bone white, the lips a deep blood red. Eyes glistening with barely contained power flicked to Kellan.

He shuddered under that gaze.

The figure solidified. Those long fingers reached around Ayre Byrne's neck to caress the thick-linked gold chain of the amulet.

The witch didn't have a proper hold on the entity she was trying to manifest. Not at all.

When Ayre Byrne's eyes flew open, they were blown out black, edge to edge. With a flick of her fingers, she pushed the power she'd gathered from the outer circle toward Neve and Lile.

The twins stiffened—then dissolved into a lazy fit of giggles. Ayre was trying to cheat, trying to coerce their compliance.

Neve and Lile had to accept the entity steeped in darkness and currently standing at the witch's shoulder. They had to believe in it in order to willingly submit themselves. To hand themselves over to be transformed.

"There, there," Ayre crooned, still unaware of our presence. "Now, that feels good, doesn't it? You know what else feels good? Letting your magic loose."

I could tear through the outer circle and have my blade at the witch's throat in three long strides. But I had no idea what doing so might do to the seven people currently holding that circle. Fueling it.

Which was why Kellan was also hesitating.

Neve and Lile giggled again, quietly chanting between peals of laughter. "Be the wolf, the wolf, the wolf. Let the wolf loose."

The twins were too young to transform, weren't they? Their magic too immature?

"No!" Sisu's sharp cry came from near the twins. From under the table? I couldn't see him. "Don't give in!"

"Hush!" Ayre snarled, kicking the leg of the table—and momentarily disturbing the containment ward placed around its base. As I focused on it, I could see that ward anchored in the dirt floor with sporadically placed small round stones.

Ayre's kick and the accompanying push of power reverberated through the concealment spell on the table, momentarily revealing the small white-blond figure beneath it.

Thank the gods.

The magic driven by the witch's kick shoved my brother back, driving him to the far side of the table.

Lile cried out, "Stop it, you nasty witch!"

Then she and Neve dissolved into a fit of giggles again. Sisu laughed as well.

And my fear of seeing him trapped, contained, eased with that sound. The thing—my own beast?—that had been wild and flailing in my chest since I'd first heard the chirp of Uncle Beckett's watch over Kellan's phone settled into a low simmer of anger.

Now that the concealment spell had been revealed, I could see through it clearly. I had no idea what Ayre's plans for Sisu were, or why she'd placed him under the makeshift altar. But I knew he wouldn't be there for long.

"Enough!" Kellan roared. His voice reverberated with power around the room.

Ayre's mouth dropped open, reacting as if she'd just seen him. And Gitta.

The kids stopped laughing.

The chanting paused. But just for one heavy beat.

Snarling, Ayre twisted toward the figure still hovering at her right shoulder. She grabbed the amulet hanging around her own neck and barked a single word of power.

The partially manifested figure reeled back as if punched. It faded, then struggled to reform, to solidify.

I'd been right about the power dynamic. The construct of the death goddess was trying to break Ayre's hold, working without her knowledge. It had opened the door to invite us into the basement. And it had somehow cloaked us from Ayre's senses.

"Kellan Conall." Ayre Byrne turned with a flourish of her cloak to greet the shapeshifters in a singsong voice. "Gitta Conall. Perfect timing. I will add your power to the circle as I call forth our goddess and her divine companions. What a blessing for your family to have been so chosen."

Neve and Lile spun around to see their uncle and mother, then dissolved into more giggles—a stark contrast to the terror etched across their faces.

That contrast did all sorts of terrible things to my insides. And for the briefest of moments, I almost lost hold of myself. I almost forgot that collecting as much information as possible before acting was always the best course, the best choice.

Sisu, still sitting, started systematically kicking the leg of the table farthest from Ayre.

She hissed, displeased, then flicked her fingers toward the twins a second time. They stiffened and then fell, convulsing on the table. In pain this time.

Kellan snarled, reaching up with clawed hands to tear through the outer circle. But the shadowy figure backing Ayre thrust itself forward, practically wrapping its dark energy around the witch.

A pulse of power tore through Ayre, hitting the outer circle. In response, energy undulated through the stones. The chant picked up speed and intensity, the seven Adepts no longer sounding quite as peaceful.

Ayre stumbled as if the wind had been knocked out of her. She had just expended a whack of magic. And not willingly.

The edges of the figure solidified further. Tall and slender, it was wearing a hooded cloak.

The chanting increased. Then the energy holding the outer circle reached out and tried to draw Kellan and Gitta within it.

Kellan snarled, twisting away.

Gitta yipped, then began sliding toward the circle's stone-tiled edge.

The twins were mewling in pain, struggling.

Ayre's magic was forcing them to change into their wolf forms—a transformation that neither of them were anywhere near able to achieve on their own.

I stepped around the beast that was Kellan, keeping my gaze on Sisu as I revealed myself. I paused at the edge of the circle between the spokes created by River's and Ridge's supine forms, bone blade in hand.

Ayre Byrne reacted to my presence with a strangled protest of unarticulated rage, raising her hands toward the outer circle and pumping more power into it. The chant grew even louder, voices straining now. The notes no longer sweet.

The shadowed figure grew more and more solid.

Gitta snapped at the power trying to draw her into the circle, severing its hold. Kellan shook his massive head and twisted his shoulders to do the same.

Sisu spun, taking me in with a wide grin. Then he waved. "Hey, Dusk! We've been waiting for you."

"I'm sorry it took me so long," I said calmly. Then I kicked the stone tile set in the dirt before me with a wallop of dragon-fueled power.

Three sharp kicks to three stone tiles, launching each across the circle. Directly at Ayre.

The witch snapped up her hands, shielding herself just a moment before the stone tiles would have caved her head in. But doing so cost her another whack of power.

Neve, Lile, and Sisu remained tucked safely behind the secondary circle, but the Adepts trapped within the outer circle fell silent.

It was possible that I had just hurt the adults—badly—by disturbing the outer circle. But I didn't doubt that each one of them would sacrifice themselves for the kids if that was what it came down to. That was most likely what had gotten them trapped, forced to fuel Ayre's invocation, in the first place.

I surged through the opening I'd created in the outer circle, feeling that magical boundary trying to compensate and close behind me as I jumped over River's and Ridge's outstretched arms. Gitta and Kellan followed me, though Kellan's shoulders snagged on the edge of the opening, slowing him.

With a masterful sleight of hand that would have made his demigod father proud, Sisu pulled a short steel sword out of his backpack. The sword I had expressly forbidden him from bringing to the sleepover. It was stupid of Ayre to let him keep the backpack—but she thought he was just a five-year-old witch.

Sisu started slashing the blade over and over again, bringing it down next to the far leg of the table. Slowly but surely, he was cutting through the magic that he'd already weakened with his kicks.

The witches and the werewolf who made up the spokes of Ayre's main spell suddenly bucked in pain, then started screaming.

I glanced from Sisu to Ayre. The entity stood behind the black witch with two hands on her shoulders now. Ayre was gathering power from the circle, channeling it through the death goddess incarnate, then amassing it in her hands.

She released all the raw power she'd siphoned from the outer circle and the Adepts within it with a forward thrust of her hands.

It slammed into me first, forcing me back a step.

Then it hit Gitta and Kellan, throwing each of them to the edge of the outer circle, where that circle's power once more tried to pin them in place.

I stumbled again as the same spell tried to grab me, tried to leech my power from me. Standing within the circle, I'd made myself an easier target.

I acknowledged the pain with a snarl. Then I flung out my arms and gave the spell a better taste of my magic.

It flooded the room, searing the edges of the outer and inner circle alike. Under the onslaught of my power, those boundaries dissolved, freeing Kellan, Gitta, and the other adults.

Kellan made it to his knees, clawing at himself as if tearing through the spell that Ayre had first hit him with. Gitta and the other adults stayed down, though. Hopefully only unconscious, not dead, but I didn't have the time to check to see if they were breathing.

Sword still in hand, Sisu slashed through the residual of the containment spell trapping him under the table. He crawled out, glancing from me to Neve and Lile, who were now caught in the middle of the transformation from human to wolf. The twins were mewling in pain, limbs disjointed, faces distorted. They were too young, their magic too immature…

Sisu climbed up on the table, placing himself on the corner between the twins and the witch.

Ayre was gathering another mass of power. This time, I could feel her pulling energy from the entity that was practically draped over her shoulders now. She glanced from me to Sisu.

And in that moment of indecisiveness, I brought the bone blade into play. Or perhaps I just let it loose, letting it guide my hand.

Ayre unleashed the spell she'd taken from the death goddess incarnate on me. It was even less effective the second time, but it came with more pain. I cut it away, feeling Kellan slowly gaining his footing, stepping back into the fight behind me.

Lunging the final steps between myself and the witch, I slashed forward with the bone blade.

Ayre danced back, actually laughing.

The entity's form thinned, then reformed just a few steps away, its black glittering eyes glued to the witch who held it captive.

"Missed," Ayre said mockingly.

"Not at all," I said.

Eyes widening, the black witch looked down to the amulet that had fallen to the dirt floor between us.

Ayre screamed—in anger, not fear—as she lunged forward to grab it.

The entity-that-yearned-to-be-a-death-goddess got there first, plucking up the amulet and laughing darkly.

The magic-laden sound of that laughter skittered through the room, making the hair stand up on the back of my neck.

Ayre got hit harder, actually convulsing. Then, blackened eyes widening, she dropped her mouth open in a silent scream of utter terror. As if maybe the binding she'd forced on the entity—the bond I'd just severed with a flick of my blade—was generating some sort of torturous feedback.

Kellan lunged past me, reaching for the black witch.

Despite her terror, or maybe because of it, Ayre hit him with something malicious. An utterly noxious spell.

Kellan stumbled under the assault but barely slowed down. He grabbed either side of Ayre's head as even more of her wild, tainted power pounded him.

The would-be death goddess stumbled back and looked around—its gaze finding, then fixing on me.

Then it fled. For the door. With the amulet.

Even as I spun to go after the entity, I saw a tiny wolf stumble to her feet on the table from the corner of my eye. She was shaking. But not in fear. Standing over her sister, she threw her head back and howled in triumph and warning.

Darting around the other Adepts still struggling to gain their feet, I blew through the door, running for the stairs beyond. Sisu leaped off the table, chasing after me.

I heard the snap of Ayre Byrne's neck from halfway up the stairs. But I couldn't pause to acknowledge it as I chased the construct of a goddess of death through the house and out into night-shrouded Dublin.

A construct I had released. To stop Ayre Byrne.

Now I had to quell the would-be death goddess before it wreaked any further havoc. So I needed to work quickly—and without any witnesses.

CHAPTER TEN

A TRIO OF WEREWOLVES, INCLUDING AISLING CONALL in human form, raced by Sisu and me, sprinting into the house as we exited. Cars were pulling up to the house and disgorging witches, including Mesa Byrne.

Sisu and I ran by them all, cutting through the obfuscation and distraction spells they were hastily casting. Not one of them reacted to the partially actualized goddess of death streaking through their momentarily unified ranks. The shadowed entity's magic must have been hiding it from unattuned senses, though I saw Ravine shudder as it slipped past her on the sidewalk.

I was forced to slow so I didn't barrel into any of the newcomers, but I didn't lose sight of the would-be death goddess for a single second.

"Dusk!" Ravine shouted.

I glanced back as I passed the metal mage. "Basement!" I kept running.

"Sisu!" Ravine cried in disbelief behind me, then instantly firmed her tone. "You stay here with us!"

I caught Sisu's grin and the wave he gave the confused witch as he skirted past her, climbed over her tiny car where she'd parked it on the sidewalk, and continued after me. His steel sword was still firmly in hand.

The entity veered right, then right again, heading along the same course we'd followed to find it, away from the docks and Dublin Port. I tried to close the distance as I followed, even as my mind feverishly worked through all my options. The bone blade in my hand was warm. Just a degree or two higher than my body temperature, but enough to notice. It was impossible to ignore its…eagerness. Its delight in the hunt.

As I chased it, the entity manifested more strongly, pulling power into itself and solidifying further. A long black cape was streaming behind it now as it fled.

Or as it deliberately led Sisu and me away from the others?

Yeah, that possibility was part of my ongoing assessment of the situation. My brother and I would make epically powerful celestial beings if our magic could be utilized in such a way. And if the entity understood that we were dragons, not witches. Thankfully, I was fairly certain that neither supposition was true.

I was equally certain that I wasn't dealing with the manifestation of an actual death goddess. Even a hint of that sort of event would have been picked up by Chi Wen the far seer ahead of time. Nothing magical on that epic a scale could hide from that guardian dragon's gaze. And even if it somehow did, Suanmi, the guardian of Western Europe, would have immediately intervened.

No. This was something else, something lesser. And my mess to clean up.

Well, it was the Byrne coven's mess, ultimately. But I would take responsibility for containing the entity.

The would-be death goddess glanced back as it veered onto another street. I caught a glimpse of its glittering eyes, mostly blackened but with a sharp-edged silver ring around each wide iris. Those eyes were too large for its thin, pale face, but it was otherwise manifesting a human form from the waist up.

It propelled itself upon a shadowed cloud of power that continued to thicken as it fled down the center of the street, spreading out toward the sidewalks. It was deep into the early-morning hours now, and only a few cars traversed the streets with us. Most of the drivers were thankfully oblivious to our passage. But when we turned right for the third time, I saw two drivers slam on their brakes as the entity passed, pressing their hands to chest or mouth in horror.

The entity was touching them somehow, even through steel and glass. Telepathically? Visually?

Besides the early-morning travelers, there were hundreds of people sleeping peacefully all around us. And the dark energy undulating, swelling, around the would-be goddess racing through the city was curling over the sidewalks now.

If its energy kept expanding, the entity would be able to reach tendrils of its power into homes and apartments, affecting the occupants as it had the drivers we'd just passed.

"We're going to herd it," I said to Sisu, making a snap decision based on the path the entity appeared to be taking. I didn't bother to shout. My brother was only a few steps behind me. "Toward the water. Next left."

Grinning, Sisu broke off, shifting to the right until he was running along the sidewalk.

The shadowed cloud of power that propelled the would-be goddess began condensing at the edges. Forms appeared within, remaining even after the entity had passed.

Shades. Of the dead.

Those shades didn't move, didn't react to my passing. They were only echoes of the dead, not true creatures. But they were substantial enough that it might not take magical senses to see them. Or feel them.

Any mundanes in the area might already be able to see or sense the power the entity had called forth. The shades were appearing along the sidewalks, hovering above stoops, clustered at the street corners.

The witches were going to need to call in a necromancer. Or several.

I loosened my hold on my magic, letting it all go. For a brief moment, that energy crackled around me. The sensation was odd enough that I almost dropped my focus from the entity fleeing before me. Then my power rushed forward, flooding the street.

Apparently, I had just torn through Jiaotu's glamour.

I'd have to worry about that later.

Sisu, already radiating power like a small, fierce star to my own senses, copied me. His golden glow instantly pushed back the shades attempting to form on his side of the street.

The entity shied left, away from the energy Sisu radiated while I pushed it from behind with the flood of my power.

Then it veered left at the next street. Exactly as I'd wanted.

I picked up speed. I'd been holding back from the worry of leaving Sisu too far behind. But the would-be death goddess was generating too much power even without its celestial creatures. I had to end this chase through the city quickly.

The entity glanced back at me. I caught a glimpse of those silver-ringed black eyes again, now topped with dark eyebrows and even darker hair.

The would-be death goddess flicked long, black-tipped fingers toward me. A section of the miasma of power it propelled itself within broke off, staying in place.

I barreled forward even as shades formed within the dark cloud of power the entity had left behind.

An attack of some sort. Or a trap.

I had the briefest moment to note that the shades were wearing clothing of different eras, then realized that I could no longer see my actual surroundings.

I'd been swallowed within the dark cloud.

I'd also lost sight of Sisu and the would-be goddess.

The shades rushed me, actually grabbing hold and trying to stop me, to pin me in place.

The bone blade wasn't interested in having its hunt cut short, though. I was spinning and slicing through the substantial shades before I'd even thought to execute the first strike. They didn't disperse or dissipate, but I damaged them enough that they lost hold of me. Perhaps because I'd severed their connection to the entity?

The darkened city street once again opened up around me. Sisu, ahead of me now, had herded the entity to the left again. As I tried to close the distance, another chunk of the entity's power broke off and attacked my brother. It formed into two massive creatures—some sort of cross between a bulldog and a lion. Perhaps manifestations of former celestial creatures?

Either way, the beast shades lunged for Sisu. I couldn't stop myself from shouting a fear-laced warning, but he didn't even falter.

My brother leaped up onto the cars parked at the side of the road and kept running. The nearest of the beast shades tried to scramble after him, but Sisu's higher-ground advantage let him easily bring his sword down across the back of its neck, disabling it. He didn't even slow down.

I attacked the second beast shade as it tried to swipe my brother's feet out from under him. It was weighty and substantial in a way that should have been impossible when dealing with a shade—normally a mere shadow of a formerly living creature.

But we were dealing with an entity that believed itself to be a goddess of death. And I had no idea what that meant in terms of the power it could wield.

Shadowed claws caught in my sweater, and the shade's teeth actually clamped down on my forearm. The bone blade vibrated with what felt like glee as I stabbed it in the eye to free myself. I pulled back, readying another strike—and acutely aware that the blade would have pulled me off my feet to make that last attack if I hadn't already known how to move, how to wield a weapon.

But since I was the one wielding the blade, not the other way around, I remained in control.

I would just keep telling myself that until it was wholly true. And I would remind myself that it was possible that wielding the blade—forcing it to do as I willed—was actually the only way to tie its power to me. To fully claim it for myself alone.

I chopped off the head of the second beast shade, then moved to the shade that Sisu had disabled. It appeared to be trying to knit its essence back together, struggling to close the wound at its neck. That was...surprising. I had no idea how that was even possible after the would-be death goddess had severed the shade from the miasma of power that propelled it. Unfortunately, I didn't have time to ponder that mystery.

Quickly finishing off the second beast shade, I ran, drawing on all my speed as I made another left turn. Just ahead of me, Sisu dashed across a wide road. Traffic was sparse, but still amounted to more cars and people than

I would have expected to be out in the deep darkness before dawn.

I steadily closed the space between me and my brother. I could smell saltwater now, even over vehicle exhaust. Sisu was almost within reach of the would-be death goddess, driving it straight ahead.

More brakes squealed. The sounds of car doors slamming and people shouting followed in our wake, but no one appeared to notice us. The drivers were arguing with each other.

The dark miasma of power around the would-be death goddess wasn't as substantial now, as though its decision to attack Sisu and me directly had used too much of what it had managed to collect through Ayre, the first celestial creatures, and the interrupted invocation. But tendrils of that dark-tinted energy were still streaking out from it as it fled, still influencing the drivers.

"Sisu!" I cried, pointing toward the tendrils nearest him.

"I see!" He brought his steel sword down, severing their magic.

And yes, I'd finally figured out that my brother's weapon was much more than it appeared to be. I should have known that Jiaotu wouldn't give his son a simple steel blade.

Continuing to drive the would-be goddess toward the water, we were suddenly cutting through warehouses. The fact that the entity was allowing us to direct it so relatively easily made me wonder what it could assess of the world in which it had been set loose. Could it scent or smell the ocean? Without its celestial creatures, it wasn't gathering power as quickly as it was shedding it, forced to flee and to defend itself.

Of course, being chased by two dragons, even as young as we were, might just have been that distracting.

Side by side now, Sisu and I chased the entity through the warehouses, through the port gates, past outbuildings, and down to the water's edge.

The would-be death goddess dashed onto a wide wharf, wood and metal jutting across the water's edge and over the sea.

Three meters out, it shrieked, realizing that we'd corralled it over water. Deep water.

The entity whirled around, spinning to a stop. Its hood fell back, revealing a pale face with blood-red lips and blackened eyes. Power condensed tightly around it until it stood on two legs, two feet. Its bare toes were tipped with black, just like its fingers.

She. Not it. The entity's still-skeletal form was now distinctly female. As was the case with so many of those among the decreed divinities who claimed power over death.

Her cloak still undulated around her, rife with dark energy. But I had guessed correctly. The seawater on either side of the commercial wharf restricted her reach, its salt content disrupting her power in the same way a barrier of salt would have. Preventing her from gathering the energy she needed to fight us.

Sisu and I slowed, then stood side by side, blocking the way back to the shore. The wharf stretched ahead, far out over the deep water. A number of ships were docked farther down. The would-be goddess might still try to run, if she knew how to pilot a boat. If being completely surrounded by water didn't terrify her.

She shifted back a few steps, her gait smooth despite having manifested legs and feet only moments before. The cloak settled around her as she cinched her power tighter and tighter. She took Sisu in with a flick of her silver-edged black eyes. Then she dismissed him to stare at me for a long moment.

It was those silvered eyes that were truly giving me pause. A manifestation of her true self? I'd never seen an Adept with silver-tinted magic. But I'd read about it—of course and always—and it firmly placed her in the category of divine creatures, even if I didn't know her exact place in that order.

The bone blade urged me to dart forward, to attack before the entity got its bearings.

But I was an archivist. I didn't destroy what could be preserved.

So we stared at each other.

"Call me Morrigan." Her voice was a harsh rasp, pushing air she didn't actually need to breathe through vocal cords she hadn't used in centuries. I couldn't distinguish an accent, but was more surprised that she spoke English at all.

Adaptable. That could be a good thing, meaning she was capable of rational thought, of a discussion. Of understanding consequences.

"You will kneel before me," she added.

Alternatively, she might simply be an automated avatar, destined to repeat a set series of manipulations and attempts to...what? Conquer? Rule a world in which her magic no longer thrived?

"No," I said. "You're not the sisters. Not the Morrigan herself, and naming you such would give you too much power."

The self-proclaimed goddess hissed indignantly, her magic churning around her viciously enough that it lapped against the water. She withdrew as if pained, taking a few more steps back. She looked around for an exit. Or a weapon, perhaps. Her movements felt a little unhinged.

I tightened my grip on the bone blade, bringing it forward. Sisu brought his sword up, holding it near his right shoulder in both hands with the blade pointed upward. Ready to follow me.

The entity stilled as if catching herself. Her attention was pinned to the bone blade ready in my hand. Then she began gathering her power again.

Except she was standing over saltwater, and it didn't hold the type of power she wielded. She needed the echoes of death, if not outright death itself, to fuel her. Numerous workers had likely died on these docks over the centuries, but not nearly enough, nor was there earth here to bind them. So she needed her celestial creatures. To siphon magic from, and to guard her.

"You're alone," I said gently. "Alone in what must be a confusing world."

"I have taken what I needed from the witch," she snapped.

Enough power was pooling around her feet to obscure them again. She was either going to use another chunk of what little remained of her reserves to try to kill me, or at least knock me out. Or she was going to attempt to dart across the water. If she could do so, I couldn't follow her. I could probably take whatever spell she might throw, though. Presumably a death curse of some sort.

But the silver rings around her otherwise blackened eyes worried me. The hint at some connection to the divine. Even without her celestials, even without the power of the dead to draw from, there was a chance she could hurt Sisu.

"The witch dared," the would-be goddess snarled. "To try to use me, tame me. Rule over me."

She was wearing the amulet now, the chain restored where I'd severed it. It swung forward through the opening of her cloak as she brought both hands together before her, fingertips pressed into an open pyramid. The energy she'd gathered crackled between her palms.

"I wouldn't," I said quietly. "The witches and pack wolves are on their way." I tilted my head thoughtfully, momentarily bluffing as if I could sense them. Though I had no doubt that the others were in the process of cleaning up while they followed the clear trail the would-be goddess had left in her wake. "And when they get here, they will destroy you."

She curled her blood-red lips, revealing teeth that hadn't been so blackened a moment before. She was pulling power solely from herself now, and she couldn't fully manifest while doing so. She couldn't hold her preferred form and fight me, fight us.

She unleashed her spell.

Sisu shouted.

I was suddenly holding Infinity in my left hand, the bone blade still in my right. The spell—a darkly malignant promise of death—sped toward me. And without truly thinking about it, I allowed Infinity to fall open in my hand, then flipped it forward directly in the path of the death curse.

Infinity absorbed the malignant power, swallowing it eagerly.

The would-be goddess fell to her knees, barely catching herself on one hand to avoid toppling over.

I snapped Infinity shut, tucking it against my chest. My archive shuddered. Then its magic…stretched as if reaching through dimensions I couldn't even feel. That disconcerting otherworldliness quickly snapped back, fading until only Infinity's soft humming power remained.

Sisu threw his head back and laughed with utter glee. The warm sound rolled across the water, splashed against the steel hulls of the ships, and echoed back.

The would-be death goddess's chest was heaving, though I wasn't sure whether she was actually winded like someone who needed oxygen to survive might have been. It was more like she was spell spent. Deprived of the magic she needed to manifest, and struggling to maintain her form.

I pressed Infinity tighter against my chest for a moment, belated fear streaking through me. Had I called my archive forward? To take a death curse that might possibly destroy it? Or had Infinity somehow chosen to…take the spell itself?

And in that case, was the would-be goddess more powerful than I'd thought?

Had my archive decided that the curse would have seriously harmed or even killed me? And then…chosen to sacrifice itself?

I felt a little faint. At the thought of any of those options.

So I stepped forward and kneeled across from the death goddess. I placed Infinity before me, the bone blade to the side—deadly end still eagerly pointed toward our foe. According to the blade, not me.

Sisu stood at my side with his sword still at the ready.

The entity's attention flicked to him, and an almost-amused smile curled her blood-red lips. She looked back at me, then allowed her attention to fall to Infinity.

"Dragon," the death goddess wheezed, "I'd mistaken you for a lowly witch." Her form had solidified enough that she looked almost human. The silver ringing her eyes was only a glint now, as if it had fueled the spell she'd flung at me.

The spell Infinity had swallowed.

That was going to have ramifications. And maybe it already had. Because I had the distinct impression that my personal archive had actually allowed the spell to pass through it into another dimension.

A personal archive opening into other dimensions? Or even a dimensional pocket such as the nexus? That was unprecedented as far as I knew. Especially not without the archivist first establishing an anchor point in that dimension.

I wrenched my thoughts back to the present, caressing Infinity's front cover under the so-called goddess's steady gaze. "Archivist," I corrected.

"Oh, yes?" Her amused smile stretched to reveal teeth that were back to being mostly white. "I understand."

If the entity had drawn from Ayre Byrne's knowledge—as was seemingly the case with her knowing English—then it made sense that she had originally identified Sisu and me as witches. But having figured out that we weren't—and knowing that the black witch hadn't known that—she was now treating that as a secret she could manipulate.

She wasn't wrong.

Magic tickled my senses at the very edge of my range, power amassing. The witches and the shapeshifters were on their way.

"We don't have much time," I said, keeping my gaze on the would-be death goddess.

"Make your bargain then, archivist."

I was in over my head. I'd been mostly in control of the situation for most of the evening. Scared for Sisu, but assured that I'd get to him, Neve, and Lile in time. Sure that I was capable of cleaning up Ayre Byrne's mess.

Now Ayre was most likely dead, and I was chatting with an entity who just might have been what she claimed. And I was exceedingly aware that I'd only gotten this far because the death goddess had been thrust into a world she didn't yet understand.

Yet.

My gaze fell to the bone blade. This was one of those moments all archivists loathed. The moment of weighing the greater good.

"I value all…magic." I had almost said 'life,' but I wasn't actually certain that the being across from me was alive in the traditional sense.

"It's knowledge you truly desire, archivist."

I smiled, pleased that she was at least willing to listen. "Yes. But you cannot wander where you will."

"You would cage me?" she spat, clutching the amulet around her neck. "Use me?"

I allowed my power to flow out of me again, not realizing that I'd instinctively contained it. "What need do I have of your power?" I whispered. "I doubt it's even compatible with my own."

She tilted her head, then reached out one hand, curling and uncurling her fingers as if she was stroking something. My magic, presumably, though I couldn't see or feel her touch it.

"Yes, my sweet," she purred. "A bargain, then. A vow between an archivist and her…goddess."

I shook my head at her, grinning despite myself. She really wanted that title, which confirmed that she gained power from it.

Sisu pressed against my shoulder, whispering, "They're close."

"Make quicker words, archivist," the would-be goddess snapped.

"A deal," I said, conscious of needing to keep the wording as simple—and as free from potential loopholes—as possible. "A cage, yes. But on my estate—"

"Free to walk the entirety of the property and all buildings, to interact with who I will," she immediately countered.

"A tower with windows in all directions," I said steadily.

"A luxurious suite! With as many servants as needed."

"No. Though the tower is large enough, and furniture can be provided."

"A tiny cage," she murmured distastefully. "With only two children for company."

"Well..." I smiled. "You never know who might drop by for a visit."

An answering smile sharpened all the hard edges of her face. And in that smile, I could see that she would not only try to escape at the first opportunity, but that she would kill me if she could. Or try to corrupt me, at least.

"For life," I added silkily, tendrils of magic stretching between me and the would-be death goddess. Our bargain, but yet to be accepted and anchored.

She lost the smile. "You will provide me with entertainment, food, as requested. Conversation."

"Within reason. And you will answer my questions."

Her grin reappeared, along with a playful but malicious glint in her eyes. "To the best of my knowledge. You will not use my power for your own."

"You will not harm anyone under my protection."

She opened her mouth, to protest I thought. But I cut her off with a raised hand. "Residents and invited guests. If anyone tries to harm Sisu or me, you may strike against them as you will."

Sisu glanced toward the buildings behind us. I could sense what he was feeling as well. Kellan was near. A handful of others were lingering farther back. The witches, likely cleaning up the last of the mess with the drivers using whatever magic they had on hand. Or perhaps the Byrne coven had access to a strong telepath?

"I will walk with you to your abode."

"You will return to the amulet," I said, flipping Infinity open to the back cover. "You will place the amulet in Infinity, and I will walk you home under cover."

"And if I don't agree to your terms?" she snarled. Her sudden anger was vicious and sharp.

It was the idea of being contained in the amulet again that bothered her, I thought.

I didn't blame her in the least.

I laid my hand on the bone blade and just looked at her. I let her see what I would do if she didn't agree—albeit unwillingly. But I would do it as my duty, to protect the city, to protect the world from her.

"For the span of your life," she said, suddenly in control again, her gaze penetrating, "I will reside in your tower. I will not harm anyone under your protection, residents or invited guests." She gleefully snapped her teeth on the last two words as if already anticipating consuming the life force of any uninvited guests. "I will answer your questions...as I will. You will shelter me from the witches who would use me as if I were nothing but an endless power source."

Kellan, still in his massive beast form, leaped onto the wharf behind us, actually causing it to shudder underneath me. Even Sisu stumbled.

The would-be death goddess's magic flared, spreading out before me in a terrifying display of dark power. She emanated pure pain, and a promise of destruction.

Utter terror flashed through me—but the entity was projecting all her will toward Kellan, not me or Sisu, so it didn't grab hold.

It was an impressive manifestation. She was going to completely burn herself out if she wasn't careful.

Kellan roared like a vicious, wild beast. Then he crouched, leaning into the onslaught and clawing his way forward until he was within arm's length of me.

And all I could do was stare at him, unable to speak even just to call him off, to reassure him.

His eyes glowing a brilliant green-gold, Kellan took in the dark vortex of power that was the goddess of death, then me with Infinity, then Sisu. He unhinged his toothy jaw with effort. He howled, "Run!"

Then he snatched Sisu, slung him over his shoulder, turned and ran. Sisu shrieked in protest.

He had just rescued my practically immortal brother. From a situation I had completely under control.

Now that was awfully sweet.

The moment Kellan's feet hit the shore, the death magic trying to quell him snapped back into the entity. She was smaller now, slumped across the wharf, her pure-black glittering gaze on me.

"Well," she whispered with a hint of a smile. "Wasn't that interesting."

Kellan Conall had not only stood against a full-out onslaught from a death goddess incarnate, but he had moved into it just to rescue my brother. That made him not only powerful magically—which I'd already figured out—but mentally.

"We are in agreement," she said.

"Yes, in agreement."

The tendrils of power that had been building between us twined around the wrist of my right hand, then solidified. Anchoring our bargain.

The self-proclaimed death goddess somehow melted back into the amulet that hung around her neck. Not even a wisp of her power remained. The amulet hung suspended in midair.

I quickly shifted Infinity under it, still open to the back page. "To hold," I said. "Just long enough to get us home."

The amulet fell through the pages, instantly swallowed by my archive.

Infinity shuddered for the second time that evening, growing so heavy for a moment that I had to strengthen my hold on it. Which was completely and utterly contrary to the well-established fact that magic didn't have mass.

I was a big advocate of learning the rules…if only to see which of them could be bent. But the amulet, the would-be death goddess, adding that much weight to Infinity? That was a little too much to handle in the moment—especially when added onto an evening that had been full of just a little too much already.

I tucked Infinity into my backpack, sheathing the bone blade. Standing wearily, I returned to the shore while carefully tucking my own power neatly away.

I just had to collect my brother and make it back to the estate, navigating all the questions I was sure to get from werewolves and witches alike, without outright lying about the death goddess incarnate I was carrying around in my backpack.

And I needed to do so quickly. Judging by how seriously the straps of the pack were actually cutting into my shoulders, it felt like a very good idea to not force

Infinity to hold a being with divine origins for a moment longer than necessary.

Ravine threw her arms around my neck, actually managing to startle me. I'd made it only a block up from the water before being swarmed by witches and werewolves for the second time that night. They were all heading down to the wharf, following in the would-be death goddess's wake—literally.

They didn't stop to question me. Presumably, the interrogation would come later.

I stopped, though. Because my attention had snagged on Sisu riding around on Kellan's broad shoulders. It might have had something to do with the fact that the shifter had transformed into his human form but was currently wearing only black sweatpants. Leaving far too many glorious handspans of muscled light-brown skin exposed, but nary a tattooed rune in sight.

Handspans? Was that even a proper measurement?

I needed to sleep.

But I couldn't sleep until I solved the issue of securing the death goddess incarnate in the tower I'd promised her. I really couldn't leave her in Infinity, and I certainly couldn't just release her in the main house.

So Ravine got her arms around my neck, with little inclination of letting go, while I was distracted. And I found myself hugging her back. A misty rain was falling again. I hadn't noticed when it started.

"Is everyone okay?" I asked, finally allowing myself to take a breath and acknowledge all those who'd been caught up in Ayre's insane attempt to harness the power of a goddess.

I scanned the block, not seeing Gitta or Neve or Lile. River and Ridge had been among the mass of witches racing down to the wharf.

"The witches are spell shocked, but okay," Ravine said into my hair. "I haven't gotten a recent update about the werewolves. Bethany, Len, and Odane were caught up in it all, but alive. But you were…you were…" She loosened her hold, lowering her voice. "I saw you chasing that…shadowed creature. You were magnificent."

She pulled away before I could respond. Not that I knew what to say. I had been exceptionally focused. And, as I was ready to admit only now and only to myself, hanging on by my fingernails.

And I wasn't done.

Kellan was striding toward us with a look of pure intent. I wasn't certain what that intent was, but I knew I needed to either stand firm or step out of his path.

I stood.

Even pretending to be a witch, it wasn't ever going to be any other way.

In a complicated move that might have seriously hurt a less powerful steed, Sisu swung down around Kellan's neck, holding on with only his legs. He flung both arms toward me, then kicked off Kellan's chest into a backward flip.

I caught my little brother under his arms, practically shoving Ravine to the side in order to do so.

She swore, stumbling.

Sisu landed in my hands with his back to me, facing Kellan, who was still glowering. Then my brother thrust his hands into the air, conjuring golden sparks out of nowhere and shouting, "Ta da!" as if he'd just done a magic trick.

A five-year-old witch shouldn't have been able to backflip off the neck of an uber-powerful werewolf, to be subsequently caught perfectly by his sister, who was also a witch.

We hadn't even made it a month without blowing our cover. I was just waiting for someone to call us on it. On any of it.

I mean, honestly…the estate? The box of treasure? Chasing a self-proclaimed death goddess through the city? How was I supposed to come up with plausible explanations for any of it?

But Kellan just grinned at Sisu, as if my brother was completely brilliant. And Ravine clapped, laughing.

Sisu thrashed around in my grip until he had his arms around my neck and his head on my shoulder. While doing so, he almost smashed me in the chin with the hilt of his sword, which was once again sheathed and invisible in his backpack.

I just hugged him back. Barely contained, pent-up fear flushed through me—enough to actually weaken my knees. "You're in so much trouble." I struggled to keep a flood of tears at bay. "For too many things to count."

"You don't need to count." He patted my cheek sweetly. "You got me back."

I huffed. I had barely rescued him at all. And if Bethany was right, he could have stayed behind in the park with her and not needed rescuing in the first place.

Another witch called Ravine away, beckoning toward the wharf. She squeezed my arm and left to join the other witches. I could feel them trying to cast something, magic rising from the earth at their bidding, then moving outward…seeking out the goddess? Or perhaps feeling the residual from the display she'd put on for Kellan and trying to nullify it? Hopefully they would think that was the last of it, that she'd burned herself out.

I had to clear the area in case they decided too many questions hadn't been fully answered.

"Bethany?" I asked Kellan, who stepped so close that he was practically sheltering Sisu and me from the misty rain with his body.

I didn't step away.

"She'll live," he said. "But she isn't going to be happy about moving for a few days. Neve and Lile are safe. Sleeping it off." He cleared his throat, looking over my shoulder toward the wharf, then back at me. "The pack has you to thank for all that."

"I was just doing my job," I said, my tone weirdly stiff. It felt wrong to be thanked when an entity of utter chaos was currently tucked away in my backpack.

No, I corrected myself. Ayre Byrne had been the chaos maker. The would-be goddess had simply been her tool.

But I was almost certain that Kellan wouldn't see it that way.

He lowered his voice, dipping his head slightly to force eye contact. "You got away," he said.

I needed to be truthful. He might smell an outright lie. "She wasn't interested in keeping me."

He narrowed his eyes doubtfully. But his face blanked when I spoke again.

"Ayre Byrne?"

"Dead."

I nodded. I had heard her neck snap—but that sometimes wasn't enough to kill a black witch.

"Let me get you home." Kellan raised a hand, waving down an SUV that had just pulled up. Owen Brady was driving, in human form. A wiry woman with dark-blond hair and light-brown skin was in the passenger seat. She looked enough like Gitta that I guessed she was Kellan and Gitta's half-sister, Erin. The werewolves hopped out, leaving the SUV running.

Brady nodded to me, then to Kellan, who waved in response. Then he and Erin jogged down the street to join Aisling. The alpha was slowly walking up from the wharf. With Mesa Byrne.

I needed to go. Quickly. "We'll walk, thanks."

Kellan snagged my elbow—lightly, but enough to make me pause. "You're dead on your feet. As am I. Let everyone who hasn't been running around the city clean up." He side-eyed me, a slight smile on his face. "Think of all the magic you've drained. All the spells you used…for speed and strength, breaking wards, and cornering death goddesses."

His tone was soft, almost seductive. I couldn't figure out if he was threatening me or teasing me, so I just looked at him.

Releasing me quickly—almost as if I'd burned him—he raised his hands to the sides in mock surrender.

I turned to walk away, not at all interested in playing games. Sisu raised his head from my shoulder, looking at Kellan who hadn't moved to follow us.

"I'd like to ride in the car," my brother said quietly.

I sighed and relented.

Kellan somehow got to the back passenger door of the SUV before me, opening it so I could tuck Sisu inside, making sure he belted himself in after removing his backpack.

I closed the door and climbed into the front passenger seat, not avoiding Kellan's gaze but not engaging it either. I placed my own pack in my lap, feeling the energy Infinity was burning even through the fabric and my dragon leathers.

The night wasn't anywhere near over yet.

Kellan climbed into the driver's seat and pulled the SUV onto the street, quickly getting up to speed as he set a course for the estate.

And for some odd reason, while he and Sisu quietly chatted about some game they had played together on the iPad earlier in the week, I closed my eyes and fell into a deep, refreshing sleep.

Apparently, I was unexpectedly comfortable with the idea that Kellan could be trusted to get us home, and even to guard us—or at least Sisu—on the way.

CHAPTER ELEVEN

I SLEPT FOR THE ENTIRE FIFTEEN-MINUTE RIDE HOME, waking oddly refreshed. Kellan insisted on walking Sisu and me to the gate, though he'd parked illegally and it was only a few steps away.

The misting rain had stopped. The crescent moon and a few tiny pinpoints of light had appeared in the sky as the cloud cover eased, but the lights of the city blocked most of the stars from sight.

"Thank you," I murmured to Kellan, reaching for the gate.

"I'll walk you to the door."

"You're just as tired as me, Kellan. We'll make it to the house unscathed."

But he had crowded up behind me to follow us onto the estate, and didn't back off. I looked up at him, slightly peeved that I had to tilt my head quite so much to meet his gaze. I likely looked like prey. And even with the nap, I was tired enough that I felt a little vulnerable.

Actually, it might have been residual fear from losing Sisu that made me feel that way. I tightened my grasp on my brother's hand, and he leaned against my leg for a moment.

"So you really aren't going to tell me," Kellan finally said.

"What specifically am I withholding?" I asked—actually needing the clarification because I was hiding a multitude of things at that particular moment, including exactly how heavy my backpack was across my shoulders. Even heavier than it had been when Infinity had first absorbed the amulet.

Kellan laughed, a quiet, husky sound that made me feel all the more vulnerable. But not necessarily in a bad way. "Well now, that's a long list, isn't it?"

I snorted. "What am I not telling you that as a member of the Conall pack and my contractor you have the right to know?"

"How about as someone who had your back all night, no questions asked?"

"No questions?"

He flashed one of his grins that was really more a baring of his teeth. "Minimal questions."

"This is odd, isn't it? Actually, all our conversations are odd."

"Odd how?"

"I can't figure out if you're flirting with me or interrogating me."

He leaned over me, growling. "I know you aren't a witch."

"I know you aren't a shapeshifter."

"I change shape."

"And I cast spells."

Something flickered behind Kellan's softly glowing eyes. Shards of magic. They looked sharp, dangerous.

I grinned in anticipation, not quite understanding my own reaction. Except I knew that Kellan was trying to decide something...something that might result in him attempting to silence me before I mentioned to anyone else what I'd picked up about him. And about Neve and Lile.

How deep and desperate was his secret? The pack's secret? Was it worth killing over?

What about my own secrets? How far would I go to try to keep them?

The shifter's eyes narrowed, gaze falling to my mouth. Then a slow, lazy grin softened all his hard edges.

My belly fluttered. Again.

Damn it.

Still, flirting was definitely better than attempted murder. Especially since if Kellan ever tried to attack me, it would become really, really obvious who I truly was.

His phone buzzed. Not breaking his gaze from mine, he pulled it out of his pocket, silenced it, and put it away.

"Are you going to kiss or kill each other?" Sisu asked.

Though I was still holding my brother's hand, he startled me. We both glanced down at him.

Heat flooded my cheeks. Kellan cleared his throat, momentarily stymied.

Then, prompted by the phone call Kellan had just muted, I remembered the picture of Bethany on his phone. And my embarrassment turned into mortification.

I shouldn't have been flirting with Kellan—assuming that was even what we were doing. I shouldn't have been staring at him nearly as much as I did. I'd had no idea that he and Bethany were seeing each other. Though of course, that made Kellan staying late when she covered evenings for me make more sense. I'd assumed that he simply wanted to spend more time with Neve and Lile, and was a little obsessive about his work. But if Bethany was his girlfriend…lover?…then that made even more sense.

Bethany might even be Kellan's mate. A fierce, strong woman who'd put herself between a black witch pulling power from a death goddess and my brother, as well as the twins. And it had almost cost her her life.

I reached for the gate, getting it partially open before Kellan recovered from Sisu's question.

"Dusk."

"Please let me know if Bethany is okay. I'll check in with her as well."

"I already told you she was going to be fine."

Nodding, I pushed the gate open.

"Good night, Kellan," Sisu chirped.

Kellan stood like a silent sentinel behind us. So silent that I glanced back at him, almost instinctually, to make sure he was okay. His face was only partially illuminated by the light over the gate. His gaze was on Sisu, and thoughtful.

He nodded to himself before looking at me. "Is Sisu yours?"

I blinked, completely thrown by the question. Of all the secrets my brother and I were trying to hold onto so tightly, Kellan had put two and two together and come up completely wrong.

"Is Sisu my…child, you mean?"

"No," Sisu scoffed.

Kellan glanced at my brother, then back at me. His eyes narrowed in suspicion, and a knowing smirk crossed his face. He was looking at us like he could read magic.

I wondered how many cracks we'd both put into Jiaotu's glamour. I was still assuming I'd burned completely through mine, as Jiaotu had warned me could happen.

"I don't normally like kids." Kellan stuffed his hands in his pockets, likely in an attempt to seem less intimidating, but the gesture only made his shoulders seem broader. "But I like Sisu."

"That's nice," Sisu said.

"I'm not...following. Sisu is my brother."

Kellan just huffed doubtfully.

"Dusk...is...my...sister..." Sisu said slowly. As if Kellan were an idiot.

"I'm just saying, that if that is one of the secrets on that long list of things you're obviously hiding, I...I don't have any issue with it..." He trailed off, frowning. At himself, I thought.

He'd either said too much or realized he wasn't articulating himself well. The confused look I could feel etched across my own face probably didn't help.

Kellan cleared his throat, then shook his head.

"I'm going to go inside," I said.

"I'll escort you."

"We already had this part of the conversation, Kellan."

"Yes, but everything else is unfinished."

It clicked for me then. Just a couple of the pieces. Kellan was worried I was going to say something about his unusual magic. And maybe he was trying to find out a few of my own secrets for leverage.

"Don't worry," I said, stepping through the gate. "I collect magical creatures."

Kellan huffed. "Collect?"

"Oh yes. I currently have a death goddess in my backpack."

A snarl overtook his smile. "What?"

Smirking—because it was apparently my turn to do so—I crossed through the boundary wards with Sisu at my side. As we passed through the magic that sealed the estate, I informed the wards that no one else needed entry until after sunrise.

The gate clicked shut behind us. As expected, I felt Kellan try to open it, to pursue his point. The gate resisted.

Sisu and I continued up the path toward the house, my brother's attention glued to the gate over his shoulder. A window on the ground floor radiated light, as did another upstairs. Zeke must have commandeered the bedroom a couple of rooms down from mine.

Something hit the barrier of invisible energy behind us. It felt like a single punch, powerful enough to reverberate through the wards.

Wow.

Well, that was rather…sexy.

And there was definitely no way that Kellan Conall was just a werewolf.

"You made him angry," Sisu said, twisting his hands together worriedly.

"Don't fret, my brother," I said glibly. "He'll get over it."

"Okay," Sisu mumbled, trailing slightly behind me as we continued up the path to the house.

"We don't have to answer all those questions," I said, trying to assuage the weird discontent I felt, as well as to soothe Sisu. I didn't like lying. "That is our personal business."

I'd been trying really, really hard to not outright lie. But my mouth tasted a little sour now, after walking away and locking Kellan out of the estate.

"It's just that I like the Conalls," Sisu whispered. "And I'm…I've been careful, like you and Papa asked me to be. And now Bethany is really hurt, and…Neve and Lile…I thought…"

Sisu's voice broke.

I dropped to my knees on the stone path, hard enough that I felt it, sweeping him into my arms. "They'll be back. I promise. Werewolves heal quickly, and I don't think the twins were seriously hurt..." I hid my own uncertainty about that, still not sure what it would mean for the two to have been forced into their wolf forms at such a young age.

"But...but..." Sisu wailed. His vibrant energy contracted around him tightly. "Kellan is angry. And angry people go away...and...and...don't come back."

I pulled slightly away so I could see his face. I had no idea who Sisu was referring to—and worried suddenly that it was Mom who he thought he'd angered, sometime before she went away. I wouldn't be able to fix that until she came home.

"Text Kellan." I smoothed my hands over my brother's wet cheeks.

Sisu's lower lip trembled. "What?"

"You can text Kellan right now and ask him to come for breakfast. He can bring Neve and Lile, if they're feeling up for it. Remember we were going to go see the gnome together, with the imp eggs?"

"After...waffles..." Sisu snuffled, then wiped his cheeks with the back of his hands.

My heart felt like it had cracked open in my chest and was just endlessly bleeding. I was struggling to breathe around that purely manifested pain. I smiled at my brother, though it was the last thing I felt like doing.

"Text him?" he said.

I nodded.

"With...your phone?"

"Yes."

"And you'll make cinnamon buns? With blueberries?"

I would have to get up at five am to pull that off for breakfast. And to beg some more blueberries from the gnome, whose name I still didn't know. And I had no idea what time it already was. After getting the self-proclaimed death goddess set up in the tower, I might not be able to go to bed at all. "Yes."

A wide grin swamped Sisu's face. "Kellan likes your buns."

I frowned, trying to remember when Kellan would have had a chance to try my cinnamon buns.

"Bethany hit him on the back of the head for staring too long yesterday."

At cinnamon buns? Had I left some in the kitchen?

Sisu started chortling—through the abundant snot that had accompanied his earlier tears. "Buns! Get it?"

My cheeks flamed, though I was more pleased than embarrassed.

"Your bum!" Sisu crowed. "Neve says buns is another word for bum!"

I huffed. "Funny."

Sisu sobered. "Though it doesn't make any sense to watch you walk away. A dragon is way more dangerous when it's facing you."

I straightened, my chest still aching from Sisu's unusual tearful outburst. I would have to ask him about who he thought had left angry and never returned, but it was already going to be a long night. "We're witches, remember?"

He took my offered hand, sauntering along beside me. "And witches are more dangerous from behind?"

I laughed quietly. "It's a…an attraction thing. Between adults." Though I was surprised to hear that Kellan had looked at me at all while Bethany was close enough to catch him doing so.

And with that caveat, I knew I shouldn't have been feeling quite so pleased about Kellan staring at me, as I'd been staring at him. Of course, Bethany might have been misreading the intent of his gaze. Kellan might have just been trying to decide exactly how dangerous I was. And what secrets I was hiding.

Sisu remained thoughtfully silent all the way up to the house. Then he asked, "Like how babies are made?"

I blinked, trying to remember what point we'd left off at in the conversation. I'd been thinking about Kellan's bare chest—and the runes I thought I'd seen on him in his beast form. Not because I was obsessed or anything.

Right. Attraction between adults. "A precursor to that. Some people find certain parts of other people attractive."

"Bums?" Sisu asked doubtfully.

Oh, gods, yes. "Sometimes."

He snorted, shaking his head doubtfully.

The front door flung open dramatically, revealing Zeke. He ran his hand through his hair, looking utterly flustered. "Where the hell have you been? Never mind. We need to get that amulet back. Now. I figured out the markings, and I was just about to trigger a tracking spell—"

"Death goddess," I said. "Egyptian origins, but now convinced she's one of the aspects of the Morrigan, presumably because she's been held by Celtic witches for so long."

Zeke's jaw dropped.

"She's in my backpack."

"Excuse me?"

"In the amulet, in Infinity. We made a deal."

"Made a deal..." Zeke murmured in utter disbelief, still staring at me. Still blocking the door.

"I helped," Sisu said. "After Dusk rescued me from being kidnapped by a black witch."

"What?!" Zeke reached for Sisu, as if it was instinct to do so.

My brother took the opening to launch himself into his great-great-uncle's arms. "Well, I wasn't really kidnapped," Sisu said, grinning madly. "But I went along."

"And you broke yourself out," I added.

Sisu shrugged, then grinned at me. "And I almost chopped that lion-dog's head off!"

"Lion...dog?" Zeke said, sounding a little helpless. "You had to kill a...lion?"

"A shade," I said, finally pushing past Zeke to enter the house. He was letting all the warm air out. "Or maybe a ghost ...? It wasn't exactly clear."

Zeke pivoted to follow me into the cloakroom, still carrying Sisu. Warmth that had everything to do with magic and nothing to do with actual heat wrapped around me. The house, welcoming me back.

"Bethany was really hurt, though," Sisu said, more subdued. Tired, I thought. "And Neve and Lile were spelled. About five times. They turned into baby wolves!" His voice thinned with distress. "What if they get trapped as wolves!?"

"They won't," I said matter-of-factly—though I had nowhere near as much information as I would actually need to make that assessment. But the twins had the same color of eyes as Kellan, and he was exceedingly powerful.

Then as if just remembering he was in Zeke's arms, Sisu wiggled to be put down. "We're going to invite them for breakfast!"

Zeke set him down, still looking a little shocked. It was an unusual look for a dragon archivist.

Sisu reached for my backpack, unzipping the outer pocket even before I got it fully off my back. He pulled out my phone, furrowing his brow as he punched in the passcode as prompted.

Zeke closed the space between us, reaching for me as if he intended to pull me into his arms. Then he glanced down at Sisu's bent head and checked himself. "Are you all right, then?"

"Really scared for a bit," I said truthfully. "When I didn't know where Sisu was. But I didn't know how scared until afterward."

Zeke nodded. Then he laid his hand on Sisu's head and closed his eyes for a moment. "Why didn't you come for me? Do you know how much shit I would have gotten in if anything had happened to you two?"

"I had it under control. And I didn't have the time for a detour."

"Dusk," he snapped, "asking for help would have been the logical choice."

"She had Kellan. And Gitta." Sisu didn't look up from the text message he was composing.

Zeke's face blanked. "Excuse me? The shifter?"

"He's really big! And super strong!" Sisu said, rather unhelpfully.

Before Zeke could build it all up in his head more than he probably already had, I pulled Infinity out of my backpack.

My personal archive hummed with power far more intensely than it ever had. It was still heavy, and disturbingly warm.

Zeke's gaze instantly snagged on it.

Then the energy of the house pressed in around Infinity, as if trying to help my personal archive keep a would-be death goddess at bay.

That was good. I was going to need all the help I could get—and I was counting on a couple of the unique aspects of the house in particular.

"Want to help me secure a death goddess in the central tower?"

Zeke's gaze flicked up to mine. He opened his mouth.

"Sure," Sisu said, interrupting his uncle with a shrug, as if he dealt with death goddesses every day. "But first I want to text Bethany, too."

"You know she'll be sleeping, right?"

Sisu nodded, but he wandered out into the great room with his head still bowed over the phone.

"Let me see the messages before you send them," I called after him, slightly worried about anything that might have been interpreted by Kellan as—

"Too late!" my brother shouted back.

Zeke hovered his hand over Infinity, but was careful not to actually touch my personal archive. Archivists didn't handle each other's archives. Not without repercussions such as singed digits.

"You trapped a death goddess in your archive," he whispered, almost reverently.

"No," I said. "She went willingly."

His head snapped up. Dealing with change had always been difficult for Zeke, at least since I'd known him. Understandably. He'd been trapped in a spelled copy of *The Iliad* for over three hundred years, then had discovered that his entire immediate family was either dead or missing after he'd been rescued.

So his response to what he interpreted as nearly losing Sisu, or me for that matter, was as expected.

"The central tower?" he asked.

I nodded. "I think she'll like the view."

"She'll like the view..." he muttered incredulously. Then he shook his head. "I assume you have a plan?"

"Well...first we need a key." I exited into the great room, heading for the library with Zeke on my heels. "And then some wards."

"But you said you hadn't even figured out how to ward the bookshelves."

Thanks for the reminder, Zeke. "I picked up a clue to that tonight as well."

"A clue?"

"Yes. We'll just keep moving forward and see what magic has to say..."

He muttered something under his breath in Ancient Greek, most likely disparaging. I didn't bother interpreting. I'd learned that what Zeke didn't want to say in English, I probably didn't want to understand anyway.

Actually...no.

I spun around so quickly that he nearly crashed into me. "Are you with me or not?" I said bluntly. "I'm really tired of being questioned. And doubted. I could have had my hands on the amulet hours ago if people had been more forthcoming. And then I wouldn't have a partly manifested goddess of death to deal with!"

"I'm with you," he said soothingly. "I'm just a little...deals with self-proclaimed goddesses are..." He shook his head again, correcting what he was going to say. "Not something I've dealt with before. So...we'll learn together."

"Okay."

Sisu piped up from right behind me. "You're not going to kiss, are you?"

I spun around.

My little brother looked utterly disgusted.

"What is this sudden obsession with me kissing people?"

Sisu grinned, laughing. And then, of course, he refused to elaborate.

"People?" Zeke said. "As in more than one?"

Ignoring him, I started for my desk at the far end of the library. The still-glowing embers and the pile of books by the fireplace informed me that Zeke had spent all evening there, doing research.

Sisu held up the master key to the house, proudly.

He'd already retrieved it. From a safe I had hoped I'd secured against raids by five-year-olds.

I sighed. Heavily.

Sisu grinned. "And we're going to need furniture."

"Furniture?"

"For Morgan."

"Morgan?"

He pointed to Infinity. "Morgan. I think she'd like dark-wood accents, but light airy fabrics. I'm thinking a four-poster bed and lots of silk pillows."

He said that last part in a perfect mimicry of River Byrne.

Zeke threw his head back and laughed. Then he tossed the likewise chuckling Sisu over his shoulder and headed to the stairs, bound for the tower.

Apparently the two of them had repaired their relationship with a single hug.

With only hours until morning and no idea of when I was going to sleep, I took a moment for myself, standing in the middle of my library and just holding Infinity. Then, trying to not think of anything but securing the goddess, I allowed my archive to fall open in my hands.

Glancing down, I saw the cherry branch that had come to me in the guardian nexus, its blossoms perfectly pressed and preserved between Infinity's pages.

Yes.

I knew why my magic brought me bits of flora to preserve now. And I understood the power of this blossom in particular. I would use it to secure the main doorway of the tower.

Sisu was scouring one of the attics for items he thought a death goddess might like. Zeke had slipped away to grab a book about ward magic from his bedroom. I finished clearing out the last few items—mostly boxed artwork—still stored in the tower. Then I stood in the center of the large stone-walled room, holding Infinity.

Eyes closed, I just breathed.

Letting everything else fall away, I thought about what I needed. The house responded immediately, its energy whispering around me. I thought about how that power had been originally sourced from the earth by the guardian dragon who had built herself a manor house, most likely around an ancient church that had once occupied these lands. Jiaotu-who-was had anchored her chosen abode with the massive walnut tree that was now the front door. That tree was the true foundation of the house—as it was of the entire estate—with strength flowing through its deep roots and filtering up through branches hidden within the walls.

The house had gone dormant with no one walking its halls, sleeping under its roof. Until it had awoken for Sisu. For me.

And now I needed the house to do even more. I needed a place for a goddess of death to reside so she wouldn't try to conquer a world that no longer worshiped her kind.

Carrying the scent of honey and the taste of citrus, a breeze filtered through metal-paned windows that weren't actually open, stirring the hair that had escaped from my French braid at my temples and the nape of my neck.

I opened my eyes to see pristinely white flowers decorating the wide, deep stone sills of all four windows.

Lemon or orange blossoms.

That was all the confirmation I needed.

I stepped back to the thick wooden door and set the master key in the lock. It shifted in my hand until it fit the keyhole perfectly. Leaving the door open, I stepped out into the hall and kneeled before the stone threshold. From Infinity's pages, I retrieved the cherry branch that had come to me in the nexus. I placed it on the stone before me.

With Infinity open in my lap, I laid my fingers across the branch and fed my power into the cherry blossom, not certain if I should scatter the petals across the threshold. Would that weaken it? Still acting mostly on instinct, as I had been when removing the break spells on Bethany, I used the branch as an anchor, then pushed my magic through it and into the stone threshold.

The energy of the house reached for my power. It emanated from a deep reserve that I could now acutely feel underneath the house's entire footprint, as well as along the deep roots of the walnut tree. Or perhaps it was less sentient than that. Simply power responding to power.

I wove my own magic with that of the house. The blossom yielded to the pressure of my fingers and somehow sank into the stone.

The power...settled. Still present, but not active until someone unauthorized tried to pass in or out of the tower.

I hoped.

I opened my eyes. A flower pattern was cleanly etched across the stone before my knees, in a smooth but almost indiscernible design.

Zeke was crouched beside me, a book in his hand. His gaze was on the flower design. I hadn't felt him return.

"Well, then," he said, his voice oddly rough. "You don't need this." He straightened, then reached over my head to press his hand to the open doorway, acting as if he felt resistance. "Strong." He looked down at me. "Impressive."

It was meant to be a compliment, but apparently Zeke and I had too much going on between us for me to accept it as one. I straightened. "The house helped. Being built by a guardian dragon and all."

Zeke made a noncommittal noise in the back of his throat. "Windows?"

"Yes." I stepped into the tower, belatedly realizing that I'd have to invite Zeke through with me. I reached back for him, but he shook his head.

"I'll check the wards when you're done, if you wish."

I dropped my hand. "Thank you."

"I'd better check on Sisu. He's been gone for a suspiciously long time."

Had he?

My confusion must have shown in my face, because Zeke added, "You were sitting at the door for about fifteen minutes. At least."

Ah, okay then.

It was going to be a long night.

And I still had cinnamon buns to make.

Zeke carried Sisu into the tower room in an ornate antique chair I wasn't certain I'd seen before. But apparently, Sisu had earmarked it for Morgan. By falling asleep in it. Fast asleep. A simple nod was all it took for the new wards to allow Zeke and Sisu to enter. I had anchored that magic at each of the windows with the citrus blossoms, then woven it all together like a net that completely secured the almost perfectly square room.

In my hand, Infinity was putting off so much power that it felt like it was overheating. "I have to hurry," I said.

Zeke nodded, setting the chair—with Sisu still in it—at the center of the otherwise empty space. He glanced around, likely noting the faint flower design that now ringed the room, on the floor at the edge of the wall, on the wall about a half meter up, and over top of all four windows, about two meters from the ceiling.

"I'm going to step out," he said, scooping up Sisu. Completely limp, my brother muttered in his sleep, then curled into Zeke's arms. "But I'll stay in the hall."

"In case she gets by me."

He nodded, but then said, "She won't. But I rigged a trap. Modified it with what I could decipher from those ridiculously garbled runes."

"They held a self-proclaimed death goddess for over two hundred years," I said ruefully.

"But not against a black witch."

"True. Though ironically, I'm fairly certain she only went black over a matter of hours. In order to crack the amulet."

Zeke looked at me for a moment, his gaze almost tender. "I don't think it's a sudden choice, Dusk. When someone chooses to turn to darkness."

"The trap?" I asked, keeping him on track. Though it wasn't totally clear what direction the conversation had been threatening to go.

He flashed me a knowing grin. "Your mother taught it to me when we were hunting down those sorcerer-bred serpopards outside Cairo."

"Thank you."

Zeke nodded, stepping back into the hall with my brother in his arms.

I opened Infinity to the back page, standing with the warded but still-open door at my back. I had thought about locking myself in the tower with the…with Morgan, as Sisu had dubbed her, but decided it was a bad idea.

She shouldn't have been able to pass through the wards. But an open door might be tempting enough for her to actually try instead of biding her time. A good test for magic I was just learning to wield.

I silently requested the return of the amulet from Infinity. My archive spat the artifact out so quickly it nearly hit me in the face.

I caught the chain, immediately stepping forward to deposit the artifact on the chair. I didn't want to get caught up reading it by touch, not when a would-be death goddess was residing within it unsecured.

I stepped back, pausing halfway between the chair and the open door, then said quietly, "Welcome home."

Energy spilled out of the amulet, steadily accumulating until it was a shadow, a form. Then it resolved into a goddess of death draped across the chair as if it were her throne. As if she'd always sat there, as if she always would.

She was clad in layers of deep red silk slightly darker than her lips. No hint of the black cloak that had propelled her through the city. Of her pale skin, I could see only the tips of her toes and a hint of collarbone, as well as her long fingers and narrow face. Her fingers were blackened as before, from the nail to the second knuckle.

She wore the amulet around her neck. Her black glittering gaze held only the barest trace of silver now. She'd spent a lot of magic.

Her gaze flicked to the open door behind me, then she smiled. "Tricky, tricky, youngling."

"You may call me Dusk."

She stiffened for a moment, and I thought she might rebuke me. Then she simply touched the amulet lightly and grimaced. "As you wish."

"And Sisu has named you Morgan."

She blinked, but then quickly hid her surprise behind one of her calculated smiles. "The littlest one. The pretty morsel? Sisu. Delightful."

"I think you'll find dragons don't make the best meals."

She laughed. And for a moment, the walls and windows of the tower darkened, becoming deeply shadowed.

I didn't intercede, understanding that power plays were necessary for this sort of creature. This entity that had decided it was to be obeyed as a goddess.

But the house wasn't happy. It pressed back with its warmth and acceptance, actually pushing the shadows from the walls as the windows also lightened.

Morgan hissed, displeased. But then she relented, tapping her long fingernails on the arm of the chair. Pulling back on her dark energy, she stood abruptly, pacing to the nearest window and looking out.

Dawn was the barest hint of light on the horizon.

Morgan laid her hand on the stone casing of the window. Then she slowly paced around the room, running her fingers along the walls. I didn't bother turning to watch as she crossed behind me, past the open doorway. She walked easily on her manifested feet, the silk of her dress undulating around her prettily.

Though perhaps she meant to be intimidating?

She did a complete circuit, pausing at the east-facing window again, power shifting around her. She grimaced, the bone structure of her face shifting as if it needed to accommodate the expression. "You are annoyingly proficient."

"Yes."

"Though without the house, you wouldn't be able to hold me."

I shrugged. "A good archivist uses all the assets at her disposal."

Another of those slow, thin-lipped smiles transformed her face into something wholly inhuman. "Is that what I am now?"

"Bring harm to anyone under my roof or on my property, and I won't hesitate to destroy you."

She sneered. "You already made your threats, archivist."

"You seem hard of hearing. An affliction that often affects elders."

In an instant, she appeared utterly wrathful, pulling her power around her in a dark cloud. If I tilted my head, I could catch flashes of silver shot through it.

Interesting.

Morgan laughed huskily, sounding almost human. "I've already conceded, Dusk. I'll need more furniture. And...entertainment."

"Sisu picked out the chair for you."

"Did he?" She crossed to the chair, caressing the top rail with her black-tipped fingers. "Yes, I see why. It will do. What a delight. Shall we be friends, Sisu and I?"

There was a threat in that question. I answered it with a smile full of promise, then kept us on topic. "I'll bring up some books."

"And a plant…a flower of some sort. Something…rare…and deadly in the wrong hands. For the north-facing window, where it will get as much light as it needs, but not burn under the touch of the sun. Ask your gnome what it recommends." She flicked her gaze to me, looking for a reaction.

I kept my expression impassive. "Deadly in the wrong hands isn't going to happen."

"Everything…anything is always deadly in the wrong hands."

I grinned wickedly, raising Infinity from my side. "Like a book?"

She huffed. "If you won't play with me, I'll get bored."

"You will endure."

She sighed dramatically.

"Another chair," I relented. "Some pillows and blankets." Then, remembering a chess set that River had uncovered in one of the attics, I added, "And a board game."

As if called forth by my pronouncement, energy shifted through the room—but not my magic.

Another chair appeared in the center of the space. Slightly smaller than the first, but clearly from the same era. Oak arms and legs, gold brocade on the seat and back. It was followed by a small matching table, with the chessboard already set up.

Well, that was new.

Apparently the house was listening in on the conversation.

That was what I got for installing a death goddess in the tower.

"Ah!" Morgan cried. "Perfect. Now I can entertain guests." She wound her power around the chair Sisu had brought her, almost like her cloak was now invisible and she was laying it over top. A ward of some kind, maybe? Or perhaps just a claiming. Then she sat down and peered at the chess set. "And this?"

"I'll get you a manual."

"A manual?" she asked with a sneer.

"The rules. To teach you how to play."

"It's set up for two people, yes?"

"Yes, but you will play yourself."

"What about the boy, Sisu? Does he play?"

"Not with you."

"And how will you enforce that?"

I tilted my head thoughtfully. "I won't. You will."

She huffed. "And the other dragon waiting on the stairs with a wicked trap for me?"

If the gnome reference hadn't tipped me off already, I would have been surprised that she could feel Zeke's presence in the hall, through the wards.

I glanced toward the open doorway just as Zeke stepped up to casually lean on the stone wall. He grinned at Morgan, open and friendly. The kind of smile a dragon offers prey to soothe their fears—right before running that prey through with magic-imbued blades.

Morgan leaned back in her chair languidly, flicking her fingers toward him in acknowledgement. Then she pointedly dismissed him, looking at me expectantly. "The books?"

"I'll see what I have to spare." I turned away without another word, utterly weary of pretending I wasn't drained. Zeke stepped away from the door so I could pass.

Power shifted behind me as Morgan tested the ward line. For the second time, though the first attempt had been far more subtle. But the wards held again. Easily.

That didn't mean I wouldn't be checking them. Daily.

"I look forward to our conversations, archivist."

I almost didn't answer.

But then I thought about what a valuable resource an ancient being could be for an archivist. Would be.

And here I was with a practically empty library to fill.

I smiled at Morgan. "Perhaps tomorrow, over tea?"

She looked pleased, as if she'd expected more resistance. Then she turned her head offishly. "That would be acceptable."

I closed the heavy wooden door behind me, locking it and pocketing the master key. The wards would keep Morgan in, and the master key would keep everyone else locked out.

Sisu was curled up at the top of the stairs where Zeke must have set him. I scooped him up and carried him to bed. Zeke, having disabled his trap on the stairs, left us without a word, but the light from the room he'd claimed was still on when I headed for bed myself.

I was too tired to talk. And still feeling way too vulnerable to even consider doing anything else. I went to bed, though I desperately wanted a shower. My phone informed me that I had only an hour to sleep before I needed to be proofing yeast and kneading dough.

Then I saw the text message from Kellan.

>I'll be there at 10. With the twins. And yes, I'll ask Bethany. Sleep well.

Ah, so I didn't have to get up until 7:00 A.M., then. Lovely. I climbed into bed, noting through my slightly open door that Zeke's light winked out only moments after I shut mine off.

But instead of wandering down the hall and climbing into my occasional lover's bed—or whatever he'd cobbled together in lieu of a proper mattress—I fell asleep thinking of the power that had radiated from Kellan Conall. And of tracing the markings I thought I'd seen on his chest with my fingers...while on top of him and making him groan my name in that deep husky tone.

CHAPTER TWELVE

THE GUARDIANS OF NORTHERN EUROPE AND WESTERN Europe were standing at the base of my bed.

I sat up abruptly, all vestiges of sleep wiped away under an onslaught of adrenaline. Thankfully I was fully clothed. Sure, I was in flower-printed pajamas, but it was better than being naked. I'd been up twice already, first to make the dough for the cinnamon buns, then to roll and slice it. I had just crawled back into bed for another thirty minutes after setting the buns in a warm oven to rise a second time.

Arms folded and eyes narrowed, Suanmi appeared to be contemplating slaughtering me where I slept. Though as in the nexus, I couldn't pick up a single drop of her actual magic. She was outfitted in dragon leathers with an unusually long katana sheathed across her back, radiating a cool determination. She also wore a gorgeous dark-gray sweater that I thought might have been knit from fine metal thread. And magic, of course.

I instantly lusted after that sweater with a surprising amount of intensity. A tangible desire. Though that might have just been residual from the absolutely yummy dream I'd just been having about a certain hard-bodied contractor and—

Jiaotu cleared his throat. Pointedly. The white-blond guardian was leaning against the bedpost, appearing relaxed, yet completely ready to strike. But whether he was expecting to have to stop Suanmi from following through on slaughtering me or was planning on aiding her, I had no idea. He was wearing a long coat with a short collar over a shirt and worn light-blue jeans. The coat looked vintage in design but was pristinely preserved.

"Is there a particular reason you have a death goddess lurking in your central tower, archivist?" Suanmi asked icily.

I opened my mouth to explain. Nothing came out.

She snorted derisively. "A message would have been helpful."

Again, I just stared at her. It hadn't even occurred to me to message the guardian, even though this was her territory. I also had no way to do so.

Then I realized with a dawning sense of terror that Morgan was powerful enough, enough of a threat, that she had come to Suanmi's notice while dashing through the darkened streets of Dublin. The death goddess had twigged that sense that every guardian had for their territory—a sense of wrongness was how my Great-Grandfather George had described it in his journals.

And I'd been triggered in a similar way, though I hadn't understood it.

I'd also let Sisu…

I groaned internally. There was absolutely no way Sisu wasn't going to tell his father that I'd let him hunt down a self-proclaimed goddess of death at my side.

My gaze flicked to Jiaotu.

He raised an eyebrow at me. "You know you can call using the telephone on the desk?"

"It's…it's hooked up to the portal system…" I muttered miserably. I loathed feeling like an idiot. I should have put that together from the telephone call with Pearl Godfrey—as well as Jiaotu mentioning that the doorways in the nexus had ears.

Suanmi huffed.

"Guardians…" I tried to straighten as best I could while in the middle of a soft bed, folding my knees under me. "I would never wish to waste your time. I was able to retrieve the entity with minimal effort." I didn't mention that I'd likely outed myself to the pack and the coven at the same time.

Infinity was suddenly in my lap, rather than on the bedside table. In my attempt to be professional, to compose myself, I had subconsciously called my personal archive to me.

Suanmi's gaze flicked down to take in Infinity. Then she glanced at Jiaotu, smirking.

He ignored her—as much as a predator ignores another predator. Or possibly an even bigger predator.

Once again, I had no idea how to read the situation, but I tried. "I apologize for—"

"The house is barely furnished." Suanmi deliberately flicked her gaze around my room, lip curling in a hint of contempt. "A brownie or two would be helpful."

Before I could address that statement, she turned on her heel and strode toward the open door to the corridor. "I have always preferred the bedroom that overlooks the rose garden. You may have your people update it and the adjoining bathroom accordingly."

My people?

She paused in the doorway, looking back over her shoulder at me and hitting me with an utterly charming smile.

The transformation was so unexpected that all I could do was stare at her dumbly. Which was probably fine with the guardian of Western Europe. It was fairly clear that she preferred to issue orders rather than be addressed.

"The delectable boy at the end of the hall," she purred playfully. Golden shards glinted in her hazel eyes, then immediately disappeared. "Does he belong to you?"

"Um, Zeke?"

"Zeke..." She tested out the name with delight. "Ezekiel. He looks so familiar. In the best of ways."

"You knew his sister, Diana," Jiaotu said—with enough wryness that even I picked up that he meant 'knew' in the fullest sense of the word.

Suanmi tilted her chin in my direction promptingly. I hadn't actually answered her question.

"No, guardian. Zeke doesn't belong to me. He is—"

She waved me off. "I prefer to figure him out for myself." Then she turned away as if intending to immediately start figuring Zeke out. In his bedroom. Where I was fairly certain he was still sleeping.

The guardians might have been able to slip through the house without notice, but I was tuned into Zeke's magic.

Suanmi paused one step into the hall, tilting her head as if listening. Then, with a huff, she stepped back into the room and closed the door, leaving her hand on the doorknob.

"See to my room, Dusk." She shot a look toward Jiaotu. "I don't share."

"As well I know," he said stiffly.

She smirked at that, but kept her gaze on me. "You may contact me through your telephone. Though a brownie would be more reliable. But…I am pleased that the death goddess was no match for you."

Shocked at what I thought might have been some sort of praise, I simply nodded.

Suanmi opened the bedroom door and power blasted through the room. A portal was now neatly tucked within the doorframe. She stepped through it. The magic snapped shut, dissipating as quickly as it had manifested.

I blinked, belatedly remembering to shut my mouth.

Jiaotu was smirking. Like, perpetually. "The death goddess lurking in your tower?"

"Lounging," I said, somehow finding some snark with which to counter being constantly on the edge of overwhelmed. "Lurking would be beneath her."

He grinned, wickedly pleased. Disconcertingly so. "Suanmi scoured the streets of Dublin for the entity…for hours. Apparently, she couldn't get past the wards on your estate without tearing them down."

"I'm glad she didn't." I still had no idea how to erect boundary wards over such a vast area. I would have to collect a lot of flora. And it might still take weeks. Plus the house was unique—especially the tree that had been carved into the front door. A guardian tearing through the wards might damage it all.

And that was why Suanmi hadn't done it. Because she valued the house for some reason as well. What with her demands for the bedroom and brownies and all.

"Yes." Jiaotu snorted doubtfully, heading for the door. "Very kind of her. You may introduce us now."

He'd crossed into the hall before I fully absorbed his words. He wanted an introduction to Morgan.

I scrambled out of bed, grabbing various items of clothing and hoping they came together into a passable outfit. Then, instead of the shower and blow dry I would have preferred, I ran my fingers through my hair to comb out the now seriously ratty French braid—after a moment of fighting to free the tail that Kellan had tucked so tightly. Then I followed the guardian of Northern Europe.

I found Jiaotu in Sisu's room, being regaled with the tale of foiling kidnappers, protecting his new friends, and containing death goddesses.

I paused in the doorway, watching Sisu, still in his pajamas, enact his heroic dealings with the shades Morgan had used to attack us. The bed was my brother's stage, and his sword punctuated each glorious detail.

Jiaotu listened to every word with a slight, delighted smile on his face.

My chest ached. Logically, that was a product of the burst of adrenaline wearing off. But also…I had put Sisu in terrible danger. It was one thing to be arrogant about my own abilities, but…

"I shouldn't have let him come with me," I whispered, forced to give voice to my regret. Even if acknowledging it to someone as powerful as the guardian, someone as invested in Sisu as his father, might mean…

I hadn't even thought…

Jiaotu might decide I was unfit to take care of—

"Why?" Jiaotu asked.

"Yeah, why?" Sisu bounced on the bed, sword hanging by his side. "I helped!"

"You did." I tried to smile but didn't quite manage it. Then I looked steadily at Jiaotu, steeling myself for his judgement while forming an argument in my head against him taking Sisu.

"I had to deal with a multidimensional being the last time Sisu and I had a weekend together," Jiaotu said casually.

I had no idea what a multidimensional being was. But it sounded like something really nasty to fight, if it could cross through those dimensions at will.

Sisu stopped bouncing, his gaze pinned to his father. His expression was suddenly serious. This was the incident that had given him nightmares that still hadn't gone away.

"We didn't know who our allies were." Jiaotu shrugged. "And calling the treasure keeper was rather abruptly not an option."

"I helped," Sisu said quietly. His eyes were wide.

Jiaotu closed the space between them in a single step, laying his hand on Sisu's head gently. "You have good eyes, my son."

Sisu gazed up at his father for a long while. Then, apparently, not needing any more reassurance, he thrust his sword up in the air and announced, "We're having blueberry cinnamon buns for brunch!"

His demigod father chuckled, allowing his hand to fall to his side. "May I join you?"

Sisu looked to me.

"Of course, guardian. I just need to bake them."

Sisu leaped off the bed, abandoning his sword and snatching Uncle Beckett's watch from his desk in the same motion. "I can do it. Twelve minutes, then rotate."

"That would also be helpful," I said, though he was already barreling past me.

He shouted from the hall, "And I left a note asking for fresh orange juice."

Jiaotu raised an eyebrow. "Left a note?"

"For the gnome, I suspect."

The guardian twisted his lips, amused. "Gnomes don't usually take…direction."

I grinned. "Sisu just has a way about him."

Jiaotu closed the space between us, touching me lightly on the shoulder, then immediately allowing his hand to fall away. "You both do."

I nodded, not even remotely believing him.

"You've burned through your glamour," he murmured. "I already fixed Sisu's."

As he'd done before, the guardian pressed his forefinger and middle finger to my forehead, and a whisper of energy passed between us. With regret—and, frankly, a lot of doubt—still lodged in my chest, I found I couldn't hold his gaze. I stared steadily at his right shoulder instead, tightening my hold on Infinity.

"Keeping Sisu with me was the best way to keep him safe," Jiaotu said softly. "Even though I know he was far too young to witness what he did. Just as I know he is safe by your side." He brushed by me, stepping into the hall without another word.

I followed him, feeling a little lighter than before.

"Hello, old one," Jiaotu said. He had opened the door and entered the tower without the need for the key. Not unexpectedly, given that the estate had been built by Jiaotu-who-was. But still a little disconcerting.

"Guardian." Morgan sniffed, still swathed in blood-red silks and reclined in her chair. "Your youngling has me well in hand. No need to bestir yourself on my behalf."

"Fledgling," he corrected, looking at me expectantly.

"Jiaotu, guardian of Northern Europe, of the guardian nine," I said—as formally as I could manage while wearing mismatched socks. "This is…Morgan. Originally from Egypt, but now a permanent resident of Wilding Manor." The name for the estate tumbled out of my mouth without thought. But with a bit of binding magic behind it.

The death goddess's attention was fixated on Jiaotu, as if trying to read him inside and out in a single steady gaze. But she flicked her silver-rimmed black eyes to me with a smirk, presumably for the 'permanent resident' comment. Then she nodded imperiously, acknowledging my introduction.

Jiaotu arched an eyebrow. "You claim to be the Morrigan?"

She shrugged one shoulder, lounging back in her chair. "I have no quarrel with the name your exceedingly delightful child bequeathed me."

Jiaotu glanced at me. "Sisu?"

Not certain what other child he thought she'd be referencing—the resemblance between father and son was striking—I nodded. "No power in a nickname."

"Indeed."

Morgan deliberately transferred her attention to me. "I require more reading materials." She picked up a book from the top of the box set next to her chair. A bare-chested male wearing a kilt and wielding a large sword dominated the front cover.

I had dropped off a box filled with various fiction titles that I hadn't managed to unpack before I'd gone back to bed—twice—while letting the dough rise. The death goddess had homed in on the historical romances. That was…unexpected.

I, of course, read all the modern fiction I could get my hands on, which was never as much as I wished. It was part of my job as Archivist of the Modern World, after all. Bare-chested, sword-wielding men were just a bonus.

"More of these," Morgan continued imperiously. "Though…not necessarily so…male dominated." She grimaced. "So much…unnecessary penetration. Some is expected, even necessary in the advancement of the story…" She waved the book. "The need for children, for securing the throne is one thing." She flicked a sly gaze toward Jiaotu, then continued addressing me. "But it is more than obvious that the heroine should have also taken her chambermaid to her bed."

"All right…" There was a used bookstore just up the street that I'd been dying to visit. I could happily spend a few hours scouring the shelves. "More diverse relationships. I can find that."

"And a goat."

"As a…character in a book?"

Morgan huffed. "As a sacrifice for your goddess!"

"No goat. I can order you Middle Eastern or Mediterranean food, though. If you are…feeling displaced."

She snorted delicately, weaving more of her magic around her chair. It was looking more and more like a throne with all those added layers of power. "I'll have one of those cinnamon buns the youngest was talking about." She opened her book to the first page, presumably planning to reread it. "And an orange from your gnome, if it is so inclined." Magic glinted wickedly from the corners of her downcast eyes.

"You don't need sustenance to survive," Jiaotu said, mildly chiding her.

"But I do need to…experience life," she said loftily. "If I'm to be of any use to your Dusk."

Jiaotu smirked at me, still emanating that distinct sense of pride. "Bargained, did you?"

"I did."

"Well, this should be interesting," he said. Then he crossed out of the tower without another word.

Morgan raised her head just enough to watch him go. Then she glanced at me out of the corner of her silvered eyes, slyly. "And I'm the one you've caged."

"In a palace," I said blandly.

She chuckled. "Your seat of power."

I deliberately let my gaze fall to the amulet strung around her neck. "We all make the best of the choices offered to us."

"Yes." She returned her attention to the book. "Do let the guardian know I'd be delighted to beat him in chess. After you get me that manual you promised."

I let her dismiss me, carefully turning the key in the lock and laying my hand on the door for a moment to check on the wards.

I found Jiaotu at the window midway down the stairs, looking out toward the greenhouses and the forest. The windowsill was deep enough to perch in with a book. And a blanket. Sitting on the stone was chilling, despite the near-perfect view.

I had plans to test out multiple possible reading nooks throughout the house. Though I suspected this window was now too close to the death goddess to achieve the total comfort that was one of the bonuses of getting lost in a good book.

"A goat?" Jiaotu asked, completely amused.

"It's part of the power games."

"Indeed. A former necromancer…" he mused.

"I thought so as well. But gifted with some sort of divine power."

He nodded. "She is weakened from your encounter."

"Truthfully, I don't believe she'd fully manifested."

He turned to look at me then, bright-blue eyes drilling through me. "Not overestimating yourself, or underestimating your opponent, is always the correct path. She is a valuable addition to your collection. Though upgrading from a gnome and a few imp eggs to a death goddess is very…ambitious."

"I was only doing my job," I said stiffly.

He chuckled quickly. "I'm not questioning you, Dusk. Though you might. You've made yourself even more interesting in the eyes of Suanmi now. There are very few who are allowed to contact her directly. No one outside of her ward and apprentices."

Well, that was…overwhelming all over again. And I had no idea why Suanmi was interested in me in the first place. I'd actually thought it was to simply play games with Jiaotu. Maybe that was still part of it.

Jiaotu sniffed knowingly. "Come. The buns will need icing, yes? Like your mother makes them."

"Yes, guardian."

I followed Jiaotu down into the basement kitchen, where Sisu had already pulled the buns out of the oven. My brother appeared to be texting. On my phone. Which I would have sworn was by my bed.

Jiaotu slipped away without saying goodbye, to me at least, a few minutes before Kellan arrived. The dark-haired shifter was laden with pastries, special coffees, hot chocolates, and Neve and Lile in tow—both looking perfectly healthy and seemingly unfazed by what had happened.

We set up in the dining room, nary a word passing between Kellan and me other than good morning. If he sensed the death goddess or the new wards in the tower, he didn't mention it.

In between pastries and cinnamon buns, Neve and Lile tore around the house with Sisu, reenacting the events of the previous evening. As far as I could tell by watching and talking to them, the twins didn't bear any apparent residual—magical or otherwise—from their kidnapping and forced transformation.

And there was fresh-squeezed orange juice.

Zeke joined us, greeting the others absentmindedly as he grabbed a cinnamon bun, then settled in midway down the table with a book bearing hieroglyphs on the spine, making notes in his archive.

I caught Kellan glancing between Zeke and Sisu multiple times as if comparing them, but he didn't broach the subject of my brother's parentage again.

If Kellan thought I was keeping secrets, him mistaking me for Sisu's mother was a far more logical leap than the actual truth. That I was an all-but-mythical creature. A dragon in disguise. With a death goddess tucked in my tower, and an uneasy relationship with at least two of the most powerful beings in the world.

Under the cover of two large black umbrellas, Sisu and I walked Zeke to the gate. A taxi was already waiting to take him to the airport, from which he would fly into London, step through the Dunkirk witches' magical door to the British Museum, and then cross through the museum stacks to Giza. He had shelved a few of the books he'd brought in the library, claiming his own bookshelf. Without permission. But I forgave him after he promised to send any more info he uncovered on death goddesses of Egyptian origin.

There wasn't much I wouldn't forgive if the apology came with books.

Kellan had left a couple of hours earlier, carrying the exhausted Neve and Lile. The twins had literally crashed after eating their fill of pastries. Magical exhaustion was often like that, hitting unexpectedly and lasting for seemingly random amounts of time. I had offered my bed so they could nap, but Kellan wanted to get them home to Gitta, who had stayed to watch over Len. The twins' father had been hurt almost as badly as Bethany, caught in the break spell that Ayre had used to rip the front door from Gitta's house. But Kellan was still confident that both Len and Bethany would heal fully, given time.

At the gate, Zeke crouched to exchange a complicated handshake with Sisu, then hand off his umbrella to him. I had no idea when they'd had the time to come up with the handshake.

Straightening, he brushed a kiss across my lips, almost absentmindedly. I was fairly certain he wasn't looking forward to the flight or being surrounded by mundanes, as he called nonmagicals.

I thought about warning him about Suanmi's interest in 'figuring him out,' but didn't. If I didn't want Zeke involved in my love life, then I shouldn't mess around in his…not that I had a love life outside of Zeke, of course.

Without another word, he stepped through the gate, crossing quickly through the rain toward the illegally parked taxi waiting for him. He spun back to wave, and Sisu and I reciprocated. He climbed into the taxi, and it pulled away.

Prompted by a push from Sisu, the gate clicked shut.

We were alone.

Just the two of us on the vast property.

Well, the four of us. If I counted the gnome and the death goddess watching everything from the central tower.

"Do you want to take the eggs out to the gnome with me?" I asked as I held my hand out to Sisu. Neve and Lile had fallen asleep and been carted off by Kellan before we could head out to the greenhouse together.

"Yes! I'll get them." Abandoning his umbrella, Sisu took off for the house.

Grabbing and collapsing the umbrella before I had to chase after it across the property, I followed at a slower pace, just enjoying the feel of the energy of the estate around me. Wilding Manor. That felt right.

Sisu joined me before I made it to the front door, carefully carrying the mason jar that held the imp eggs in two hands. The eggs, barely as big as the tip of my fountain pen, twinkled behind the glass, tiny pulses of possible life. I wasn't certain whether they would be as light-sensitive as the adult tooth fairy had been, but I had Sisu tuck the jar in his jacket for warmth and darkness anyway. Together, we skirted the house and headed for the greenhouse.

"Neve says it hurt," Sisu said quietly, tucked next to me under my umbrella.

"Changing?"

"Yeah. But Lile says she doesn't remember, but I think she's just trying to be brave."

"It's okay to admit when things hurt," I said casually, feeling Sisu look up at me, then away.

"I like it when Papa visits..."

"I'm glad."

"But...I still miss Mom."

I touched him lightly on the top of his head, fighting through a press of sudden tears. "Me too."

Sisu held the mason jar up to eye level, blinking at the three eggs as they randomly glinted with tiny pulses of magic. "But this place is cool. And maybe the imps might want to live here too?"

"Maybe. Yes."

Sisu bolted ahead to grab the latch of the greenhouse door, then waited for me to pull it open. We stepped inside quickly to avoid letting out too much warm air.

I tucked both umbrellas to the side of the door, breathing in the scents of earth and citrus blooms.

Sisu darted forward. "Dusk! Look!"

I turned. Three long, low wooden benches, grayed with age and wear, ran the length of the greenhouse. As before, the outside two benches were covered with various potted trees, grouped by type. Oranges, limes, lemons. Even coffee, vanilla, and cacao plants. And blueberry bushes, of course—some of which were the size of trees. The greenhouse was most definitely larger on the inside.

But a plywood box I hadn't seen during my previous visits was perched at the end of the central bench, directly across from the door. The plywood looked brand new—and had presumably been purloined from the stacks the Conalls seemed to have delivered at least once a week. I was fairly certain the gnome didn't have a credit card. Or get deliveries, for that matter.

The front of the box and the lid were partially meshed and coated in magic. Perhaps to ease the ambient light? Or perhaps, as I'd guessed, the eggs needed magic to be sustained. A heat lamp was set over one end, hanging from the rafters. It was mostly likely battery powered or magic, because the greenhouse wasn't otherwise wired.

"Hello," I called as I stepped forward. "Thank you for the orange juice."

Sisu, grinning ear to ear, set the jar with the precious eggs next to the box. Climbing up onto the bench, he peered at the heat lamp—which wasn't on—then lifted up the lid.

"It's an incubator!"

"Yes." I was grinning ear to ear myself.

We had hatched chickens in something similar at the family estate. Or rather, Job, Mistress Brightshire's younger brother, had. That incubator had been lined in pine shavings, but the gnome's was filled with what appeared to be fluffy wool batting.

A scrawled note was pinned to the side of the box, bearing my name.

I opened it.

I watch over eggs.—G

G wasn't a full name. But it might have been a sign that the gnome was going to trust us.

My throat tightened. With joy, I thought, but it was an unusual enough reaction that I could only watch as Sisu carefully placed the jar in the incubator and opened the hinged lid.

Then my brother set the meshed lid back on the incubator, crouching down to peer at the eggs as if they might hatch instantly.

The heat lamp winked on, throwing a soft glow of red across the box and Sisu.

"We are very lucky," I whispered.

"Yeah," Sisu said agreeably, most of his focus still on the eggs. "But Mom says luck is mostly hard work, with a bit of magic mixed in."

She did say that.

I tucked the note from the gnome in my pocket and stepped forward to crouch down and peer at the imp eggs myself. I would head back to the house in a moment. I had letters of my own to write, and historical romances to buy for a death goddess. But for now, I would take this snippet of peace.

And maybe, just maybe, the imp eggs would hatch.

ACKNOWLEDGEMENTS

With thanks to:

MY STORY & LINE EDITOR

Scott Fitzgerald Gray

MY PROOFREADER

Pauline Nolet

MY BETA READERS

Anteia Consorto, Terry Daigle, Gael Fleming,
and Megan Gayeski Pirajno.

FOR THEIR CONTINUAL ENCOURAGEMENT, FEEDBACK, & GENERAL ADVICE

Nicole Deal – for the illustration of Kellan
SFWA
The Office
The Retreat

ABOUT THE AUTHOR

MEGHAN CIANA DOIDGE IS AN AWARD-WINNING WRITER based out of Salt Spring Island, British Columbia, Canada. She has a penchant for bloody love stories, superheroes, and the supernatural. She also has a thing for chocolate, potatoes, and cashmere.

For recipes, giveaways, news, and glimpses of upcoming stories, please connect with Meghan on her:

New Release Mailing List: http://eepurl.com/AfFzz
Personal blog, www.madebymeghan.ca
Twitter, @mcdoidge
Facebook, Meghan Ciana Doidge
Email, info@madebymeghan.ca

Please also consider leaving an honest review at your point of sale outlet

ALSO BY MEGHAN CIANA DOIDGE

NOVELS

After the Virus
Spirit Binder
Time Walker
Cupcakes, Trinkets, and Other Deadly Magic (Dowser 1)
Trinkets, Treasures, and Other Bloody Magic (Dowser 2)
Treasures, Demons, and Other Black Magic (Dowser 3)
I See Me (Oracle 1)
Shadows, Maps, and Other Ancient Magic (Dowser 4)
Maps, Artifacts, and Other Arcane Magic (Dowser 5)
I See You (Oracle 2)
Artifacts, Dragons, and Other Lethal Magic (Dowser 6)
I See Us (Oracle 3)
Catching Echoes (Reconstructionist 1)
Tangled Echoes (Reconstructionist 2)
Unleashing Echoes (Reconstructionist 3)
Champagne, Misfits, and Other Shady Magic (Dowser 7)
Misfits, Gemstones, and Other Shattered Magic (Dowser 8)
Gemstones, Elves, and Other Insidious Magic (Dowser 9)
Demons and DNA (Amplifier 1)
Bonds and Broken Dreams (Amplifier 2)
Mystics and Mental Blocks (Amplifier 3)
Idols and Enemies (Amplifier 4)
Misplaced Souls (Misfits 1)
Awakening Infinity (Archivist 0)
Invoking Infinity (Archivist 1)

NOVELLAS/SHORTS

Love Lies Bleeding
The Graveyard Kiss (Reconstructionist 0.5)
Dawn Bytes (Reconstructionist 1.5)
An Uncut Key (Reconstructionist 2.5)
Graveyards, Visions, and Other Things that Byte (Dowser 8.5)
The Amplifier Protocol (Amplifier 0)
Close to Home (Amplifier 0.5)
The Music Box (Amplifier 4.5)

DOWSER SERIES BOOK 1
CUPCAKES, TRINKETS,
and other
DEADLY MAGIC
MEGHAN CIANA DOIDGE

DOWSER SERIES BOOK 2
TRINKETS, TREASURES,
and other
BLOODY MAGIC
MEGHAN CIANA DOIDGE

DOWSER SERIES BOOK 3
TREASURES, DEMONS,
and other
BLACK MAGIC
MEGHAN CIANA DOIDGE

ORACLE SERIES BOOK 1
I SEE ME
MEGHAN CIANA DOIDGE

ORACLE SERIES BOOK 2
I SEE YOU
MEGHAN CIANA DOIDGE

ORACLE SERIES BOOK 3
I SEE US
MEGHAN CIANA DOIDGE

RECONSTRUCTIONIST SERIES BOOK 1
Catching Echoes
MEGHAN CIANA DOIDGE

RECONSTRUCTIONIST SERIES BOOK 2
Tangled Echoes
MEGHAN CIANA DOIDGE

RECONSTRUCTIONIST SERIES BOOK 3
Unleashing Echoes
MEGHAN CIANA DOIDGE

THE AMPLIFIER SERIES: BOOK 0
THE AMPLIFIER PROTOCOL
MEGHAN CIANA DOIDGE

THE AMPLIFIER SERIES: BOOK 1
DEMONS & DNA
MEGHAN CIANA DOIDGE

THE AMPLIFIER SERIES: BOOK 2
BONDS & BROKEN DREAMS
MEGHAN CIANA DOIDGE

Made in the USA
Las Vegas, NV
14 December 2024